S L E E P   O N,
B E L O V E D

C E C I L   F O S T E R

O N E   W O R L D   B O O K S

Ballantine Books • New York

A One World Book
Published by Ballantine Books

Special thanks to the Ontario Arts Council for its assistance.

Foster, Cecil.
Sleep on, beloved / Cecil Foster. — 1st ed.
p.   cm.
ISBN 0-345-39015-6 (alk. paper)
I.   Title.
PR9199.3.F572S57   1995
813'.54—dc20   94-44069 CIP

Manufactured in the United States of America

First American Edition: May 1995

10 9 8 7 6 5 4 3 2 1

FOR

GLENYS

AND

MENSAH KAFELE

SLEEP ON, BELOVED

CHAPTER 1

GRANDMA NEDD LOVED to dance, but only on the right occasions and in the right places. Otherwise, she hated dancing, banned it from her home as too corrupting, too sacrilegious. When she did perform, nobody stood in her way; nobody defied her. She took second place to no one, not even when the occasional arthritic flare-up left her joints swollen and sore.

It was as though dancing in the presence of her God was an instant cure. That and a good slicking down with Vicks VapoRub mixed with turpentine. Sometimes, she used two castor leaves from the trees beside the house, singeing them lightly over a fire and, while they were still hot, tying them to the top of her head to sweat out any demon illness.

It seemed to Suzanne that no time was better for her grandmother's dancing than when Pastor Grant took his small flock on a *journey*. "Who are we to ignore the instructions of our God as uttered to the prophet Jonah?" Pastor Grant would ask rhetorically, signaling his plans for the outing a few days later. "Arise, go unto Nineveh, that great city, and preach unto it the preaching I bid thee, according to the Word of the Lord." They always set up the tabernacle at the intersection of the two roads that ran through the village, the paths previously used by both the fleeing rebels and the faint of heart.

The two-lane highway, the one tarred and made smooth, was reduced to a series of gaping potholes every rainy season. This happened about the same time the fields bloomed with sugar canes, yams, cassava, beans and peas, when the mosquitoes invaded. This highway was the main route from the village to the defiling city and the wider world. It was a road of sweet enticement. But it also invoked memories of betrayal and disappointment. Grandma Nedd told Suzanne that centuries earlier it had been the highway traveled by the colonial armies formed to control rebellions by the slaves who were forefathers of these latter-day journeyers.

The other road was an unpaved track for cows and goats. It became a swamp about the same time potholes appeared in the main road. It led into the very heart of the village and then just stopped, a dead end. Here the forefathers, neutered of their rebellious sting, were allowed to set up hamlets. Here they were permitted to live free of hassles as long as they never incited insurgence or bothered with matters beyond the borders of their village. As long as they let the dream wither and die.

Pastor Grant and members of his Immanuel Tabernacle of a Risen Christ journeyed to the intersection ostensibly in search of souls for Christ. At this place called Cross Roads on maps of the area and Damnation by residents of the region, they bore witness to His name and glory. They did it with pride and foresight, with unshakeable faith in the righteousness of their cause and certainty of purpose. A belief that at the end of the painful journey would be a great feast, a remarkable celebration for having the courage to keep their eyes on the prize and their feet on the straight and narrow path. The reward for bringing home the dream. They journeyed underneath the village's one street lamp, a naked bulb hanging from a rotten pole, puncturing the darkness for miles around, with bats and moths circling hypnotically. Grandma Nedd had explained it was customary for African people to gather at these crossroads, at the place where the paths of communications between the human and spiritual worlds were joined.

Members of Immanuel Tabernacle assembled, always dressed in white cotton gowns that hung down to their ankles. Their clothes stiff with starch from the cassava roots and pressed smooth with hot irons. Pastor Grant alone dressed in a full-length black gown, with a white cord around his waist. The cord's ends, tied in bows, fell majestically to his calves.

The women wore white head ties, with the ends rolled around the crown and knotted at the front. At the specified hour, as if with a single mind, the members formed a circle, addressed one another as *bredren* and *sistren* and began their journey among the foreigners and sinners, a group that included everyone not saved by the redeeming blood of the lamb, as taught at the Immanuel Tabernacle.

Suzanne remembered that Pastor Grant would start the proceedings by calling on a boy or girl to read from the scriptures. Then on one of the elders, usually Grandma Nedd, for an opening prayer. "The Holy Spirit be upon us," Pastor Grant intoned as an introduction for Grandma Nedd to take over. "In our faith the woman is always exalted, made equal to her brethren to shelter and to give sustenance when the men had to flee the darts and slings of Babylon or to seek protection and refuge. For as the Holy Book says in Acts two verse seventeen: 'there shall be an outpouring of the Holy Spirit, the Comforter, on the men servants and on the *maid* servants.' Again, it is written by the Prophet Isaiah: 'in the last days the women shall compass the men.' This is the faith of our fathers and mothers that goes back to Mother Africa; faith that gives unto women the right, indeed the calling, to lead and to prophesy. The true faith of our fathers and mothers living still."

Then the congregation of saved souls would begin their witnessing with song, Bible reading and personal testimony. They spoke in strange tongues, uttering words and phrases Suzanne never understood, even when she heard them flowing uncontrollably from her own mouth, words that apparently only someone of her grandmother's calling and anointment could decipher.

Every so often, Pastor Grant, in his long black gown, picked up a large silver bell. Like a man about to flog himself, he raised the bell repeatedly over his shoulder and let it drop under its own weight, issuing a clarion call across the village, a summons to worship, to praise God. He threw holy water from a silver cup toward the four corners of the earth. With every toss of the water, he rang the bell, calling on the Holy Spirit to enlighten those of the true faith who had journeyed to the four corners of the earth, who were exiled in foreign places or even among the dead. Someone read from the Psalms. Pastor Grant prayed and rang the bell again for sanctification, to cast out evil spirits that might have crept into the midst of the faithful with the first summons; corrupting spirits of another culture and place that could defile the insecure and unwilling, possibly driving them to permanent delirium. They had to be banished with the bell of exorcism.

The men and women of the congregation began to sway, slowly at first, then more frenetically. They moved rhythmically to the music, clapping hands, shuffling their sandaled feet, swirling the long white gowns, talking in strange undecipherable tongues. They were primed for a night of hard labor, for their journey into the early hours of the morning. They were prepared to labor until exhaustion of strength and voice, if that was what it took to save just one solitary soul, to conquer all things foreign and alien.

A *humba-humba humba*. A *humba-humba humba*. The men chanted hypnotically from the depths of their chests, from their very souls. As the rhythm quickened, sistrens swooned under the influence of the Holy Ghost; the eternal life-giving Spirit took residence in their bodies and caused them to move

6

and cry like animals. The women slithered like snakes or leapt like panthers, the blackest and most beautiful of untamed creatures, to the center of the circle. There, a white tablecloth had been spread on the ground, held down by four symbolic stones at each corner. The Holy Bible, The Unabridged Seven Books of Moses and the kerosene storm lamps all lay in the center. A *humba-humba humba*, chanted the brethren. A *humba-humba humba humba*.

Above their heads fluttered the flag of the faithful and saved, a banner of red, green and yellow with the star of the Conqueror and a Christian cross in the center. The flag was a symbol of veneration for the past and the future, recognizing the presence of a carnal sovereign and a spiritual deity. A time when the past, present and future were one. The red told the world of the tribulations caused by fire and blood. The green signified peace, bountifulness, and yellow the empowerment of the Holy Ghost. Nothing was done without first raising this flag.

Pastor Grant and his followers might appear part of the wider society. But at the appropriate time they gathered under their flag and declared themselves separate. The true keepers of the flame and religion of their forefathers. The flag of the Conqueror told the world these people had overcome centuries of outcast, had remained firm in the face of fire and brimstone, hurricane and gale of repression, degradation and discrimination. They had survived the fiery furnace, had outlasted the crossings. They lived to nourish the dream.

They danced in celebration, in unity and love. They danced, like generations before them, in hope of ultimate redemption and deliverance from the hands of the wicked and ungodly. They danced until the women collapsed from exhaustion and the brethren had to hold them up, preventing them from falling to the ground amidst the dust and marl. Their bodies writhed as the Holy Spirit reluctantly left them, and they abandoned themselves to the other spirits, those of the universal powers of powers and those of all their ancestors in the Caribbean and, particularly, Mother Africa. It was only in this listless daze that the women fell silent, unable to talk, argue, fight or predict with certainty. When they were no longer the representatives of the African *vooduns* Ogo or Isis, they became as weak as the men, broken by the spirits and abandoned. Only then were they free to return to their daily chores and fit right back in with the ungodly until it was time to drop the mask again.

This was the only time the Rastafarians participated in the worship, attracted by some unspoken communication that demanded a gathering even of those who chose other ways to honor their true heritage. The Rastas usually kept to themselves, in a community apart. But they always returned. Especially for these celebrations, when their bodies were reclaimed by the ancestors. Like the worshipers, the Rastas always traveled with their flag of red, green and gold, with the emblazoned head of the Lion of Ethiopia. Everybody knew the Rastas attended for the music and dancing, but Pastor Grant continued to pray that they would see the light and integrate fully. Grandma Nedd, however, always welcomed the Rastafarian elders and rapped with them as if one of their own, as if their colors of red, green and gold had the same liberating meaning for everyone. She led them in familiar songs.

As the night wore on, the village resounded to the drums: big drums, small drums, long drums, thin drums, especially the drums made of goat- and sheepskins, drums being the preferred instrument of the Rastafarians for their chanting and dancing. Drums the instrument used by Pastor Grant, along with the bell and tambourine. They made a joyful sound. Everybody knew the Rastafarians and Maroons, the original slaves who fled from slavery to the hills and mountains beyond the reach of the indoctrinating masters, were the ones chosen by the ancestors to preserve and propagate the art of drumming. Their task was to safeguard these dynastic mysteries and to keep them safe for all African offspring. And to guard these

secrets particularly for the captured peoples such as the Pocomania and the Shouters, the special minders of the true faith,
the people they taught the intricacies of drumming to in the
wee hours of the journey. Over the centuries, these unlettered
people had been denied the right to use such instruments in
their worship. They were forced to hide their God behind the
skirts of other people's idols. At Cross Roads, in the late stages
of the journey, the sons and daughters of both the enslaved
and the runaway were joined in a coming-home dance, all
summoned by the bell and drum, all hoping for deliverance
from damnation. They were joined in the dream of ultimate
triumph, some great day. But even then they knew that in
these latter days, when the master's whip was lifted from their
backs and the shackles from their ankles, they dared not talk
too openly about the great day coming. They had to be decep-
tive, use a language only few understood—the mother tongue
of the drum.

There was absolutely nothing so unifying as the universal
language of drumming. Suzanne always remembered one of
the anniversaries of independence back home in Jamaica,
when something called Carifesta—Caribbean festival of the
arts—brought together African people from the African conti-
nent, from Haiti, Cuba, Martinique, Curaçao, Suriname,
from every English-speaking Caribbean island. It attracted
southern Baptists and Shouters from the United States, with
their jazz musicians and famous dirges. The festival opened
with one big jam session at the Jamaica National Stadium, after Pastor Grant had given his benediction and rung the bell.
Nothing in Suzanne's life ever surpassed the intensity and sat-
isfaction of that moment.

Years later, Suzanne still remembered vividly the drums, including the steel pans from Trinidad and Tobago. She still
marveled at how they spoke one common language. She
never forgot Carifesta: the drumming and the men and
women dancing—dirty dances, too, like those she performed
years later on tabletops. The men and women in their multi-

colored national costumes had given an unrehearsed outpouring of their rich common culture. She revered the drum, the
harmony and unity it brought to Carifesta, to Pastor Grant's
open-air meetings and to all in St. Ann's. How she missed
such music, such spontaneity, in sterile Toronto and all North
America. How she wanted to see Grandma Nedd dance again.
Only in those overpowering dreams, the quaint mixture of reality and memories, was she given this pleasure of watching
her grandmother's intricate movements. And only in her
nightmares was she reminded of the seriousness of the curse.

At the open-air meetings back home, by the early hours of
the morning, only the white gowns of the Pocomania and the
long braids and dreadlocks of the Rastas told the difference between the groups. They appeared as one in worship, in sound,
in dance and fellowship. Even the elders of the Rastafarians
were less strident when they railed against the sins of the capi-
talist world, against those who oppress African people—the
lost tribe of Israel. The elders put aside their prophecies of
doom and their demands for the separation of different cultures so the people could practice their religions free of deception. Under the cover of darkness, they did not have to hide
and pretend.

For one night, the Rastafarians didn't expound their belief,
as the Prophet Marcus declared, that any person lucky enough
to be born in the Caribbean should be happy to die there. The
only alternative would be the promised land of Africa, particularly Ethiopia, the spiritual home of all black people. No de-
scendants of African slaves should be happy going to another
country, where even the weather was hostile and only the
fittest and fairest survived.

But when the Rastas took up the issue, Suzanne found it
frightening. "Tell me, sister, but when we, the children of
African kings and queens, going to stop this foolishness of
picking up weself and running away to a next man's country?"
the Rastafarian asked when Grandma Nedd and Suzanne
stopped at the stall at Cross Roads to buy oranges. Grandma

Nedd wanted to remind the Rasta to leave the area clean of the nutshells and the skins of oranges, bananas and mangoes at the end of the day, clean for the journeyers from her church when they praised God later that night. The Rasta had inquired about Suzanne's mother. Grandma Nedd's response that she hoped Suzanne would soon join her mother in another country did not please him. "After all these years, we still can't answer the damn question: where's home for we niggers, for Africans like you and me? Why any o' we have to leave where we born and bred? And all the time we running, we saying still with the other side of the mouth that this is supposed to be a new and independent country we building down here in this Caribbean! To me, it just ain't righteous to have the daughters like you running off all the time to a next man's house, to be the unwelcome lodger in somebody else's bungalow when you can be the mistress of your own lean-to. We got to try our levelest best to make this here place better by staying right down here, you see what I mean?"

"Why do the Rastafarians say these things?" Suzanne had asked when her grandmother joined her in bed after the open-air meeting. The girl was worried about what might happen if her mother in Toronto kept a promise and sent for her to live in the strange city, the land of Babylon, according to the Rastafarians.

"Don't worry your head, chile," Grandma Nedd had said. "Them Rasta boys taking things a little too far. Them like they never hear you can take a horse to water but you can't make 'im drink. Because you live in a next man country, don't mean you gotta be ungodly like he, not if you got the proper training, not if you got the love of the true God in your heart."

"But they keep making it sound like the worst thing that could happen to me," Suzanne said. "I don't mind staying back here with you, Grandmother."

"Remember the Hebrew boys, chile: they refused to bow down to another man's god. Our religion teach us the same thing too," Grandma Nedd whispered as she pulled the sheets over them. "You can be in this world, but not part of the world. You can pretend to be one thing if you have to do it to get by. But in your heart, only you know who you really is. Only you know that the God we worship is the one true and living God, even if people in them big churches and cathedrals down the road like to think we worship the same God as them."

The words of Grandma Nedd quickly lulled Suzanne into a deep and peaceful sleep. Suzanne never forgot what her grandmother had explained in the early hours of the morning, when both of them were exhausted and Suzanne was scared: that she could be in the world, but not a part of it. She patterned her life on this tenet and did not feel guilty. "Mark it on the soul case of yuh heart, beloved," she always remembered her grandmother's advice. The voice in her memory was so soothing; everything she said made such sense. "Go to sleep now and don't worry about them things and conflicts. Sleep on in the assurance that when you awake it will be to a new life and you will be at peace with yourself." Suzanne had inscribed it so indelibly that years later she was able to appear naked on tabletops and still sincerely believe she was not a lewd dancer. She was a dancer, but not in the dance-sex business. Except seldom did she find the sleep of peace, of waking and knowing who she really was.

Her mother, her stepfather, her teachers, all the people she knew in Toronto, complicated things for her. They made her doubt everything she had been taught. Made her question everything she cherished and took on faith, even the teachings of Grandma Nedd and Pastor Grant. Stripped her of things so innate and integral to her very being. Nothing the people in Toronto said squared with the teachings in Suzanne's heart.

At least once a month, even now, ten years after her arrival in Canada, after she had gone through the Children's Aid Society's foster homes, and six years after she started to live on her own, Suzanne still dreamed about the drums, about how she was twelve years old again, back home in St. Ann's preparing for her first trip abroad.

In the dream, she attended a farewell prayer meeting at the church in her honor. But it wasn't the happy thanksgiving service she expected for someone embarking on a personal journey. It was a somber mourning that included praying, meditating and self-sacrifice. In the dream, Suzanne found herself in the mourning room with just one attendant, her spiritual pointer, and with nothing to eat.

"You must be like the Hebrew boy, Daniel, prepared to live among the sinners, yet apart from them," the faceless woman advised. "As Daniel said: 'I, Daniel, was mourning three full weeks. I ate no pleasant bread, neither came flesh nor wine in my mouth, neither did I anoint myself at all 'til three weeks were fulfilled.' "

The regular worshipers and the Rastafarians were singing, beating their drums and dancing. She was pulled between Grandma Nedd and the Rastafarians. She didn't want to get on the airplane, the menacing metal bird, that in the dream was always waiting for her at the side of the road, right where they liked to journey. Obviously, it was too impatient to wait at the airport. Suzanne was in no hurry to leave and kept seeking out someone new to wish an elaborate good-bye, even though she knew she was holding up the flight.

Near the end of the dream, Grandma Nedd and Pastor Grant always took her by the hand and, begging her not to be afraid, firmly led her toward her destiny. Yet they always left her at the bottom of the stairway to the plane, as if they dared not enter it themselves.

As she put her foot on the first step, the Rastafarians always began a solemn drumming and chanting. The words trailed her up the stairs, like the anguished cries of forefathers torn from their homes and families to board a slaver for a journey into the unknown. The words of the traditional stanzas were clear over the drumming:

13

Hear the words of the Rastaman say,
Babylon's throne soon fall down, fall down.
Babylon's throne soon fall down.
Hear the words of the Iahman saa-ay
Babylon's throne soon fall down.

Her mind focused intently on the drumming, her leaden feet moving slowly as the drums spoke directly to her:

Boom-uh-boom-uh, boom-uh-boom-uh boom,
Boom-uh-boom-uh, boom-uh-boom-uh
Boom-boom-boom.

As she climbed the stairs, the drumming and singing got louder. Even when she was inside the belly of the beast, she still heard every word, every drumbeat, as clearly as the thumping of the heart in her chest.

I'll fly away to glory, (Boom-uh-boom-uh boom boom)
I'll fly away. (Boom-boom-boom)
Some bright morning when my work is done
I'll fly away. (Boom-uh-boom-uh boom boom boom)

Inside the plane, naked and dancing, was Suzanne's mother. Her face had been painted with so much makeup it became a demonic mask, just like one of the trickster goddesses Grandma Nedd always warned Suzanne against. It was nothing like the African mask Grandma Nedd wore to celebrate the birth of a baby, a wedding or when a family moved into a new house. Nothing like the mask Mira Nedd wore when she became more than just Suzanne's grandmother. Inside the mask, Mira was transformed into the spiritual power that was represented in all women, all mothers, in all things fertile in the air, in the water and on the land. When Grandma Nedd said she was just like Mother Earth.

14

The strange mother on the plane was dancing and drinking and smoking and playing with her pubic hair, while beckoning for Suzanne to come to her. Just like the tricksters that were always trying to undo the good of the other gods and goddesses. The creature had so many hands, too many perhaps. Or they were moving so fast and frenetically, they appeared more than two as they groped, reached and confused like a magician deceiving the eyes. Every time the light changed, the features of this woman that was Suzanne's mother altered. At times a smiling woman; other times cackling, demeaning and ugly, the hands flaying every which way, seeking whatever was in their reach to transform into the shaper's likeness.

When the girl stopped in her tracks, with all the passengers laughing, her mother began to approach her, snarling menacingly as she drew near. The masks that were her faces changed faster than Suzanne could blink. Something about this woman was so frightening, just as the Rastas has warned. At the same time Suzanne knew she had to trust her grandmother's promise that Ona Morgan, her *new* mother, would never harm her. As she stood transfixed in the aisle, her mother bore down on her. All the time, her mother danced, pulled at her breasts, at the pubic hair, swung her legs like a young woman dancing naked under the lights.

The plane's doors were closed, cutting off Suzanne's escape. Still, she heard the drumming and chanting. They got louder, reverberating in her head as the aircraft gathered speed for the takeoff. When her mother reached out to touch her with talonlike hands, like an eagle swooping down on prey, Suzanne screamed and jumped up from the dream.

Awake, she knew she was no longer a child. But her heart would still be beating too fast and blood would pound in her ears. The bedclothes would be soaked with sweat. It happened every time.

Usually, she did not get back to bed until she had read the Bible and written to Grandma Nedd. Most nights she cried and pined to be back home, in the warmth of her Jamaica. To be in the bosom of Grandma Nedd where she might escape the pain of the cursed.

Something was troubling about this last dream. Ominously, it happened in broad daylight, in the chair where she had dozed off. As if the demons of the nightmares were now so anxious, so uninhibited, they were unable or unwilling to wait until the cover of darkness before preying on her.

CHAPTER 2

SUZANNE GRABBED THE phone on the floor beside the chair. The dream had been so real, the drumming so spiritual. Now, a strange gruff voice was barking in her ears, piercing the warm sleepy haze. "I'm on my way over," the harsh voice said. "Twenty minutes. I'll be downstairs at your apartment building."

She heard the click of the phone before she even thought what to say. Glancing at the clock on the wall over the television, Suzanne realized she must have fallen asleep after the surprise lunch with Henderson. It must have been more than a snooze. Those dreams only occurred in deep sleep, particularly when she was really exhausted. But the phone and her manager had intruded. And she had not even started to pack. Soon the manager would be downstairs, fretting as usual about how he was doing her a favor; how he was running such a huge risk by having Suzanne in his troupe; how he would not be showering such kindness on her if he didn't like her so much, if she weren't such a good dancer.

"Bullshit," Suzanne said aloud. The only reason he kept her was that she was his best dancer. The most expressive and un-

17

inhibited, she had heard him say. Sometimes, this life was too tiring, so hypocritical, she thought. Nothing like back home in Jamaica. She never remembered feeling so tired in Jamaica, so weary physically from having to dance seven nights every week; so mentally tired from not being sure if what she was doing was right. On top of this was the heavy strain of not knowing if Grandma Nedd would approve of her granddaughter's lifestyle if ever she found out.

Still, she had to pack. Suzanne ran into the bedroom and started stuffing the unfolded clothes into the bag. The manager had told her to travel lightly. Otherwise, suspicious immigration officers at the Peace Bridge might question her closely. Also, he warned her to bring enough *reasonable-looking* clothes. Those were his actual words. The clothes should convince anyone she was on her way to spend a week in Brooklyn with her fictitious cousin Avril.

"You're the only one I'm a little worried about," the manager had said. "The American immigration people are more likely to suspect you. It happens with you black girls all the time. One look at you and they start thinking you're not Canadian. Once they hear your accent, they automatically think you're planning to become an illegal alien. It always happens."

Suzanne hefted the bag for weight and tried to be cheerful and optimistic. She reflected fondly on how the early part of the afternoon had gone. It was strange how things happened in this life, she mused. As if they were preordained. Otherwise, what was the explanation for Suzanne, on the spur of the moment, deciding to go for a walk in the early spring sunshine? And why was it that as soon as she stepped through her apartment door, she ran right into the very man she had tried so hard to elude the previous night? If she didn't know better, she would have sworn Henderson was looking for her. They just stared at each other. The surprise on their faces quickly melted into smiles.

They understood what was going on. She explained she was taking a walk before leaving for Buffalo in a few hours, that she had been in a hurry to get home last night, and anyway she didn't like talking about events at the tavern when she was not there. The tavern was her work and she liked to keep her personal and professional interests apart. He invited her to lunch. Suzanne surprised herself by accepting, as if her strength to resist was already sapped, or suppressed by some all-powerful force acting on her behalf. In the end, she knew she had spent more time with Henderson than she had planned, than was good for the two of them.

By the time they left the Bellair Cafe at the corner of Parliament and Wellesley, they were both tipsy, talking too loudly, touching too much. They were happy and would definitely get together again when she returned, she promised. Of course, this promise was not cast in stone. She still wasn't sure Henderson was worth more than a good flirt. And she knew he had other ideas, the kind of notions Grandma Nedd had warned against.

Suzanne remembered the first time she saw Henderson. Even then, from that encounter, she knew he was different. And this was frightening. As scary as if Grandma Nedd was standing behind her and warning her to stay clear of this stranger. She would always remember how, for some unexplained reason, her eyes were drawn to the door, to where three black men were entering the tavern. One of the waitresses was showing them to the only table where the three could sit together. Somehow, Henderson stood out. He was the only one of the three not wearing a suit, obviously the least sophisticated and roughest looking. It was a packed house, but nobody was drinking and the boss was cracking the whip. "I'm relying on you to stir up some activity. Work your magic for me tonight," he said to Suzanne.

The three men weren't buying any drinks. Two of them were talking, but not showing any real interest in the show. Henderson, meanwhile, was looking around the room. He whispered something to the two men. His eyes locked on Suzanne. She felt them. And irresistibly, she looked in his direction, had to see him smile and say to the other men something she had no chance of hearing from this distance, but which she still yearned to hear. What he said must have been important. It had to be about her. All heads, including the waitress's, turned in Suzanne's direction. That was what Suzanne hated about black men. When they came into the tavern, they always acted as if they possessed her, as if she were letting down the whole black race by dancing naked for white people. Now they were asking for her, so they could condemn her in person.

Suzanne knew what was up, what had to be avoided. She stood on the stairs by the stage, readying herself for when the music stopped and her name was called to walk up the stairs for the next performance.

"They want you to dance for them," said the waitress tersely. Suzanne felt her heart scream. Before she could answer, her name was announced. Suzanne glided onto the multicolored stage, grinding and pumping, not even bothering to hide her raging anger. From the corner of her eyes, she saw them pointing and laughing. The three of them. Perhaps they really thought she was dancing for them. She was sure she heard their lewd voices over the noise and music. These three jerks sitting by the deejay's booth, in the worst seats in the house. They were not going to distract or unnerve her. Not this Suzanne who was so free dancing, whirling and grinding.

Then the music ended, leaving her naked to their eyes. When she came off the stage who should she see talking with the three men but Philmore Leach, the owner. He was laughing, looking in her direction, then back at the men, talking a bit and then looking back at her. And now he was coming in her direction.

"Suze," he said, "these three guys at the table over there, they want you to dance for them. See what you can do." She had no choice.

As it turned out, they did not pillory her with obscene talk as she had expected. They were kind, actually, enjoying themselves. She perched her little box on their table and danced freely. Surprisingly, she fell easily into conversation. They offered her a drink. They wanted to know her name and introduced themselves as David, Whitney and Henderson. As to be expected, no last names. How long was she in Canada? Why did she like to dance? Would she perform at their private parties?

Her answer to the last question was a firm no. But they didn't give up, continuing the friendly probe but putting no pressure on her. Ultimately, the song ended. They paid the five dollars, plus a tip of fifteen dollars. She stooped on the box in front of them, talking some more. Throughout it all, Henderson said nothing, but never stopped watching her. She found it impossible to look him straight in the eye. Two hours later, the three left together. No other woman had danced on their table.

Until this encounter she would never have admitted there was any truth in Grandma Nedd's prophetic words: the women in her family were destined to relive their mothers' lives. Just as Grandma Nedd had ended up the same way as her mother, so had Ona ended up like Grandma Nedd. And Suzanne like Ona? It seemed to be an unbreakable cycle of pain and suffering unless fate intervened, or God forgave the youngest female of the family for the sins of the preceding generations.

"It's only the cold hand of death that can end this curse," Grandma Nedd had said. "For as long as we have a girl child in this family, the curse is bound to continue."

Suzanne breathed a sigh of relief to see the three men leave after she had finished dancing. Henderson had unnerved her. She felt him fondling her breasts and buttocks with his eyes. Something in his movements told her he was married; but even that did not lessen the strong physical attraction, particularly when he looked in her eyes and smiled. At that moment, she felt destiny's strong hand on her back.

Later that night, Henderson returned to the tavern. With her eyes, Suzanne followed every stride, every movement of

21

his head. He was alone and he had liquor on his breath when he ordered a beer. He had come to give her a ride home after work, he said. "Okay," Suzanne stammered. While he sat in the dark waiting for her, Suzanne gave him the slip. She dashed up the stairs at the back of the tavern. They would re-peat this pattern for several nights, with Henderson refusing to give up.

Then, as fate would have it, she spent most of her last day in Toronto with this man, of all people. Suzanne had to admit there was something exhilarating, almost magical, about this chance encounter. The fact Henderson's wife—he was mar-ried with two young sons—could have seen them standing at the corner from her sixth-floor apartment didn't bother Suzanne in the least. Neither did it seem to worry Henderson. If it did, he hid it well, the same way he hid just about all other personal information. Maybe he meant it when he said there was no longer anything between him and his wife; that there never was. That he only married her and endured living six years in wintry Thunder Bay because that had been the only way for him to get back into the country once the author-ities had kicked him out. And maybe it was true that Hen-derson's wife understood that this arrangement was ending, especially now that they had moved to Toronto. All that he told her was believable. Suzanne had seen how similar mari-tal arrangements had expired, like a contract no longer use-ful enough to be renewed and just left to lapse. The good-bye kiss on her lips, the firm squeeze of her ass didn't betray any fear of being caught, any hint of guilt. The only tinge of ap-prehension came from her wondering whether Grandma Nedd wasn't right about the Nedd women and the curse of married men.

Realizing it was almost three o'clock and that they had lin-gered too long, she had dashed across the street against the lights, narrowly avoiding a cyclist. When she looked back, Henderson was still on the pavement, watching her. His ac-tions portrayed carefree happiness, as if he had won the lottery. She too was happy and excited. Perhaps happiness—and alcohol, which always made her drowsy after lunch—had caused her to doze. And to dream, with her mind creatively mixing up the fear and apprehension of the past decade. Those dreams always left her feeling spent and helpless.

Now she was ready to leave, sitting in the living room waiting for the intercom to buzz. Absentmindedly, she flipped on the television. The room was flooded instantly with the laughter of "The Cosby Show." After all these years, this situation comedy about a black family achieving it all—good family life, parents with professional jobs, living in the best neighborhoods, loving their children—seemed farfetched and stale. No wonder. But it was always a favorite in the Morgan family. Or was when they were a family. Before she had learned real life was different from what she saw in the Huxtables' household.

Suzanne switched off the set. There was no need to be sad or to endure this paralysis by nostalgia. No need to dream the unattainable. Or even to think of her family. Instead, she decided to check again to make sure she had everything.

Suzanne remembered the manager's warning to bring her passport. She checked her handbag to make sure the document was there. Although she was a landed immigrant in Canada, and had spent more than the requisite three years to qualify for citizenship, she never thought of herself as anything other than Jamaican. She felt no acceptance in Canada. That was why she had never applied for Canadian identification. Nobody she talked to ever assumed she was anything but a temporary visitor to this country. Fortunately, Jamaica was, and always would be, the country in her blood, the place of friends and family, of the memories that erased any craving to belong elsewhere.

In Jamaica, she was not *alien*. She had a strong national pride—imbued by Grandma Nedd's wonderful stories about life in the old days, about how Suzanne should be proud to be Jamaican, West Indian and African, to be part of a small but proud nation and a region where black people were the majority and ruled themselves. Her Jamaican passport was more than her only identification.

Her first experience at a Toronto school made her realize the term *Jamaican*, despite what Grandma Nedd taught her, was never a badge of honor in this country. Rather, it was a confining label flung, whether deservingly or not, at all black people, unjustly signifying inferiority and backwardness.

Suzanne realized she had not placed the fading black-and-white photograph of Grandma Nedd in her passport, something she did every time she traveled. She went to the bedroom for the picture, her precious traveling companion. When she wasn't touring, the picture graced the upper right-hand corner of the mirror on the wall. From there, Grandma Nedd kept an eye on the bedroom and maintained guard over Suzanne. Sometimes Suzanne was sure she saw the old woman frown when certain people came into the room.

Right beside Grandma Nedd's picture was Telson's, whom she knew was now so much bigger than the baby in the photograph, the baby she still cherished. She wanted an up-to-date picture of her little brother, but her mother would never oblige. In reality, these two, Grandma Nedd and Telson, were her only family. Because of distance and differences, both caused by her own mother, Suzanne could never be with her grandmother or brother.

The deep familial feelings she had for Grandma Nedd were totally absent for her mother, Ona. Suzanne felt guilty about this. Maybe Ona wasn't totally to blame, if anybody at all was wholly responsible for the gulf between them. Remembering Grandma Nedd's warning that she must always honor and respect her mother, Suzanne felt doubly guilty. Her grandmother had warned her to make allowances and to be patient, but above all, to remain true to herself and to the ways of her living God.

"Remember the ten commandments," the old woman had said when Suzanne rebelliously professed she didn't know the mother she was going to live with in Toronto.

"How should I know what to do?" she had asked. "Same thing with this mother-and-father business. I don't know if I can handle that kind of thing."

"Let the commandments be a guiding light unto your feet, chile. No matter how you feel, just remember the fifth commandment, the one that tells you to honor your mother and father, that your days may be long in the land which the Lord thy God giveth thee. The new land the Lord giveth thee." But that was back in Jamaica. Grandma Nedd never knew the truth of this new land. So it was impossible for her to understand what had caused the rift with Ona. Someday, God willing, Suzanne planned to explain everything to her grandmother and to set the record straight. Maybe life would be normal after that discussion, after Grandma Nedd illuminated a way out of this darkness, a route out of this blind alley, by giving both Ona and Suzanne the benefits of her wisdom, thoughts and even clairvoyance.

The intercom buzzed sharply. "You ready?" the manager's voice boomed from the speaker. Again he had interrupted her reverie. He had taken almost an hour to arrive. "We're running late. We gotta hurry."

"Just a minute," she said, hoping he didn't hear the tears in her voice. She hated traveling and being alone. Were she to achieve her dream and return home permanently, she would always remember this about Toronto, the loneliness, isolation and cold.

"Hurry up," he said. "I'm parked illegally in front of the building. I don't want another fucking tick—"

Suzanne pressed the intercom button, cutting him off in midsentence. "I'll be down," she said. She dropped the passport and Grandma Nedd's picture into the handbag of black imitation leather and slipped into her running shoes. The telephone rang again.

Who the arse is calling me now? she wondered. Should she answer? It might be Ona. On the fourth ring the answering machine clicked in. It was Mrs. King downstairs, just calling

25

for one of her interminable chats, or perhaps another damn fight.

Suzanne sucked her teeth; she wished it had been Ona. She would love to tell her good-bye. But her mother never called anymore and she knew her calls were no longer welcomed. As Mrs. King's voice trailed on, Suzanne closed the door behind her and locked it. She put on dark glasses and walked briskly toward the elevator.

The trembling had returned to her limbs, but Grandma Nedd had taught her always to put on a brave face, to laugh when crying. She put that training to the test once again, calling on the discipline that enabled Suzanne to split herself in two, to hide and protect the soft, vulnerable spirit that was her soul.

The carefree Suzanne must walk boldly out to the car and, later, onto the stage in Buffalo, she told herself. On her way out, one of the Suzannes dropped four postdated checks into the landlord's mailbox. It was a precaution: just in case she had to return to Toronto and needed a place, as Grandma Nedd would say, to rest her head.

CHAPTER 3

THAT HER MOTHER bluntly refused to post the bail, even though she knew she would be repaid, didn't surprise Suzanne. It only made her wish that back in Toronto she hadn't been so hasty putting all her money toward the rent. She should have kept some of it for an emergency, or as Grandma Nedd often said, for a rainy day.

It had been a long time since her mother did anything, good or bad, for her. After all, this was the same woman who left her behind in the Caribbean while she gallivanted all over Canada and let her rot in a home for delinquent children. Why then should she expect her mother to change on hearing the news that her whoring daughter—for that was how Ona Morgan so contemptuously described her own flesh and blood to strangers as well as those stupid black women she hung out with—was in some decrepit American jail?

A home or a jail, what was the difference to her mother? Such things as a temporary loss of freedom had no effect on Ona. Not since she had washed her hands of her daughter. Not since she had found out what had gone on with her husband behind her back. Rather, Ona had argued that jail, or

27

confinement in any institution, was one way of keeping Suzanne out of trouble, from harming herself. And it was also a way, Ona claimed, of sparing her the pain of having a policeman knock on her door in the middle of the night. The agony of not knowing where her offspring was, what she was doing and with whom.

Suzanne imagined what her mother did on receiving the news from Buffalo. Ona once foretold with great certainty that since Suzanne was under the same curse as she and Grandma Nedd, Suzanne was bound to end up going from jailhouse to jailhouse, her body riddled with diseases.

"I'm washing my hands of you," she had said, dusting her palms as though they were covered with invisible flour. "So from now on, when you get in trouble with the police, or your belly swells up to your mouth, or you're too sick to help yourself, or one of them wicked boys you like to hang out with in them gangs smoking dope shoots yuh up, I'm telling you right now, don't bother calling my name."

A part of Suzanne refused to get angry with her mother. She had given Ona justification enough. That side was willing to blame Suzanne for purposely making life difficult for her mother. It rejected categorically any suggestion that, by being difficult, Suzanne was only trying to teach her mother a lesson. Nothing more. Even in the throes of this internal struggle, Suzanne recognized some basic truths to life. Everybody understood that the bonds between a parent and child should be strong enough to withstand anything. Except that, Suzanne was forced to concede, in her case there had to be that strong link in the first place. And by leaving her at such a tender age, Ona had ensured there wasn't any real attachment. Yet Suzanne still felt she had to keep reaching out, had to pretend some bond existed. Whose name leapt automatically from her lips when the stern-faced jailer asked for her next of kin, as if she were just a lifeless body to be delivered to whomever wanted to claim it for disposal? She could only turn to her mother, not the woman she discovered on arrival in Canada, but the loving and kindhearted angel Grandma Nedd had always told her about when she was back home. The only problem was that Suzanne never got to meet the kind mother Grandma Nedd had led her to expect. Therefore, there was no real surprise when Ona's answer came back.

Her mother was so typical of all those West Indian parents. Suzanne remembered what her friends had said some years earlier. They were standing around the plaza in front of one of those twenty-four hour convenience stores, smoking a little grass, sharing a few cans of pop. It was cold, the middle of the night, and they were hungry. Yet none of them wanted to go home. Just then one of the guys broke the tension. It was intended as a joke. "Can anybody here think of one youth born in the West Indies that is happy right now? I'm thinking of, say, a youth who was raised back home and came up here when he or she was almost a teenager. Any of them happy?"

Suzanne remembered thinking how the stony silence confirmed the validity of this observation, how the speaker had emphasized one word—yewts as he sneeringly called the young people. Nobody laughed. Even then, she had wondered what her mother would have said if the same question were put to her. Maybe she would have dismissed it by saying if the yewts weren't happy it was because they didn't know what to do with themselves; that they were ungrateful and without ambition; always disrespectful and following the wrong crowd rather than turning to their parents for advice and guidance. Ona had said that much to her, even when nobody asked her opinion.

Years later, simply thinking of that cold evening and how they all felt back then still sent chills throughout Suzanne's body. She remembered the looks on the faces of her friends, how their countenances so clearly showed the impact on their hearts of the statement: how it had ripped the scabs off the wounds; how their gazes and unfocused stares demonstrated the vulnerability of every last one of them. The dynamics of the group changed instantly once those words were spoken.

They stood around in the cold for a while. But even then their spirits were broken. The intended joke had deflated them. One by one they drifted off into the night, into the shadows with only the glowing cigarettes pointing them in a specific direction. Some of them just left, even though they had nowhere to go. Suzanne was among the last to leave. Fortunately, when she got home Ona was out.

Even as she sat in the jail, that cold evening and its implications played in her mind. No, Suzanne reflected, she still couldn't point to one happy buddy, and this was years after the question was asked. None of them got along with their parents. Particularly those who had been left behind in the Caribbean to be raised by family and friends. The story seldom varied. When they arrived in Canada they found themselves dealing with strangers, particularly fathers and stepfathers, some of whom they had never heard of until they joined them in Canada.

Suzanne had been no exception, and because of this she believed she and all the immigrant children like her were a lost generation, drifting aimlessly without ties or a sense of belonging. At least this was one thing on which she and Ona agreed. How could they not agree when Ona was among the first to point out how the school system had been so good at making immigrant children feel out of place? But the schools were not the only problem. The parents themselves were too. And that was where she and Ona disagreed. Just about every one of her buddies complained about the same thing: how they felt unaccepted by their parents and resented by pampered brothers and sisters born in Canada who never understood what life was like back home. There was never a closeness, never a bond.

Many of the West Indian immigrants her age were long-term inmates of the jails. Several carried the scars from shootouts with drug dealers, other gangs or the police. Despite her faults, Suzanne knew she had done well to get as far as she had. Staying alive this long was an achievement, even if her mother didn't understand and had become so vehement in her condemnations.

It was best if Suzanne and her mother continued to have nothing to do with each other, if they simply kept to separate paths, Suzanne thought. Except that at a time like this, stranded in a dilapidated Buffalo jail, she had nobody but her mother as next of kin.

After giving Ona's name to the jailer, Suzanne had specifically instructed the American lawyer provided by the manager to tell Kevin Jenkins in Toronto to make any arrangements necessary to get her out. Although she was not a fan of Jenkins, Suzanne had used him from time to time, his usefulness stemming from the fact that her mother knew him. Jenkins was the only real inheritance from her mother, and he wasn't even much. Still, he was a lawyer, the only one that her mother really knew, or was willing to trust and confide in. Whenever there was trouble, Ona instinctively turned to him instead of dealing with another lawyer whose faults she didn't know.

Suzanne had insisted that under no condition must Jenkins approach her mother. The last two times Suzanne was in trouble in Toronto and needed bail, true to her word, Ona had refused to help. It was unlikely she would help now.

Not surprisingly, the word had come back from Jenkins that the lawyer should give Suzanne a clear message from Ona: Suzanne didn't have a mother and, certainly while in jail, she was fully on her own. Suzanne told herself she didn't really care. Somehow, she was glad her mother had reacted this way. The rejection proved how right she had been all along. Why she didn't trust this hardhearted woman who had brought her into this world, but had abandoned her to flee overseas. Suzanne had been right when in anger she had screamed at Ona that she didn't know what the word "mother" meant. "You're not my damn mother!" she had shouted. "Grandma Nedd is my mother. She'll always be."

Suzanne's choice was to get the bail posted, pay the fines and leave Buffalo without anyone in her family knowing. Her preference was that the lawyer, if he were unable to arrange payment himself and had to approach a member of her small family, should go to her stepfather, Joe. But he too should be left out of this matter for as long as possible. She and Joe had caused enough trouble for each other. Even so, Joe hardly had any money to help even himself.

Her reluctance to call on Joe went deeper. Suzanne still wasn't sure of her feelings for her stepfather and didn't want to complicate matters by being beholden to him. As Suzanne sat thinking, she realized her few options were shrinking. The young American lawyer refused to let the manager post the bail. It would only make matters worse for the girls, the curly-haired bespectacled man reasoned, if someone were to realize the same man was bailing out all these Canadian girls from the same jail for the same immoral offense at the same bar. And in the case of Suzanne, here was a woman traveling on a Jamaican passport and working in the United States without a green card. "It's not going to work," the lawyer said. "Some smart person in the district attorney's office starts to investigate everybody's background, makes this discovery and nobody benefits."

Suzanne insisted on risking everything rather than asking her mother for help, and adamantly told him so. The lawyer smiled the same belittling smirk she had seen on lawyers' faces many times. Without his uttering a word, Suzanne knew what this attorney was thinking. That here was this smart-ass woman, a whore at that, who didn't know American law, but who felt she had the authority to tell him what to do.

"Let's try for your mother," he said impersonally. "In my opinion, for what my opinion is worth, it could have some effect on the judge if I stood up in court and said that your mother, an irreproachable hardworking woman in Toronto, had hastened to send the bail money for her misguided daughter. That Mrs. Morgan, a Christian woman to the bone, a hardworking immigrant making a life for herself in a new country, so blinded by her long hours of work she didn't know of her daughter's line of business, was terribly distraught at the news and was waiting at the border to take her unfortunate and misguided offspring home. These things have a way of affecting judges."

Suzanne didn't even bother to explain to the lawyer that such arguments had long stopped having an effect on her mother. He didn't know her mother, the things she had gone through, and what had contributed to Ona's rock-hard decision not to be caught near a prison or court if Suzanne was inside it. However, everything the lawyer did convinced her his patience was running out so she decided to just listen and make him think she was being impressed. She knew he had fifteen other women waiting for him. The others didn't care who provided the money as long as they got out of jail.

"Suzanne," he finally said, sitting on the chair and looking her straight in the face. "Listen to me. Number one: it's just not possible for the man who brought you across the border to help. Number two: we can't borrow the money from Kevin Jenkins in Toronto. As I gather, he's not only your lawyer in Toronto but some kind of family friend. Your manager told me this lawyer is also an associate of the man who owns the tavern in Toronto where you performed last, is that right?"

"Yes," she said, "he helped my mother to immigrate to Canada."

"I'm sorry, but it's not wise for him to get involved with this kind of thing, especially since he's involved in other business over here and has to cross the border often. Can't you think of anyone who might help you? We're trying to get your mother or father and that's the best we can do so far," the lawyer said. Up to this point, Suzanne didn't even know the name of this attorney. She didn't want to find out either. At first sight, she didn't like him. "If your mother doesn't have the money, your lawyer friend at the nightclub in Toronto can lend it to her and we can settle this thing. So don't tell me not to call her."

As he left the cell, his body language clearly indicated he was in a hurry to be rid of this troublesome client. Suzanne sat on the edge of the cot and began to read some writings on the wall. Someone had left phone numbers with the 416 and 905 area codes. Maybe she wasn't the first whore from Toronto to get busted and thrown into this cell on a charge of defiling Buffalo's public decency.

The numbers might have been left by someone like Bobby Ali, the young Guyanese gang leader who was her first school friend. Bobby was in prison most of the time. Suzanne had visited him in Toronto's Don Jail after the last drug bust. He was once arrested in Buffalo when he had almost cleared the border with the shipment in the lining of his Mercedes Benz car. Bobby said the arresting officer's eyes popped when he saw the amount of coke stuffed behind the panels. Until then, Bobby said it had been an uneventful trip from the pickup in Miami.

On his return to Toronto, Bobby had told friends that the worst jails were in Buffalo. "They treat you like a piece of shit, man. I'll tell you guys something, stay away from the U.S. jails if you can. Ask to be transferred to Canada to serve out your time at home." Bobby had gotten his wish to be transferred and was right away given parole for time served in the United States.

Eventually, the lawyer came back asking if Suzanne had thought of anyone else to call. They were unable to get through to her mother. Ona had hung up abruptly and refused to answer subsequent calls.

"Look, this case is taking up more time than I expected. I thought this was going to be a simple matter," the lawyer explained.

He had important people waiting for him at his office, he said, checking what looked like a gold watch under the white monogrammed shirtsleeve on his left wrist. Suzanne remembered Bobby's advice about the Buffalo jails. She wondered if the same counsel of avoidance applied to American lawyers. Bobby had to spend eight months in the jail before getting home; she wasn't looking forward to staying that long.

"What about this cousin, Avril, in New York?" he asked. "Can you get hold of her? The other girls are ready to leave, and you're holding things up."

"There's no cousin," Suzanne said scornfully, wondering if this so-called lawyer was so naive not to know that even if there were a cousin in New York, she would never give anyone the name. Otherwise, she would be exposing the poor girl to all sorts of abusive calls from people in the courts, from the police who made a habit of following through on these matters, from immigration people who automatically assumed she was an illegal immigrant. People would naturally believe the cousin was in the same line of business and pester her. The disrespect in her voice finally got to the lawyer.

"Look, I'm trying my best to help," he snarled back, "and I'm not getting any help from you. As far as I'm concerned, you can stay here with that attitude, if that's what you want. I have to think of the others waiting for me to clear up matters with you. But I must tell you something before I go. They're thinking of holding you in immigration detention and then shipping you back to Jamaica. Not Canada," he said slowly, "but to Jamaica, since you are traveling on a Jamaican passport."

When he turned to walk out of the cell, Suzanne panicked. He sounded so much like her mother. She saw herself alone in the jail while the girls paid their bail and returned to the motel to await word that their lawyer had entered the guilty pleas, paid the fines and they were free to leave the county, never to return. Then they would bundle into the van and head for some other town, maybe even in the same state. She was going to be left behind, alone in this jail, until she was transferred to the detention center. Back in Jamaica, Grandma Nedd would be absolutely startled to see that they sent back the wrong person—some dancer. Suzanne wasn't going to sit back in all her pride and let them inflict this disappointment on her grandmother. Suzanne recalled her mother's horrific stories about immigration detention centers.

"What did she say when they called?" Suzanne asked the lawyer, desperately trying to stall him from leaving her alone and cut off.

"What *who* said?"

"My mother. What did she say?"

"How am I to know? I wasn't there," he snarled.

Suzanne sat up on the cot, sulking. The lawyer softened a bit.

"Look, I gather she hung up the telephone before anyone *really* talked to her. I told you that, didn't I? She didn't say anything. Just hung up."

"Bitch," Suzanne muttered. "What about Joe, my stepfather?"

"If nobody will answer the phone, we can't reach them," he answered. "Look, isn't there anybody in all Toronto, in New York, in Buffalo you can contact? Somebody willing to do a favor for you? A friend. Somebody from school, who's working legitimately." She thought hard. There had to be somebody. She wasn't going to risk Grandma Nedd having the wrong person sent home to her.

"There's one person," Suzanne said in a panic. "His name's Hendy. Henderson. I'll give you the number. Maybe he can get the money from Philmore. Maybe you can call him and help make the arrangements for him to pass 'round by the club and borrow the money from Mr. Leach for me."

Rummaging through her purse, she located the piece of paper Henderson had given her with his name and telephone number.

"This is at home or work?" the lawyer asked, taking the slip.

"Home."

"Is he likely to be there? Doesn't he work?"

"I don't know."

The lawyer shrugged and walked out of the cell. The guard, impatient with the lawyer's goings and comings, slammed the door shut loudly.

Suzanne sat biting her nails, hoping Henderson was home

on this Victoria Day weekend, the first long holiday of the new year.

ON THE BUS back to Toronto, Henderson and Suzanne talked very little. She looked scared, deep in thought. Eventually, he gave up trying to start a conversation. For most of the trip, she slept with her head on his shoulder.

The lawyer, Jenkins, and Philmore Leach were waiting for them at the Toronto bus terminal. When they saw her coming down the steps, the two men got out of their car and walked over. They kissed Suzanne on the cheeks and led her away. Leach took her black bag. They were walking to the white Cadillac when Suzanne turned and waved to Henderson.

The lawyer took the wheel and pulled out into the traffic. He headed up Bay Street to Wellesley and then crossed over to Parliament, making the trip in five minutes. He pulled up in front of her apartment building, but didn't cut the engine.

"By the way," Jenkins said, looking into the rearview mirror at Suzanne's reflection, "any idea how you're going to pay Phil back the bail money, plus the usual interest?"

"I'll stop payment on three of my rent checks now I'm back. I'll bring the money tomorrow. 'Bye, Mr. Leach. Thanks for the help."

"Don't mention it," Leach said. "If I didn't know you, I'd swear you were a different person. There's something a bit strange about you."

"Yeah?"

"Like hell," he said.

Suzanne slammed the door shut. One good thing about such a short trip to Buffalo: she was now able to make Mrs. King think she was taking the old woman's advice to get out of the business. On the negative side, Suzanne now had to find some way to make money to buy food and pay the rent.

It had been a long journey to this point where Ona no

longer helped her, Suzanne reflected, still smarting from the
hurt of the rejection and the near miss with her grandmother.
It had been so different when she first arrived and Ona was so
anxious to impress and protect her. Sometimes, Suzanne
wished she were free to fly back to that junction, to the crossing in the roads leading to this estrangement, to earlier times
when Ona was always ready to fight for her even against the
greatest odds. Maybe, just maybe, she had taken the wrong
track, Suzanne thought as she threw the bag into a corner. She
dived into the bed hoping to sleep quickly, to further numb
her mind to all around her, anesthetized to all she had lost,
and to willingly offer herself up to the demons in the nightmare lurking in the apartment.

CHAPTER 4

ONA IMPATIENTLY RANG the intercom buzzer a third time. On evenings like this, when she was in a hurry, she hated waiting. Even for old Mrs. King, with her swollen arthritic legs, to drag herself to the intercom, to inquire two, three or even four times who was at the door, as if she were going deaf or suspiciously taking absolutely no chances, and then after a long pause to let her into the building.

If Ona were lucky, and she seldom was, a tenant entered the apartment building ahead of her, letting her slip into the main foyer without having to buzz the old lady.

Then she waited an eternity for one of the four elevators, positively the slowest in all Toronto. Invariably, Ona would be checking her watch, counting the minutes to the six-o'clock Toronto Transit Commission bus. It ran to the subway every fifteen minutes until six sharp. After that there was a thirty-minute wait for the next bus. The half-hour interval held no appeal for Ona, especially in crime-riddled St. James Town, home of violent drug dealers and, unfortunately, her only daughter.

Thirty minutes' waiting always threw off her entire schedule, so that well after nine P.M., when Joe got home from work at the same TTC, from the job she had pushed so hard to get him, she would still be slaving over a hot stove. Even after they had stuffed their faces while silently watching television, her work for the day wasn't finished. She had to iron Joe's transit uniform, without much effort because of the almost rumple-resistant material, thank God, and then bathe little Telson and put him to bed. Bedtime stories came only on weekends no matter how much he begged. And, of course, the dishes had to be washed. Her mother had drilled that much into her. It was a slack woman of the house who went to bed leaving in the sink dirty dishes to attract ants and other vermin. And in any Nedd household, her mother had instructed, women always took their leadership roles very seriously. So even if she were dropping with tiredness, she still had to finish washing the dishes before taking a shower and going to bed.

Ona preferred to slip into the apartment building unannounced, but Mrs. King didn't like it. She seemed to feel Ona was creeping up on her, as if trying to catch her mistreating little Telson, or to spy on Suzanne and her. There were aspects of Mrs. King that reminded Ona of her mother in Jamaica. Conflicting things that caused Ona to cling to this old woman who could be so gentle and then just as quickly repel her. What Ona really hated about this old dried-up and suspicious woman was how quick she was to lecture her about life; telling Ona to settle for less than she aspired to; to stop running her blood to water; to try to relax and enjoy life.

Every time Ona turned up unannounced, Mrs. King made a point of saying, "Oh, I didn't hear the buzzer. Maybe it ain't working this afternoon. I must tell the super." Suspicious. She was too damn suspicious and private, just like Mira Nedd.

In any case, Mrs. King's message couldn't possibly be lost on her visitor. When she was in a really cranky mood, probably from an arthritic flare-up, the same Mrs. King was likely to grumble that although she always loved children, and although they brought joy to her apartment and some extra cash to her pocket every week, at her age, which the Lord had seen fit to bless her with three score plus ten years and then three, she shouldn't really be testing the limits of the law by turning the one-bedroom apartment into an illegal day care center. Then, just as quickly, she would be talking of doing her little bit, as long as God kept breath in her body, to help Ona see her way in this life. That she, Mrs. King, would be available for her as long as Ona needed her, because Ona was a kind, good-hearted woman who only needed a chance or two and a few good friends.

One way or another, Mrs. King drove home an unmistakable point: Ona Morgan needed her more than the old lady needed Ona Morgan. Such was the case in the past, the present, and would be in the future. When all was said and done, poor, sickly Mrs. King was the only true friend Ona had. Worse, Ona knew the old woman was right.

The thought of putting two-year-old Telson into a proper day care center, where he could at least learn to count and spell his name, avoiding the fate of his big sister, appealed to Ona. But for the moment such luxuries, like so many other things, were beyond reach. Certainly, some of the dreams would be attainable if her husband helped her more in the home, planned a life with her and acted as though Telson was as much his responsibility as hers. If he kept away from those losers he called friends.

As far as she knew, Joe made good money at the TTC, even if he did claim, with some justification, that it was the world's most boring job. All he did was sit in a glass booth, selling tokens and tickets, making sure people presented valid transfers before entering the subway station. She understood and empathized with his frustrations. It took no brains to collect tickets and transfers. This wasn't fulfillment of the dream that had brought Joe to Canada from Barbados. She knew how much Joe believed in his own ability. In his job, in their marriage, and in wider Canadian society, Joe felt trapped, unable to flex his muscles, unable to implement any of the ideas bubbling in his mind. Every day at work was frustrating, he told her. It wasn't as though he was driving a bus, where the challenges of driving or meeting new people broke the boredom.

Ona sympathized generously. She too knew what it was to feel unfulfilled, to struggle against the oppressive reality that one's life dreams would never be attained, certainly not in this life, when all that was left was the cold inner void of untapped potentials, a grave of its own. She kept these thoughts to herself because nobody believed her when she said she understood the effects of the abortions of dreams. But nobody believed she was genuine, not Joe, and certainly not Suzanne or her friends like Bobby Ali. Sometimes not even Mrs. King. They were too quick to argue that Ona and her generation should never have made such sacrifices to be accepted into a new culture.

Ona knew certain realities of living in a white-dominated city like Toronto had to be faced and endured by black people, and the less complaining, the better. In this aspect, she agreed with Mrs. King and her lower levels of appeasement. If she wanted to, she could make the same criticisms about her job as Joe did of his. Still, boring or not, the work paid the bills and gave them the chance to make sure that, with a bit of sacrifice and astute planning, Telson would have a better choice of jobs than his parents ever had. With luck, he would turn out better than his sister.

That was why Ona wanted Joe to be less tight-fisted and accept his responsibilities. She had read in the newspaper that with benefits TTC workers were making something like thirty dollars an hour, but for all she knew, Joe was working for nothing. At the end of the month, he placed on top of the fridge $920 for the rent. It was always in cash, usually crisp, hard-to-separate bills. As far as she knew, the man didn't even have a checking account.

The $920 was all he spent on the home, even at Christmas when everybody needed a bit more. Whenever she asked him to add a few extra dollars, he angrily pointed out that with the

payments for his car, stereo, television and family commitments back home in Barbados, he was fully extended. If she
wanted, she was welcome to think of the $920 as half the rent
and half the food and heating bill, because he didn't live
alone, neither did he eat all the food in the apartment. Indeed,
he might be able to shave a few dollars off the rent if he leased
a one-bedroom apartment somewhere in the city, a place just
big enough for himself and the occasional visit from Telson.

Of course, he knew Ona didn't like talking about such matters. She preferred to suffer in relative silence than to engage
in such poisonous and belittling conversations. Just the threat
was enough to get Ona to drop the topic. Painfully, Ona had
learned it did her no good to argue. Not with Joe, Suzanne,
Mrs. King, lawyers or even her supervisor at work. Even back
home in Jamaica, she never won an argument with Mira
Nedd, the thought of which still ate her guts out. Instead, she
was always planning how to stretch her measly salary of $560
every two weeks. Some months, she skipped the loan payments for the furniture. This was a loan that ten years later was
still strangling her. So many times she had had to consolidate
and renegotiate the repayment terms. Or, as she did only a
week earlier, she would skimp on the food bill to buy Telson a
much-needed article of clothing. Thank God, he was off baby
food and starting to take solids and she didn't have to spend all
the money every week on plastic diapers and milk formula.
Yet every week before she received her pay, it was already
spent. Ona couldn't remember the last time she had treated
herself with a tin of powder or a good hairdo. Or when last she
had sent her mother in Jamaica a little something. How was
Ona to do any of these things when she could never tell when
Joe was likely to ask her to lend him the same rent money he
had given her, because often he needed to make the payment
on his car. Joe was always so broke, Ona swore, that he had to
be giving his money to some outside hussy.

Otherwise, Ona suspected Joe was either salting away his
money, stuffing a kitty for when he inevitably left her, or he

was simply blowing it on drinking and gambling. She had good reason to believe the latter was true and prayed to God Joe wasn't also involved in the growing drug trade. On Friday nights he went to the homes of his friends, not the white colleagues from the TTC where Joe said he never felt fully accepted, but people in similar circumstances as him from back home. These lowlifes drank heavily and played poker well into Saturday, breaking only to come home to dress and head off to the Hole for an all-night dance. Then Joe would come home smelling of stale smoke and alcohol, most times angry and broke.

Once in a while, he stumbled home in high spirits with piles of crumpled bills that looked like they had been shuffled through several hands before being stuffed into a pocket at the end of the long night. Usually, he dumped the uncounted money on the dressing table. While he took a bath, Ona often sneaked into the bedroom and picked out four or five of the twenties. Such windfalls were rare. Most times, he begged her for money to see him through the next week. When he slept, she checked his arms for needle marks.

Yes, it would definitely be easier on her if Joe helped out in the home. She didn't mean such unmanly things as shopping or washing, but maybe reading a story to Telson, taking him for a walk or even playing with the child once in a while, instead of coming home and putting on the stereo and then plugging in the big leather headphones as if to tune out the world around him. That was what she really hated: the way he picked up the headphones with a smile on his face and slipped them over his head, as if daring Ona to complain. Telson had learned not to approach Joe when he was listening to music. Instead, he hung around Ona's feet, asking her to fix broken toys, to button shirts and even to wrestle with him, until, in exhaustion, she dumped him in bed.

"God, these elevators slow, nuh?" said a black woman standing next to her with several plastic shopping bags. Ona had seen her in the building before, had seen her at some black women's meetings, and believed she lived there. When passing, they said nothing, but smiled at each other. An unspoken bond as strong as any. Now, having heard her voice for the first time, Ona knew she was definitely West Indian, perhaps Vincentian. But from which island, she wasn't sure.

"I can't understand why every elevator gotta go down into the damn basement first," the woman continued. "Why the apartment owners can't make it so that at least one of them can stop on the first floor and then go back up without going all the way to the basement where it only gets full up with people from the underground garage and then leaves us here when it comes back up?" she asked, sucking her teeth in disgust and casting a glance at Ona.

"I know what you mean," Ona answered. Her thoughts were still on the bus and the dwindling time.

"What I say makes sense, don't it?" the woman asked. "Watch and see what will happen to the one that just gone down into the basement. Mark my word, when it gets back up here on the first floor, it's going to be full up with all sorts of people from the underground garage. By the way my name Anita, Anita Watkins."

"Mine is Ona Morgan."

"I know. I know your daughter too. She's the one that used to live in this building. Sometimes, she used to talk to my Debbi. I think I talked with her once or twice. Nice girl you have there. My Debbi really likes her a lot."

The elevator opened right in front of Ona. She squeezed in and the woman stood beside her, putting some of the bags upright between the insteps of her feet. Ona pressed sixteen and the button lit up.

Every time she pushed that number, Ona felt guilty for exposing Telson to unnecessary danger. The fire department got angry when it found out that, despite dire warnings, people kept children above the eleventh floor, the highest point the department's ladders could reach. Of course, the fire department didn't think about the financial realities for working people who just couldn't afford proper day care.

There had to be a meaningful tradeoff between safety and financial necessity, Ona told herself. The sixteenth floor in this building was the tradeoff, the optimum point where the available money bought the minimum risk. Still, the fire department was likely to hit the roof if it found out Telson was taken care of by an old woman with swollen legs, a keeper who probably couldn't run as fast as the child walked.

Ona stared at the panel of numbers to stifle her thoughts. What choice did she have? She wasn't going to leave Telson all alone in the apartment. She had learned from making that mistake with Suzanne. The silence addled the brain. In any case, Telson was a mere baby. She couldn't abandon him too.

Almost every button from five up was lit. Anita Watkins had pushed twenty-three. When the elevator couldn't hold one more body, after some people had tried to force their way in, the car began to buzz impatiently and the door closed. For what seemed an eternity, they were entombed in the slow-moving machine, listening to one another's breathing and smelling one another's sweat.

Finally, the light on sixteen went out and the elevator stopped with a slight bump. When Ona stepped out, the Watkins woman said, "See yuh later," as though they were friends. It surprised Ona. She thought the brief exchange had ended with the opening of the elevator door. She returned the farewell gesture, then looked at her watch. She had just enough time to pick up the little boy, place the plate and soup bowl in her bag, button up the child's coat and run.

"The elevator kinda slow today, eh," Mrs. King said, waiting at the open door to the apartment. "I was standing here long time waiting for you."

The little boy was watching television. On hearing his mother's footsteps, he jumped up and ran to meet her.

46

"How was it at the credit union today? Hectic?" Mrs. King asked.

She seemed to be in one of those talkative moods that hit her when the shut-in loneliness got to be too much, but Ona had no time. Those talks tended to be long and rambling. When she did have a few minutes, Ona didn't mind chatting with the old lady. She understood how frustrating, how trapped it must feel to spend every day in a little apartment in a large building—not venturing outside, seeing nobody but the child and talking to nobody unless the phone rang. Her mother back in Jamaica would go bananas cooped up like that. Ona knew she would too.

Ona tried to put aside some time to talk with Mrs. King, usually when she delivered the groceries on Saturday. Every second Saturday, Joe allowed her to use the silver-gray Buick to shop for groceries. By noon, with the newspaper advertising supplement and coupons in hand, she would have hit all the discount shops—Bi-Way, Bargain Harold's, Valdi, Franklin's— to stretch every dollar. She always kept an eye out for a few inexpensive things for Mrs. King, such as house slippers to protect her feet from the cold apartment floor. Then came the long drive to the cavernous Knob Hill Farms store, where it looked as though the food had just left the farm and not made an intermediary stop for packaging. This was where she did the major shopping for her family and Mrs. King, making a point of picking up a tin of English biscuits and a bag of sweets for the old woman to munch on while sitting alone at home.

"You know when my husband was still alive, God bless his soul," Mrs. King was saying, "he wouldn't let no bank touch one red cent of his money. Not one blind cent. Used to be a porter on the railway, the only job black people could get in them days, on the Canadian Pacific. Bertie was a staunch union man, he and Uncle Donald and brother Gairy, and he always put the few dollars he worked for in the railway brotherhood credit union. Don't know why he did, but I was young in

47

them days and didn't used to ask too much questions. Did everything he told me. You know when yuh young, new to a country and you and a man struggling to make a life together, especially if the man was born here and knew everybody. Besides, he was the only one that used to work and support his family, not like the so-called men o' today, if I might say so. Those were the days when a woman stayed home and minded the children or got a job as a domestic servant for the white people. A proper man found some good, stiff, hard work. What we got nowadays ain't men, but something else. Anyway, one day my Bertie comes home with his chin on his chest and tells me 'Moms, we lost everything.' The credit union gone bankrupt or something, so . . . "

"That won't happen today, Mrs. King," Ona interrupted, still hoping to make a quick exit. No matter how close she and the old lady were, West Indian respect dictated she always call her Mrs. King. No first-name acquaintances here.

"These are different days. The government does put insurance on all the money at the credit unions. Just like the banks. You can have faith in the banks these days. In the credit unions too," Ona explained.

"I don't know. Insurance or no insurance, you can't trust the banks. This ain't like back home in the West Indies. Anyway, that ain't a problem for a poor woman like me who ain't got no money, except for the few pennies from you and the pension left by Bertie. One time, I used to get a pass on the railway. Went all over this country Canada here and the United States, way down south where the black people does live worse than some o' we back home in the West Indies, even worse than places like Halifax out east. But they stopped givin' the wives of pensioners the passes now, and anyway I'm too old to make use o' them. All I can say is thank God they ain't stop the pension Bertie worked out his soul case for. At least, they ain't stop it yet. But you can never take anything for granted. You shouldn't trust anybody neither. I remember when black people like we couldn't buy a house on most streets in this Toronto. You just couldn't get the land title in your name if your skin wasn't white, and this Mr. Harewood at the railway front office told my Bertie he would buy this house for him if Bertie gave him the money. Then he would give it back to Bertie on a lease forever. Bertie gave the man the money, and just like that he disappeared. Gone with the money. We couldn't even call the police. They would have laughed at us. We had no proof. It was from that day that Bertie and me decided to put everything down in writing and to trust nobody, why I'm always keeping notes on everything I see and do."

The old woman paused briefly, then changed the subject. "Talking about writing down things, take Suzie," she said. "I know she's mad with me, but I can't help it if people always taking offense at me, 'cause you know me, I like to speak my mind even if it does offend people. But everybody got to know by now that old Mrs. King don't mean no harm when she talks in a certain way. I just speak my mind. God loves the truth."

"Suzie don't like listening to nobody, not even she own mother, Mrs. King," Ona said, easily tossing aside the formal language of her workplace for the more expressive vernacular. "I don't know what to make o' the young people o' today. You can only try yuh best and pray."

"Well," Mrs. King said, "as you just say you'self these is different times. Thank God, I ain't no part of them. I mean, I only got so long to live on this earth. That's why I'm so glad that Rev. Lucas does still drop by and visit me on Sundays. A real nice fellow. I even took the liberty of suggesting that maybe Suzie should go and have a chat with him. He said: anytime, that he'd do it just for me. That's when she got vex. I think she got upset because Rev. Lucas is from one of these establishment church as she put it, not from the Pocomania she's used to. So she got vex and I ain't heard from she since."

Ona saw this conversation dragging on forever, now that the old woman was sitting and making her legs comfortable. Ona shuffled her feet, checked her watch and cleared her throat. Mrs. King got the hint.

"Run 'long now," she urged. "Don't let me keep you back any longer."

"Come, Telson," Ona said, grabbing the chance to escape. "Tell Grandma good evening. The bus soon come." '

" 'Bye, Grandma," Telson said.

"God bless yuh, child," Mrs. King said, rising slowly to close the door behind them. "I does really feel sorry for West Indian children like little Telson here who ain't got no grandmother or grandfather, no aunty or uncle. That ain't the way we does bring up children in the West Indies, where everybody does live like one big family. The poor children up here don't even know who they is or where their family come from, no sense of belonging. Then they go out in this society out there like so many lost ducklings with nobody to lead them across the road. Just a mother, and father if they're lucky. I does feel too sorry for them. How can we expect them to make anything of themselves when they start out so lost and bewildered?"

Absentmindedly, Ona began digging at the little boy's nose to dislodge a piece of dried snot. "You'll make the boy's nose bleed," Mrs. King scolded. Ona stopped. "How can these children learn anything, with their parents so busy cutting and contriving to survive, and no grandparents around to give them a view of the bigger picture, to tell them that life won't always be as hectic as it is for their parents? How will they learn times and seasons to life with no grandmother or grandfather? African people always left these teachings to the grandparents, but in this society, there are no teachers. That's why I keep telling Suzie to talk to Rev. Lucas. It hurt my heart when I hear older black people like myself saying, just like they're white, 'I don't want anything to do with the grandchildren. They can come and visit but they must leave at the end of the day.' And they're so proud saying that, not knowing their history or culture. That's why I try so hard to be friendly with Suzanne and to point her in the right direction even if she doesn't like it. That's why I don't mind looking after the little boy so that you can go off and try to make a life for yourself."

"I know, Mrs. King," Ona said. She blinked to hold back the tears and the memories of *that* voice whispering over her shoulder so often these days. In a strange way, when Mrs. King talked about helping Ona by looking after her child, the old woman was only repeating what Mira Nedd had said two decades earlier. Even the voices sounded the same these days. "You've always helped me out. You've always been there for me, Mrs. King, even with Telson here. But I got to go now. We'll talk another time. I'll telephone, if I'm not too tired tonight."

"Don't bother yourself if you can't call. I understand how it is," Mrs. King said. "If you hear from Suzie, tell she to visit me sometime, nuh. I left a few messages on she machine, but she ain't call me back."

"If I ever see she," Ona said, grabbing the child's possessions and stuffing them in the bag, not giving the old lady a chance to start another conversation. "You know very well Suzanne don't speak to me no more. And I'm her mother."

"I know. I was still hoping things changed," Mrs. King said sheepishly. "I keep hoping you and that girl will make up real soon. Both o' you need one another. That's why I think both of you gotta talk to somebody that can help you. I mean, I've tried my best, but I can only do so much. I'm an old woman."

"See yuh on Tuesday, bright and early, after the long weekend, Mrs. King," Ona said, opening the door.

As usual in Ona's life, something went wrong. Before she reached the stop, the bus pulled up. The driver, seeing her running with the child on her hip, simply looked down the road and drove off. She cursed the driver blue under her breath. He could have waited a few seconds. Instead, she had to wait thirty-five minutes for the next bus.

That night things simply got worse. Telson had come down with a cold and fever and kept her up all night. For the next three days, Ona stayed at home caring for the baby while Joe went about his business, staying out half the night, listening to his music and sleeping. So much for the first long weekend of the new year. During this time, Ona saw Joe for no more than a couple of hours and that was on Monday morning when he came home to dress for work. The anger inside her just bubbled over and she exploded. The frustration of being saddled with the boy all weekend, of being confined to the little apartment like some damn prisoner while Joe had his fun, was too much for her.

Their voices rang through the building in bitter argument. Finally, he left the house in anger, slamming the door behind him. That night Joe didn't return home. For the first time, Ona felt she really meant it when she told herself that she didn't really care if he ever came back. What a wasted long weekend. She must have been really crazy to think it was going to be different, to believe for even the most fleeting of moments that Joe planned to spend at least one of the three days with her and Telson. That they could have gone walking in the park, maybe for a drive to Niagara Falls or across the border into Buffalo for a bit of shopping. Or that Suzanne might find some excuse to visit or even call.

Still, it might have been worse, Ona consoled herself as she prepared to return to work Tuesday morning. It might have been different if it had been a regular weekend when the little boy was so sick. She would have had to rack her brain deciding whether to skip work yet again to nurse the sick child or to send him to Mrs. King and worry all day.

After traveling forty minutes by bus to Mrs. King's apartment, Ona found it crawling with policemen. Mrs. King had been found dead in her apartment. She had not changed from the clothes she was wearing the last time Ona saw her. Already running late for work, Ona had to hurry back home to search for a makeshift baby-sitter, not knowing who to turn to, knowing she couldn't afford to miss another day in the already shortened week. The supervisor would fire her on the spot.

For a moment, in desperation, she thought of telephoning

Suzanne and asking her to look after her brother for the day. She always professed he was the apple of her eye. Over the weekend, Ona had thought about trying one more time to bridge the gap between them. Holidays, supposedly times for family, always had this effect on Ona, always made her notice what was missing in her life, always made her want to wrap her family around her. Maybe Suzanne wouldn't mind having Telson over, if Ona reached her on the phone. In any case, because of her filthy job, Suzanne slept most of the day. So it wouldn't make any difference if the little boy was in her apartment or not. It shouldn't affect her sleep.

These thoughts were going through her mind when Ona pushed open the apartment door to hear muffled voices and laughter coming from the bedroom. She must have left the television on, she thought at first, but the voices weren't continuous. There were soft words spoken between suspiciously long breaks. Leaving Telson in the doorway, she tiptoed to the bedroom and threw the door open to find a long-haired white woman, about half Ona's age, naked on the bed, with one of Ona's large towels between her legs. Like a spent force, Joe was on his side, lazily caressing her breasts. They froze when they saw Ona.

"Jesus Christ," the startled woman swore, jumping up from the bed, "I thought you said she went to work."

"You slut," Ona shouted, charging at them. "In my own apartment."

Joe intercepted her rush and the two of them fell onto their now-defiled marriage bed, struggling. The woman hastily picked her dress off a chair and pulled it over her head and was gone, grabbing her bag on the way out. She left the panties and bra behind on the floor.

"I'll burn them, you stinking bitch," Ona screamed after her.

The phone rang. It was Kevin Jenkins, the lawyer, Ona's former boss, calling to say Suzie was in trouble again. She had to be bailed out of jail. It would take $5,000 this time, plus his fees and money for a lawyer in Buffalo. Ona mumbled something incoherently, then slammed down the phone, cutting him off in midsentence. Almost immediately, the phone rang again. The voice started on something about going to Buffalo for her daughter, to which Ona said something about a motherless child and again slammed down the phone. Then sitting on the edge of the bed, she held her head in her hands and cried silently while Joe dressed. Neither of them seemed to hear the phone which never stopped ringing. Joe left the apartment without saying a word, without even apologizing.

As he left, more out of frustration, Ona shouted after him not to come back and began to throw his clothes into the hall behind him. He didn't look back, but strolled imperiously toward the elevator.

Even when the elevator's door closed behind him, Ona continued throwing the clothes, the stereo headphones, records and tapes, everything that was his, into the hall until it was cluttered and she was exhausted. Maybe Joe felt she was just acting up again. Perhaps he didn't realize she was serious, that she had had enough. Everything around her had collapsed. The damn phone kept ringing. She wanted nobody to intrude on her world. She refused to answer. But she held Telson close in her arms and tried not to cry openly.

Ona's head was beginning to throb from the tension. The pain started behind the right eye in sharp stabs and then it spread around the crown to the back of the head. A migraine and a big one. Maybe it was time to give in, to stop struggling, to come back to her roots and the things she had tried so desperately to shake all her life. Maybe it was time she went to church again and became a regular, steady member. It was time she admitted defeat.

She tightly embraced her only worthwhile possession, the frightened child with his heart fluttering in his little chest. She couldn't care less what her supervisor said the next day. There were some things she had to straighten out that morning, a few things she had to do for the special woman that mothered her. When the women assembled in Mrs. King's apartment, Ona knew she had to be there to welcome them, to keep the small talk going and to sing the praises of the departed. She had to represent Mrs. King because there was nobody else to do it. And now, with Mrs. King dead, there was absolutely nobody for Ona to turn to for help. Nobody capable of understanding the heaviness she felt in her chest every time she thought of Mrs. King. She knew how much she was going to miss that crabby old woman, a loss second only to the way she expected to feel if her birth mother had died.

When Joe returned home, the locks had been changed on the door. His possessions were carefully packed in a cardboard box and placed by the garbage chute in the apartment hallway.

CHAPTER 5

FOR AS LONG as Ona remembered, life was difficult, even back home in Jamaica. She never felt in control of her life but that she was always trying to please someone. When it wasn't her mother, it was the pastor or the headmistress at school. They were always making demands, forcing her to do things she wasn't interested in and preventing her from pursuing those she really wanted.

Her mother, in particular, had nagged her constantly about going to church and taking an active role. She pressured Ona to set an example by keeping her school uniform clean, to take part in the young people's meetings at the church. And she never let Ona forget how she should prepare to eventually take over from her mother, and how she had to be mindful of the curse that haunted the Nedd women.

Ona hated the life and all the brooding it caused her every time her mother spoke. It was unreasonable to expect her to grow up to be anything like her mother. It was too much asking her to be always cautious, never taking a chance by displaying her emotions, never being free to be just herself, free to be just like other children her age. She wanted to dance professionally, but at first her mother simply refused to let her. No matter how much she tried to please the woman, she was not allowed to dance simply for pleasure. Not even as a compromise when Ona agreed without protest to be baptized by Pastor Grant in the ocean at six o'clock one rainy morning. Not even this apparent first step toward eventually taking over from Mira Nedd in the church and village could change her mind.

Ona became addicted to dancing at the village school, under the direction of Mrs. Small, or Miss English Woman as everyone disdainfully called her. The name stuck even though she was as Jamaican as any of them. Mrs. Small had returned home to teach after living and studying in England. Yet there was something strange about this woman living alone. Something different that never allowed the children, the teachers or even the people in the market to accept her back fully. In her big house, she was apart and alone, with her quaint practices of foreign and local ways, and her honorific title of mistress even though she had never married.

Mrs. Small was in charge of arts and cultural affairs. Even in the junior classes, they were taught that self-fulfillment had to come from overseas. They had to accept the education offered, so that when they immigrated, they could fit easily into their adopted land. This was the only way they would be successful like all those past students living abroad, the role models fulfilling their dreams and contributing to their new country, while helping the less fortunate back home.

The day Mrs. Small brought to school an old gramophone and some scratchy records was magic. They were to discuss dancing as the expression of cultures around the world. As though introducing the girls to something illegal, Mrs. Small closed the door to the small arts room. Ignoring the heat from the scorching afternoon sun and the suffocating room, she played the records and enthralled the students.

The record covers showed beaming young women from around the world dancing in colorful costumes and obviously having fun. Mrs. Small played music from Africa, carefully explaining the role of the drum. The music sounded familiar to Ona. Finally it made sense when Mrs. Small said that the Pocomania dancers, whose freestyle dances Ona and her mother danced at Pastor Grant's church, were from Africa. This gave new status to these dances everyone took for granted and considered low class and of no cultural significance. Anyone who danced Pocomania danced West African folk, asserted Mrs. Small.

Ona now had another reason for going to church. She practiced and watched the older women going through the movements. She noticed how they grunted and shuffled their feet effortlessly, how they swayed their protruding behinds and wound up their hips. There was so much to learn from them. Every night she raced through the Bible lesson so that her mother could quickly dispense with the opening prayers. So that the congregation could get on with worshiping in song and dance. And every time they journeyed to Cross Roads, Ona was the first to arrive, the first to link hands in the circle under the lone street lamp.

At school, she performed in the dance troupe, but didn't dare let her mother know. She was so good, the moves coming so naturally, that she was the automatic choice as lead dancer. At the end of the weekly workout, her white blouse was always stuck to her back. The sweat ran down her face and neck, under the intricate cornrow plaits. She felt utterly exhilarated. But as soon as the school door opened, she had to pretend such dancing did not exist. As a professed Christian, saved by the redeeming blood of the Lamb, she had to show absolutely no interest in such behavior.

Then came the first crisis with her mother and Pastor Grant. Mrs. Small announced three weeks before the end of the school year that she had talked to the director of the Jamaica National Dance Troupe. She beamed with the good news: Ona and six other girls were invited for a tryout. Because of their ages, they had to get permission from their parents or guardians for the trials.

Mrs. Small said the troupe's director, a lay preacher in the city's Anglican Cathedral, was very strict. He accepted new dancers only if they were of upright character and acceptable social standing. None of the girls needed to worry, Mrs. Small said, adding that she had vouched all of them were virgins. "And all of you better not prove me wrong," she said with a nod of the head in acknowledgment of the mischievous giggling, "or be foolish enough to own up otherwise. Just keep your mouth shut and always mind your own business." However, one thing she could not change or hide, Mrs. Small said. The girls had to agree to abide with the troupe's strict rules and moral code if selected. Such an agreement was mandatory for both the boys and girls. "But that shouldn't be a concern to any of you," Mrs. Small said. "Your main task is simple: pass the audition and we'll deal with anything else afterward. And as I said, don't go pushing your mouth in anybody's business, if it doesn't concern you."

Ona ran home with the permission letter and shoved it in her mother's hand, thinking Mira Nedd could not but revel in the good fortune. She had to feel proud that some big shot in Kingston, the capital of the entire country, wanted to see her daughter dance. The selection of her daughter from among the hundreds of thousands across the island was surely an honor for a woman like Mira Nedd. After all, Ona thought, her mother found it so difficult to contain herself at the sound of the drums. Without trying, she had passed on the love of dancing to her sole offspring; she had to be happy her daughter had learned it so well.

But Mira Nedd didn't see it that way. She said dancing in Kingston wasn't for the honor and glory of Christ. It was the work of the Devil to increase lust and wickedness in this sinful world. Just like the corruption of the Pocomania music by those singers in the dance halls, people who on Saturday nights sang only about love and sex, she said. Just like all those rebels and hypocrites who defiled the Word of God by making records and performing reggae music around the world while talking glibly about love and fellowship. This was not for a baptized child of God who had dedicated her soul to Christ. Ona wasn't going to have any part of it, not if she still wanted the only thing her poor mother could give her: rich, plentiful blessings for the rest of her life. More than that, Mira Nedd said Ona was simply a country girl and wasn't ready for life in a bustling city like Kingston. And, she said, it didn't surprise her in the least that other people thought Ona a dancer. These weren't compliments, but simply statements of the obvious. Dancing ran in her blood, one of the many manifestations of the curse.

After throwing the letter into the wood fire cooking the evening meal, Mira Nedd told Ona to prepare for the church service and to put all dreams of going to Kingston out of her head. The girl walked away with warm tears running down her face, hoping her mother wouldn't see them and administer one of her almost frantic floggings.

Mrs. Small knew how to get her way, though, even after Pastor Grant, too, had denounced the auditions as Satan's work. On the last evening of the school year, Mrs. Small took the walk home with Ona. The teacher sat with Ona's mother on the bench in the backyard as if she had come calling on a friend to gossip. They talked about everything under the sun, while Ona kept inside the house, out of sight, but within hearing range. Finally, Mrs. Small got up to leave.

"So Sister Nedd," she said, "tell me, nuh, you going to sign the piece o' paper for the pickney to go dancing or not?"

Mira didn't answer, even though she must have anticipated the question.

"Come on, talk to muh," the teacher pressed. "You done

know it won't hurt the little girl none. 'Cause, you know she's getting big. Fifteen in another two months, leaving school soon, making her own way in the world. You can't keep her for much longer, not if it's dance she really want. Listen to me, Sister Nedd, you can't hold her back. So what you say? Sign the paper for me, nuh!"

"Let me look and see if I can put my hand 'pon it. I can't even remember where I put the piece o' paper," Ona's mother said, showing the first sign she was bending. Ona suppressed an urge to clap her hands.

"Don't bother with the looking, Sister Nedd. I have another one right here. Just sign it," the teacher said, pulling the pen and paper from her pocket. "And you don't have to worry about buying fancy clothes. 'Cause I know that's what bothering you. Just make sure the girl clean and neat, that's all. Don't go spending no money, you hear me."

"But she'd be alone in the city. . . . "

"Don't worry, Sister Nedd," Mrs. Small said, putting an arm around the mother's shoulders. "Think of it this way: this is one of God's talents we are taking from under the bush. We letting it shine for all the world to see."

Ona went to Kingston and passed the audition. The next step was the formal dancing courses in a large hall near the university. This meant Ona had to move to Kingston, where, as a country girl, she knew no one. It was Lawson Heron, already a senior dancer with the troupe, who befriended her. They knew each other. His father owned the St. Ann's village shop. Although he had never spoken to Ona in the village, Lawson was glad to be friends with her in Kingston, if only because all the teachers said she was the most gifted of the students.

They started dating and even talked of getting married. But for the first year and a half they had to keep their affair a secret because, Ona thought, of the director's strict moral code. Only very close friends knew they were lovers, and when the full troupe was together, the junior and senior dancers, Lawson always distanced himself from her.

Ona remembered what Mrs. Small had said about the director and how easily all her opportunities could be jeopardized by even the smallest indiscretion. She enjoyed the double thrill of dancing and living dangerously, knowing what would happen to her and Lawson if the director heard of their secret. For the first time in her life she enjoyed freedom and a liberation from her mother's watchful eye. For the first time, she felt in control. And she was glad Mrs. King had warned all the newcomers about keeping their mouths shut for this was the way all the dancers liked it. Nobody bothered discussing personal matters.

Almost two years later, a month before she was to give her first important solo performance, Ona got grim news. She was pregnant. There was no choice but to leave the troupe and return in disgrace to the village.

Lawson didn't even bother seeing her off. She never spoke to him again. One year later, Ona read with horror in the *Gleaner* about the elaborate celebration to mark the fifth wedding anniversary of the troupe's lead dancers, Lawson and Mavis. The minister of culture had lauded the artists for keeping their love alive in spite of the demands of their profession. The two of them had kept their marriage a virtual secret out of fear that disclosure of such knowledge would affect their careers. Knowing the likelihood for gossip, the minister said, he could understand the concerns that people would think it was some big collusion to have a man and his wife as the lead dancers of the same troupe.

Now Ona understood why Lawson had kept their affair secret, why her mother muttered so much about the curse of adultery. The first time her mother hinted at the matter was when Ona let slip once that she was meeting Lawson at his father's shop for a ride back to Kingston. The muttering got louder when Ona came back home for good.

"I know it. I know I should've followed my mind," Mira

Nedd said when Ona walked into the house, feeling as if the word shame was emblazoned on her face. "I shouldn't have listened to no sweet-mouth talk, all these people saying this and that, how I should let you go to Kingston and dance. But like a fool, I listened. Even though I could see this thing happening, how it had to happen once a young girl like you start living in Kingston. And you're to blame too, 'cause you wanted to go, didn't want to listen to me, didn't think I am a mother and know better. Maybe, now that things change so, maybe you'd really believe me when I say I know better; when I say it's all because of the curse."

She took the bag with Ona's clothes into the bedroom. Ona looked around the house, into the yard behind, and at the neighbors' houses where the tale of her return was probably the current topic of discussion. "I keep telling you there are certain things in this life that we Nedd women like we can never avoid," Mira Nedd's voice returned to Ona. "It's the same way we can unscramble dreams for other people but not for weself. The same way we can tell people things that will happen to them; the same way we bring about our own destruction by letting these lying married men have their own way. But what can I do? All I can do is to accept you back. 'Cause you're my only child. But at the same time, I still got to make sure that you understand what you're dealing with, so you won't have the wool pulled over your eyes another time. 'Cause, to tell the truth, you ain't ready yet. Not at all."

But Mira Nedd did not maintain that level of anger. Later in the evening, she took a good look at her daughter and pronounced with bemused pride that she was carrying a girl. "I only got to look at the way your stomach developing to know you got to be carrying a girl," she said. "Which only proves my point about this curse thing. It can be passed on only through a daughter. And let me tell you again, if you ain't careful, the little infant there in your womb will face the same thing soon. Unless we break this cycle. That's why I'll do my best to see that you get your life back in order, so we can help that little angel you are carrying."

Ona decided there and then that the child, if indeed it were a girl, would never be as naive as its mother. Neither would it ever feel cursed. Not if she could help it.

CHAPTER 6

FOUR MONTHS AFTER Suzanne's birth, Ona was back in Kingston working in a branch of Barclays Bank International. The job of running errands, copying documents and filing reports had been secured with the help of her former teacher. Mrs. Small was obviously disappointed with what had become of such a talented student. Nonetheless, she was still willing to give the young mother a second chance and was happy to make the recommendation.

"I won't say it's the kind of job you'd want to spend the rest of your life doing," Mrs. Small had said when Ona told her of the interview in Kingston. They were standing in the center of the main room in Mrs. Small's bungalow on the affluent side of Cross Roads. On the walls were framed pictures and paintings of scenes from overseas, along with the parchments and educational scrolls with Mrs. Small's name on them. Those scrolls, and the experience from living abroad, were what made the difference in Mrs. Small's life, what gave the teacher freedom to do as she pleased despite what others thought, a fact that Ona found impossible to ignore as they talked. If Ona wanted to redeem herself, there was no doubt she had to find a way other than just getting baptized by Pastor Grant. Un-doubtedly, she would have to seek redemption away from St. Ann's, or even Jamaica itself.

"At least it's something to get you started," Mrs. Small con-tinued. "Especially since that good-for-nothing man has shown no sign of living up to his responsibilities as a father. Take the job they're offering you, but as soon as you get a chance for something better, take that too." Miss English Woman shook her head. Ona looked at her. There was noth-ing more to say. Finally, she told the teacher good-bye and thanked her for helping.

"This isn't the kind of job anyone with ambition would want to do for too long, you hear me," Mrs. Small called after her. "And remember, whatever happened, you're still very smart. So be brave and keep your eyes and ears open. Other opportunities will come."

Every weekend, Ona made the long trip from Kingston to St. Ann's for two short, tiring days with Suzanne, the child she had to give up right away because nobody believed she was old enough to nurture an infant. Her mother was firmly in charge of raising the baby, even overruling some of Ona's decisions for the child. When Ona returned home, the two days were spent in a constant struggle with her mother. Ona started to re-sent even having to make the trip to St. Ann's.

Her mother had decided that because of experience, she was the best person to raise the infant. In any case, she said, one of them had to work to feed and clothe Suzanne while one of them took care of the little girl. "After all, that lit-tle child resting there in that box so peaceful and quiet ain't nothing but a little angel," Mira Nedd explained. "She can't be responsible for what's happening to she." Ona's contribu-tion was to work in the city for the money to buy the milk, the baby powder and skin creams for her offspring.

"This is the least I can do for you," Mira Nedd had said. "Now you know how expensive babies can be. And I can't stretch any further what little money I have. So it's up to you to go and to start something of a life for yourself. Leave the baby here with me to look after it. Things are tough, but I'll get by. The people around here won't let me suffer. Now and then, somebody'll give me a sweet potato, a pumpkin or a few eggs. So I can get by. But it's different feeding a child so young. You can't give it cassava and yams. And when you go to Kingston, this time you try and make it different. Now, you know what not to do in Kingston. And in any case, since you're woman enough to have a child, you ought to know the hardship of struggling to feed her."

"But I was planning to take the baby with me."

"Don't make me laugh," Mira Nedd said. "And do what with it? When you look so clumsy holding the little angel, like you want to drop it. Leave the child with me. Just go and try to make a life for yourself. When you're good and ready, the child can join you. That's the best I can do for the two of you."

This was said with such finality, Ona had to keep any objections to herself. It was true she wasn't as good at taking care of Suzanne as her mother. But at the same time, this was her daughter they were talking about. And while the child was a mistake, Ona still wanted to get to know her, to take care of her. She yearned to provide more than just milk formula and powder. The public health nurse had advised Ona that the best food for Suzanne was her breast milk. But even that she couldn't provide. Not if she was away in Kingston. Not when her milk had dried up so soon after the birth because, as the nurse said, all the quarreling and crying at home had caused her not to make the milk. Still, there was no way to argue with her mother and win.

On Monday mornings after the weekend with Suzanne, Ona took the first bus, always crowded with people and fowl, from St. Ann's to the city. She always arrived just in time to begin work. Often, she started the week feeling tired from a restless weekend, exhausted from crying silently on the long ride, hungry because she couldn't afford a proper breakfast before joining the long line for the bus.

Most mornings, Ona cried when she thought of her mother. Ona felt Mira Nedd was deliberately separating her from the baby as punishment for the shame brought on the Nedd house and Pastor Grant's church. There was no other reason for her mother's behavior. Somehow, it appeared as if her mother always had to be in control, as if she felt that Ona in some silent way was trying to challenge her. Nothing she did pleased her mother and everything she said brought only a stern rebuke or rebuff. The claim, even by Mrs. Small and the public nurse, that her mother was simply trying to help her to start life afresh without the daily burden of raising a child did not ring true for her. Rather, it made her think that Mira Nedd was simply proving how ignorant her daughter was, how Ona had so casually slipped under the curse that she had for so long been warned to avoid.

Ona loathed the treatment but, even if she cried silently, she tried not to antagonize her mother. In her mother's presence, she pretended to have changed and to have learned from her mistakes. Where possible, she acted as if she had returned to the Christian fold and was now mature enough never to be lured away again, not even in a place like Kingston. For a while, the conciliatory strategy appeared to work. Her mother began to soften her attitude, but Ona still felt terribly alone and cut off from her daughter.

She longed to return to that brief period when she had first lived in Kingston. To those halcyon days before the mistake, when she felt so free and liberated, when she genuinely believed she was capable of achieving anything. When she was beyond the reach and control of her mother. The mistake had not only ruined any chance of her becoming a professional dancer, but it had destroyed her mental tranquility by propelling her back into the clutches of her mother. And there was no way she could see herself escaping again.

Every time she took the bus to Kingston, Ona felt disintegrating what little bond there was between her and the child. One morning as she bottle-fed the baby in the darkness, Ona made a solemn promise to Suzanne and herself. She swore that Suzanne, no matter how many mistakes she made, was never going to feel this isolated and trapped. She was never to bury her emotions and dreams, or be fearful of expressing herself to anyone. This was never going to happen to Suzanne, she vowed, not as long as Ona was alive. She and Suzanne would grow up as friends, eventually sharing clothes and always talking and joking, with neither of them pressuring the other. No one mistake was going to mar Suzanne's life forever, causing her to forgo dreams, to sit back feeling ambition gnaw at her insides. Suzanne would get the chance to realize her dreams, and through her own life Ona hoped to prove to her daughter that all things Suzanne's mind conceived were possible. She was going to be the person to help Suzanne fulfill her dreams and aspirations. She was going to make her daughter proud. In the process, Ona would prove to her own mother that she was made of sterner stuff. That although she might bend under the strain of youthful indiscretion, she was flexible enough to bounce back and to keep reaching for the stars. That nobody, least of all her mother, should think of giving up on her. And she made the promise to have Suzanne for herself as soon as it was physically, and financially, possible.

In Kingston, Ona kept to herself, refusing to make friends. She divided her time between work and the small windowless room rented in the converted four-bedroom house that housed eight. She had to save every cent to buy food and clothes to take home on the last bus to St. Ann's on Friday nights. Her only self-indulgence was newspapers, which she took from the mailroom to read in the rented room and on the journey home.

This was how she found herself reading a short item about a new Canadian immigration policy. Affluent Canadians were looking for dedicated young women to work in their homes as live-in domestics. Beside the story was a picture of a beaming prime minister. The words attributed to him said such breakthroughs in foreign policy were only possible because Jamaicans and other Caribbean people had claimed their sovereignty and independence almost two decades earlier. The domestic servants scheme was a chance for young women to make a better life for themselves, she read, and the Jamaican government was encouraging women of good character and responsibility to make use of this program. The newspaper said a list of potential employers was available at the Canadian High Commission in Kingston. That weekend, Mrs. Small told her there was nothing to lose by applying.

The following Monday, dressed in her best working clothes, Ona walked the short distance from the bank to the High Commission during her lunch hour. By the end of the day, she had completed and returned the application form. Three months later, she received a letter from Kevin and Mary Jenkins, offering her employment as a live-in nanny for their two sons. Apart from looking after the children, Ona was expected to do light housekeeping, the letter said, and must be willing to work irregular hours. If the conditions were agreeable, she was to take the letter to the High Commission and the process of getting her to Canada would begin immediately. The pay was $600 a month, less room and board. Ona gleefully focused on the gross amount. What she was likely to earn in Canada in a month or two, when converted, would take her almost a year at the bank. With that kind of money, she would be able to buy really nice things for Suzanne. And in Canada, both she and the baby were going to be out of her mother's grasp, so that if Ona clumsily dropped the infant while feeding her nobody was likely to know or reprimand her. Free of her mother, Ona could once again create the happiness she had enjoyed when she first left home. And with this freedom and the money from a steady job, nothing should get in the way of her going back to school and probably ending up with a scroll or two like her mentor, Mrs. Small.

Only when the final letter of acceptance came back did she tell her mother she was thinking of leaving the country. But even at the height of her success, failure lurked. Sitting in the line at the Canadian High Commission, she heard the older women talking about the interviews they were attending.

"Remember what the politician say," one woman was saying to another ahead of Ona. "If any o' them Canadian people in there don't ask 'bout children, then don't mention nothing. What they don't know won't hurt. 'Cause this program is only for women without any children, not for people like me and you who only looking for the chance to work hard so we can send back home a little something to put rice in the children mouths. The Canadians ain't looking for women like me or you, people who might drag two or three children behind them easy so. From what the government politician tell the group o' we yesterday, the Canadian officers in that room won't even look at yuh if they think you got one child, far less two or three."

Ona felt her face getting warm. She was sandwiched between the two women. Both of them were old enough to be her mother, seasoned enough to counsel her on the ways of the world.

"You don't have to tell me that, Nester," the other woman said. "If they don't ask, I ain't telling. And even if they ask, I'd done plan in my mind what to tell them. They can't trick me."

At that point, Ona's name was called. Ona wasn't sure, in light of what she had heard, if she wanted to continue the process. It had never occurred to her to leave Jamaica without Suzanne. In fact, one of the main reasons for leaving Jamaica was to get Suzanne for herself.

"In any case, once we're up there in Canada, it's then we can let them know we have children, not before," the first woman was whispering. "The trick is to get in. Once you're in, you can make arrangements to have the children join you after a few years. Once you have your landed immigrant papers in your passport, it's a different story."

The immigration officer didn't ask about children so Ona didn't volunteer the information. Later, she didn't even recall having said anything at the meeting. It happened so quickly and she was so frightened dealing with this imposing authority of foreignness.

"At seventeen, you're the youngest one I've seen so far," the officer said. He looked threatening and authoritative. "A few months younger and you wouldn't even qualify. The child labor law would get you."

He speedily processed the papers, gave Ona several forms and a letter to present at the Toronto airport. She had a month to report for employment. Mira Nedd wasn't happy that Ona had waited until the last minute to inform her of her plans. Still, she saw Ona off with her blessings and the promise to take care of Suzanne in Ona's absence. "Don't you worry," she said. "Go and make something of yourself. Whatever you do always ask the true and living God to guide your footsteps. Me and Pastor Grant will always remember you when we pray." Mrs. Small promised to faithfully perform her duties of god-mother to Suzanne.

Even as Ona boarded the plane, she felt swept along by events over which she had no control. She was leaving quickly only because she didn't want to run the risk of someone re-opening her file and discovering her secret. Still, it had never occurred to her that she would be leaving her ten-month-old baby behind, or that she would have to leave the morning that the child came down with a roasting fever and runny nose from teething. The only thing that made sense was the aim of whatever she was doing. It was all in the hope that she and her daughter could live together without anyone intervening, the chance to build a new life for both of them. Never in Ona's wildest dreams did she think it was going to be almost twelve years before she set eyes on Suzanne again.

CHAPTER 7

ONA SAT TREMBLING on the edge of the sofa bed in her little basement room. Kevin Jenkins was showering. Ona could hear the deep baritone singing upstairs and the water running down the pipe outside her room. It filled her with dread. She knew what to expect on nights like these. It always started the same way, with the shower and the singing.

Mary had left for New York earlier in the evening, for a fashion show at some big hotel, and Jenkins had returned home after taking her to the airport. For most of the evening he lazed around, drinking beer and watching television. He seemed anxious for Ona to feed the children, bathe them and put them to bed. To get them out of the way.

As she moved from room to room, Ona felt his eyes on her. When she tried to delay putting the kids to bed, he politely reminded her that the children were to be asleep by 8:30 P.M. In their mother's absence, it was even more important they got to bed early. "Shouldn't they be in bed by now if they want to ride with me to school in the morning?" he asked. "I think they should be, because they have to be up early in the morning."

Those were the only words he had said to her all evening,

but she knew what was on his mind. The fact he was home so early was proof enough of his intentions. Jenkins seldom came home when his children were awake.

Having placed the children in their beds and read the mandatory *Cat in the Hat* story as slowly as possible, Ona walked downstairs, passing Jenkins's outstretched legs, and went to her room in the basement.

"Good night, sir," she said, not bothering to look at him.

He said nothing. Ona carefully locked the door and prayed for this night to be different. Nervously, she picked up the blue big-tooth comb from the small table and began to comb her hair. Her trembling fingers parted the hair to plait it in tight but fine cornrows so she wouldn't have to comb it again for the rest of the week.

Suddenly the house went quiet, except for the soft humming of the central heating. Kevin Jenkins had turned off the television. She heard his footsteps on the tiled floor of the kitchen above her head, on the carpeted living room and on the creaking stairs to the second floor. When she heard the water and the singing, she knew there was no escape. The lock had proved ineffective in the past. She would only have to pay to have another lock installed the next day if she bolted the door.

THE FIRST TIME it happened, Kevin Jenkins had come home late, obviously half-drunk, after taking his fashion-designer wife to the airport for a flight to Europe. When he came in, Ona was already in bed, but the door to her room was open in case one of the children cried out for her in the night or crawled into the bed to sleep with her.

When Kevin Jenkins appeared in her bedroom, she thought he was checking in to make sure everything was well with the children. From the slurred words, she knew he had been drinking. The plane had been delayed and they had passed the time having a few drinks, he said.

74

"You should try, sir, and get some sleep," Ona said. "You look tired."

"I don't need sleep," he said.

"Do you want something to eat or drink? I can make a cup of tea," she said.

"That would be fine, after I've had a bath."

They walked upstairs together. Ona had no reason to suspect Kevin Jenkins wanted to hurt her. In the six months she had been with the Jenkins family, he hadn't shown any interest in her. Mostly, he had hardly said anything to her. All his orders were relayed through his wife. She seldom saw him in those early months. It was different with his wife, who seemed to expect a domestic servant to be at her beck and call twenty-four hours a day.

Soon after Ona arrived, Mary stopped doing everything for the children, handing them over totally to the nanny, while she did her fitness exercises, looked after her career or entertained. These events were important to their image, Mary had explained. "Kevin is even worse than me," she said. "He'd kill if anyone were to damage his reputation. And I don't blame him. In this country, you make your money through your reputation. That's why we have people over to the house so often." Late into the night, Ona cleaned up after them. There were some disagreements between the two women, particularly differences over interpretation of the employment contract and what constituted reasonable expectations.

Their first disagreement was over the hours of work, whether Ona should be on call night and day, every day. Then, whether making breakfast and supper, cleaning the kitchen, dusting, doing the shopping and laundry and tending the children amounted to light housework. Ona contended it didn't. Kevin Jenkins did step in once to explain his wife's demands were not unreasonable or outside the intent of the contract. He gave an assurance he was not the type to exploit Ona. He was a lawyer, he said. "I can't have people thinking that I am capable of exploiting the very person looking after my kids.

What would that do to my reputation if something like that starts getting around?" At the same time, he said, he wanted to make as clear as possible that breach of contract was a very serious matter with painful consequences. It could result in Ona being sent back home.

Ona instantly dropped her protests. Working seven days a week for six hundred dollars a month wasn't what she had expected. However, the alternative, as explained by this lawyer, was simply unimaginable.

Still, it would have been worse had Ona demanded she be given the two free days from work every week as was written in her contract. But she didn't press this matter, because she knew no one in Toronto and had nowhere to go. It was just as well she stayed home and saved what disappointingly little money she received. By the time Mary Jenkins subtracted rent, board, taxes and such things as health insurance, workman's compensation and payments for the plane fare to Toronto, Ona had sixty-five dollars in her hand at the end of the month. After her personal expenses, there was hardly anything to send home to her mother and Suzanne, let alone anything to save.

Ona left the tea bags steeping in the boiled water and returned to her room. Just as she was about to turn off the lights, Kevin Jenkins appeared, sipping a cup of tea, bare-chested with a big, white towel wrapped around his waist.

"Something else you want, sir?" she asked.

He didn't answer, but kicked the door shut behind him and walked toward her, silently sipping the tea. Jenkins finished the beverage and put the expensive cup and saucer on the small table, beside the combs and the bottle of yellow hair grease. Ona was cornered.

"Mr. Jenkins, please, don't do this to me," Ona pleaded. "Please. I don't want to cause no trouble."

He continued to advance until he was standing directly in front of the frightened woman.

"Don't worry, nobody will know anything," he said. "Only

the two of us are here tonight. You must know by now that I like you. I'll be nice to you. I could help you to stay in Canada permanently. You just be nice to me."

"No. No. Please, Mr. Jenkins."

He reached for her, but Ona backed herself against the wall. He laughed and this time measured his lunge so well she couldn't escape. They struggled and fell, knocking over the table. The expensive cup and saucer shattered on the un-carpeted floor. Jenkins slapped her face so hard she saw multi-colored lights. In her pain and fright, she could only cry out and grab her bleeding nose.

There on the cold floor, he ripped open her flimsy house-coat. It seemed like an eternity before he groaned in pleasure and collapsed heavily on her. He tried to kiss her, to wipe away the blood from her face with his hand. But defiantly, even af-ter defeat, she clenched her teeth so his tongue couldn't enter her mouth.

Finally, he got up, picked up the towel, threw it over his shoulder and, without looking back at her, walked out. Half an hour later, she was still on the floor, weeping and listening to her heart pounding loudly in her ears. She thought about marching upstairs to his room with one of the sharp knives from the kitchen. Ona wondered what her mother would say. What would Mira Nedd tell Suzie when she was old enough to understand why her mother didn't come back for her? How would Ona explain why she had to suffer the consequences and put an end to all her dreams? It was only because of Suzanne she didn't carry out the thoughts in her head.

Finally she dragged herself from the floor, ripping off her soiled underwear and trying to flush it down the toilet. But they stuck at the bottom of the bowl, choking it. She spent an hour under the shower in her room, trying to wash away his touch and the memory. Hard and heavy, the water beat down on her head, sounding in her ears like a drum. It was then that Ona remembered how her mother had taught her to pray.

When Mary Jenkins returned home, she was incensed with

Ona. In front of her husband, she shouted at the servant, demanding that she pay the cost of replacing the expensive china in her precious set and for repairs to the toilet. The money would be deducted from Ona's wages. Such was the penalty, Mary Jenkins said, for being so clumsy.

After that, Kevin Jenkins had raped Ona again and again. The last time, she missed her period and was almost frantic with fear. When her fears were confirmed, she called Kevin Jenkins at work. She definitely didn't want the baby. And having a baby while on a domestic worker permit was certainly courting trouble. It meant having her contract canceled and being sent back home. Ona imagined returning home with a big belly, going back to St. Ann's for a second time to have another bastard child. And she imagined having to listen to her mother's rants about the curse on all the women in her family. The fact that Kevin Jenkins was a married man and white weighed even more heavily. Mothering the only half-caste child in an all-black village would be a curse worse than any inflicted on her ancestors, a mistake that perhaps even Mira Nedd could not forgive.

"Mr. Jenkins," Ona said, her voice shaking. Kevin Jenkins sounded annoyed at being interrupted by his secretary's putting the call through. "I'm in trouble and I don't know what to do."

"What kind of trouble, Ona?"

"Pregnant, sir," she blurted out with a sob.

"What do you mean, *pregnant*? Have you been going with anyone?"

"Only you. You're the only man that troubled me since I'm in Canada." As much as she wanted to, she didn't tell him the housework didn't leave her time for anything extra.

"I don't think we should discuss this on the phone. I'll see you when I come home."

That night, he came to her room after his wife had gone to bed. He gave her $1,000 in a brown envelope that also contained the telephone number of a doctor he knew. There was no discussion. He told Ona to go away on her vacation. Half the money should cover the operation. The remainder was for a motel where she could recuperate.

Three days later, she had the abortion. The doctor's fee was $800. The medication was another $60 and the remaining $140 wasn't enough to pay for a two-week stay at even the cheapest motel. Ona had to use her small savings to cover the bill. That was the only month during her first three years in Canada that she didn't send home anything, not even a five-dollar postal order, for her daughter.

Not once did Jenkins ask how things had gone. So she didn't tell anyone how her belly had ached so badly. There was no-body to share the story of how she had bled so much she thought she was going to die alone in a musty motel where no-body knew her. In the middle of the night, she had to call the doctor at his home so she could be admitted to a hospital. To protect the doctor who had performed the abortion she had to pretend she had been to a backstreet butcher. She stayed in the hospital for three days, but still had to pay for the motel room.

Now, only a few months after the painful and degrading experience, Mary was away and Kevin Jenkins was coming after her again. She couldn't let it happen.

CHAPTER 8

ONA TRUDGED THROUGH the puddles and stinging rain from the November thunderstorm. She had no idea where she was going to spend the night.

It wasn't until she had left the house, with a light fall coat wrapped around her, a small suitcase in her hand and forty dollars in her purse, that she finally realized what she was doing. She was running away. Every step was taking her deeper into trouble and the unknown.

The struggle with herself began almost immediately. The insecure side of her panicked, entreating her to return and endure the suffering a bit longer. Why was she risking everything? How could she destroy every chance of achieving her dreams? Running away made all the suffering, loneliness and deprivation a waste of time. And the end was so close. Surely she could hang on a bit longer, could suffer a bit more. After all, the contract called for only three full years of indentured labor. She was tough enough to survive the remainder of this test. Then she would get the landed immigrant status, the first step toward becoming a Canadian citizen, the first step to bringing Suzanne to join her. It would be stupid to lose everything for no good reason. Particularly if she had mistaken Jenkins's intentions. And she was so close to getting her wish now that she was only months short of the three-year anniversary. Mary Jenkins had just helped her to fill out the application forms for landed immigrant status and Kevin Jenkins had spoken to someone in the department for her.

But oblivious to the doubts, her determined feet continued to take her further away. With every step, she knew she couldn't go back. She also realized that if she didn't retrace her steps, Kevin Jenkins had every right to terminate the precious employment contract and send the immigration department after her.

The immigration officer had been very specific: any change in status, no matter how minor, had to be reported immediately for reassessment of status. Also, because the application was a bit premature, he had warned, Ona should not assume she had been approved as a landed immigrant. "Don't do anything until you receive notification in writing," the officer had said. "What we're doing is simply putting your application on file until the qualifying period is up. You shouldn't even assume that we have accepted it, because we probably can't."

On their way home, Kevin Jenkins explained further. "You mustn't tell anybody about this. It's just that they're doing a favor for me, so that when your time comes you won't have to spend the long hours waiting in line for a number and then an interview."

Ona knew what he meant. The times she went to the immigration office for her reviews twice a year always left her drained. They were always all-day affairs, so that an officer could spend fifteen minutes stuffing paper in a file, reviewing her bank book and asking if she had any problems with her employer. But to get this evaluation meant joining hundreds of people lining up outside the immigration office at the crack of dawn.

It was particularly distressing in the winter with thousands of people huddling in the cold, but standing their ground. People were afraid to leave the spot in the long line to pee or buy a cup of coffee. Otherwise they would lose their place and would probably have to come back another day because the immigration people stopped handing out numbers for interviews around one o'clock. Those without a number were sent home, no matter how much time they had invested in the queue. They were forced to start the process all over again. But Kevin Jenkins had his contacts around the immigration department. And Ona was grateful for them.

Ona kept walking toward a main intersection where she could catch a bus. Once on board, she hoped to decide what to do for the night and for the future. But no matter what, she wasn't going to spend the night in that house with Kevin Jenkins. She wouldn't let him defile her and then cast her off, leaving Ona to tremble at Mary's return, wondering whether she somehow sensed that Ona had been with her husband.

On the bus, Ona sat near the exit, in case she came to her senses and decided there was no use running away. In case she wanted to make a quick retreat before she had gone too far.

Back in Jamaica, her mother had told her how frightening it had been for the slaves fleeing along the same dirt tracks in St. Ann's where Pastor Grant later worshiped and journeyed into the small hours of the morning. Mira Nedd had said that often many of the freedom seekers turned back, defeated by the sheer thought of the unknown, retracing their steps to be back in the barracks before daylight. They changed their minds, opting for the certainty they knew and the pledge of emancipation someday soon. They retreated before the dogs and the soldiers caught up, before they reached the safety of the mountains, that promised land with the Maroons.

But she didn't change her mind. Ona sat watching the bus driver scrutinize her in the rearview mirror, until he pulled into the subway station transfer area. "This is the end of the run for me," he said. "I'm finished here. You'll have to transfer to the subway or another bus."

"Thanks," Ona murmured.

Water was running down her face from her soaked hair, only half of which was plaited, she had left in such hurry. She picked up the suitcase and walked past the driver into the rain.

"Are you okay, lady?" the driver asked.

"Yes," she whispered. "I'm fine. Fine."

She pulled the light coat tighter around her, entered the main area of the subway station and leaned against a wall, trying to think, until she realized people were staring at her the way they looked at crazy people on the transit system.

Ona went to a big map on the wall. She acted as though she were looking for directions. In reality, she was buying time to collect her thoughts. Finally, when it was obvious she couldn't study the map forever, she again went out into the pouring rain. In her head, she heard her mother's stories about the fleeing slaves and about the fainthearted ones that gave up. It was almost as if that culture and history were her only references. And she remembered how the best stories by her mother were always about those who kept going into the darkness, into the unknown, following only a dream, fleeing the terror.

Ona walked aimlessly along the partially deserted street for at least three hours, by which time she was tired, soaked and cold. She felt numb. Most of the anger was washed away. Maybe she should return to the house and creep in silently. As a precaution, she could wake the children and take them to sleep with her. In the morning, if their father questioned her, she could say the children were crying, maybe the rain and lightning had frightened them. But she had to go back. As soon as she had rested for a minute. She was too close to being landed to risk it all.

Ahead, the beckoning sign of a doughnut shop offered rest and warmth. She entered and sat on a stool at the semicircular counter. Absentmindedly, she stared at the lighted menu boards and the scores of meaningless names of doughnuts.

"Coffee?" a black woman about her age asked from behind the counter. Ona didn't answer, because she hadn't really heard her. A mixture of rainwater and tears was streaming down Ona's face. Her hands and lips were trembling.

"Coffee?" the waitress repeated, raising her voice.

"Yes, yes," Ona stammered.

"Cream and sugar?"

"Yes."

"Anything else?"

"Yes."

The waitress pushed the coffee in front of Ona and went to the end of the counter to clear the bill of the only other customer. She returned and found that Ona hadn't touched the mug.

"There's a washroom in the back. Why don't you go back behind there and dry yourself off. Use the paper towels. 'Cause right now, girl, you look like a real mess. Like something the cat dragged in outta the rain."

Ona did as she was told, without protest, without taking offense. In this frame of mind, she was likely to do anything anybody told her, even going back to the Jenkins family if some sign appeared to assure her that turning back was the correct thing to do. Her mother always said God sent a signal, sometimes a dream for a reader to decipher, sometimes a burning bush, when his children were in need, other times a guiding light. She found a pile of paper towels by the sink and began to rub her head and neck with a handful of them. When she left, the wastebasket was filled with wet towels. Her hair was knotted and matted like the Rastafarians'.

When she returned to her seat at the counter, Ona started to tell the waitress the story of her life, every sordid detail. She didn't need prompting to get three years of hurt off her chest. The listener made it easy. She was black, West Indian and a woman, and Ona felt a bond between them. Her name was Fanny.

"What you gonna do now?" Fanny asked.

"I don't know."

"You know anybody in Toronto?" Fanny refilled the cup with coffee. "Somebody you can spend the rest o' the night at, so that you can think things over?"

Ona shook her head. There wasn't anybody, not a single soul in this big city, in this big country.

Fanny thought for a moment. "I knock off from this place in another hour. I know a nice old lady that live near me. She might be willing to put you up for the night. But let me warn yuh: she does talk a lot so you might not get much sleep. Her husband died a few years back, so she's kinda lonely. A Barbadian who married a Nova Scotian man. If you like, we can pass around there when I knock off work and see what she says. If she says no, then you might have to try the YWCA and see if they'll give you a room. I'd take you home with me but I don't think the three roommates I share with would like that. They're students."

Mrs. King, fortunately, didn't say no. She took Ona in, gave her a nightgown and told her she could sleep on the old sofa in the apartment's living room for the night. Thankful, Ona curled up and was soon fast asleep. As she drifted off, she remembered hearing Mrs. King and Fanny talking in their Bajan accent, in low voices by the apartment door. In the morning, Mrs. King woke Ona to a cup of hot chocolate, the kind Mira Nedd used to make for her most mornings in Jamaica. She told her that after a night of thinking things over she had decided Ona wasn't going back "to them advantage-takers."

"You ain't going back," she said with determination. "You can stay here with me until you catch yourself, until you save some money and get your poor life back on track. Good Lord, what them think people is? Lord knows, I laid down in there on my bed last night and I heard you crying and crying and talking in your sleep. Talking about somebody or the other named Suzie. Suzie this, Suzie that. So much pain and anguish in your voice. I almost wake you up to see if you okay. And I had to say to myself no young woman should have to go through nothing so. You don't deserve it."

Mrs. King paused briefly. "And I don't even know yuh from the man in the moon. But Fanny brought you here and you look all right to me. So you stay right there where you are right now, drink that cocoa and catch yourself."

Ona had found a temporary home, but that wasn't the end of her troubles. Overnight she had been transformed into an illegal alien, without a secure identity. She was unable to work legally or to see a doctor without being exposed. Ona was reduced to constantly looking over her shoulder when walking the streets and to wondering when Mrs. King's benevolence might run out. Which morning was the old woman going to wake up and tell Ona it was time to face life on her own? When would she start demanding Ona pay the rent instead of just contributing to the food? Which night would be the last she slept comfortably in a warm bed? In this city, Ona had learned, no kindness should be expected, because none was usually given.

Her mother in St. Ann's never knew of these developments. The letters with the postal orders continued to arrive from Toronto every month, with Ona writing to tell how good Canada was to her, how she was going to church every Sunday and how she was returning soon for Suzie.

Ona's only request was for Mira Nedd to address all her letters to Mrs. Hilda O. King. Her mother never suspected the O stood for Ona. This arrangement helped Ona to identify the mail intended for her, while disguising her identity. In these dark days, Ona's only sustenance was to recall the stories from her mother, the tales of how even after they had escaped, it was the mere dream of freedom, someday a great and total emancipation coming, that stopped their foreparents from willingly returning to captivity, to the cotton and cane fields or to cleaning, cooking and caring for the children in the exploiters' homes. And it was in those days that she remembered Mira Nedd's instructing Ona to always ask the only true and living God to guide her footsteps and to make her worthy and willing to accept the outpouring of the Holy Spirit.

WHEN ONA CAME to Tiltman's Garments, the company was happy to receive 185 pieces of work weekly. The quota had risen steadily every week. There appeared to be no limit to the supervisor's demands. The previous maximum automatically became the following week's minimum, although the lump sum payment remained unchanged.

The growing demand forced her to work late almost every night, leading Mrs. King to believe Ona was finally seeing a man, beginning to live as a young woman should. Ona had been so frightened of being caught by the authorities she had cut out all social life, even the cinema or going dancing with Fanny.

By being so careful, Mrs. King had explained, Ona was making it too obvious she was illegal. She wasn't behaving like a young Canadian woman, but too much like someone with something to hide. "Somebody only have to take one look at you to know that things ain't right," she said. "Why you don't listen to me and start mixing with people, and making out as if you're just like anybody else. You got to stop behaving as if you frightened for yuh own shadow."

Mrs. King didn't like Ona's lifestyle, not one bit. Only rats lived that way, scurrying secretively from one hole to another, she nagged. She reminded Ona so much of her mother in Jamaica. As with her mother, she could never win an argument. When Ona started to come home late, Mrs. King reduced her badgering, thinking Ona was beginning to emerge from her cocoon. Ona kept the real reason to herself.

At the back of her mind was the hope that if she worked hard enough and made no waves, Harold Tiltman, the rarely seen owner of the company, might make Ona a supervisor and help legitimize her immigrant status. The supervisor, an old friend of Mrs. King's husband, had mentioned this possible reward for her hard work. He had said it was even possible for Mr. Tiltman to ask the Immigration Department to allow him to take over the contract from the Jenkins couple. Only that instead of Ona working as a domestic servant, she would continue at the garment factory.

"Mr. Tiltman is a good man," the supervisor had said. "I have seen him help out a good few people around here. But you got to be willing to show him you can work hard. When the time is right, I personally, as a favor to Mrs. King, will approach Mr. Tiltman for you. That is why you shouldn't be too strict demanding any pay for overtime that you work. Not that you won't get it, but just wait your time. Don't rush things."

But apart from the supervisor's promise, nothing much had changed in more than a year. Eventually, Ona realized that Tiltman had probably never heard of her, didn't even know she was on his payroll, let alone that she was his most prolific worker. Ona knew she was at a dead end with only one possible outcome. From the way the supervisor watched and treated her, Ona realized what other women in her position already knew about the supervisor: that they shouldn't trust him. That it was only a matter of time before an illegal immigrant faced the inevitable.

THE MEN IN the blue trench coats came on a rainy morning in late fall, just as Ona and the seventy-eight other immigrant women at Tiltman's Garments sat at their sewing machines. Ona immediately saw the futility of trying to run. She surrendered without a fight. Only tears betrayed her emotions.

Ona thought that she had mentally prepared herself for the day when she could run no more, when every avenue was blocked. After all, it had been more than two years since she went into hiding, enough time to prepare herself. Ona thought she began steeling herself for the inevitable mere weeks after she had first arrived in the sweatshop. An arrest took place at the very machine in front of her where a Trinidadian woman was working.

One day after lunch, some men had turned up at the factory door. They marched straight down the aisle, in full view of the supervisor. Ona sensed how every woman froze, each wondering if the men were coming for her. None dared to look up from her work to make eye contract with the intruders. The men's heavy boots crunched the trimmings and paper on the floor. Ona had to suppress the urge to run as she heard the men approaching and then passing by her. At the Trinidadian's station, from where they could reach out and touch Ona, they stopped.

"Immigration," one of them had said. The woman jumped to her feet and somehow slipped past the men. The hunt began, between the bales of cloth, the sewn garments, up and down the aisles. They ran, the woman screaming and crying, like a frightened animal. Ona instantly thought of the times back home in Jamaica, when as children they had caught a mongoose in a trap, how it ran from side to side screeching and bouncing off the sides of the wire trap, until exhaustion caused it to collapse. That was the point at which they applied the kerosene and the lighted match to the cage; when they ran away as the animal burst into flames, how her mother had scolded them for such wickedness.

The woman, whose name Ona didn't know, finally fell to her knees, begging, swearing at the supervisor for betraying her after stealing her wages. Her long sobs echoed eerily around the cavernous hall. Nobody was working. Nobody could help. The men dragged the woman away. She was still on her knees when she passed Ona's workstation. When her turn came, Ona vowed, she wasn't going to lose her self-respect.

Now it was Ona's turn. Despite the brave plans, when the men came, the tears took over. Everything she had promised to do, like hiding her feelings and not begging for the chance to collect her outstanding pay, not demanding the overtime wages from the supervisor, was put to the test as soon as the men came to her station and addressed her by her real name.

"Ona Nedd," said a man authoritatively, flashing a badge. The woman known to everyone watching as Edna Harris rose, trembling, tears involuntarily sliding down her cheeks. Ona knew she had no control over the tears, but she wanted to keep her pride. To accept defeat but to go out holding her head high. To let the tears be her only defeat. So she gritted her teeth. She was not going to lose any more of her composure. Neither would she beg. Ona said not a word, nothing about her back wages. Neither did she try to protect the real Edna Harris, whose social security number she had rented for forty dollars a month to get the job. That was the arrangement. The owner would simply report her card lost and swear she never heard of anyone named Ona.

She cried because of what was ahead. She knew derision and scorn awaited her, in Canada when the immigration officers grilled her, and in Jamaica, when the Air Canada plane would deliver her like a piece of tainted meat insultingly thrown back at the butcher. She also cried because she was glad it was over, the insecurity, the sleepless nights, the pressure from surviving like a rat in a hole, the wondering about who might betray her.

The worrying had made her as thin as a matchstick, no matter how much Mrs. King had tried to feed her. The old woman had begged her to be of good cheer, assuring her that things were going to work out in God's own time. The Canadian government would bow to the pressure someday and grant another amnesty to illegals, emancipating them from the daily trials, or Ona would fall in love with some fine gentleman who would marry her. "And what's the worst that could happen to you?" Mrs. King had asked rhetorically. "You're young and strong. If you want, you can slip across the border to the United States. I hear that it's a lot easier to get a green card down there than to get your papers up here. So I don't know why you keep worrying so much all the time. Besides, I don't think I have to tell you that you can spend several lifetimes illegal in New York without anybody catching you out."

Ona had wanted to believe Mrs. King. She needed encouragement to face each new day in this tough city. But her appetite still declined. Going to New York wasn't a solution: how would Suzanne join her? What kind of life could she offer her daughter in the New York slums?

Now she didn't have to worry anymore. As a tall officer slipped the handcuffs around her wrists, she accepted that everything was over for Ona Jessica Nedd, everything except trying to explain her failure to her mother and, eventually, to her daughter.

The officer opened the leg irons to slip around her ankles. Ona flinched at the indignity. When the man in charge of the arrest compassionately shook his head, the young officer stood up and closed the shackles. They led her away, past the supervisor, without incident, and with dignity.

SIX HOURS AFTER the arrest, the officers let Ona call Mrs. King. The old woman came at once to the airport hotel where the top four floors served as a detention center.

"This boyfriend you're supposed to be seeing," Mrs. King said as soon as they were alone. "He know that you're in trouble? He's willing to do anything to help you out, like getting married?"

"I don't have no boyfriend," Ona said, dropping her eyes.

She stared at her hands, unable to look the old woman in her face. "I keep telling you I wasn't seeing anybody, but you won't believe me. So I stopped telling you anything different."

"So what you'd been doing all them nights when you used to come home so late? I'm talking 'bout all the times I thought you were out with some man?"

"Working. Every night. I had to work late."

"Hum," Mrs. King said.

She got up from the bed and began to pace the room. Ona didn't know what to expect. If Mrs. King couldn't help, there was nobody else to call on. Ona was already feeling uncomfortable for misleading Mrs. King.

"This don't sound too good to me," Mrs. King said. "With no boyfriend, things ain't looking too good. You got any money of your own? In case we can arrange something?"

"Only what I got in the bank. But they won't let me get it. They say that I worked for it illegal so I can't take it out of the country."

"What about all this overtime work at Tiltman you just talked about?" Mrs. King asked. "What you do with all that money?"

"They still got it."

Mrs. King showed no reaction. "And this worthless lawyer fellow you come up here to work for, you think he'd help you? Suppose we approach him about arranging something about your contract?"

"I don't think so," Ona answered. "It's over two years that I left them. I don't even know if the contract is any good, 'cause we would have had to renew it. And I don't know if he would even want to help me now."

"You know something," Mrs. King said. "We're wasting valuable time here. You see what you can do to help yourself. I'll see what I can do. I soon come back."

Ona's heart sank. Nobody could help her. Overhead, somewhere on the outside, she heard the screaming sounds of departing and arriving aircraft. The following morning, she was going to be on a plane to Jamaica, without even a doll for Suzie.

WHEN DARKNESS CAME, Ona gave up on Mrs. King. She had waited all day for the old woman's return. The hours had passed slowly, giving Ona too much time to reflect on her life. At twenty-three, she was an outcast, with a fatherless child who now had no chance of living the good life in Canada.

Ona was sitting on the bed, lost in her thoughts, when a guard unlocked the door and pushed it open. The woman stood in the doorway with a tray in her hand.

"Time for supper," she said. Ona didn't respond. She continued to aggressively twist her bed sheet in her hands.

The guard took a close look at her. "Don't feel so bad," she said. "This time tomorrow you'll be back in sunny Jamaica. In a few months' time, when it's still snowing like hell around here, I'll be the first to want to switch places with you."

"I ain't going back home," Ona said, twisting the cloth. "I can't go back. Please don't let them send me back home." She jumped to her feet and grabbed the guard's hand. The woman was bigger and stronger, but allowed Ona to hang on rather than wrestle with her. "Somebody gotta help me. I paid too much to be going home like this."

The guard set the food on the table beside the bed. Unbeknownst to Ona, she had pressed a little transmitter on her belt. Seconds later, the room was crowded with guards stripping the covers from the bed.

"Take them off," one of the guards ordered.

"What?" Ona asked in bewilderment.

"Strip. We can't take any chances. Last week one of you people up for deportation used a belt to hang himself. A few

93

weeks ago another one tried using the bed sheets. Take them off."

"But I can't undress, not with everybody watching."

"Take them off, or we will!"

Ona took off her clothes, but stopped at her bra and panties.

"Them too," the guard barked. "Everything. Lorna, take the food tray out of here."

Ona was left alone all night, stripped of everything, watched by a closed-circuit TV camera. The food had been returned on a paper plate with no knife or fork. It was the most degrading night of her life.

AT THE BACK of the Air Canada passenger lounge, Ona waited for the boarding announcement. Mrs. King had not returned to see her at the hotel. She wasn't even there to see her off at the airport.

Ona had hoped Mrs. King had thought of packing a valise with some of Ona's clothes to give her something to take home. Ona was about to sever all ties with Canada. There was now no chance of even getting her savings, the $584.20 she had diligently saved. The money wasn't enough to pay her fare home to prevent deportation, but to give her some dignity at home. Her scalp began itching. Ona raised a hand to scratch the spot in her uncombed hair. She had forgotten about the handcuffs. It was impossible to scratch adequately. The handcuffs were to remain on her wrists until the aircraft was well on its way to Jamaica, the guard had said. "Count yourself lucky it's only handcuffs," the guard added. "At one time, they used to drug troublemakers to keep them quiet. But the courts stopped that."

A tall slim woman, older than all the workers but wearing the same red and blue uniform, came into the waiting area. "Boarding complete," she announced. "We can clear the aircraft for departure."

Another flight attendant entered the lounge. "We can board our special passenger now," she said, glancing at Ona.

"Does she have any carry-on luggage?"

"Nothing," the boarding agent replied. "In all my years working at this airport, I've never seen any of them with luggage."

Conspicuous in her rumpled dress and stained running shoes, Ona got to her feet. She walked behind the flight attendant with her cuffed hands stretched out like a zombie's, one of two guards close behind and pressing into her back. On the plane, she was placed in a seat between two talkative Jamaican women returning home for a vacation. The trip was going to be worse than Ona had expected. She looked up and saw the flight attendant swinging the heavy door closed. It was all over.

ONA HAD SETTLED back in her seat with her eyes closed when she became aware of a commotion at the front of the cabin.

"Ladies and gentlemen, this is your captain," a voice on the plane's public address system said. "We will be delayed a few minutes to allow someone to deplane. We apologize for the unexpected delay, but it will be brief."

A flight attendant came to Ona's side. "Miss Nedd," she said, "please come with me." She bent over and whispered something in the guard's ear.

Ona walked out of the aircraft to see Kevin Jenkins, Harold Tiltman, a grim-faced Hilda King and the immigration officials who had delivered her to Air Canada an hour earlier.

"Thank God we got here in time," Mrs. King said. "Come chile. Come. God is a good God."

Ona placed her head on the old woman's shoulder.

"Would somebody get those damn handcuffs off my client," Jenkins said. "Here are the letters stating that she was granted landed immigrant status eighteen months ago. Boy, is somebody ever going to pay for this little mistake before I'm through."

He held up copies of Ona's immigration papers and the brand-new social security card. An immigration officer came forward. After several attempts, he found the right key. "I mean," Jenkins held forth, "didn't anyone *actually* stop to check the immigration records before acting on this so-called tip? And who is this supervisor that called, anyway? Is this how things are done around here these days?"

Ona and Mrs. King walked away from the crowd, leaning on each other. When they were out of earshot, Mrs. King told Ona how she had approached Jenkins and Tiltman and convinced them to rescue her. After all, she had argued, it was better for the Jenkinses' reputation if nobody found out what Ona had endured at his hands.

After a night of searching through his old papers and letters, the lawyer came across the letter from Immigration completing the process the Jenkinses had started to make Ona a landed immigrant. The letter had arrived a year after Ona ran off and Mary had thrown it into a storage box.

"As for Tiltman and this supervisor, I hope the day soon come when all o' them advantage-takers get what's coming to them. I don't know who tell them they got any right to keep exploiting all them women from poor countries," Mrs. King said. "Just look at him standing there with all your money in his pocket. We should march over there and make him hand it over right now."

Just when Ona expected Mrs. King to spin on her heels and to confront Tiltman, the old woman stopped and looked at her. "Right now, the money ain't important. We got what we want. We got you back. And believe you me, I did mean every word when I tell them that I was going to the newspapers, the police, the government, to whoever it take to help you. You didn't deserve this treatment. You don't deserve it."

"Thank you, Mrs. King," Ona whispered.

"Don't thank me," Mrs. King said. "I only hope that you

learned some out of all of this. 'Cause this is a real strange country for black people."

Five years later, Ona found herself reliving these experiences when the telephone rang and someone said Joseph Morgan needed help.

CHAPTER 9

WHEN SHE AND Fanny walked into the darkened dance hall in the dead of winter, Ona was still wishing she had stayed at home in her warm bed. To make matters worse, Fanny instantly left her in a corner by herself. Just like Fanny, Ona thought. First, out of the blue, she had telephoned and in one of her most determined moods had persuaded Ona to go with her to the dance.

"Look, girl, switch off the blasted TV set and get your fat arse up from sitting on that sofa all night long," Fanny had said bluntly. "I mean, this is your twenty-fifth birthday, think I didn't remember, eh? Put on a dress, girl, and come let we go and shake up your waist in celebration. A quarter century, girl! I was that age three years ago and I danced down the city. You know nobody in the damn Hole can put down a dance step like you, so I don't see why you have to keep moping around that damn apartment, letting an event like this pass by."

True, Ona loved to dance, but she didn't like the idea of turning up without a male partner, particularly in the Hole. Everyone automatically assumed an unattached woman came to the dance only to get picked up. As soon as they entered, they felt the eyes of the men, married and single, running up and down their bodies, assessing and undressing as they weighed possibilities. When two women arrived together, as was usually the case with Ona and Fanny, it looked doubly obvious. And the fact that Ona was a woman with a good job, working as a teller at the credit union, put her head and shoulders above many men in the Hole. That she also had her own apartment and maybe a few pennies in an account somewhere added to her status. She was definitely the kind of woman any man wanted to take home, or hoped was desperate enough to dip into her savings for a small loan, a shirt or even a few months of rent.

Fanny had argued that Ona needed to get out of the apartment, to drag herself away from the television and the salt-and-vinegar potato chips. It was the same argument Fanny had used several times in the year or so since Ona finally moved out on her own in the hopes of laying the groundwork to receive her daughter. The apartment was small, with just a pull-out sofa bed, a washroom and kitchen, but cheap and clean enough to make the owner proud of her possession. Occasionally, Mrs. King dropped by to spend an evening. She still called almost every night, sometimes twice a day on weekends even when Ona dropped by with the groceries.

When Ona least expected it, her so-called best friend would call her up on the phone and they would chat for hours. But Fanny was some best friend. Months went by without a chat and then one day the telephone would ring. Usually, Fanny was on the other end beaming and bringing Ona up to date with all the excitement in her life. Fanny had taught Ona two things: the excitement was always in anyone else's but Ona's life; and best friends in Canada were not the same as in the Caribbean, where friends saw and talked to one another almost daily.

"Look, I'll pick you up in an hour," Fanny said. "Be ready, you know. Don't keep my arse waiting downstairs, 'cause I'm a busy woman with no time to waste."

Ona had glanced at the clock on the wall above the television. Another hour made the time 11:40. They wouldn't reach the Hole until well past midnight, when technically the dance should be all but finished by the one o'clock deadline to stop selling booze.

"I can't afford to spend the little money I have set aside," Ona protested. "I have my commitments back home." Ona did some quick mental arithmetic: an admission fee and the cost of a drink or two from the bar. A good twenty-five dollars minimum. The price of asserting her independence in the presence of the men. However, it was money she couldn't afford. It would simply cut into the already meager remittances for her mother and Suzanne.

"I'll pass on it tonight," Ona pleaded. "It's late and the dance soon done anyway."

Ona should have known the outcome. Somehow, Fanny always got her way. That night she was even more persistent than usual, as if she was on some kind of mission. And she was quicker to arrive at the apartment than planned. The two women joined a stream of people flowing into the basement of an ugly building, in the darkness about one hundred yards off the street. The dance was, in fact, just beginning. From the look of things, it was going to be a long night. Then, as soon as they were inside, Fanny abandoned her. She was off seeking excitement with her male friends over by the bar.

As she looked for a chair, Ona immediately felt the jitters. The tingling of her nerves told her she had made a monumental mistake. Nothing could shake the uneasy foreboding. So she chose a table in the corner farthest from the door. From there, she hoped to spot the first sign of trouble. Anything was likely to happen in the Hole: a fistfight, a fire, even a police raid. She knew something bad was going to happen and she didn't want to be in the midst of it. Despite her premonitions, she didn't know in what form to expect this trouble. When it showed up, she was totally unprepared.

FOR ONA AND hundreds of fellow immigrants, the Hole was an affectionate name for the long narrow basement of St. Mark's Church on Queen Street West. This was the only place in all Toronto Barbadian immigrants could rent for all-night dances on Saturdays. Over time, it had become an informal social center, a gathering spot for West Indians and friends.

Almost every weekend, something went on in the basement. This was particularly true in the winter, when for a fee of two or three dollars—a mere fraction of the cost of more formal balls and galas across the city—the immigrants for a few brief hours could escape back to the warm tropics of rhythmic language and strong fragrances, even if the odors were those of perspiring bodies bathed in cheap perfume. They wrapped themselves up in one another for one night and got on as badly as they wanted.

Ona liked going to the Hole. Like other people her age, she found the church hall to be free-spirited, where a young man and woman could afford to spend an evening having fun. In those days, it never once occurred to her that the innocence of such a place could be spoiled by the arrival of the black youths, the rebel dancers who wouldn't listen to anyone and who turned up unabashedly with guns in their pockets looking to inflict damage. It was a time when the women dressed their best, not like in later days when the young girls, even her own Suzanne, began turning up almost naked, their demeanor established by bleached blond wigs or discolored hair on their heads, with pins in their nostrils and no dreams in their heart.

Ona also liked the dancing, especially the typically West Indian alternating of fast bouncy calypso rhythms with slow hold-me-close ballads, when a man and a woman actually *danced* together, actually touched each other, communicated through movement. Not like at the later rebel sessions that began cropping up all over the black community, where, because of the anger and distrust for both friends and strangers alike, the men and the women acted as if everyone were untrustworthy, as if afraid to touch one another. These were not the sessions with every man and woman lining up against a wall and dancing alone, a beer bottle locked between their fingers and a ganja joint glowing in the dark. In the Hole that Ona cherished, everyone was part of a community.

Most of the faces in the Hole were black, but some men brought white women. Everyone seeing these mixed couples recognized a black man using the woman as a trophy to prove he had attained a high level of acceptance, an accomplishment that remained a dream for so many. The doting woman on his arm, who seemed so keen to learn his culture and spend her money on him, was the symbol of this elevation.

Ona knew there were times when symbols mattered more than reality. In the Hole, the appearance of a fawning white woman with a strong black buck was one of those times. And from their conversations, Ona knew that just like her all the black women recognized this posturing as symptomatic of the weakness and feelings of inferiority that still dogged their men. They talked about it, sometimes gathering in the women's washroom to laugh at the scrawny white bitch so-and-so left his wife at home to be with. Or on their way back home, they joked in the cars about the *piece-o'-woman* some man had spent the night proudly introducing to everyone, the same kind of man who wasn't likely to be caught dead standing beside a black woman looking so bad and half dead.

With time, Ona began to feel the same pain that she saw on the faces of so many black women in the Hole. As they got older and more settled, ironically growing more financially secure and estranged from their black brothers, the gibes in the washroom or at the tables while waiting for a dance became less funny. Gradually, Ona understood what was happening, how the expectations of these women were transforming and dying. More and more, the women realized the psychological change that would cause the men to put black women on the same pedestal as their white lovers was not likely to happen in their lifetime. There was nothing for them to hold out hope for, except for the odd dance or meeting the occasional stranger. So they stopped going to the Hole as often, even though the cravings to combat loneliness and boredom by being with their own people, to re-create the friendly cultural setting if only for a few short hours, only intensified when they stayed away.

For West Indians, men and women alike, the Hole was always a place of dreams—those that they still carried in their heads and the ones that had been shattered. When Fanny telephoned, Ona was sure she had purged herself of all the usual immigrant dreams. She believed she had set aside all those unrealistic fantasies, had replaced them with harsh practicality. She had tried to stifle every one of them, but for the dreams of a future for her and Suzanne.

In reality, the basement, with its overflowing washrooms and folding steel chairs and tables, was a drab pit. It had no decoration and poor ventilation. One door served as entrance and exit. Invariably, the doorway was crowded with men, milling around inside and outside, where even in the middle of winter shivering people escaped the infernal heat on the crowded floor.

Inside the door was a large desk, partially blocking the entrance, where the sponsor of the dance collected the admissions and sold tickets for drinks and food. The doorway was also where those not dancing congregated to talk and to greet newcomers. To enter or leave was like running a gauntlet of faces, hands, and in the case of a woman walking alone, catcalls and whistles.

Particularly in winter, with the church buttoned down, and the bodies in heat and gyrating to the loud calypso and reggae music, the basement was a fire trap. The virtually sealed room held several times the maximum one-hundred-and-fifty people sanctioned by safety regulations. The carelessness with which even sober men threw away still-lit cigarette butts

103

scared the hell out of Ona. The drunks trying to guide flaming matches or lighters to the shaking cigarettes in their mouths terrified her.

Ona expected to perish one of those nights in a blaze. How was the news going to play back home in the Caribbean? How would her mother explain to Suzanne that Ona had died in a fire, in a church of one of the denominations that frowned on Pocomania, in a place called the Hole, no different from dance halls of the heathens back home with their worship of the devil and the flesh?

Every so often, a pair of policemen, usually white, and the occasional immigration officer walked through the hall. Ostensibly, the police were there to enforce liquor-licensing rules and to discourage rowdy behavior or desecration of church property. But everyone knew differently. No matter how the immigration officers tried to blend in with the crowd, they could always be spotted at a distance. They always looked anxious to leave, to be out of the trap, as though they expected some of the beefy men to pounce on them. The cops walked with their shoulders hunched, their elbows bent and their fingers brushing the tops of their holsters. When they found nothing amiss, they were soon gone from the scene. Otherwise, the revelers were left alone.

Once or twice squadrons of police cruisers descended on the Hole and dragged people away. Ona later heard that these raids usually came when complaints from neighbors and real estate agents concerned with the value of their homes and properties were most acute and the local politicians had to do something about the pressure. Dances were suspended for several weeks after the raids. Special pleas had to be made to the authorities for reinstatement of liquor licenses.

The dances were the only entertainment for Fanny. "Where else can you go to eat some good West Indian food?" she asked. "I mean you can only eat burgers, fries and greasy chicken and doughnuts, that good old Canadian favorite food, for so long without getting a real good longing for some nice, nice food: a plate of green peas and rice, real fried chicken, beef stew, curried goat and roti. Where else can you get a really good beer: a Red Stripe, Banks or a Carib? Or a good rum punch with real rum, not the watered-down tasteless thing they sell in this country?"

In the Hole, West Indians played their recorded music as loudly as they wanted and danced as lewdly as they liked. They didn't have to adjust or temper their ways, unless they had brought along some outsider they wanted to impress. All of them were the same, sharing the same cultural background, tastes, fears and failures. Buried in the Hole, cut off from the wider society, they had no apartment neighbors ready to call the police at the first sound of the reverberating bass signaling the start of a good West Indian party. It was like going home to the Caribbean for a respite, for the renewal that came from just basking in West Indian songs they never heard on Canadian radio.

The Hole was a refuge full of imported nostalgia, as well as the source of news that really mattered: news of childhood friends still back home, information more meaningful and useful than what they read in Canadian newspapers, where there was hardly any mention of back home. In the Hole, they met new friends and renewed acquaintances. They welcomed newcomers to Canada, grieved over a death or misfortune, caught up on the latest scandals and on cricket scores back in the islands. And for sure, it was the place to pick up a man or woman for the night or for a lifetime.

Although every fiber in her body warned her to stay away, Ona felt at home in the Hole. The only place more West Indian in Toronto was the Spiritual Baptist Church, but she had stopped worshiping. To have even a remote chance of achieving the last of the dreams remaining of all the thousands she had brought to this country, Ona had no choice but to put aside the religion she professed when Pastor Grant had ducked her little body in the ocean. Ona wasn't the only immigrant in her community to make this decision. How else could they get ahead in an adopted society when they always seemed to be held back by mores from a different time and place? How else would they break the cycle? Every time these immigrants felt they had changed and adjusted their expectations so as to catch up with what was the norm in their new society, the standards changed. Just like a target that moved in wide, expansive jumps. Each move left the immigrants lagging further behind than the previous one, left them running as fast as possible but never catching up. Even if she really wanted, there was no way Ona could possibly hope to catch up while remaining faithful to the religion of her mother and Pastor Grant. It was simply incompatible with her life in Canada. And she wanted nothing, especially any baggage from back home, to hold her back.

Visiting the Hole kept her spirit alive and reminded her who she really was. Occasionally, she even became someone's partner for the night. On the Monday morning, without any pangs of conscience, she could pretend the Hole didn't exist and return to reality. For in so many respects, the Hole represented the basement of Ona's soul. It reminded her how much she had started to get behind in her dreams; dreams she never even thought of sharing with anyone back home, especially not her mother.

ONA THREW HER heavy coat on the back of a chair and sat in the darkness, waiting for her fingers, toes and ears to thaw. In minutes, her eyes had adjusted and she could make out the faces of people she had met through Fanny. Over by the makeshift bar, she saw Fanny in conversation with a group of men, laughing. The music stopped and another record began. The music was familiar but seemed even louder. Ona instinctively began tapping her foot to the beat, but under the table.

One of the men took Fanny by the hand and led her onto the crowded dance floor. In a moment, they were lost from sight as they whirled around the room. Ona smiled and settled in, accepting that it would be a long time before Fanny rejoined her, but she didn't mind. The tension was easing. She was enjoying the music. Maybe Fanny was right. She ought to get out of the apartment more often, even if she had to go some places alone.

"You dancing, miss?" a soft voice asked.

She looked up at a tall man, smiling, with his hand outstretched in her direction. He looked a bit younger than she, dressed handsomely in a white *shirtjac* and black pants.

"Can I interest you in a dance with me if you don't mind me asking?" The shirtjac was a sure sign he was just off the boat. The combination of a shirt and regular suit jacket was uniquely West Indian and one of the first pieces of clothing immigrants dispensed with once settled in the new country.

"Sure," she replied, eyeing him approvingly as she rose, almost tripping over her chair in the semidarkness.

"Be careful now, my dear. Don't break your pretty leg. Give me a chance to dance with you first." His speech too betrayed a new arrival; it still had the rough edges that had nothing to do with diction or grammar but with the fact that back home people talked differently, louder, and usually had to adjust the tone and force once they had spent any time in North America.

His teasing broke the ice. She liked to dance, but usually felt uneasy dancing with strangers. It usually took her time to know whether to abandon herself to their control, or, if they were making too many false steps, to gently take over the lead. Ona could easily switch from following to leading without threatening her partner's ego.

They danced the remainder of the tune. When she made as if to return to the table, he held her firmly, refusing to move. The next record was an old favorite, Ben E. King's "Seven Letters." Almost everyone was on the floor. This was quickly followed by Al Green's "Stealing Love." In the crowd, Ona and the stranger stood on one spot, grinding their bodies together.

Ona liked the feel of the man, the tenderness in his long fingers rubbing her back and shoulders and the way he danced. The two of them had moved perfectly from the first step.

Eventually, they returned to her table. Ona wasn't surprised when he pulled up a chair. She found out his name: Joe Morgan. He had arrived in Canada only a week earlier, supposedly on vacation.

"I could have told you that from the shirtjac," Ona said, laughing. "You only wear them in the West Indies, not up here. Certainly not in the winter."

"I see," he said. "I guess I got to buy some new clothes quick, quick then." He confirmed he wasn't thinking of going back home, that he was spending some time with the man who had waltzed off with Fanny and who now appeared very intent on keeping her from interrupting Ona and Joe.

They laughed, and he continued with his story. "I really like what I see a'ready in Canada," he told her, wiping the perspiration from his brow with the back of his hand. "A partner of mine back home did tell me about these dances, but he was talking about New York, not here. He works for the airlines and does travel all over the world. Every weekend or the other, he's flying somewhere or the next. And when he comes back home, he's always telling me how every Saturday night in New York, West Indians like to head for these basement parties. The same is true in England, from what he tells me. But I didn't expect nothing so in Canada, 'cause you know people don't associate Canada with fun, except at Caribana. So I didn't expect anything like this. In fact, this place is almost like back home. It remind me of place we call the Drill Hall in Barbados."

"I'm glad you like Canada," she said.

"Yeah. That's why I want to try to get an extension of my visitor's permit. So I could look around some more; see how things work out. But tell me: How long you've been in Canada now? You are still a landed immigrant or a Canadian citizen? Do you come to this place the Hole a lot?"

Ona answered politely, not giving too much information. But she did tell him she was a Canadian citizen, had been for one year. However, although she had spent seven years in this country and had applied for citizenship on the very day she qualified, she always thought of herself as more Jamaican than Canadian. The dual citizenship was an insurance policy, she said, so that nobody would ever be able to throw her out of this country. "Otherwise, to tell the truth, I don't really think the citizenship business means a whole lot," she said, surprising herself that she was so open with a perfect stranger. "It's not like people like we from the West Indies can't go back home if we want sometime in the future. It's not like we gotta hold on to this citizenship here because we have nowhere else to go."

"And it got other uses, too. Maybe I should marry you and take care of my problem." He laughed at what he must have intended as a joke, or even a mild probe. "I could get my landed from you."

She forced a smile and dismissed his remark. Ona had heard such jokes before. She had heard of countless women stupid enough to do such a crazy thing, some for money, others for love. In the end, every one of them was sorry. None was happy. Deliberately, she decided to not even acknowledge the statement.

When he asked her to dance again, Ona declined. Something about him was too brazen and had momentarily turned her off. Joe went to another table and found a dance partner who kept him busy. Ona thought she had seen the last of him. He appeared to be thoroughly enjoying the conversation with his new partner.

Later, however, he returned to Ona with his face bathed in perspiration. She later found out that he sweated a lot, even on the coldest nights. He bought a gin and tonic for her and a scotch on the rocks for himself. They talked some more and danced. Ona felt she was beginning to warm to him again. She bought him a drink, a plate of rice and beef stew. They were eating when there was a stampede for the dance floor. The Drifters were singing "Save the Last Dance for Me." They didn't bother to stop eating. Suddenly, the music ended; it was time to go home. The Hole was awash in bright light. People, mainly couples, were making their way to their cars. With the lights on, Ona had her first comprehensive look at Joe. They lingered talking while some people cleaned up the hall, folded the chairs and wheeled out the hi-fi set. Fanny, finally, left off from her partner to come over and join them.

By then, Ona had agreed he could phone her. If she wasn't too tired or busy, she could take him around Toronto. They might visit one or two of the usual tourist places. Or they might take in a movie or have a drink together. Neither made a commitment. It was up to him to call. She retained the option to decline.

They went out several times. Then she began sleeping with him. In the second and third months, he was at her apartment almost every night and certainly every weekend. By then, his visitor's permit had expired, and the immigration department had refused to extend it. Joe had no choice but to go underground. Around this time, Ona also felt Joe was getting a bit tired of her. His eyes started to wander but she accepted this as expected of men, who felt they still had to play the field. Women started calling her apartment; some hung up when she answered. Somehow this didn't bother her that much. She had never felt there was any permanency in the relationship.

Joe was working at a furniture factory and he had a friend who was willing to take him as a roommate if Joe paid half the rent. Soon after he went underground, Joe walked out on her. This did not surprise her. What did was that, coincidentally, on the very week that Joe left, Immigration formally told Ona in a letter that conditions were not right for her to bring Suzanne to Toronto. This disappointment was so great, so unexpected, that she had no time to even think about Joe. She had to find a strategy, any design, to get her daughter.

Ona forgot about Joe until the morning she ran into him on

the bus and he sat beside her. She suspected he had just left some woman's bed but she certainly wouldn't ask, not even jokingly. She didn't want him to think she was interested enough to pry into his business.

At his bus stop, he promised to call her to arrange a date for Saturday. He had lost weight and looked deeply exhausted from being illegal, from constantly matching his wits against the system, uncertain of whom he could trust. Ona had seen the symptoms in others and in the mirror: the smile rubbed off the face, the briskness and confidence gone from the walk. Pitifully, some illegals hacked and ached with influenza for days, too frightened to visit a doctor, even if they could afford the treatment.

"Maybe we could go back to the Hole for old times' sake," he had said lethargically. "Just like the first time, remember, when we met ten months ago."

Ona had agreed, not really expecting to hear from him. If he did call, it would be to cancel. Joe had two very good excuses for canceling. The Hole was the first place the immigration officers looked when rounding up illegals. Secondly, the last thing illegals needed was such a potent reminder as this basement of what they had given up for the mirage of a better life in Canada.

The telephone call came at work but it was not the cancellation she expected. Joe was in trouble and wanted to talk to her, the caller had said.

"Where he is now?" she had asked.

It would have been easy to ignore Joe, just as he had forgotten her until the chance meeting on the bus. That would teach him a lesson. He hadn't as much as telephoned her once since that Monday morning five months earlier when she woke up and found him gone. But as Mira Nedd said: God moves in mysterious ways his wonders to perform; everything happens for a reason. Maybe it was God's plan she had to be at work an hour earlier that week to meet the annual rush before the registered retirement saving plans deadline expired. As it turned out, he had been picked up on Tuesday, and had waited two and a half days before getting a message to her. Obviously she was now his last resort. All others had turned him down. It would be so nice to let him stew in his own sauce, just to walk away from him, but Ona believed there could be gold in every misfortune. She preferred to look on the bright side: as his last resort, she dictated the terms and suddenly she thought of something that Joe Morgan could give her.

"I don't know where he is," the caller said. "All I know is that they got him at one of the stations downtown. I think they picked him up as soon as he came in to work in the morning. Seems they were waiting for him, one at each door. Somebody must've squealed on him."

"But you don't know which station?" she asked.

"No."

"All right," Ona whispered, anxious to get off the phone to escape the inquisitive looks of her supervisor. "Okay, I'll try to find him."

Ona had no idea where to start looking. Several calls to the immigration department's inquiry number brought only busy signals. When she tried again, after closing her wicket, she was put on hold and then the woman who answered said that kind of information was not given out over the phone. It was forbidden under the privacy laws. However, Joe could be at any of the holding centers in Toronto, and Ona might have to call them one by one. By this time the supervisor was throwing hostile glances in Ona's direction. Everybody was aware that the dragon lady monitored the length of telephone calls.

Then Ona thought of calling Kevin Jenkins, the lawyer— the man who was responsible for her coming to Canada in the first place, the man with contacts in the immigration department, but also the only lawyer she knew.

Ona had promised herself she would never have anything to do with the Jenkins family again, particularly Kevin. And now she was breaking her word for Joe Morgan, almost a stranger. Even before she thought through what she was doing, Ona found herself on the phone, talking calmly, frankly with Kevin Jenkins and listening. "As you know, Joe's immigrant status can't be changed within Canada," he said. "He'll have to go back to his homeland, but that might not be so bad or for too long."

If she and Joe were to marry, the lawyer explained, Joe could be back in the country in six months to a year, more likely six months. She would have to sponsor him immediately. The government would give them three months to get married on his return. Suzanne could follow a few months later.

"Is that something you really want to do?" Jenkins asked. "I understand how much you want your daughter, but isn't what you're thinking a bit drastic?"

"Well, you know, it's been a long time I've been without my daughter," Ona said softly. For a moment, Ona thought she detected a note of concern in his voice, but there couldn't have been, not after what he had done to her. Nothing in this life could be as bad as what he had done, at a time when she was so fragile and vulnerable. She quickly dismissed this thought. "So I'm hoping something like this would help clear the way."

"It would help you satisfy the immigration requirements for your daughter. No doubt about that," Jenkins said.

What the lawyer suggested sounded reasonable to Ona. Joe was a big boy. He understood what he had to do, what he was getting into. He was a smart fellow, and she knew he didn't want to go home. She also realized this was the best chance she had to convince the same immigration people deporting Joe to let Suzanne join her.

CHAPTER 10

FOR A BRIEF and rare moment, the dark clouds had lifted from Ona's life. Everything she had hoped for appeared to be within her grasp; her life was making a more meaningful turn this time. Joseph Morgan, tall and handsome, had asked her to be his wife.

It was 5:30 in the morning. The Sunday sun had not yet risen and the aircraft was fueling a mile away for the eight o'clock departure when she went to him and he agreed to her terms. They had settled the few outstanding details in a businesslike manner. In six months, if everything went as expected, and there was now no legal reason to expect otherwise, she was going to be able to write home and tell her mother the good news. She would be able to send dispatches from an alien land that for the first time were true, not make-believe. No longer were they going be a figment of her imagination or elements of somebody's life she was enviously reporting as her own. The end was near for the separation of mother and child. But there was more: she was getting a partner, someone with whom she could build a future, someone to help her and whom she could help.

Finally, after all these years in Canada, bouncing from one lonely apartment to another, she was going to have a family. Just the thought of this was so sweet. Finally! She was on the verge of having a home with a male partner in it, and Suzanne could finally join her. She could be a mother, at long last taking on her responsibilities, ending the separation and denials, completing the vicious cycle. Ona would be able to begin creating anew by raising a beautiful girl into a fine woman. They would do it in a land with so many opportunities for anyone willing to grasp them. With all her experience, Ona planned to show Suzanne how to grab those chances and hold on to them. Unhurried, Suzanne would have all the possibilities of success, chances that Ona never had because she had never really gotten her life under control, at least not until this moment of promise.

The marriage proposal wasn't as romantic as she had dreamed or hoped. But what was to be expected with the two of them standing in a sparsely furnished hotel room with bars and wire mesh on the windows? The two of them pretending not to be negotiating, ever mindful of the closed-circuit television camera overhead and the urgency of the waiting plane. Who could be romantic under such conditions? It wasn't as if either of them had any real choices, or as if she was any longer the young princess waiting for Mr. Right. Realism and the need for practicality had long driven these thoughts from her head. The reality of the situation was that, individually, each of them was at the end of the road. Everything in the room reminded them of this. They had to decide whether they were going to retrace their steps together, in the hope of eventually getting out of the dead end in which they found themselves, or remain eternally trapped.

Sure, she could have turned Joe down. But what was that likely to prove? What good would be created out of being spiteful for some past treatment? More years of fighting to get her daughter; more years of tiring uncertainty, just fighting, fighting, fighting, one issue after another.

Ona had known Joseph for ten months and, from what else was available, thought he was worth the effort. She believed the two had nothing to lose. He held some potential and there was some value in him. There couldn't be too many surprises they hadn't already encountered. In time, they might learn to get along and appreciate, if not love, each other. If their relationship came to love, so much the better, but that wasn't something she was pinning her hopes on. If it happened, it happened. She knew the odds. Two out of every three marriages in Canada ended in divorce, but Ona felt her chances of success were better than most. Ironically, the same statistics showed that arranged marriages, supposedly devoid of love, tended to rank highest among the survivors, or so she had read in the newspapers. And this was where she saw the value in Joe, their recognition of the stark reality facing each of them, the realization that they had to stick together to re-create their lives, and the fact Joe would give her the validating name Morgan to put on Suzanne's immigration forms.

With tears in her eyes, she accepted their fate together. In her heart, Ona knew it was an unvarnished gamble, with as much potential for disaster as for happiness. But there could be no turning back. Time was marching on. Every year she was getting older, another year away from her daughter. This arrangement was going to help her to reclaim her daughter. That alone was worth the gamble.

Mentally, and to a lesser extent physically, she was tired. So weary of gambling alone, so burnt out from not having anyone to share the winnings with or to console her in the losses. If she lost again then she could walk away knowing that at least she had had the guts to give it a try, to risk another embarrassing failure. At least she was making a stab at getting her daughter back.

Should worse become worst, she could always withdraw into herself, among her few friends, and resume the old uneventful life she despised. Time would march on. Suzanne would turn ten. And only God knew what would happen next.

But if she won; ah, just the thought was delicious. She was going to earn her mother's smile, and again hold her daughter. She would no longer hear the relentless ticking of the clock or notice the passing of another month, another week, another day.

The immigration officer had returned to the room with the handcuffs and leg irons. She had made her decision. Now it was up to Joe to divulge his.

"What it's going to be, Mr. Morgan?" asked the officer, an old man with a deep smoky voice and weather-beaten face. "Have you made up your mind?"

"I think so," Joe replied. Then he hesitated. Joe's face had turned firm, almost defiant. For a moment, Ona wondered if he were having second thoughts. But she quickly dismissed this notion. One look in his eyes told her the truth. Joe was simply trying to hold out for as long as possible. He wanted to relish the few fleeting moments of what was left of his pride and manhood, savoring the last of the freedom to make a decision before the door was slammed shut.

"As you know, you can sign the form," the officer said pointing to a file folder on a desk in the hallway. His voice suggested that he expected Joe to accept the worst. "By so doing, you agree to leave Canada of your own free will, to repay the government of Canada the airfare for sending you back to your homeland, and to promise that you won't try to enter Canada illegally again. Under those terms, you'll be able to come back to Canada through the proper channels or on vacation with the appropriate guarantees, of course."

"I understand," Joe said. "I'll sign it."

The officer paused, then continued as though he hadn't heard. Obviously, protocol demanded that he spell out all the legal ramifications of the decision, or maybe Joe had spoken too softly for him to understand. But Ona had heard what she wanted. She felt like telling the dried-up old man to take his rules and stuff them. That what he was reading didn't apply to them and to stop wasting their time. But speaking up was

117

likely to serve no purpose other than embarrassing Joe Morgan. She kept quiet.

"If you choose not to sign," the official droned on, "which you're free to do, we will have no choice but to deport you when we put you on the airplane this morning. You must understand that once a deportation order is signed and executed, once the word deported is stamped in your passport, you may never return to Canada again for as long as you live, not even for a vacation."

Ona looked at Joe's face and saw the small grin breaking out at the corner of his mouth. He must have known the officer wasn't telling him the full story. Surely he must have heard of cases like this, where people felt they were leaving in good faith only to find out differently later on. Even if the immigration officer didn't say it, Ona knew that once Joe left Canada, voluntarily or otherwise, he would never be allowed back into the country unless he also agreed to Ona's terms. That's why, she thought, he was smiling at all this bullshit.

Joe Morgan had to know he was now marked for life. As soon as he turned up at a Canadian airport, his name and passport number were bound to register on the computer screen telling the immigration officers to bar his entry. No reasons had to be given. An illegal immigrant like Joe Morgan must know that.

Joe Morgan was tainted meat in the eyes of the Canadian gatekeepers. There was always going to be suspicion in the immigration officials' minds because he was black, but every West Indian had to live with that possibility. More telling, though, he had lied before; and as far as the immigration people were concerned, he was likely to do anything to live in Canada, including lying again. Therefore, he would be barred from the country permanently. The look on his face told Ona that Joe knew fully what he was up against. He knew he was beaten, except for her proposal.

They both knew people carrying the word *deported* around their necks like an invisible millstone not even time could erode, far less remove. It had happened to friends with whom Joe had hustled white tourists on the beaches in Barbados. Some of whom were simply rounded up at subways or shopping malls, all of them arrested when unable to show proper identification in these random raids, and sent straight back home.

While being romanced on the tropical sand or in the discos at night, the women promised the young men anything they wanted in return for a few weeks of fidelity. In moments of ecstasy it was easy, or perhaps convenient, to promise a plane ticket to Toronto or Montreal and the marriage license to make them permanent residents of a new country.

Having gone the same route as some of these men, Joe Morgan now had two clear choices if he wanted to get back into Canada. One was to marry Ona. She was promising no less than what another woman had offered earlier. The difference was that Ona was willing to keep the promise and invest her money as a sign of good faith. The others had not even answered the phone after the first desperate call. Ona was different. She knew how badly Joe Morgan wanted to stay in Canada, in Toronto, where friends had sheltered him when his visitor's visa ran out. He could marry her and stay in Toronto. The second choice was simple. He could fall on his own sword.

"How much this plane ticket gonna cost?" Joe asked, glancing at Ona with a tepid smile.

"Six hundred and eighty-seven dollars. Then another twenty dollars a day for five days of room and board at this hotel. Unless you can pay it all now, we'll have to deport you. You've already told the judge you don't have any money."

"All o' that money!" He seemed to be panicking. "I don't have so much money on me."

"Unless you can pay it all now, we'll have to deport you. I know you have already told the judge you don't have any money. So I don't understand why you're even asking about the costs."

"I have money," Joe fired back. "But all of it is in the bank. That's what I tell the judge, but none o' you won't believe me. Nobody won't listen. Not even the judge." He turned to Ona as if he expected her to verify his statement, to raise an argument that some leniency should be exercised to allow one of them to make a quick trip to get the money.

On cue, Ona injected, "I have the money." She sat on the hard bed and opened her handbag. "I'll pay for it. How much you said it was again?"

Something fell loudly outside. Ona thought of the bags she had left in the hallway. Behind the locked door were suitcases packed with things she had just bought in bargain stores. There were shirts, pants, dresses, running shoes, toothpaste, deodorant, soap, candy, cheap toys and a big bag of red apples.

She had thought of these things as soon as she received word that Immigration had busted Joe and was going to deport him. Everybody returning home to any island in the Caribbean had to bring these things. If Joe were to turn up at the Barbados airport empty-handed, with just the clothes on his back, everybody would know instantly what had happened. It would crush Joe's pride. She had decided, even if he said he didn't want to come back to marry her, that Joe couldn't go back home without a few possessions and gifts.

Ona took a roll of bills and began to count them, slowly and carefully. She had cleaned out her savings accounts, including the rent money, and borrowed $500 from Fanny. Kevin Jenkins, the lawyer, had told her to take along her checkbook as well, because of minor charges the government might add. Failing to pay any of them could lead to deportation.

The officer took the $787 in cash and Joe signed the papers. He gave Joe the yellow copy, threw the carbon in the wastebasket and kept the white and pink sheets.

"Keep that in your passport," the officer said.

The officer prepared to leave for the room next door. But he lingered long enough to mumble how he was sure to find some weeping woman with a bag full of money trying to save the man who had been picked up with Joseph Morgan. He shook his head.

"There ought to be a law against such exploitation," he muttered, loudly enough for anyone to hear, "and to stop these people from coming into this country in the first place."

"What's that you say?" Ona snapped, daring him to repeat the statement.

"Nothing. I'll be back in twenty minutes," the officer replied.

He turned his back on Ona in a demeaning gesture as he faced Joe. "You should be ready to leave when I get back. We still gotta be at the airport for seven."

"HOW MISTRESS ONA Morgan sounds to you?" Joe asked, teasingly.

"That ain't my name, at least not yet," she said with a laugh. "I's still Ona Nedd. I ain't give up my Nedd name yet. Anyway, I got a few little things for you. I thought I'd buy a few pieces clothes so you can take them back for the children you got at home. I hope they fit."

Very quickly, she was serious again. "First thing tomorrow, I'm going to get the papers from Immigration. First thing in the morning before going to work. Then I plan to fill them out tomorrow night, after work. The lawyer wants me to bring the papers for he to take a look at them before I carry them in. We gotta get the ball rolling right away."

"Don't worry too much, Ona. I plan to keep myself to myself when I get back home. I can swear to that right now. And when I come back up here, it's gonna be just me and you. Just the two o' we together. We'll work out things in we own way, 'cause you know something, Ona, nobody in this country would do for me what you're doing. I don't mind telling you that, because it's true, true, true."

He kissed her lips and they embraced. Playfully, he ran his

hand down the front of her skirt and pressed the spot between her legs, something he was prone to do whenever they hugged.

"None o' that touching-touching business, skipper," she said, playfully pushing away his hand. "You gotta wait. You gotta try and come back up real quick, so we can be legal. Why don't you try on the pants and shirt I bought for yuh, 'cause the man soon come back? And by the way, I want to thank yuh for taking me dancing last night. It was a real good dance."

Joe smiled sheepishly as if to confess he really had had no intention of showing up. "Don't mention it," he said. "There'll be other nights. I promise you."

"No problem. Start getting dressed. See if this dungaree pants and the shirt fit yuh?"

"I'll be a good husband to you," Joe said, opening the plastic wrappings.

"And a father too?"

"A father? You ain't planning to get . . ."

"To my Suzanne," Ona said.

"Oh, yeah. Oh, yeah," Joe said, sounding somewhat distant. "For a moment, you had me there. I didn't think o' that."

He had just slipped into the shirt and pants when the door opened and the officer came in. "We're ready to go. We have to deport the other fellow we picked up with you."

"Christ, not Albert!" Joe exclaimed. "You mean he ain't get nobody to help he out?"

"Does the luggage out there belong to you, Mr. Morgan?" the officer asked.

"Yeah," Ona said.

She handed Joe a small wad of bills. With one hand, he placed the cash in his hip pocket, and with the other pulled her close to him and squeezed. He said nothing. His trembling body thanked her for sparing him from the fate of his best friend, the man marching down the hall between two immigration officers, handcuffed and humiliated. Ona had intervened to save him from going home like Albert, with only the clothes on his back, to laughter and ridicule for not being able to buy one drink at the village rum shop. She had saved him from that, and he was grateful. He hugged his wife-to-be again.

"We have to get to the airport," the officer said.

"Thanks," Joe whispered, releasing her from his arms.

"Have a safe trip. Call me when you get home. The three dresses in the valise for your mother, my mother-in-law. Tell her I sent them. When you get home, tell her that I say she got to come up for the wedding."

"Come on, let's go," the officer said.

Ona picked up the dirty clothes, the ones he had been arrested in and had worn for the six days in detention. She folded them, sniffing his strong perspiration, and placed them in a plastic bag. She planned to wash and iron the clothes and to keep them in her bedroom to remind her of the man she was marrying. They were to be the promise of his eventual return, the positive sign that she was so much closer to a reunion with her precious daughter.

CHAPTER 11

JOE DID NOT return from Barbados in six or even twelve months. It took all of thirty long months before the Canadian High Commission in Barbados finished the paperwork to allow him back into the country. Ona had lost another two and a half years before she could start proceedings to send for her daughter.

For Ona, it was unbelievable that it took anyone so long to process a few pieces of paper. But it happened. The High Commission in Barbados unexpectedly dragged its heels on what Ona was promised was a routine matter. In the first few months, whenever she telephoned the Immigration Department in Toronto somebody was always saying everything was going fine. It was always up to this or that official in Barbados, maybe the visa counselor or the medical supervisor, to verify something or the other, they always told her.

The Toronto office had sent Joe's file to Barbados. Although it was out of the hands of people in Toronto, the officers in the downtown branch always assured her of a speedy response. Canada was committed by law and international human rights codes to the reunification of families, and Ona had complied with all the regulations, the officers repeated. She was to call back in a couple of weeks if she hadn't heard anything, they always suggested. The same story was repeated over and over. Call in a few weeks.

Although exceedingly frustrated, Ona did not hesitate to contact the immigration people whenever they missed a deadline, or just to keep them on their toes. Eventually, the receptionists at the Immigration Department would recognize Ona's voice as soon as they picked up the phone. They put the call right through to whoever was supposed to be handling the case, few questions asked.

In Ona's eyes, the results of the setback were near catastrophic. It took the bloom off everything, stripped the budding relationship of its newness. By the time Joe rejoined her, everything was so tainted, so jaded and without any spontaneity.

Worse, she felt the unexpected delay laid the groundwork for the greatest damage of all—the later troubles with her daughter. "If anybody had to ask me to point out what I think caused me all these problems, as God is my witness, I would have to say it's them immigration people," she finally told Mrs. King.

If the immigration people had worked faster, she would have gotten Suzanne before she was ten years old. Every West Indian mother knew ten years was a crucial age, when a young girl was still in a shape for a mother to influence her. Ona still could have reconnected spiritually with Suzanne; make it up to her for being away from her so long. To help ease her into the new environment of big city life. But after ten years, what could she do? Any child has already formed its character, has its own opinions, knows it all. Nothing anyone, especially a stranger, did would be good enough. By that age, children are rebellious. They no longer think they need mothers, despite their parents' ability to guide them in a new situation, to pass on the benefits of their experience and hardship. Every month that passed was another in which Suzanne was hardening against Ona for leaving Jamaica.

The way the Immigration Department treated her had other effects on Ona. It made her almost paranoid when dealing with people, even those she should be trusting. How could she keep facing friends? How could she continue to tell them her man was coming back *any day now* to marry her? How often was it possible for Ona to repeat it to herself before the statements rang hollow, before her so-called friends began to suppress mischievous grins and whisper among themselves? How long was she to keep up writing to her mother, saying she was planning to send for Suzanne, knowing the Canadian authorities were never going to allow this single woman to bring a child into the country? And these were the same authorities that were doing everything in their power to stop her from changing her marital status.

In anticipation of Joe's early arrival, Ona had arranged a loan from the credit union where she worked. It was enough to cover the airfare from Barbados, to paint and wallpaper the apartment and to buy a bed, television set and stereo.

She knew the owner of the furniture factory was willing to give Joe his old job back. He had assured her personally. So she took out the loan, without telling Joe. She simply took the initiative as she was so used to doing. She wanted to surprise him by fixing up the apartment. Their home was to be comfortable and liveable. They wouldn't have to waste even more time with meaningless details of setting up a home before getting on with the bigger plans for their lives. That was the least she could do while waiting for him. But this too proved a problem. She had counted on having two salaries to pay back the loan and to cover the usual expenses of running a home. Instead, she found herself dropping deeper into the hole, having to consolidate old loans and praying that help would come soon with Joe's return.

Throughout it all, the only thing that kept her going was the few pictures she received of her daughter. Bringing her to

Canada became a compulsion, an addiction. She dreamed about it every night, and on the subway and the buses. She had to get her daughter, had to do whatever it took to reclaim her. Often Ona found that people had been talking to her, but that her mind was elsewhere, drifting.

At the end of the first six months, Ona began to worry, especially when Joe told her he had not been contacted by the immigration people at the High Commission in Barbados. Every week she phoned him, or he called her collect. They talked for hours. At the end of the month, when the bill arrived, Ona was always shocked by how expensive talking was.

Eventually, she got Kenrick James, her legal counselor, to call the Immigration Department to threaten legal action on Joe's behalf. In desperation, and after she felt Kevin Jenkins turning cold on Joe's case, she had picked this counselor from a list in the black newspapers. Kenrick also threatened to ask Ona's Member of Parliament for help when the department reported Joe's file had been misplaced. Ona had to make another application and start the process all over again. The arrival was now postponed for at least another six months. The department promised to speed up the process, giving her special attention, because the delay was entirely its fault.

The process dragged on and the bills piled up. Every morning, she went to work to face her colleagues, knowing someone had started another nasty rumor. The prevailing gossip was that the man Ona was going to so much trouble to marry didn't want to come back to Toronto. Another had it that she was too embarrassed to face the truth: Joe had given up on getting his papers and was back to his usual self, living off Ona and hustling white women on the beach.

When they called her "Mrs. Morgan," Ona knew it was with malice. She hated going to work. Only the need to cover the crippling loan payments and Suzanne's remittances kept her from leaving the credit union.

As usual, Mrs. King was the only person to commiserate. At first the old woman, always one to speak her mind, told her what a fool she was to be sponsoring any man from the West Indies. Particularly, she said, a man so lazy he had no intentions of finding work.

"You don't need this kinda man so bad that you got to be doing all this stupidness," Mrs. King said.

"How else can I get Suzanne? I can't think of no other way to get her. Don't forget they keeping telling me I'm a single woman. I mean the last time I talked to them, they went so far as to tell me I should think of adopting my own daughter, Suzanne. Can you imagine asking a mother who grunt and groaned to push out her child into this world to do something like that?"

"Well, you gotta know what you're doing," Mrs. King said. " 'Cause, to tell the truth, I don't. All I can say to you is that it's too bad you didn't put Suzanne's name on them papers when you first come up here. But I guess you didn't know any better. And back then nobody wasn't taking any chances."

"Maybe I should've risked putting down the name," Ona said. "But that was back then. What can I do now? In a few years, I'll be pushing thirty. Can you imagine that, Mrs. King, and ain't start living yet?"

But it was about Joe that they really disagreed. Mrs. King told her she was leaving herself open to heartache; she didn't see why any woman had to go to such extremes for a man, especially one like Joe.

"As for you saying you sending money to this Joe fellow every month," Mrs. King said, "I don't like it one bit. It's a bad beginning, if you ask me. A fellow like that, you better train him right from the very start. Otherwise, he'll walk all over yuh."

"It's only a few dollars I'm sending him. So he'd got something in his pocket to get by on," Ona explained. "You know how tough things is in the islands."

"What I know is that any strapping young man like Joe got to able to find work, no matter how meager, in the land of his birth," Mrs. King said. "He should be 'shame, 'shame to sit at home longing out his chops just waiting for immigration papers and for a postal order every week. When he could be out looking for work. No man like that should be putting all this financial burden on a poor woman. Especially on a poor woman like you with a growing child back home to support."

Still, Ona looked forward to the talks with the old woman. She visited Mrs. King almost every Saturday night, knowing if she stayed at home, she was bound to pick up the telephone and run up a big bill. Going to the Hole, even when Fanny invited her, was out of the question. The rumors were circulating there too.

"Sometimes I find myself wondering suppose you're right, Mrs. King," Ona said late one Saturday night when they were in front of the television. The commentators were screaming their lungs out about some fantastic game on the Hockey Night in Canada telecast. But they had hardly watched. They didn't know anybody who took hockey seriously, but there was nothing better on TV. It was as if they were watching a show intended for other people, a telecast that could very well have been in a foreign language and about foreign places. "Suppose all this waiting ain't worth it."

"Don't sit there on a night like this sulking yourself," Mrs. King said. "You've done do all you can. And a person can only do so much. That's why you have to leave some things in the hands of God." It was the first time Mrs. King had sounded so resigned. They sat in silence for the rest of the night, sipping from Mrs. King's big pot of green tea and nibbling on her favorite butter cookies and quality sweets in a can. Finally, the commentators announced the end of the game. They had not followed any of it. They had not participated like so many Canadians from coast to coast in the ebb and flow of this national game, this Saturday night ritual. Ona decided it was time to walk to the bus stop, where she was bound to hear the screaming voices of Canadians spilling onto the street from the hockey temple nearby and from bars and taverns across the city.

As happened so often, when she got home Ona picked up the phone. As soon as she entered the bedroom, she called Joe. But that night, he wasn't home. Where was Joe so late in the night? she thought, as she undressed and made ready for bed. Was he with that woman with the children for him or was he out with friends? Ona told herself he was with friends. She couldn't expect the man to stay at home drumming his fingers, waiting for the airplane ticket, the visa and a telephone call. It was all the gossip and stares from people that were putting doubts in her head. All of them were so wrong, and she shouldn't let them make her think bad things. And as Mrs. King had said for the first time that night, things had to work out in Ona's favor eventually.

In the end, it was the letters from Joe that kept her sane. She rushed home from work every evening and headed straight for the mailbox, even though she knew Joe never wrote often enough. But she needed those letters.

The letters told her what she wanted to hear; they fortified her resolve. He too was finding the separation difficult. Like her, he was going through uncontrollable moods of elation and despair. He lurched between believing there was no way the government could deny him a permit and the fear that eventually, if the government waited long enough, Ona might change her mind.

He demanded assurances from her. He yearned for reinforcement. He needed her to end his despair. He even suggested that she come down to Barbados for a vacation. That they could get married in Barbados, if only to prove to the immigration authorities how determined and how much in love they were. Ona never took this suggestion seriously, if only because of the huge cost of a Barbadian wedding. Secondly, such a wedding was likely to spawn even more rumors in Toronto.

130

Finally, in the depths of hopelessness, two and a half years later, she received the telephone call saying the permit was in his hand. It was a good thing she was at home and not at work. She screamed at the top of her lungs.

"They send me the visa this afternoon," he explained. "They give me three months to make things right with you in Canada and to report to the immigration people up there."

"Good. Good," Ona shouted, not fully realizing everything Joe was telling her. "Listen. Tomorrow, I'll go to the Air Canada office near where I work. First thing in the morning. I'll pay down on the ticket for you. So you can get your sweet arse up here real quick."

The news, coming at the end of another tough workday, made her feel so good and liberated. As if she were finally expelling a demon sapping energy from within her chest. When she called Mrs. King, the old woman didn't have to ask anything. The tone of Ona's voice said it all. And when Ona went to work the following morning she had a triumphant smile on her face.

Joe came back on probation. Full sponsorship was deferred until some all-knowing person in the government felt convinced he and Ona were genuinely in love, confident that their union, although blessed by the priest at St. Mark's Anglican Church, was capable of lasting. Other conditions were more onerous. They had to marry within sixty days, not ninety as expected, of Joe's arrival in Toronto. Joseph Mathias Morgan had to agree not to leave the city for a year. If they stayed together for four years, he found gainful employment, didn't get into trouble with the law or require social assistance, he would then receive full landed immigrant status to complete the sponsorship.

Ona didn't care about the stipulations. The thought didn't even occur to her to challenge the damn conditions, even after a lawyer advised her to. Unfortunately, this advice didn't come until Joe had been back for two or three years. By then, things were already going downhill and they had actually sought advice on a legal separation. Ona just wanted to get her life back on track so Suzanne could join her.

But for a while, it appeared the wait had been worth it. Life wasn't too bad for them soon after Joe arrived. The modest marriage ceremony and reception went off well. Joe started to regain the weight he had lost at home. He teased her about losing some of her size. He liked small, bony women, the way she was when they first met, he needled her. The two of them went to the Hole to dance and meet people and so Ona could clear her name.

Sometimes they stayed at home, turned off the television and turned up the stereo to top volume. They held parties for just the two of them. Many times, Fanny dropped by and the three of them just danced and danced. The snow would be coming down outside the window, covering everything, but they were warm and comfortable inside, like in the womb, totally oblivious of all the problems of the world.

The first really big problem was finding a job for Joe. The furniture company had given up on him by the time he returned. The new foreman didn't know Joe. Most of the men Joe had worked with had moved on, most just one step ahead of the immigration officers. The new foreman didn't seem too keen on employing people like Joe, anyway, not immigrants with a more permanent legal status. Not people demanding at least the minimum wage and payment for overtime and who didn't want to be paid in cash at the end of every working day. And Joe wasn't really willing to do all that lifting, hauling heavy boxes, loading them into trucks, dragging them up narrow apartment stairways and into elevators. He wanted another type of job, maybe in an office, so he could get up in the morning, put on a suit and go to work.

So he began looking elsewhere, without any success, for work more suited to his expectations. Every morning, Ona left Joe at home to go to work. She came home in the evening to find him looking bored, after sitting up all night watching television and sleeping all day. One good thing about Joe, though: he was even better at cooking than dancing. Ona regularly came home to a fantastic meal, which she ate enthusiastically. Then she went to sleep, waking in the morning a little fatter, only to have Joe tell her to lose some weight.

Joe just couldn't find a job; no Canadian experience, they kept saying. All the time Ona kept looking at the calendar, remembering the four years of probation hanging over Joe, wondering when this shit would settle down and let her get her daughter.

Small problems began to arise as soon as Ona had taken care of Joe's immigration. The fact that Suzanne still had to be legally adopted, as if she were a stranger, was the next frustrating problem Ona had to solve. It further delayed Suzanne's joining them. But when Suzanne did finally arrive, well after her twelfth birthday, they clicked as a family. The little girl had no problem in answering to her new name—Suzanne Morgan.

Except she wasn't really little anymore, but a young woman coming into bloom, with long slim legs that reminded Ona of Suzanne's father. That was Ona's first shock. In her mind, even after all the years that had passed, Ona still thought of Suzanne as the baby she'd left behind. Meanwhile, the real Suzanne was fast becoming a woman, having lived through a childhood Ona never shared. It was a good thing she didn't buy those little dresses in the shop windows. That was what the years had done to them.

Still, Ona couldn't have been happier having her daughter back. Suzanne and Joe liked each other and got along well; in fact, better than Suzanne and her mother. At first, Ona didn't mind the coldness that she started to detect. Suzanne must have come to Canada with high expectations and quite likely had been disappointed to discover that her mother didn't live in a big house or drive a car. All West Indian immigrants had to be purged of those expectations, and time was the only solution. Everybody knew how these anticipations grew out of proportion back home, Ona thought. Suzanne, she surmised, might even be angry that Ona had taken so long to send for her. If she was, Ona was confident that, because of their special bond, the two of them could leave the past behind and move forward together.

CHAPTER 12

ONA AWAKENED SUZANNE early in the morning and put a bowl of corn flakes and milk on the table in front of her. This was Monday, Suzanne's first full day in Toronto. The previous night had been awful. The plane had been delayed and didn't arrive until after midnight. When Suzanne got to bed, the dream was relentless, as if, as Grandma Nedd used to say, some *duppie* or ghost had decided to ride the poor girl for the entire night, robbing her of sleep.

"I left some food in the big pot in the fridge," Ona said, as the girl settled herself at the table. "I cooked it last night. I was so nervous waiting for you to come, I had to do something. It's in the pot with one of the handles off. So you only got to warm up a few spoonful o' the rice and stew when you're hungry."

While she talked, still standing in the kitchen, Ona shoveled bits of bread into her mouth. She hastily sipped from the cup of coffee she was drinking black as part of another diet. "At lunchtime, put some of the food on one o' the plates up there in the cupboard. Warm it up in the oven, and try not to burn yuhself, and eat it. I got to be going now so I can't stop to fix it up for you now, as I would like."

Suzanne noticed Ona talked a lot, never stopping to let her get in a word. The night before was very much the same thing, with Ona constantly proclaiming how happy she felt, how glad she was to have her daughter, never once giving Suzanne the chance to say what she really felt, how much she was already missing her grandmother. So Suzanne decided to keep her mouth shut and just listen to her carrying on.

"The God above done know," Ona continued, pulling the big-tooth comb through her hair. "But I'm already running a little late for the people's work this morning. It's like the morning does come so quick these day, yuh can hardly shut a' eye before it's time to get back up again. Anyway, if Joe's up when you feel hungry, you can ask him to warm the little morsel for yuh. Maybe when I come back home this evening, we can have a real meal together. I was thinking that would be the first real meal the two o' we ever had together. Can you imagine that? I was searching my brain, all the while I was cooking last night and killing time to go to the airport, and I keep saying to myself I don't think I've ever cooked a single meal, not even a green banana, for that chile. Imagine that."

Minutes later, Ona bundled herself into a coat and ran out of the apartment. The door slammed behind her. Suzanne became aware of the room's silence, not a lack of noise, but an overpowering quietness. In Jamaica there was always the sound of a bird in the trees, a cricket in the grass, someone singing loudly next door, the wind just blowing. Not this stillness that was so alien and frightening in a strange land. Not this dry apartment heat, and the funny unnatural smells of another country. It was like a prison. Nobody to talk with; no friends in the neighborhood; nobody next door she could shout to if she got frightened or just needed to gossip. At home, there was never a separation between the noises in the house and those abroad in the land. They just merged, with the outside sounds, songs and noises drifting on the wind into the house. Or the wind carrying the sounds from within one house into another and then another, mixing them with the outside strains as it went along. Nothing was sterile, isolated, buttoned down or clinically self-contained.

Down below in the winter's darkness, Suzanne saw people huddling together at the bus stop. She tried without success to make out which of them in the indistinguishable gray coats was her mother. They all looked like one mass of gray with several heads, hands and legs; too many limbs for one body. Then the bus was gone. The street was as empty as the room, as the entire world of this new country, as the jail that was the apartment building.

Suzanne finished the corn flakes. The milk was cold, straight from the fridge. She had never drunk milk like that. Grandma Nedd stopped offering her milk a long time ago. And when she used to, it was never cold. They did not have a fridge back home. Instantly, Suzanne felt like belching, like vomiting. Something rumbled loudly in her stomach. The pain of the movements caused her to wince. Her stomach grumbled loudly.

The few times she drank milk at home it was directly from Mr. Heron's shop, straight from the cows in the pasture behind his house. She never liked milk. Even when it was warmed. Grandma Nedd always scalded the milk, skimmed off the skin for butterfat and added some vanilla essence to make the milk drinkable. The public health nurse on visits to the schools had recommended milk. But try as she might, Suzanne couldn't help feeling sick just at the sight of it. Eventually, her grandmother gave up trying to make her drink milk, except for the canned sweetened condensed milk they also bought from Mr. Heron's shop and used in tea or chocolate. Occasionally, when her grandmother wasn't looking, Suzanne poured the thickened sweetness into the palm of her hand and licked it like a cat.

Suzanne sat on the couch and flicked on the television. Nothing interested her. Nothing eased the pains in her bowels. There was nobody to tell how much her belly hurt, nobody to rub it like Grandma did whenever Suzanne walked around barefoot on the damp earth after a heavy rainfall back home and caught a cold. The previous night, Ona had explained how she had tried to take a few days off from work, so she could spend with Suzanne her first days in Canada. But, as she explained, she had used too many days already. What was left of her vacation would best be used in the summer when Ona, Suzanne and Joe could roam around Toronto together. They might even make a trip or two to the United States, maybe even to New York, just for Suzanne.

"But don't mind. I'll be able to spend more time with you when I sort out things," Ona had explained. "It's just that I can't take any chances with these people at work and with the piece o' job I still need. But one of these evenings I'll come home a little bit earlier, and one o' the first places I'll take you is to the Eaton Centre. Everybody that come to Toronto does go there. Every immigrant got to stop there for inspiration, to look at the statue there, at the proof that anybody coming to this country can make it just like the Eatons."

As she talked, Ona rolled her hair in curlers in preparation for the next day's work. Suzanne didn't realize her mother's hair was that short, not even as long as hers, or Grandma Nedd's. Not as long as the pictures back home of the young girl with long, shiny braids down to her shoulders, or looking so beautiful in intricate cornrows. Healthy-looking hair that needed care and attention to maintain its luster. Not putting it in curlers twenty minutes before bed. And in curlers with rubber foam on them that would destroy the ends of the hair. Suzanne also noticed her mother didn't look at her much, not even when she talked. Not like Grandma Nedd who was always looking her in the face, looking at her from head to toe, reaching out to touch her so often, searching her head to pick out bits of lint, or just caressing her hair with the palms of her hands while she talked.

"That Eaton Centre and the statue got to be the real symbol

of everything that's big and powerful in this city o' Toronto,"
Ona continued. Every word seemed to serve notice to Suzanne of a widening gulf. "A real institution around here, that
Eaton Centre. I'll let you see how people does go up to this
damn statue and rub the shoes or kiss them so that the Eaton's
luck will rub off on them. I don't know if it does work for
them, but I sure could do with some of that luck."

Suzanne yawned unintentionally. Ona said she knew it had
been a tiring day, with the travel and all. She took Suzanne
into her bedroom and gently pulled the sweetly scented covers
up to the girl's chin. Ona turned out the light and, bending
over, softly kissed Suzanne on the forehead.

"Good night, baby," she whispered. "Welcome again to
Canada. If you only know how glad I is. It's just that I can't explain everything. But we'll spend some time talking and getting to know each other."

"Good night," Suzanne said.

"Sleep tight, beloved," Ona said even more softly. "You
know, I couldn't wait for the chance to say them words to you.
Just saying them makes me feel that I am really your mother,
'cause I always remember how when I was a little girl my
mother always used to say the same thing to me. And when
she said it, it always made me feel that no matter how angry
we was with each other before, no matter what I did, that
everything was now right and nice. Everything forgiven and
we can start all over again because there was nobody in the
world as precious as the two o' we. Me and she were at one. I
always slept so soundly after she said it."

When Ona closed the bedroom door, she left the lemonish
smell of her hair grease in Suzanne's nose—a smell Suzanne
would always associate with her mother. Unfortunately, the
dreams wouldn't let Suzanne sleep but for a few winks. Finally
exhaustion overcame her and she fell asleep, just before she
heard Ona calling her and saying she had to leave soon for
work.

Suzanne got up from the chair and went to the window

again. Her stomach was still hurting and she felt like going to the bathroom. Outside, it was snowing, ice building against the window, cold and heartless. This was not Jamaica, warm and sweet and comforting. In Jamaica, the sun was high in the sky at eight o'clock in the morning. At this hour, she knew her friends were playing in the schoolyard, the boys pelting the mango trees for its fruit, playing soccer or a quick game of cricket. The girls skipping, playing rounders or jacks in the shade of the tree. From every direction, the laughter was ringing out across the schoolyard until the bell rang and they assembled for prayers and the national anthem.

For four hours, during which time she made six trips to the bathroom, Suzanne sat at the window fascinated by the falling snow, and because she had nothing else to do. She wished Grandma Nedd would come and get her. She longed for Delores, her best friend, to talk to her. She wondered what Delores was thinking at that very moment, thinking as she recited at the top of her voice the national pledge to build a strong independent country, a pledge Delores would make this morning like every other morning to start the school day. And she wondered what her best friend and all her friends really were thinking as they listened to the daily promises that, even as children, they must join hands together to build a strong Jamaica, to fashion a prosperous and independent Caribbean community. How she would love to know if Delores was still envious, believing that Suzanne was truly blessed to be in another country. Eventually, she heard the water running in the bathroom. Joe was up. The streets down below were still empty, except for the cars and buses leaving black, snaking lines in the white snow on the roads.

"I'm going out now," her stepfather said. "I'll be out for a little while. Remember what we tell you last night: don't answer the phone. If anybody knock at the door, don't answer it. You're not supposed to be left alone until you are fourteen, I think. Be a good girl until I get back. Okay?"

Suzanne was glad he repeated the rules. In the previous night's confusion very little she was told had actually registered in her memory. In Jamaica, she didn't have to sit alone inside. She went out to play whenever she wanted. She called to anyone passing near the house; in fact, it was expected that she did as a sign of good manners. And if someone showed up while Grandma Nedd wasn't home, she simply took a message, or even conducted business on behalf of her granny. Suzanne was used to such responsibilities. What she wasn't accustomed to was this quiet and loneliness.

The room seemed even quieter with Joe gone. In the coming weeks, she found out that it was a long time between her mother leaving for work and the time cartoons and children's programs started showing on the television. Her entertainment didn't start until it was almost time for Ona to return home. For most of the day, Suzanne sat at the window and stared out. Other times, she found comfort in the Bible, hearing her grandmother's voice as she read. When she got home, Ona was usually tired and always in a foul mood. Most times she was angry Joe had left Suzanne alone for so long; she was frustrated there was nothing she could do to help Suzanne during the day; she was angry Suzanne had not touched the food.

"I don't know why I keep wasting all my time cooking every night if nobody isn't going to eat it," Ona said on the third day, as her frustrations blew up. "Why didn't you eat anything, chile? You don't like what I cooked?"

"I didn't feel too hungry." Suzanne didn't want to tell her that the cooking was nothing like when Grandma Nedd turned her hand, certainly not in the area of taste.

"A whole day gone by! And you didn't feel hungry? I don't know why I bothering myself so much seeing that I'm up so late at night racking my brain finding something to cook. But what am I saying: you're just a child. You don't know any better. Lord knows what I went through when I first came to this country so that other people's children wouldn't have to spend

141

a whole day alone. But that's my luck. I got to keep working. And my poor child, she got to stay home alone. But that will change. It will change once you start going to school. You won't have to spend every damn day all alone in an apartment by yourself."

These moods did not allow either of them to carry on the kind of conversation that would help them to get to know each other; to allow Suzanne to tell Ona about the troubling dreams. Attempts at talking, at touching, at probing each other were too awkward. It soon became routine: Suzanne went to her room and read; Ona busied herself in the kitchen or downstairs in the basement laundry room. Joe came home late at night. This was not the life Grandma Nedd and Ona had promised her, Suzanne thought. Most nights, alone in the apartment and in the world, Suzanne was haunted by the nightmares. The drums calling her offered the only hope of rescue.

SUZANNE PRETENDED SHE wasn't really disappointed with the Ona she was encountering. But she could only make believe for so long. Suzanne knew Grandma Nedd wouldn't knowingly lie or exaggerate. But this definitely wasn't the woman she had described to Suzanne. It had to be Ona who had purposely deceived her own mother.

Grandma Nedd had done her best to prepare Suzanne for life with a man in the house. In this case, Grandma Nedd was closer to the mark. Funnily enough, Suzanne thought, she had described a man she had never seen nor met better than her own daughter. Joe simply kept to himself. He gave Suzanne her space, allowed her to ask questions and to discover things for herself. He left her alone to think and brood. Not like her mother who always seemed so impatient, so uptight. Always pressing Suzanne, inundating her with information, challenging her to learn fast, to plan a strategy to quickly go out and conquer the city. Life was easier with Joe just floating around, smiling occasionally and once in a while offering her a Jamaican beef patty or a Ting soft drink from the West Indian stores.

One Saturday evening, when Ona was out shopping, Joe took out the Christmas lights and ran them through the apartment and into Suzanne's bedroom. Just to cheer her up, he said. Just to lighten up the gray drabness of evenings that came so early. And he cooked a fantastic Jamaican meal. They sat around the table as a family. For the first time in Canada, Suzanne cleared her plate. The lights stayed up until well into summer. Grandma Nedd was so right about that one thing.

"Grandma, how come I don't know who's my father?" Suzanne remembered asking her grandmother while they were talking casually in the calm of the evening. In less than two weeks, Suzanne was to board the plane for Toronto. Grandma Nedd felt it was her duty to prepare the young girl for her new life, to let her know what to expect. Suzanne had to condition herself to learn to live with all the luxuries awaiting her without showing off or forgetting to be humble, or sacrificing her pride. Grandma Nedd said she had had a similar talk with Ona before she left the island twelve years earlier.

"It does please me so much when I think how your mother has taken to her heart all the things I tell her," Mira Nedd said. "I remember it clear, clear to this very day. It was on an evening like this, inside this very yard, when your mother tell me how she was planning to go up to that Toronto to live. Up to then, I didn't know one thing about what she was planning. I was too busy minding you as a child. So what could I do when she tell me, but give she the best I could? I looked your mother straight in her face and said: girl, put your faith and trust in God, in the true and living God. Not in man. Read your Bible when things get hard for yuh and when things aren't hard. Always go to the Lord in prayer. Sanctify his name in good time and in bad. It look like she took my advice. I only got to read her letters to see this. And it does make my heart so proud to hear of the bountiful blessings God bestowed upon her in a new country."

Her conversation with Suzanne had touched on many things before raising the question of paying honor, as the commandments instructed, to her parents. Honor and pride come before a fall, she had warned, and it was only proper that Suzanne learned to give respect to her mother, and to her new father.

"How can I honor anybody if I don't even know who my father is from the man in the moon?" she asked.

"Different story that, so don't bother with it now," the grandmother had said swiftly. "The good Lord, in His wisdom, planned it that way. So you wouldn't have any trouble giving honor and respect to your new father, even though he ain't your real, real father. When you get up in Canada to join your mother, let me tell you, you will definitely have to treat her husband like a father. Give him full respect. No foolishness now."

"Is that why they change up my name to this foolish Morgan? The children at school does laugh at me when the teacher start calling out my new name. They keep saying, ain't nobody in all St. Ann's with a name like that. I like Suzanne Nedd better. I want my real name back."

"Don't mind what them forced-ripe womanish and mannish children say, chile. They don't know no better. You'll get used to the name. Just remember you're better off with that name than with Nedd. All of we women carrying this Nedd name are born cursed. Sometimes I think it had something to do with how we left Africa. How some o' we Nedds helped sell out our culture to foreigners; we come from a line of leaders in Africa. One thing good you can say about the Nedd women is that we are readers, born fortune-tellers, and that's why we have a place in the church. As a reader, I can tell you that things will be good for you up in North America. So you don't have to be frightened 'bout anything. It's like God anointed this family for this calling. When it hits you, nothing you can do 'bout it. So you should be happy to change the name and to live in Canada where you can make something of your life, something to help you get away from this curse. Just look and see how things are turning out so good for your mother, especially after she changed her name."

"Who is my real father, Grandma?" Suzanne had asked. "You keep telling me the same things you'd tell me before. But you like you don't want to tell me the truth."

They were sitting in the backyard. The sun had gone down minutes earlier and a sudden tropical darkness enveloped them. Above them, the sky was dotted with what seemed to be several billion stars. The crickets were chirping and a strong breeze was singing in the trees. They wouldn't have to worry about rain that night. But Grandma Nedd would still sleep with an ear cocked, ready to rush out to rescue the washing at the sound of the first drops on the galvanized tin roof of the one-room house.

In the mornings Suzanne ironed her uniform, a navy blue skirt and white blouse, on the bed. Grandma Nedd made the breakfast and a lunch, usually of boiled rolled-stick chocolate with dumplings and maybe a piece of fish from the night before. That was if the ants hadn't carried away the fish while they slept. Grandma Nedd floated a dish containing the leftovers in a pan of water to prevent this. In the morning, the pan was full of drowned ants. When she forgot, the fish was devoured to the bones.

Grandma Nedd was adding rice to the pot on the wood fire when Suzanne asked the question. The old woman seemed not to hear it. From an early age, Suzanne had learned that her grandmother's first reaction was never an indication one way or the other.

Nobody could tell with Grandma Nedd; she was so good at hiding her feelings. Suzanne should learn not to put her emotions on display so people could trample them, the older woman would warn. Concealing her emotions was one thing Suzanne had learned well. And there was no better teacher than her granny.

"When we finished putting some food in we stomachs, we'll put on rubber slippers and go 'long to Pastor Grant's open-air meeting. You got to full up your tank with his blessing, 'cause you don't know what will happen when you leave this place," Grandma Nedd said, refusing to rise to the bait. "I hope the Holy Spirit's ready to move in the hearts of the people tonight. 'Cause in my own heart, I can tell this is redemption time, as sure as there's a God above, a time for all o' we to start journeying for the Lord."

"Who he is?" Suzanne insisted. She knew when there was latitude, when to persist with a specific conversation. She also knew when it was absolutely essential to drop the subject on the spot. "Somebody must be my father. Who he is, unless you don't know yourself?"

"I know who the vagabond is," Grandma Nedd said, continuing to stir the pot. "But I don't know if I should tell you."

She placed the cover over the pot. Reaching into a bowl on the ground beside the fire, she lifted out the salted slab of cod soaking in the water since early afternoon. She broke the fish open and tasted it with the tip of her tongue. It had soaked enough. Most of the salt was out.

"I don't know if it's any good for you to know at this stage of your life. 'Cause I can only look back and see that when you were little and wanted a little help from a father to get by, he wasn't any use to you. So you don't need him now, if you ask me."

"But everybody wants to know who their father is, right?"

"I don't say not. Only that I ain't sure if it would do any good telling you. To tell the truth, I was thinking 'bout the same thing a couple o' days now. Ever since the good-for-nothing man came up to me and says he's a changed man, that he gave his soul to Christ and wants to make things right in he life. He wants to own up to all his children. So he up and beg me to let him take you out and have a little talk with you, father and daughter, although he knows he wasn't much of a father to you and you're now getting big and going up to Canada and thing. I still don't know if I should tell you, 'cause I don't know how his wife of all these years will behave if she catches him making much of you."

"So he's married, which means I must have more brothers or sisters."

"Lots too. He was married even before your mother had you, but that didn't stop him from dropping outside children all over this island. After all, he was the best male dancer on this island. The women just loved him. It's just that he didn't tell your mother anything. It was only after he swelled up her belly with you that she know he had a wife and children. The curse, I tell yuh. We Nedd women always seem to have these married men running after us. The Bible says you're truly *curs-ed*, committing 'dultry if you as much as look on another woman's man with lust in your heart. Check the ten commandments for yourself. The tenth commandment: *Thou shalt not covet thy neighbor's house nor his* . . . You can read it for yourself. And let me warn you right now: as sure as you're standing in front me, if you don't watch yourself when you become a woman, the same damn thing will happen to you too. That's why I have to keep asking the good Lord above to have pity on me and forgive me my sins. When you get up in Canada, I pray to God that this stupidness stop, the same way like it already stopped with your mother. If it never happen to you, that'll be the end of this curse."

"Who he is, Grandma?"

"Lawson Heron," the grandmother said, not looking at Suzanne. "The one dancing for the National Folk Dance Troupe in town, the same one that travels all over the world, dancing for kings and queens."

"You mean the son of Mr. Heron that got the shop up the road? He's my father?"

"The same one. He asked me last Sunday, right after church

147

when there was still a prayer in my heart, if he could take you to the National Stadium in Kingston to see him dance at this Carifesta thing Pastor Grant will be at. I said to him that I didn't know. For in truth, I didn't know if you would want to go with him, but at the same time I only tell him that because I didn't know what else to tell him."

"So that's why Old Man Heron always giving me sweets. Why he won't take no money from me. I always used to wonder why he does measure the sugar and flour heavy, heavy for me alone." Suzanne paused. "Can I go Grandma, to the stadium for the dance?"

"Sometimes I wonder 'bout you, chile," the grandmother said, turning to face the girl. "The more I look at you, the more I see your mother. It makes me real frightened. Nobody did have to tell me you would want to go; you have dancing in the blood. Not only from your father, but from your mother's side. That mother of yours could dance rings around anybody that got in she way, even that pissy father of yours. Ona was a born dancer. Nobody had to teach her nothing. That was how she ended up getting herself in trouble in the first place. And it wouldn't have happened if she had listened to me, if she didn't show up how much she could dance and had kept to herself. All the same, if you hadn't come along, she would be a big star in the National Troupe today. If she didn't let that married man get her in trouble. That why I keep saying the very same thing could happen to you. I only have to look down at you sitting there beside me in the House of the Lord, when the singing and music gets hot, hot, and I see you tapping yuh foot and getting ready to dance. You're a born dancer too. I can see it in you. I only pray you use it as a talent for God and not, like your mother, for the pleasure of man."

"Just like you, Grandma Nedd. The people around here say that even in your old age, nobody in the whole of St. Ann's, in all Pastor Grant church, can hold a light to you when it comes to making a jig and dancing around in the spirit."

148

"Go away from me, gal," the older woman said, flashing a look of false annoyance. "You're getting too feisty, yuh hear. I would never be a dancer, not the way you thinking of. Never. Not the type you're thinking, moving and scandalizing to devil music."

Then Grandma Nedd smiled. She knew the truth had fallen undiluted from the child's mouth. Grandmother Nedd was also right: Suzanne loved dancing, and she loved her grandmother. The old woman reached out and hugged her, resting Suzanne's head on her shoulders, letting the girl's long plaits fall across her breasts.

"You know I love you like a daughter," Mira Nedd said. "As much as I love my very own daughter. I had so much hope for Ona. And thank God, she ain't disappointing me. She turned out to be a good Christian woman. I couldn't have asked for more, especially after what happened when she got you. Now it's the time for you to complete the circle, to give the respect due to your mother. That's the best I can hope for you starting out on a new life."

Suzanne always remembered that moment, particularly the sweet acrid smell of Mira's perspiration, her grandmother's signature that would always stay with her senses. Never again would she feel that close to anyone and so loved.

JOE WAS A big surprise for Suzanne. When she first arrived in the country, Suzanne had feared she wouldn't know how to react to this man Grandma Nedd said she also had to treat with honor. Until her arrival in Canada, the only men she was ever close to were Pastor Grant and her biological grandfather, the shopkeeper. But the other men she knew in Jamaica were distant. They never lived under the same roof as Suzanne. She never had to deal with them on a daily basis; she didn't have to share the bathroom or a meal with them; didn't have to decipher their moods from looks on their faces. Initially, Suzanne approached Joe with caution and waited for him to establish the rules and tenor of their relationship.

To her pleasant surprise, her new father was almost as good a dancer as what she imagined her real father to be. Except that Joe didn't do it for a living, but for fun, to make Ona and Suzanne happy on cold winter nights. And he was a fantastic cook, even better than Grandma Nedd, if that was possible. Joe was easy to talk to, and he didn't pressure her as much as her mother. He didn't raise his voice when he got angry, or smash things and bang doors like her mother did. And from early on, he liked dancing with her, often turning to Suzanne when Ona said she was tired or was called away to fix something in the kitchen or downstairs in the laundry room.

The best days in Suzanne's memory were in the first year after her arrival, the first twenty months of Ona and Joe's marriage. On cold evenings the three of them sat in front of the television with piping hot plates of food, snow falling outside the frosted windows, laughing loudly as Cliff Huxtable demonstrated on TV how her stepfather should act in the house and at work, if he found any. They felt warm and connected, believing that someday their family might be half as normal as the Huxtables. Sometimes Suzanne curled up on the floor, her head in Ona's lap and her feet spread across Joe's back. The bond between Suzanne and Joe continued to strengthen. When Ona worked late or went off to a meeting with one of her groups of women friends, they talked and laughed, sometimes danced. And he was always making something special for her to eat, baking a cake, or just trying his hand at some new recipe with Suzanne as the guinea pig for his tasty experiments.

Sometimes they listened to West Indian music blasting out of the stereo, while taking a nip or two from Joe's Mount Gay rum. It was a home and a warm shelter; a refuge for Ona from the gossip at work, a place for Joe to gather strength for another day's search for a job, and, eventually, solace for

Suzanne contending with teachers and guidance counselors at school. This was a period when, for the first time in her life, Suzanne experienced the love and tender care of a mother and the unexpected bonus of a father. This was the good life she had expected in Canada—the cinema, new clothes from the Eaton Centre and all the television she could watch.

But soon fissures started developing in the relationships, as if Ona and Joe could no longer maintain the façade. Sometimes, Suzanne saw Ona looking at her and Joe suspiciously whenever they were dancing. Ona never said anything directly to her, but must have raised the matter with Joe, because soon after he stopped dancing with Suzanne as often as before, and certainly not when Ona was at home. Instead, he sat and listened to music more frequently while Ona grumbled and nagged him for being inattentive to her. Unexpectedly, a barrier, a chill, had descended on them. There was no more laughing, no more spontaneity or frivolous fooling around.

"I CAN'T BE responsible for what you were thinking when you came here," Ona said the day she and Suzanne had their first real confrontation. The pressure had been building up and they had to let it blow. Suzanne couldn't cope with her mother's pretenses; her deliberate misleading of Mira Nedd back home. Ona was beginning to realize something was going wrong with Suzanne in school as she brought home notes and letters with growing frequency.

Suzanne thought this betrayal of Grandma Nedd was unforgivable and told her mother so. It made her grandmother look foolish in the eyes of her neighbors, particularly the worshipers in Pastor Grant's church. For how could Mira Nedd in her testimonies before the entire church, before the entire village really, keep claiming things about her daughter when anyone who got on a plane and came to Toronto, or knew a

151

friend who visited Toronto, would discover that the Ona Morgan of the old woman's boasts didn't exist, if indeed she ever had.

For Suzanne, everything flowed from a Christian understanding of life as she had been taught in Pastor Grant's church. In disbelief, Suzanne watched her mother changing the price labels on cans of food in the supermarket. Ona would wear a dress on Saturday night and return it to the store Monday morning, claiming it was too short or tight for some mythical sister and pocketing the refund.

"People up here in North America expect you to tell them a white lie or two every now and then," Ona explained. "It's only the foolish fools from the West Indies that play by the rules. The rich people take all the shortcuts and get ahead. You watch them for yourself. We have to start playing by the same rules as everybody else if we want to get ahead in this world. And in any case," Ona continued, "what was so wrong with me that I don't meet your approval? If you only knew how hard things were for me in this damn country before you come."

Suzanne was positive Grandma Nedd wouldn't be caught dead emulating Ona's disgraceful activities. Suzanne had not forgotten Grandma Nedd's stern admonition that Suzanne had to live a life creditable to her God and people. Her life was to be a candle, sending forth rays of love and sincerity so that nobody was ever to doubt who Suzanne was and what the tenets of her life were. That left no room for changing price labels on cans of peas or stuffing fourteen ears of corn into a bag and pretending the package contained a dozen. It was a teaching at odds with what Ona practiced; what Ona wanted to teach her daughter to become. It was deception. And if it could be played by one daughter on a mother, then another daughter could play the same subterfuge as punishment.

In her confusion, Suzanne wrote a letter to Grandma Nedd. But even after writing it she was still torn: she didn't want to betray Ona and feared the price of disappointing her grand-mother back home. Also, she recognized the very real possibil-ity of Grandma Nedd not believing her, of thinking she was rebelling against having to live in Canada. Suzanne agonized over posting the letter and kept it in her room while deciding what to do with it. Ona discovered the letter while putting away some laundry. This proved to be the final humiliation. She was already mad that she had to attend a meeting with the principal and that Suzanne could give no good accounting for her behavior. The same had been true when Joe attended the last meeting so that Ona didn't have to ask for more time off from work. Ona read the letter and came screaming out of the bedroom waving the envelope at Suzanne.

That was the first night Suzanne spent away from Ona's apartment. Mrs. King invited Suzanne over to her place. They talked at length, although Mrs. King was not apologetic for Ona. "You got to realize that that mother of yours hasn't had it too easy in this country," she said. "She only means good, but sometimes she can get too anxious and impatient. Ona's like that and you have to understand when she's in her moods, she don't always mean what she's saying. You just keep your head about you." Suzanne felt a growing attachment to the old woman. Mrs. King reminded her so much of Grandma Nedd.

It was an attachment that did not last too long or develop the way Suzanne had expected. Mrs. King wasn't entirely like her grandmother and at times she was as critical of Suzanne as she was of Ona. That was what prevented Mrs. King from re-placing Grandma Nedd in Suzanne's affection: Mrs. King al-ways felt she had to be equally critical, had to split things down the middle, unlike Grandma Nedd who just spoke her mind regardless of what anyone felt.

"You should be ashamed to be giving your mother such a hard time," Mrs. King said another time. Ona had said Su-zanne should call the old woman Granny as a mark of respect, but she had refused. She could not bring herself to do it, to put this woman on the same pedestal as Mira Nedd. Calling her Mrs. King was enough. "I don't want to stick my nose in other people's business or to carry tales out of school about what happened between you and your mother, but I got to say, Suzanne, you're giving your mother a hard time, giving her hell, if you ask me. I mean, she's still struggling to get used to you. Things aren't quite the way she expected."

"Not me," Suzanne had replied. "This place is too tough. It's she who's making things too tough for all of we in that apartment. Even for Joe."

"You got to remember one thing, Suzanne. You are the child and Ona's the woman. And you got to know by now just how hard it was on Ona when she left you behind with your grandmother. It's nothing like what you're seeing right now. If I had to tell you some of the things that I know for a fact that this woman went through, your head would split. It would make the things you complaining 'bout seem so small, if you want my true opinion. It wasn't easy leaving you behind; I don't know how you ever got that idea in your head."

Leaning forward into Suzanne's face, the woman looked straight into Suzanne's eyes, as though she wanted to reach into her head with every word. Her breath felt dry and warm on Suzanne's face and smelled funny.

"We were only trying to make a life for ourselves in a strange country. That's all we're doing," she said. "Trying to start over, on a new page, in a new country. After all, life was so hard at home, who could blame us for leaving and trying we hands elsewhere? And let me tell yuh right now: it was tough as hell, real tough back then getting into this country. Some of we couldn't even admit we had children. Otherwise, the immigration people would've sent us packing right back home. You think it was easy for any mother to deny having a child? It was a good thing some of us did look so young the immigration people couldn't believe we actually had children. But a lot of people, some with three or four starving children back home, had to take the chance, had to tie up them bellies, make them flat as a pancake, even if we couldn't breathe."

"Nobody had to do that," Suzanne interjected with disbelief in her voice. "Not really."

"Ona didn't have to tie she belly, but I could tell you others who did. Your mother had little choice but to leave you behind if she wanted to get ahead. Suzanne, your mother worked really hard to get you back as soon as she could. That's why, Suzanne, you should give the woman a chance. It's never too late to turn the page, if you ask me."

Mrs. King had paused to blow her nose in a cloth. Her eyes looked distant, as if her thoughts were elsewhere. When she spoke again, her voice was calmer. "I hope you can see your way to help your mother."

"But she lied, Mrs. King," Suzanne said. "I can't forget that. She lied to Grandma and to me. She didn't have to tell no lie. If she knew it was this tough in Canada, she could've tell we back in Jamaica. We'd understand. And even so, I didn't want to leave Grandma at home, anyway. I didn't have to come here only to see she crying all the time that things so tough. I could've stayed at home and ease the burden on she. But she wanted me. And she had to lie all this time. And now she wants me to keep this lie, making Grandma Nedd believe we're all one big family. Lies, Mrs. King."

"So what if she lied?" Mrs. King said. "I ain't condoning lying but, I mean, how would any of we from the West Indies survive without telling a lie, without lying to ourselves too? Sometimes it took a real good lie to fortify us, so that we could pretend and face another day. Your mother wouldn't tell everybody these things. Not when she can keep it bottled up in she chest, not when she can let people think things are better than they are. If only you knew how hard it is for even me to get your mother to unburden herself. Even now I only know what she wants me to know, nothing more. The same thing happen, I believe, with your grandmother. That's how Ona behaves. She's a very proud woman, sometimes too damn proud to let her true feelings show. Must be something she learned back at home in Jamaica."

"But she lied," Suzanne repeated. "She's a deceiver."

"That's the past, my dear chile. Your disappointment can never be as great as what all o' we went through up here. It wasn't like anything we were promised either. But we buckled down and tried to make the best of a bad situation. So you better shape up, give your mother a chance; she's only human. Look at the future she's offering you. And don't keep trying to write letters to your grandmother. You owe your mother some loyalty. After all, she's got only you. I don't know what that husband of hers would amount to."

By the time Ona became pregnant with Telson several years later, family life had virtually broken down. Ona mourned forever about making this mistake just when she was getting ready to enjoy life. Joe tried his best to ignore her, continued to listen to his music. Sometimes, he conspiratorially let Suzanne put on the earphones and playfully they danced close without touching. Through the earphones, the blaring reggae and calypso music pounded deep into her brains and she loved it.

They would laugh—just the two of them stealing some time together; they were shutting out the world and her mother, who could never understand what was really going on. Suzanne understood Joe, even if her mother didn't. Suzanne told herself that she knew how it felt to have to face this strange world every day and to meet it with a smile. Her strange world was in the classroom; Joe's was in those employment agencies and personnel departments that, somehow, always seemed to have hired the last person minutes before he showed up.

Suzanne had decided she could be just as good at deceiving her mother. In fact, it wouldn't be deception at all. Not in the least. In Mrs. King's words, no doubt an echo from Ona, Suzanne was just not telling her mother everything to form a complete picture. Ona looked at Suzanne and saw only what she wanted, not realizing, just as Mira Nedd still hadn't realized about Ona, that someone else, someone totally different, existed too. Mira Nedd could be excused because she had only letters on which to form her opinion. Suzanne planned to do whatever she wanted under her mother's very nose. That would be her repayment to, her way to honor Mira Nedd, her true mother.

CHAPTER 13

ONA WAS ALREADY sitting in the principal's office when Suzanne walked in. Her mother looked impatient, uncomfortable. The look on her face showed clearly she would prefer to be at work rather than squeezing this meeting into her forty-five minute lunch break.

All morning, Suzanne had waited nervously for the call from the principal. She had taken the letter home on Friday; it requested another meeting with her parents. The day she knew, Wednesday, but not the hour. It all depended on arrangements Ona could make at work that day. Then she was to call and confirm a time. Nobody had told Suzanne what the meeting was about. It was not necessary. A letter sent home especially after the last incident meant only one thing: she was in trouble again.

Suzanne had hoped her stepfather would attend the meeting this time, so that at least it wouldn't drag on. With him things went quickly. Joe simply sat nodding his head in agreement, adding very little to the discussion, just letting the principal or teacher unload whatever was on their chests.

But she was disappointed. Instead of having someone on

her side, she was to have her mother and the principal gang-ing up on her. Suzanne expected the worst: humiliation from the principal, lecturing from her mother that would last for weeks. "Have a seat, Suzanne," said the principal, a tall slim man in his late forties.

He closed the door to his office and returned to his seat be-hind the big rectangular desk. A nameplate read: Edward Clifford. A few framed pictures and academic scrolls deco-rated the office. Dominating the room was a picture of a smil-ing red-faced woman with long brown hair, two girls in their early teens and a boy about eight years old standing beside a shaggy dog. Next to this was a picture of the principal himself in a black academic gown and a hat.

Suzanne sat beside her mother, facing the principal, afraid to even glance at Ona. The principal made her even more nervous by tapping on the desk top with a yellow pencil. Ona was resolutely still.

"Mrs. Morgan," the principal started, speaking slowly and authoritatively, "I'm glad you found the time once more to come and see us. We wish more parents would show the same interest. You know, to come and talk to us about the education of their children, to give the staff some encouragement. We have always found you to be a reasonable and understanding parent, and we greatly appreciate the effort."

He waited for a response. Ona said nothing. Suzanne had expected her mother to say something condescending. Some-thing like how she was about to give up on her daughter, that this was the last time she would inconvenience herself this way. That no longer was she going to stop working for her daily bread to come to any school. And for what? For a child in trouble, a child foolish enough to get involved in a matter anyone with a brain in her head would avoid. Ona had said such things so often, Suzanne expected the words to pop auto-matically out of her mouth.

Surprisingly, Ona just stared back at the man with no emo-tion on her face. Suzanne held her breath. From the corner of her eye, she saw Ona fingering the black bag in her lap. Something was brewing. Not only was Ona playing with the bag, she was self-consciously shuffling her feet in the navy spike-heeled shoes that matched the navy blue and white polka dot dress.

"The reason we asked you here today, Mrs. Morgan, is to get your permission to start psychological testing on Suzanne. We—"

"What you mean by psychological testing?" Ona interrupted brusquely. Suzanne sat up straight. This was news to her, too. Maybe the meeting wasn't about what she expected. "What's wrong with she now?"

"Well, Mrs. Morgan, Suzanne's father and I have discussed her behavior several times before. Suzanne is still having trouble adjusting. She's disruptive in the classroom, and academically she's not progressing as we would expect. She's not learning anything, to put it bluntly, and her antics are preventing others from learning. We want to have her assessed: to find out what may be wrong and how we can help. Maybe there's something in her past creating obstacles. Is she having any problems at home?"

"I don't see anything wrong with she," Ona snapped. "She look okay to me, and I should know. I'm her mother. It's just that I don't understand how a child so bright in Jamaica, always top of her class at school, how all a sudden she's some idiot up here in Canada. I can't understand it at all. Maybe it's just that you have her in too low a grade to start with."

"No, no, Mrs. Morgan," the principal protested, obviously as startled as Suzanne by Ona's outburst. "We're not saying she's an idiot. Not at all. We're saying she's"—the principal paused as if collecting his thoughts—"unable to operate within the system at this school. Can you blame her? It is traumatic for anyone coming to Canada at this stage in her life and Suzanne is no exception. She isn't old enough to fully understand what's taking place in her life, all of a sudden living with a mother she didn't know until a year or so ago, having to

160

accept a father for the first time, having to make new friends in a strange country, having to deal with authority that is mostly white. It's quite a strain. That's why I'm asking if there's any problem at home. She does get on well with her father, doesn't she?"

"That's right," Ona said, "blame me. Just blame me for everything gone wrong. You think I don't have eyes to see what you and this school trying to do?"

"Please don't take this personally, Mrs. Morgan," Clifford said. "We're trying to help."

Suzanne had heard variations of the principal's speech before. The first time she and Bobby Ali were sent to the office for talking too much. Mrs. Trudel, the aging teacher with the short temper, had claimed they persisted in carrying on a running conversation, disrupting the class with their bouts of giggles.

Bobby Ali was also new to the country and to the school. Although his parents were from Guyana, they had spent some time in England before moving to Canada. Bobby Ali arrived with a thick accent, a combination of British and West Indian, which made him the butt of the class jokes. Suzanne also had problems with her accent. She found it so much easier to express herself the way she had back home.

She and Bobby Ali had arrived at the school about the same time and found themselves sitting in the back row of the class. It didn't take long for the two of them to realize they were different. In the very first math class, Bobby kept his hand in the air while the teacher overlooked him and moved on to others who she felt knew the answers. This was not the last time Bobby was overlooked. After a while, he and Suzanne developed their own system. They did not raise their hands but wrote the answers on pieces of paper they passed to each other. Sometimes they drew funny caricatures. Other times they scribbled a joke.

This communication came to an abrupt end when the teacher intercepted a piece of paper and quickly recognized the ugly caricature representing her. She was incensed and packed Bobby and Suzanne off to the principal. Since it was a first offense, Clifford had given them a strong warning and threatened to send home a note if such disrespect recurred.

It didn't take long for the notes to start coming. Suzanne got notes for incomplete homework, for disrupting class, for skipping classes or for talking too loudly and, eventually, for fighting. Each complaint, and the speed at which they arrived, seemed to overwhelm Ona a little bit more. Suzanne thought it was another complaint about fighting that had brought Ona to the principal's office. This time, they had probably gone too far.

Bobby Ali had brought a butcher knife into the class. Several of the white boys had promised to beat up on him and Suzanne, the threats resulting from angry exchanges between the blacks and whites the day previous to the fight. At first it was just name-calling with Suzanne and Bobby yelling "white trash" every time they were called "dumb niggers." A gang of white boys chased them home.

Later, when Bobby telephoned to find out if she had gotten home safely—they had been separated in the sprint—he promised he was not going to let the matter drop. "Just wait and see what I planning for them tomorrow. Just wait. They think them bad, eh. They'll see what I can do, if they think them bad."

"What you plan to do?"

"Wait till tomorrow morning, I tell yuh. In fact, if you want to see for yourself, why don't you wait for me in front of the apartment building. So we can walk to school together. Then they can come and try to run we down again. Let them come and try that again. You'd be my witness for when I do to them what I plan in my head."

Nothing happened on the way to school or during the first class. But as soon as the door closed behind the teachers, Bobby and the white boys started taunting one another. Su-

162

zanne took the knife from Bobby's bag, and seemingly oblivious to all around her, started to pare her nails.

"What you doing with that knife, bug face?" one of the boys shouted. "You think we're frightened of that knife?"

Suzanne didn't answer. The boy advanced on her. The rest of the class began shouting, stomping their feet and banging the tops of the desks. Suzanne sat placidly, watching the boy from the corner of her eye. Bobby Ali moved forward. The boy made a snatch at Suzanne's hand, knocking it and sending the knife flying between the rows of desks.

Bobby Ali punched the boy in the face and grabbed him. Suzanne kneed the boy in the crotch, causing him to double over in great pain. The whimpering boy fell on top of Suzanne, as he struggled to escape from one of Bobby's much-touted neck holds. Just then, Mrs. Trudel had come through the door and instantly assumed that Suzanne and the boys were fighting and that Bobby Ali was trying to pull them apart.

Suzanne visited the principal again. As usual, Suzanne didn't report any of this to her mother. It was still her plan to make Ona believe that Suzanne was the young woman her mother wanted, not the one that went to school every day and had to rough it out with the institution and people intent on making life difficult. In Suzanne's mind, she was only following the example set by Ona. The way she kept her mother in the dark was no different from what Ona had done to Grandma Nedd.

SUZANNE WAS GLAD nobody had told the teacher about the knife. And judging from what the principal was now telling Ona, obviously the school officials still weren't in on this secret.

Discovery of the knife would guarantee an automatic suspension and a visit from the police. There was even talk that as part of a zero tolerance proposal on violence, the school board trustees would expel permanently even first offenders caught with a weapon on school property.

Compared to the possible alternatives, a visit to the principal's for some general discussion about Suzanne's academic performance was virtually nothing. Even less threatening was the stupid testing they were arguing about, a test Suzanne knew she could always fake to get whatever results she wanted. Bobby Ali had taken the test and said he had beaten it. Suzanne had no doubt Bobby Ali could teach her how to deceive these officials too.

The only thing that bothered her was the principal's constant harping about whether she was having trouble with her father. Suzanne wondered what the principal knew that Ona didn't. Could it be that he suspected something, maybe from how nervous Joe was whenever he visited the school? But she decided not to raise the matter, to let the issue rest unattended like the time bomb she knew it was. Her secret relation with her stepfather governed everything. And it had to remain a secret to protect everyone, including the wicked girl that looked just like her and who liked Joe's touches.

Her mother knew nothing that was happening between that Suzanne and Joe. And that was the way the other person had asked Suzanne to keep it, to keep this strange character a secret. Except that with ever-growing frequency, the other Suzanne was showing up at school and taking out her frustration on everyone who even spoke to her.

"WE'RE ONLY TRYING to help, Mrs. Morgan," the principal was saying earnestly. "We're not blaming anyone."

"So you say," Ona replied, dismissing everything he had said, but pointedly refusing to comment on the question about problems in the home. "I still think Suzanne can hold her own in any school. She's a bright and talented girl, as bright as anybody else her age. We even giving her private lessons on weekends. The teacher's a member of the Black Heritage Academy, a school run by black people, and that teacher keeps telling me that she's really progressing good. It's just that she got to get some extra attention every now and then, and I'm talking 'bout attention from teachers that understand her, people that know what this little girl here wants. The same teacher at the Black Academy keep telling me over and over again that Suzanne isn't a bad girl. She ain't the best either, but she ain't the stupid fool you keep telling me 'bout. It's just that she needs somebody to keep after her to do the work. To keep her mind from straying from time to time. Not somebody branding she a damn idiot with no brains in she head. I can't understand why you keep saying she ain't progressing. I can't understand it at all."

The principal pressed his fingers together, trying not to lose patience. A look of resignation fell across his face. Suzanne imagined what he was thinking: the same things he had explained to the Caribbean Students Association whenever something happened to force him to come and speak to the West Indians as a group. His speech was always the same; the way he shifted and shuffled his hands never changed. From his body language, Suzanne guessed what he was thinking, what speech he would be making right now if the students were in front of him instead of her mother. He would start by saying that maybe he was wrong after all. Wrong for having too high expectations for this group of students and their parents. Suzanne watched as Clifford's eyes focused intently on Ona's face, as the muscles above his cheeks tensed. She imagined what he was thinking: this woman sitting across from me is no different from all the other West Indians, all the people who think that schools are where they dump their kids, where they expect teachers to be fathers, mothers and counselors.

Suzanne shifted in her seat. For a moment, she feared that the principal might announce that he knew the real problem, that Ona didn't really know her own daughter or that someone was pulling the wool over her eyes. The look on Mr. Clifford's face, as he flitted from Ona's face to Suzanne's and back to Ona's several times, indicated that he had caught on to something. It was just a question of whether he planned to expose it.

Before her mother arrived, Suzanne had canvassed opinions of other West Indian students on what she should do if the matter of the knife came up. They had all said the same thing. Deny it and stick to the same story. Let the principal and the parent duke it out. And root for the parent, they had told her. Suzanne suddenly felt proud of her mother, standing up to these school officials. She was doing a better job than Joe, whose conscience always seemed to weaken his resolve.

"Well, Mrs. Morgan," Mr. Clifford said. Suzanne watched as he leaned back in the chair and clasped his hands over his head. Obviously, his thoughts were racing. "Looks like we have a problem here. You don't see the situation the way we do. But I have the proof to back up my statements."

"Oh, really," Ona said.

"Look, don't get me wrong," the principal said. He leaned forward again. "Maybe Suzanne is a late starter, as you say. It might be no more than that. Everybody doesn't bloom at the same time. That's why we want to have the testing done. At least we would have something to work with instead of fumbling around in the dark. Maybe something in the home, I don't know what, but maybe something in her background is distracting her from her schoolwork."

"What would it prove, this testing?" Ona demanded, appearing to back down. "If we did it, if I agree to it, what would it tell me that we don't know already?"

"We'll be testing to see whether we have her in the right academic stream. Maybe, and I'm only tossing this out as an example, she might be better suited for a more basic education, such as learning life skills."

"Like what?" Ona's voice was rising again, as though she had anticipated the answer and was prepared to fight it. This was the mother Grandma Nedd had told her about, Suzanne thought. And how ironic, that it had to take a contrived situation like this for her to see the mother she had always been told lived inside the person masquerading as Ona Nedd.

"Well, you know, teaching her things like how to apply for a job, some typing and shorthand, remedial English, arithmetic and possibly ESL, English as a Second Language."

"English as a what?" Ona shouted, almost jumping from her chair. It was as though he had pressed a button connected to springs in her chair, hurling her from the seat. The bag on her lap fell to the floor. She bent over to pick it up, never taking her eyes off the principal.

"What you think Suzanne has been speaking all this time? Dutch?" Ona demanded. She reached unsuccessfully for the bag. In her haste, she knocked it further out of reach. "Tell me that. What language you think we've been speaking all these years in Jamaica, where she came from, eh?"

"Please, Mrs. Morgan," the principal pleaded, leaning forward again and resting his elbows on the desk. His voice was firmer. "We really believe this is part of the problem, a big part. Suzanne is disruptive in class because she can't understand what's being said. She can't express her feelings adequately, so she takes out her frustration in other ways. This is her way to get attention. We have to find out how we can get to, how we can reach, the real Suzanne."

"How can she express sheself any better when every damn time the poor chile put up a hand to answer a question in class, nobody bother calling on she?" Suzanne was glad she had told her mother part of the story behind the earlier incidents. However, she was still surprised that Ona actually remembered even that much. "Or when they get 'round to asking, as soon as she opens her mouth, the first thing the blasted teacher says is 'Pardon me, will you repeat that.' When the poor child give it another try, the same damn thing all over again: 'Pardon me, what did you say?' It's accent, not language, that's the problem, Mr. Clifford. English is English. People have to listen more careful. I face the same problem every day at my work. That's why we need more of our own people in these schools, teaching our children so they can understand what they are saying, not trying to fool the children that they're speaking some foreign language. As a grown woman, let alone a child, I'd stop talking if everybody was to treat me the same way every time I opened my mouth to talk. If all the children laughed at me and the teachers let them do it. I don't see why anybody got to get psychological testing to find out what the problem is. It's plain enough to me. I'd do the same thing, and I ain't no child. So I wouldn't be surprised if the chile here did something out of the way to get attention, because everybody in this damn school makes she feel she's different."

"That's definitely not the case, Mrs. Morgan," the principal said, shaking his head in apparent frustration. Suzanne had to struggle hard to resist the urge to smile broadly. The meeting was going so wonderfully. Every one of them, Ona, the principal and Suzanne, had a different agenda, and Suzanne's was coming out ahead. She pretended to be looking through the window. She couldn't wait to tell Bobby Ali what was happening, for the news to spread in the schoolyard. She imagined the laughter. And her mother would think she was the heroine! The principal's voice broke into Suzanne's daydream. "Suzanne might be your daughter, but let's look at the facts objectively. First, she has already missed one grade, and probably won't be promoted this year."

He took a sheet from the folder on his desk and began reading from it, running a thumb down the page. "Her reading is subnormal; comprehension, the same; attitude, terrible. It goes on and on, I'm not making this up. This is what her teachers and academic evaluators are saying, and it's not a conspiracy."

"What 'bout the report from the Black Academy I just done tell you about? That report is as different from that one on your desk as night from day."

"I can't account for what any other teacher is finding. But it doesn't sound correct to me. Not unless Suzanne makes a radical change under their supervision, which I suppose is possible. From what you are telling me, it would appear as if we are talking about a different student. Not the one that my staff have to deal with every day. Look, all I'm trying to do is work with what I see in front of me, to help this girl. We believe that because of her background she would do better in a basic stream. But before we can do that, we've got to test her, to see if even the basic stream would be any help."

"I don't know about that," Ona snapped back. "How come Suzanne isn't the only West Indian child to have problems in this school? How come it's almost always black people, West Indians, if I may say so, in this so-called basic stream you're talking about? Answer me that, Mr. Clifford. Explain this pattern to me!"

"Are you insinuating something, Mrs. Morgan?" the principal asked. "Is that your explanation for why some of the children you just spoke about can't even write the alphabet?"

"Yes. I'm saying that's why the students seem so different when they are in the presence of a black teacher. You ever heard this child here read the Bible? Well she can read that book cover to cover. I even have her borrowing books from the library every week and reading to me or her father in the evenings. I mean, I'm not saying her reading is absolutely top-notch, but it isn't that bad either. I think you're trying to do the same thing to Suzanne that every damn school in Toronto does to West Indian children. Put them in a basic stream, train the girls to be maids and waitresses, maybe secretaries, teach the boys to make furniture or something. But don't ever bring them too close to a computer, and don't try to teach them French or English literature. The Lord knows that if I had the money I would take her out of this school right away and send she full-time to the Black Academy. But I don't have the money."

Watching the exchange, Suzanne understood what people meant when they said she had her mother's temper and tenac-

ity. She was glad her stepfather wasn't there. Joe would have
accepted everything the principal said, and even signed the
forms. He was nice, but too soft when it came to confronting
the authorities. Only when he got home would he voice any
uncertainties and then it was usually too late. The damage was
done.

This was one of the few times Suzanne was so proud of her
mother she couldn't help looking at her. Couldn't help wondering why Ona hid this side of her personality from her, the
flaring temper and rolling eyes. This was the same defiance
that had put Suzanne in so much trouble in the schools and
which she had tried to conceal from her mother. This was le-
gitimizing her actions in the classroom. If her mother stood up
to Principal Clifford, Suzanne now had every right to stare
down the dried-up woman Trudel and tell her where to get
off.

"Are you going to sign these forms, giving us the permission?"

"No," Ona shot back and started to rise to her feet. "If you
don't want her in your school, tell me right now and let me
find another school. It's as simple as that. But she isn't going
into a basic stream and she ain't getting no psychological testing like some monkey. Nothing is wrong with this little girl
that a little time can't take care of. I'm her mother. I should
know."

"We're sorry to hear that's the way you feel," the principal
countered. "Anyway, it is our duty to see that Suzanne's welfare is taken care of, so we'll be taking other steps to do our
duty, with or without your permission."

"You can do what the hell you want. Just remember this little girl got a' owner, somebody that brought her into this
world. She will get the best things in life too. Every opportunity, like everybody else, whether black or white, West Indian
or Canadian. Good day to you, Mr. Clifford."

The principal looked relieved it was all over when they
walked out of the office. The look on his face showed what he
was thinking, that finally the mask had slipped. He could now

follow the standard procedure for dealing with such trouble-some cases. Behind her mother's back, when Clifford noticed Suzanne studying him, she glared at him long enough for him to notice the coldness in her stare. Then she followed her mother out, not bothering to return the principal's good-bye. Suzanne knew she was now virtually untouchable.

Outside, Ona put her arm around Suzanne and told her to go back to the classroom, to open her ears and eyes, not to be ashamed of anything. She was as bright as anyone else. Carried away by the situation, Ona was talking so loudly Suzanne saw heads turning and looking at them, as if Ona was scolding Suzanne publicly.

Suzanne felt a mixture of embarrassment and pride, but now wished her mother would leave. Then she was gone, leaving Suzanne to walk into the classroom and face all the stares. As expected, Bobby Ali howled with laughter. That afternoon, both of them were sent to the principal once more. And once more they took a note home. It was only when Suzanne got home that she heard her mother and Joe talking about Ona's disappointing morning. How she had gone to work only to be told she was not getting the promotion. Some "pissy gal with blond hair" had got the job even though Ona had been teaching her for the past six months. They didn't even want to give Ona the time to visit the school.

"From the time they tell this morning about the job it was all just downhill," Ona told Joe. "Then before I left for the school this hard-side supervisor called me in and start trying to make me feel good after what they tell me earlier. She said how they're recommending that I do some upgrading work. That I take some test or the other to show how much I know about the credit union business, and to find out if I have what they call people skills. Then I had to face this asshole at school talking about some damn test all over again. I just let him have it, right there on the spot. The people in this country like to test too much."

A week later, Ona received a letter from the Metropolitan

Toronto Children's Aid Society demanding that Suzanne be given the psychological test. Failure to give approval would result in the society taking the issue to court, the letter said, explaining this was the first step in asking for Suzanne to be made a ward of the state.

Ona ripped the letter to pieces, dropping the shreds in the wastebasket. But she knew she was beaten; she couldn't fight much longer against the system. Later that month, after an embarrassing court appearance, Suzanne was tested and dropped to the basic stream. Ona promptly stopped going to meetings at school. She also stopped applying for promotions at work.

Suzanne no longer had to actively try to separate herself into two personalities to survive in this cold country with the dreams from her warm island still intact. In the basic stream, it just happened instinctively. Suzanne found no difficulty moving from one character to another as the mood struck her, or when she had to adopt a specific style or stance to suit a situation. And most times she didn't even know that she had shifted character.

CHAPTER 14

SUZANNE'S DETERIORATION IN the basic stream was so thorough and quick, Ona feared she had blighted her daughter by fighting too hard against the demotion. Unable to bear the thought of raising these doubts with anyone, lest they be validated, she reasoned silently that she must have alienated the whole school, perhaps even the entire education establishment, by simply standing up for her rights.

All she wanted was the best for a daughter she had obviously left behind for too long. The damage done to the child in her absence was plainly so much greater than she had anticipated. The remedial work needed so much more time than she could give while still holding down a stressful job.

No matter how hard she tried to show him, Joe just couldn't see these things. Neither would he even try to understand why he should at least attempt to help out, or even give some support to the woman he still called his wife. He could not comprehend why he should back her fight against the school, and against a recalcitrant daughter so unwilling to help herself.

But it was about the school that she felt the most distress and failure. It was always part of Ona's thinking that a good education would be the vehicle to launch Suzanne to success. Late at night, when she pondered what went wrong, why Suzanne brought home such dreadful reports and notes, Ona was never sure how much she was to blame for creating the wrong environment.

After all, teachers, like people in any other profession, stick together. Especially against anyone as loud and proud as she, a stubborn black immigrant women, an outsider foolish enough to challenge their authority. Worse, Ona concluded, she had fought them in court, in the full glare of publicity, possibly embarrassing them. Such uppishness made her proud. But it couldn't have done her cause any good. Certainly not in the classroom where the teachers always sat in final judgment.

"I tell yuh, I think I finally learned the lessons that everybody did want me to learn. And I learned it damn good too," Ona said when Suzanne's report for the second semester in basic stream came home. It was so bad. She could no longer wrestle alone with the fears and suspicions born of self-doubt and personal questioning.

Joe was sharing the curried chicken and rice he had spent all afternoon fussing over in the kitchen on his day off from the TTC. Flamboyantly, he was ladling the food and placing the heaping plates on the table. It had been a long day at work for Ona, the length of which could not be measured simply in eight hours, or by piles of documents to be stamped and filed. And the first thing she encountered on returning home, supposedly a place of refuge and rest, had been the brown envelope containing the report.

Still dressed in her work clothes, Ona drew up a chair and started straightaway on the report. The results had not improved, even though she had shifted Suzanne to another school. Although she had succeeded, at least temporarily, in getting Suzanne away from the evil influence of that Bobby Ali. She had the right to move the girl to any school run by the educational board receiving her taxes. But it was still the teachers who conspiratorially put Suzanne right back into the basic stream, defeating the very reason for moving her. And with a phone in the apartment, how could Ona stop Suzanne from talking to Bobby Ali and other rebels? It was impossible to monitor every call, especially with Suzanne always arriving home before her on evenings and Joe not giving a damn, just spoiling the girl and undermining Ona's authority.

"But I didn't learn fast enough," she said, speaking to nobody in particular. She took up the fork and picked off a piece of the chicken wing. But she didn't eat it. The fork remained suspended over the plate. "Except for learning something 'bout this society we living in. How it's always reminding people when they're poor, when yuh got no clout, when you just don't count. Them black people that born in this country, that we came over here and find, them is the smart one. They're the one that know how to survive without giving themselves ulcers from worrying. They know not to rock the boat but to be nice, nice and quiet, just accepting anything for an easy living."

"Tell me, what bothering you now, Ona?" Joe blurted out. "Why you don't eat up the food I just put in front yuh, just *nyam* the damn thing before it get too cold? And stop fretting yourself so much, nuh. Not another damn evening of this quarreling, 'cause I can't take it no more. Tell me, how was work today?"

"Now I understand why they're so quiet," Ona continued as if she had not heard Joe. "Why they don't challenge things. This report card, the one right here on this table before me, is all I need to tell me everything I want to know. And this child that they spiting so is already fourteen years old, when she should be thinking about university, 'bout making something or the other of she life before too late. But I tell yuh something, if we West Indians ain't too careful, the children that we got up here will end up just like them black people we come here and find. Too damn passive, no real ambition. 'Cause

175

one thing this country know good, good is how to take the sting out o' people."

Suzanne kept her head down. She knew what her mother was doing and why. Ona was giving voice to the deep feelings that told her the will to grind down people wasn't strong in the schools alone, but also in every aspect of North American life. She had come to learn this the hard way, Ona had explained many times at the same kitchen table. At first, Ona said, she had been quite willing to accept that it would be more difficult for her to adjust to living in a new society. After all, she had come to Canada as an adult and never had enough time to fully integrate. She didn't know the system well enough, she used to explain. She was never confident enough, didn't have the time really or was freed of one distraction or the other, to keep experimenting and testing until she got it right. Remaining outside the mainstream was the price she had to be willing to pay for not spending her youth in Canada.

But this explanation did not satisfy her when she addressed the problems with Suzanne and her failure to make a mark in their adopted society. Her daughter sang the most modern version of the Canadian anthem, perhaps better than most people born in Canada. She had been taught Canadian history and geography and counseled on job skills and survival techniques. She acted like regular Canadian children. Was even as spoiled and ill-mannered as most of them when it suited her.

Yet her daughter seemed to be confronted by the same problems Ona faced. Growing up in Canada didn't seem to matter. She seemed headed for the same dead end as Ona and Joe, condemning yet another generation to the same cycle— maybe even curse—of powerlessness and alienation. So it had to be something else blighting their lives, something more treacherous than not having Canadian experience. It had to be something else. Something unexplainable. Maybe, Ona suspected, something to do with the way she kept driving herself to succeed, to be different from what she was in St. Ann's,

Jamaica. To transform herself into a genuine Canadian, whatever that was.

"In every battle I've had to fight up here," she said, dropping
her voice to almost a whisper, "something always happened
to keep reminding me how much it's me the outsider. It's
like when you find the money to pay to go to one o' them big-
fashion dances we always reading 'bout in papers. And it's only
when you done pay your money that you realize something is
wrong, something missing. That, although you can pay to get
in, you can't help feeling out o' place inside. Something must
be wrong with you, you keep telling yourself. Maybe it's the
way you dress—clothes too cheap, everybody can tell where
you buy them by just looking at you. Maybe it's the hairstyle.
The way people look at you. All of it telling you that you really
belong in a place like the Hole, not in the Royal York ball-
room. You can never ever graduate to anything good."

Suzanne and Joe exchanged glances. They knew this rant
was going to run indeterminately. And they also recognized
the wisdom of not trying to stop Ona, not when her frustration
reached the stage where it had to bubble over. Otherwise she
might turn on them with even greater force. Somebody, anybody actually, simply had to get it when she was in this mood.

"And then you can't trust nobody," she said. "Not when
your own flesh and blood making you look like one big idiot,
doing the things she's doing behind your back. Thinking
you're some sort of a fool. How can I trust anyone?"

Suzanne felt her heart skip a beat. She looked up at Joe, but
he didn't return the glance. This was the first hint that Ona
might be catching on to the deception.

"How can a daughter do a thing like that to a mother?" she
asked. Suzanne looked at Joe with his head bowed over the curried chicken and rice. All three of them had to be of the same
mind. Suzanne knew that Joe and Ona must have realized, as
she did, that they had arrived at another turning point, a significant one this time.

177

Suzanne felt like breaking down and telling her mother that she was glad the deception was finally over. That there was no need to carry on this battle, this hurting just to prove a point. That now Ona must understand how Mira Nedd was bound to feel when she found out the truth about what had happened in Toronto. The more she thought of her own experiences and disappointments, the more Suzanne felt like having everything out in the open for Ona to see and understand. It was on the tip of her tongue to tell Ona that it was simply to spare her grandmother such pain that she didn't post the letter. The letter Ona had used to confront her.

She felt like telling her triumphantly that the same letter was now sealed in an envelope without an address and safely hidden in her Bible. At the appropriate time, she would put the address on the envelope. Or she might just hand it over herself when the time was right. But Grandma Nedd would know the truth at some point.

Suzanne looked at Joe, noticed the grim look on his face, and decided to keep quiet a bit longer. If Ona raised the issue of Suzanne and Joe that would be another matter. A matter Suzanne didn't know how she would handle, whether she was to have someone else to deal with it for her.

It was better to let Ona get it all off her chest first. Better for Suzanne to know the full breadth of her mother's thinking, better to know how much she knew of the deception and of Joe's role in it.

"JUST LOOK AT what happened in the courts a few months ago," Ona lamented. "Did anyone care about what I felt? No, they had the power to do whatever they wanted with my child, the same way they always delayed and delayed everything in my life."

For Ona, the report card was the symbol of all that was wrong. It was in the school where Ona felt she lost not only a battle, but the war to make something of her daughter. She had come from a part of the world where she knew of countless people, poor but endowed with sharp minds, who had redeemed themselves through education. And she would never give up the dream that her daughter could be redeemed and straightened out.

Even in Toronto, every day, in the newspapers, on television, somebody was sounding off to the children that they should remain in school and do well. Practically every black baseball player was enlisted in this drive. The message seemed pointed particularly at the black children; that and the avoidance of drugs.

But it still seemed to Ona the world was against her and her drive to see Suzanne receive a decent education. She could never tell what was real. No matter how much she suspected it, there was no way of knowing for sure if Suzanne's black skin, like that of almost every other child in the basic stream, wasn't the main factor in deciding how diligently the teachers taught the girl. Still, the suspicion ran deep. It was the price Ona felt she had to pay for being an immigrant. She had to be constantly vigilant. The strain sapped her energy. It left her unable to drop her guard, to smile or relax. The load was so heavy, her points of reference so alien and diffused.

She had not gone through the Canadian school system, so she had no personal experience against which to judge Suzanne's behavior and achievements. She didn't attend the monthly Parent–Teacher Association meetings, because the participants might take her for an idiot, either by her silence or questions. Yet she had to continue trudging ahead, striving after a dream, stumbling along a road obliterated by the raging snow, comforted only by the certainty that some reality had to exist beyond the temporary blizzard.

"Just because I wasn't born up here, didn't go to their school, they take me for an idiot," Ona said.

"That's a good point you just make there," Suzanne interjected. She had held back from joining in for as long as she

179

could. "That's what I've been trying to tell you all this time: what can you tell me about the schools in Canada when you never had to sit in one of the classrooms? When all your education was back home, where everything is so different? How can you tell me anything about a school system you never experienced? That's what I mean when I say I know better than you. But you always take what I say the wrong way. But I know what I'm talking about. I've been to the schools up here and at home in Jamaica. You haven't. What you think happening in the schools up here don't and you don't know the difference. So how can you help me when you don't know what I'm talking about?"

"I know what you are *really* trying to do by asking them sort o' questions, you little brute," Ona said coldly. "You are just trying to tell me how much I failed you by leaving you behind. How I'm now doing it a second time, at perhaps the most crucial point in your life, right? That's what this is really leading up to, right? You want me to say that I ran away from you, was having a whale of time in Toronto, at the very moment in your life when I could make a difference. And you know what, Suzanne, you are right. I failed you. Not only you, but myself, too, damn it. Both o' we failing one another."

"Come on, you guys," Joe pleaded. "Don't you think that's enough? Every damn evening the same flipping thing. Every minute of the day you two going at each other. Nobody hearing the two of you would think you are mother and daughter, but two bulldogs going at each other."

"And you should talk," Ona said, turning on Joe. "Ain't you the so-called man in this apartment? Sometimes I just wish you'd speak up. Help me to discipline this girl, rather than leaving everything to me. Why is it me that always have to be the bad one, the disciplinarian, the one to do the punishing and scolding? Why? Give me some support, nuh."

"I'm only suggesting that enough is enough," Joe said, dropping his voice. "You're just going on and on and on, talking, talking, talking. The food's getting cold and you humbugging yourself too much. Can't we talk about something else? That's all I want this evening."

But Joe did not get his wish. Maybe the cuts were too deep for either of the women to ignore. Suzanne lapsed into silence, but Ona did not. She probed and pushed, exploring deep within her memory, searching for information and solutions. Most of the questions she could not answer. She spat them out and left them hanging over the table, mixing with the cold air robbing the meal of its heat while Suzanne and Joe waited.

"I give up," Joe said eventually. "I give up before you start on me. 'Cause I can see you brewing to start on me. So let me go and listen to some music before I get my arse in trouble with you."

"Anything I say about you is only the truth," Ona said. "The same way with all you black men out there, with no ambition, just waiting for some woman to come along an' pick you all up. All you black men are so useless, it makes me sick."

"Christ," Joe said. "Don't start on that now. Don't start on my arse, now."

"Here you're supposed to be the man in this piece o' apartment, you should be the one who know people of class and substance, people who can help all of us in this apartment move on in life. But what do you do? Wait on me, just like all them men you like to hang out with on weekends. Always relying on me one way or the other just like how I got you the job at the—"

"Yes. I know what you did," Joe interrupted. "Christ, you have said it so many times. How many times do I need to hear the same damn story from you, like the song the old horse died on. How it was you, Ona Morgan, who bring me up here to Canada in the first place and it was you who had to find this piece o' job for me. How often have you repeated the same damn story? How it was just luck that you was sitting at your wicket in the credit union when a group of bus drivers came in. How it was you who became damn pushy, because you have to be pushy to get ahead in this Toronto, and how you opened your big mouth that ain't got no cover and asked if they had any jobs going at the TTC. How one of them said 'sure, they're looking for drivers now, willing to train.' To which you, Ona Nedd, quickly asked, 'how come nobody never hears about these damn jobs and why they never advertise them in the papers and could just about anybody apply?' To which the man said that usually people have to have friends working at TTC to hear about these jobs. And from here, you'll switch into confusing my arse about how we West Indian people have to learn to network with other people to get ahead. Why you always got be getting mad at me for not being a man, for not knowing the important people in this country, as any real man would. For not standing up like a man. Why I'm always spending time with no-good people around Toronto instead of with people that can help me. There. I've said it for you. You don't have to repeat it. And besides, I gone from this table, before you only get my arse hotter this evening."

"Go ahead, run away from the argument," Ona taunted. "You never could stand and face the fire. Go ahead, run away. Prove to me again that you ain't a real man."

"If you had to put up with what I have to put with at the TTC, you wouldn't say them things," Joe barked. " 'Cause you think it's easy being a black man in this country; you think it's easy working at the TTC, sitting on a stool in a glass booth all the fucking day and doing nothing but taking transfers and handing out tickets and tokens. Any damn idiot can do that. It don't take no brains. When I left home in Barbados as a young man, I never believed that I would spend the rest of my life doing just that. Nobody doing that kinda work can keep any ambition for too long. It's not even as if you're driving a damn bus, where you can see different things on the outside, talk to people, actually do something. You won't know, have a life. 'Cause you, Ona Nedd, the know-it-all, never have to sit in that booth that is a damn prison. When I have to deal with somebody like you, I understand why all the black men I know hang out with white women. 'Cause they don't need this shit, I tell yuh."

Joe got up from the table and crossed over to the stereo. Suzanne stood up too and took the opportunity to ask Ona to sign the report card that was still on the table.

"You got to be kidding," Ona answered brusquely. "Me? Sign that piece o' paper? Don't kid me. You think I have nothing better to do?"

"But I have to return it tomorrow."

"Ask your father over there," she said. "See if you can get him to unplug himself. You and he deserve one another."

SUZANNE SAT ON the bed looking at the picture of Mira Nedd on the wall and wondering what her mother had really meant by her last statement. The old black-and-white head-and-shoulders picture was beginning to fade from exposure and overuse. Whenever she retired to the bedroom, she always spent some time with the old woman. Sometimes they read the Bible together, with Suzanne reading aloud the passages her grandmother suggested in her letters.

Often Suzanne heard the footsteps outside her door. Occasionally she noticed the shadow blocking out the overhead light shining through the crack at the bottom of the door. Perhaps Ona did know what was going on and had been dropping broad hints all evening. When Suzanne wasn't reading, she liked to sit in the dark, hoping the darkness would cause him to think she was sleeping and that he would go away. The only problem was that when the nightmares came, they were usually more frightening in the dark. She always seemed to board the plane much faster. The many-handed creature that was her mother always touched her more quickly, and in the wrong places. The plane ride was always so much longer. The drums too muffled to help.

Joe didn't always agree with Suzanne that he should be looking for someone else, not Mira Nedd's granddaughter, when he dropped by the bedroom. At first, he claimed to be there hoping to bring peace between Suzanne and her mother. After all, Ona kept upbraiding him for not intervening enough. It's just that he didn't like confrontation, he said, but preferred to talk to Suzanne and her mother privately. The early meetings had been short and purposeful. He spent most of the time standing, looking down on Suzanne on the bed.

This evening he sat beside her, as he always did of late. Something was different, Joe said. He had grown tired of listening to the music, of sipping the Mount Gay rum on ice alone. So he had decided to knock on her door because he felt like talking, just talking to someone, and not being screamed at for hours. And she knew that Joe was the only friend she had in this apartment. He warned her that she should do nothing, divulge nothing, to ruin this friendship, unless she wanted to deal with Ona on her own. Suzanne was too frightened, too confused to argue or resist.

THE HUMMING OF the machines in the laundry room was a relief for Ona. She knew that she had upset Suzanne and Joe by talking too much, killing the spirit for the meal Joe had worked on so hard. After all, it was only a damn report. Another report. She must have carried on for too long. But what else could she do? Just wash her hands of everything? Sit back and assume things would work out; assume that Suzanne would come around eventually; that Joe would start taking life seriously?

She placed the basket with the dirty clothes on top of the machine next to the one she wanted to use. Once again, she checked her pocket for the quarters, hoping that she had not been so absentminded again to forget the money. Otherwise she would have to drag the entire basket, clothes and all, back up to the apartment. She could not risk leaving the clothes behind. Not for somebody to *thief* them.

To her relief, she found the coins. She separated the clothes and dumped one batch into the container. As usual, she planned to wait out the entire wash, rinse and separation in the laundry room, rather than going upstairs between cycles. This was her chance to escape and to think, to reflect on everything. Some things she had said at the table had startled even her. She didn't know where they came from, except that maybe her mind was working overtime, running ahead of everything else.

She had to think through her own thoughts, and what better place for this than among the whirring sounds of the washers and dryers. Anyway, Suzanne and Joe probably didn't even notice she was out of the apartment; he with his eyes closed and his head stuffed into the earphones; Suzanne sulking behind that damn closed door.

In all her arguments, Ona felt she was always trying to get across one thing only. And it didn't matter if she were talking to Mrs. King, her boss at work, Suzanne, Joe or a principal. They had to realize she was a woman who believed she couldn't remain a human being if she turned her back on her goals. She would never be happy shackled by the same things from which she expected liberation. Her dreams and aspirations had to be attained somehow, not used as weights around her ankles.

To accept otherwise would leave her a shell, hollow and adrift in a country that was still confusing.

She would become no less than a zombie, without dreams or hopes. Without anything to keep her going in the middle of winter when it was so dark and bitterly cold and lonely that she doubted the wisdom of coming to this country in the first place. Without a burning passion, a conviction that she would ultimately triumph, and her daughter too.

That was why she didn't want to give up on her daughter, to accept that her own flesh and blood was intellectually inferior. She knew she had turned into a nag. Christ, Joe had called her that often enough, and then fled through the door when she, in reflex anger, had hurled back just as biting invectives at him. But nobody understood these things. Nobody.

So it was left to her alone to get after Suzanne. She wasn't aggressive enough, unless arguing with her. She wasn't dedicated enough, unless reading her Bible or attending some major functions at the Spiritual Baptist Church. Ona was convinced she had only limited time to turn Suzanne around. Like a person possessed, she relentlessly ordered her to stop sitting in front of the television like a vegetable, to occupy herself by reading a good book that could teach her something about life. She told her to get out of the apartment and meet people, even if it meant investing in a walk to the library. Ona even subscribed to a heap of magazines, thoughtful black publications like *Essence, Jet* and *Spear,* and left them around the room, hoping Suzanne would pick them up. She never did. The magazines remained on the table untouched, as though Suzanne lacked even the elementary curiosity to pick them up and leaf through them.

Instead, Suzanne read the Bible, locking herself in her bedroom for hours, reading, fasting and mumbling to herself. This drove Ona crazy. She was wasting her time. Ona felt her priorities were misplaced. Finally she demanded Suzanne cut back the time she spent going to church or reading the Bible. She insisted Suzanne spend more time on subjects that would be useful in later life.

Ona put the rest of the clothes in another washing machine, set the knobs and closed the lid. Just as she was reaching to insert the first coin, the machine started roaring, filling with hot water. Ona checked her coins. She must have put in the quarters before the clothes, she thought. No, she counted them again; she still had the same number of quarters.

Ona sighed and leaned against the dryer. She could not remember the last time she had gotten anything for free. She kept watching the machine, making sure it didn't have a mind of its own, didn't realize what it was doing, didn't give up midcycle. Ona hoped this was a sign. She didn't know that fifteen floors above her, Suzanne and Joe had other ideas.

CHAPTER 15

THE FIRST NIGHT in jail scared the hell out of Suzanne. Bobby Ali had assured her there was no risk. The plan was simple. They were to cut out from school after the first period, when they were supposed to have unsupervised study. Nobody was likely to miss them, or take much note of their absence. In any case, they could always argue they had been studying in the library.

For some time, they had agreed that Suzanne was ready to make a heist with Bobby. She was to be the perfect foil. White people tended to find black women less threatening, Bobby said. They didn't watch them as closely as they did black males. Under this plan, he and Suzanne would ride the subway north to the final stop. From there, they would take an inter-city bus to one of the small towns somewhere behind God's back. Nobody knew them up there, and those places were so slow and laid back that people hardly noticed strangers among them. The police never did, apparently. So it was impossible to get caught.

"Believe me, we can pull this thing off, easy, easy. Before they find out what hit them, we'd have the place cleaned out.

We'd be back downtown, in class, acting as if nothing happened," Bobby said. "Just do what I tell you. Trust me, the best place for this kind o' thing is in those little malls."

First they picked a jewelry store with a lone employee, an old and frail-looking woman. Bobby Ali produced a hundred-dollar note and offered to buy a cheap watch, asking for small bills as change. He used this opportunity to distract the saleswoman while Suzanne grabbed handfuls of chains and rings and stuffed them into her pockets. While Bobby was at the counter, she was to walk out of the store and make a left turn. When Bobby followed, he was to turn to the right. They would rendezvous later at the subway station for the ride back downtown. Later, they planned to fence what they couldn't pawn.

But Suzanne appeared nervous and knocked over a mirror. She panicked and tripped over more things. A man came out of the back and held her. Bobby Ali disappeared, as part of the pact they had agreed on earlier.

The drive in the back of the police cruiser was humiliating, as was the fingerprinting and the questioning. As Bobby Ali had suggested, the only information Suzanne gave willingly was the name of her mother and her telephone number. She didn't eat that night, nor in the morning, so that by the time she arrived in court her stomach was grumbling loudly. And she was scared.

ONA WAS GETTING ready for bed when she got the frightening news about her daughter's first brush with the law. Joe was out, only God knew where, when the telephone rang. A policeman asked if she was Mrs. Ona Morgan, and did she have a daughter named Suzanne Morgan, fifteen years of age. The last time Ona had any dealings with the law or courts was more than a year earlier, when she fought the Children's Aid Society in court.

Her heart fluttered as she listened to the voice on the phone. Ona didn't know what to expect, so she braced herself for the worst. Only a few weeks earlier, the police had gunned down a young black woman sitting in the front seat of a parked car, paralyzing her from the waist down. And another black youth had been shot in the back when he drove through a police radar trap.

Ona thought instantly about the mother, a Jamaican about her age, when she had seen her on television crying at the funeral of her teenage son. He had been shot in the back of his head in his mother's driveway. The fact that the boy was in a stolen car didn't numb the pain of the mother or the hollowness Ona felt when she saw her grief. The police had called her just as she was getting into bed, too. For confirmation, she needed only to open her bedroom window and shout down to the people gathering, to the women already making their way over to console her.

Ona felt apprehensive. These were unsettling times. There was even talk that Bobby Ali and his gang were arming themselves with guns and knives. She had tried her best to persuade Suzanne to steer clear of them, that at her age she had to be careful, she should be spending more time on schoolwork or even looking for a job after school.

Ona recalled that the newly elected mayor was among the first to make the statement that West Indian gangs were getting out of control, creating concern that the police were being given a free hand to hunt down and shoot any black youth. Every black mother with a child outside the house dreaded getting a call from the police in the middle of the night. Often, maybe while waiting in the laundry room, Ona and other mothers had tried to joke about what they would do if such a call were to come. All the while, they prayed silently that the telephone would never ring at a strange hour or that the chaplain or police would never sound the doorbell.

Now the police were calling Ona. And so late at night, obviously so urgent it couldn't wait until morning. Ona paused for a deep breath, digging deep within for the strength. "We arrested your daughter this afternoon, and she'll have a court appearance tomorrow morning in Newmarket," the policeman said. "Shoplifting."

Ona didn't have a clue where Newmarket was, didn't know that it was north of Toronto, didn't really care where it was. She didn't know what had really happened to her daughter, in which jail she was spending the night. As soon as she hung up, the phone rang again. This time it was some official-sounding woman claiming to be a lawyer and telling her to be at the courthouse early, to dress conservatively and to bring such documents as her Canadian citizenship card and bank books. "That kind of thing impresses the judge," the woman said. "Your husband can come too, but it doesn't really matter since he is not her real father." She didn't even bother asking if Ona wanted to be at the court, if she had to work the next day or if, with her limited knowledge of that part of the world, she wanted to travel that far.

Ona didn't sleep a wink that night. She kept pacing the floor, drinking coffee, watching television, listening to the radio for any bit of news about what had happened. Early the next morning, she called in sick once more. She was now relying on the grace and humanity of her supervisor to get away with such requests. All her sick days were used up due to the problems with Suzanne.

The people at the bus station told Ona where Newmarket was and which bus to take. She was the first person to arrive, even before the doors opened, so she found a doughnut shop and pretended she was interested in the bad-tasting coffee. Eventually, the sterile-looking courtroom with the hard high-back benches and the picture of the queen filled up. If anyone else in the room was as nervous as she, it didn't show.

"First time offense for your daughter," the man sitting beside her said reassuringly, after Ona had confided in him what little she knew. "I wouldn't worry my head, if I were you. They'll probably let her off with a reprimand. If she's got any

191

kind of a lawyer, she might not even get that. Not for a first offense. Shouldn't cost you anything. You got legal aid for her,
right?"

"No. I didn't have time to think of that."

"Don't waste your money when you can use the government's. Get legal aid next time," he whispered. "Sometimes
the children don't deserve your good money."

The balding judge, a man in his fifties wearing a white mus-
tache and a black robe, looked bored. One by one, the ac-
cused took their places in the box. Their actions, the smiles
flashed at friends and relatives, clearly showed they were familiar with the ways of the court and weren't in the least bit
frightened. Most of the cases dealt with shoplifting, breaking
and entering, possession of stolen goods, assaults, a few minor
weapon charges and several for drug possession.

Ona got the eye-opener of her life. Until then, she had been
totally unaware that young people were committing the crimes
to which the majority was pleading guilty. Or that they would
treat such serious matters so lightly. Ona felt that someone
had lifted a veil from her eyes. It affected her harshly, especially whenever a black youth took the stand. She felt as if all
black people were on trial, that she represented all the mothers and fathers of those children parading before the judge
with such bewildering speed. Ona looked around the room
to count the black adult faces. Only two others: the man beside her and a woman with a boy perhaps younger than
Suzanne.

It wasn't until after the noon recess that the court heard
Suzanne's case. Proceedings went as easily and quickly as the
stranger had suggested. Up to that point nothing had prepared
Ona for the shock she felt when the prosecution and defense
lawyers both turned to her as if she were the person standing
before the judge. Someone had arranged legal aid and the
lawyer was good, except that she painted a very bleak picture
of Ona and her parenting skills, telling the court how Suzanne
had been raised by a grandmother in Jamaica and had only

joined her mother a few years earlier. Both mother and daughter had been ill-prepared for the reunion, the lawyer explained. The mother was hardworking, but because of the long hours of work outside the home, she couldn't provide all the parenting needed. Neither was she able to bridge the gulf between herself and a teenager at a somewhat rebellious age.

To Ona's surprise, the lawyer produced copies of Suzanne's school records as evidence to support Suzanne and to discredit her as a mother. Suddenly, Ona was on trial. The lawyer told the judge she had all sorts of shortcomings as a mother, neglecting to recount how hard Ona had worked and how much she had sacrificed for this little girl. And when Ona thought the worst was over, the lawyer dropped another bombshell.

"The mother is willing to give Suzanne another chance, and the court should give the mother one more chance too," she said. "So the mother can prove herself."

This was unbelievable, Ona thought. She had done nothing but good and sacrifice. Now this lawyer was pleading with the judge to give her one more chance. She had not even bothered consulting Ona, perhaps because she knew Ona dared not say no. And while this was going on, Suzanne was sitting there with a bewildered look on her face. A look as if she were the most surprised person in the world to see Ona accepting blame that should rightly be placed on her own shoulders. As if she couldn't wait to get all this behind her.

"Is the mother in court?" the judge asked.

"Yes, your honor," said the lawyer, in her well-tailored black suit and red-framed glasses.

Ona rose on trembling legs. The entire world had heard her life story, even how she had fought the school system, how difficult she was to get along with, and how erratic she was. Now everyone was watching her, stripping her naked. She stood, pulling the sweater around her shoulders, more against the chill of the stares than the air-conditioning, and waited for judgment.

"Is what the lawyer told the court true, Mrs. . . . ," the judge asked, checking his notes, " . . . Mrs. Morgan?"

Ona nodded in agreement, tears in her eyes, humiliated to have to admit to the world that she was a bad mother. That she was responsible for Suzanne's going astray. And that she was the one to be punished. She cried silently because she knew somebody was bound to ask how could she be so irresponsible. How could they judge her that harshly? They did not know what had happened; how she had fought so hard to get her child back at an early age. She could not even try to tell them. Not with her daughter's future on the line. She had to absorb all the shame and go quietly. Ona nodded her head, afraid to speak lest her voice break.

"There'll be some documents for you to sign," the judge said, dismissing the case.

"Thank you, your honor," the lawyer said cheerfully. She gathered up some papers and put them in a black briefcase. The lawyer, whose name Ona never learned, signaled with her head for Suzanne and Ona to follow her. "I had to do it for my client Suzanne, not you, so nothing personal," she whispered to Ona. It didn't sound like an apology but like a clinical statement just setting the record straight. "I had to make you look worse than you are for your daughter's sake. I had no choice. I had to do whatever it took to give her a chance."

"I understand," Ona mumbled, wondering what kind of record she, as a mother, now had with the courts. The lawyer got into her car and drove off. Suzanne and Ona waited at the bus stop in silence, unable to look at each other. Suzanne felt devastated. Some youths from the court joined them, with Ona noting that not one of them showed any remorse. They acted as if this experience were cause for celebration, a rite of passage. Ona knew she would have fainted in the dock if she were in the place of any of them. On the outside, she would be hiding her face in shame, wondering who knew of her record and what people would say when the news inevitably reached back home in Jamaica. Instead, these youths were commemorating their formal arrival as criminals. Worst of all, Suzanne was officially one of them.

AS SUZANNE LOOKED at her mother from the corner of her eyes, she wondered how she could show Ona that she was glad to see her. The first person she had seen when she arrived at the court in the morning was Ona, pacing in front of the building. As the van pulled up with the prisoners inside, it stopped right in front of Ona. She was unaware that people were watching her through the dark glass and that the very person she was looking for was in the belly of this beast just in front of her.

Suzanne was grateful her mother was there. But even as she stood in the court, as they waited together for the bus, she couldn't let her mother know how she felt. She had to control her emotions too. Just as Grandma Nedd had taught them. She could not let her actions betray this happiness or even send a signal to her mother. The same way her mother had hidden her true feelings when she stood up to face the judge. When they got outside the court, Suzanne decided to remain as cool as her mother. She had no choice, not with everyone looking on. At the moment, she felt like reaching out to her mother, to rescue and calm her, but pride prevented her from doing anything to show a softer, different side.

AS THEY BOARDED the bus, Ona looked for a seat near the back. The black youths piled on and sat in the middle. A group of whites, looking just as mean, sat near the front. Soon the blacks and the whites were taunting one another. Ugly knives, brass knuckles and guns flashed around. One wrong move would have started a riot. Ona almost died of fright, especially when the black youths blocked the aisle of the bus and dared anyone, black or white, to push past them. The bus driver kept his head straight, stopping only when someone rang the bell.

As the bus sped down Yonge Street, several people in the back, of all ethnic groups, exchanged anxious glances. They obviously had missed their stops, had been too frightened even to beg the youths to let them signal that they wanted to get off. Ona was shocked this was happening, and in broad daylight, too. She could see that the driver was scared, so jaded from such repeated behavior and the results of calls that only endangered his personal safety afterward, that he didn't even bother to summon the police.

"Let's get off here," Suzanne said.

"Where?" Ona asked, looking out at buildings she didn't recognize. Suzanne saw the puzzlement on her mother's face. She had to act quickly. She had to get her mother off the bus before Ona saw what it would be like if these groups really clashed. If Ona were to find out the truth, she would never let her out of the apartment again, Suzanne thought. With such a grounding, she was bound to lose face with her friends. This would compound the disdain others had for her when Bobby explained how a well-prepared plan had been bungled because Suzanne was too clumsy and frightened.

"We can't get out here! Not in this no-man's land," Ona whispered in astonishment.

But Suzanne had already pulled the bell cord. The driver eased up at the stop and consulted his mirror to confirm that someone was actually trying to get off the bus. The youths closed ranks as Suzanne made her way up the aisle, her mother lumbering behind her.

"Ah, it's Suzie," said a white skinhead. "What you getting off here for?"

Suzanne didn't answer, but walked steadily toward the exit.

"Give us a shake, a good grind," the leader of the black group said. "Give us a dance, Suzie, if you want we to let you off this bus."

To Ona's horror, Suzanne grabbed a pole in the center of

the aisle, wrapped her legs around it, and gyrated her hips and waist sensuously for a few moments.

"Way to go, Suzie! Way to move!" the boys called out, whistling loudly. The brief dance broke the tension. Ona felt like sinking through the floor of the bus, but she quietly followed Suzanne out onto the sidewalk. She hadn't experienced a more humiliating day in her life.

When she got home, Ona made it clear she never wanted to experience such an ordeal again. Suzanne promised her it wouldn't ever happen. Ona took that statement to mean no more court appearances, no more robberies. Suzanne didn't explain any further. If she had, Ona might have found out Suzanne was merely saying she never intended to get caught or laughed at again, a promise made to herself rather than her mother.

THE POLICE CALLED again several times, and at all hours of the night and day. Every time they called, Ona still found herself being shocked by her daughter's ability to find new ways of getting into trouble. Finally, the call came that was to change Ona's attitude. The time she decided to reclaim her life. For more than a year, she had been at her daughter's beck and call, frantically rushing to aid Suzanne every time she got into trouble.

The pivotal call came at the end of summer when Suzanne was still several months short of her sixteenth birthday. Could Ona come and bail out Suzanne? the polite caller inquired. This time she was caught in a smash-and-grab at the close of the Canadian National Exhibition. Ona wasn't as surprised this time, although she still felt disappointed. Of late, she had sensed something was wrong. Suzanne was coming home weighed down with gold chains and Ona had found more money than Suzanne could account for in her room. More than Suzanne made packing groceries at the supermarket.

Ona didn't skip work to attend the trial. The lawyer called the office to find out why Ona was delayed in arriving at the court and when she could expect her. "In another hour?" she asked.

"No," Ona said. She was surprised how ready she was with an answer. "Not me."

"But she's your daughter, Mrs. Morgan," the lawyer persisted. Ona didn't answer. Finally the lawyer said: "What am I supposed to do?"

"Let her rot in jail if that is the kind o' life she wants. If she just plans to make a life for herself going from jail to jail, associating with them lowlifes, then a good long piece of prison might be the best place for her."

"The judge might make her a ward of the court, hand her over to the Children's Aid Society."

"Fine with me," Ona said. "Do what you like, but I'm not going to court." She hung up the phone.

CHAPTER 16

ONA'S EYES FLASHED in anger. Suzanne had never seen her mother like this. And all that had sparked the outbreak was her asking why Ona hadn't come to her help. Why was she so gruff with the lawyer on the phone and why had she allowed the Canadian Children's Aid Society to send her to a holding home? But instead of a civil answer, exasperation and frustration burst out of Ona, through her eyes, through her flailing hands. Seemingly involuntarily, the harsh words gushed out of her mouth, as if her tongue had a mind of its own.

"When you can tell me which daughter I'm dealing with, then you can ask me those kinds of questions," Ona railed.

The force of the reply slammed Suzanne in the face. After the few weeks apart, she had expected a different reception. Maybe a mild scolding or a lecturing of how she must try harder to get her life under control. But general happiness to have her back. The belief that by walking through the apartment door, Suzanne was giving all of them another chance for another beginning. Not the feeling that Ona was just waiting to let loose on her.

Ona too was taken aback by the strength of her reply. But

what else could she do? Continue to lie down like a doormat and let everybody walk over her? The words unmasked the feeling of being so helplessly unable to reason with this young woman who seemed hell-bent on destroying her life. When words failed, her only resort was her hands, contorting them, swinging them in every direction to aid her communication, to reach out and push away that invisible barrier always present between her and Suzanne.

"I won't be any help," she screamed. "Listen to me good, I won't be sitting here on my fat ass waiting for some call in the middle of the night. Not to get out of my warm bed to come and rescue you like some damn pimp. I ain't no pimp. And I won't do it. My God, I keeping doing my best for you, but my best like it ain't good enough. Like nothing I do is enough. 'Cause I just can't understand you. What do you think things is?"

Suzanne had no answers. She went to her room, passing Joe plugged into his earphones. Unfortunately, Ona wasn't through with her castigation. While in the Children's Aid Society's care, Suzanne had heard how her mother had taken to disowning her publicly. Her mother was even willing to take the differences in their relations outside the apartment, as if alerting the world early not to be surprised with how she planned to deal with this juvenile delinquent for a daughter. Suzanne didn't believe the news when she heard it. Mira Nedd would never have gone public with any family feud. Now she had the proof: the look on Ona's face; the way she rung her hands; the uncontrolled rage in her voice. But it was the look on her mother's face Suzanne could never forget. That stare, when Ona said she was through pimping for her own daughter.

Until Ona set her straight, Suzanne believed her mother was only appearing to harden her heart as a threat, a means of demonstrating she was not going to let this *own-wayish* girl walk all over her. Threats, never carried out, were the only way Ona knew to maintain some control over her. But the reports of what Ona was saying to other people soon dented Suzanne's faith that her mother wasn't willing to go beyond posturing. It also served notice on Suzanne that she had to come up with a different tack to remain one step ahead of her mother. And worst of all, no matter how she wished differently, that she could never let her mother know how much Joe was troubling her.

Suzanne was convinced her mother couldn't be right in her head, or that she absolutely had no feelings for her own flesh and blood. What mother would not help a daughter in prison? Grandma Nedd would, the same way she had taken care of the baby seventeen-year-old Ona had dropped on her. Back then, Grandma Nedd was disappointed, but she didn't fold her hands and turn her back. She didn't tell Ona to get lost. She raised the baby into a woman.

Suzanne found it hard to believe that Ona forgot these things; that she really understood anything about mothering. After all, when Ona got pregnant, wasn't she just one year older than Suzanne was now? So what was the big thing about not helping a daughter that had made a small slip? Where was the example Ona liked to talk so much about? And if Ona wouldn't help her with the law, how could Suzanne ever expect her mother to understand what was happening with Joe, or the bad dreams that wouldn't let her sleep at night? Ona had to know about these things, Suzanne surmised. She knew everything that was happening in their apartment. It was just, as she had told the police and the lawyer, that she didn't care. Never did care, as indicated by the speed with which she had dropped Suzanne so soon after birth and headed to North America.

No, Suzanne reasoned, Ona was missing a piece of the puzzle. After all, this was the same mother that followed her into the bedroom, demanding that Suzanne leave her apartment, obviously never to return. The same woman so willing to throw her out into the pelting rain. "If you can't live in here by my rules, then you can leave right now," she said. "Don't even bothering saying that you unpacking the few things you have in that bag. Just leave."

"I don't have to stick around for this," Suzanne shouted at her mother. "I'll find someplace to live. I won't stay where I'm not wanted."

"Suit yourself. Prove that you are as much woman as you like to think. Go on! Take your own ship to sea and see what it's like out there! 'Cause there can be only one woman in this house."

Left with nowhere to turn, Suzanne tore out of the apartment only to end up at one of the West Indian volunteer agencies for the night. She was taken there by a young woman named Brenda, who said she had encountered similar problems with her parents and was now so much happier living on the streets. Suzanne was coming out of the McDonald's with a hamburger when Brenda asked her for a piece. "I'm a bit off," she said. "My welfare check ain't come yet."

Brenda explained later that on her sixteenth birthday, the very day she became legally responsible for herself, she had left her parents' home rather than put up with their shit. She had been free ever since, although the two years had been tough and uncertain at times. "When I'm a bit stuck, when I run out of money between checks, I just go out and panhandle, maybe outside the train stations or a McDonald's like now. But you won't have to do that."

Suzanne gave half of the hamburger to Brenda, who ate it hungrily. She gave her the rest and the Coke.

"You still at school, right?" Brenda asked. "That's good. Because it means you can get student welfare, which is easier than what they give me as regular welfare. Sometimes it's like those people don't want to send me my money. But it'll be different with you. 'Cause you're still in school and they can check on you every day. Go to the welfare people and tell them you have nowhere to live. The CAS can back you up on that point. The welfare people will give you someplace to live and some money to live on."

But it wasn't that easy. Suzanne wasn't sixteen years old. The welfare people said they still needed her mother's concurrence that the relationship had broken down. Only then could they hand over the financial assistance or put Suzanne in an apartment. Having assured them there should be no problem getting her mother to cooperate, after all Ona had thrown her out, Suzanne was aghast when her mother bluntly refused.

"I didn't send her nowhere," Ona said. "I have a bedroom right here in this apartment that is Suzanne's own. I buy food and clothes for she. It's me that always giving she everything she wants. And all I ask for in return is that she gives me respect. That she start to act and behave as if she alone don't live in this world. Otherwise, she can live in this apartment 'til she grow as old as Methuselah. I mean, I might have said a few things to her, maybe one or two things a bit too harsh 'cause I'm only human, but I didn't mean for she to bundle up her things and walk out, swaggering past me like she expect me to come running after she. That bedroom in there belongs to Suzanne. She can come back and get it anytime she's ready to behave."

They were at an impasse. Suzanne was unable to return home and she couldn't get any money without her mother's assistance. Worse, it was another seven months to her sixteenth birthday, when she would be free of parental control. Once again, Brenda came to her rescue. They found another welfare office in the city. Brenda signed Ona's name to the forms. Then she took Suzanne's key and went to Ona's apartment while Ona was at work and waited for the call. When the welfare officials telephoned, Brenda said she was Suzanne's mother and that she had given her permission. When the first welfare check arrived, Suzanne and Brenda blew it celebrating all night on the town. When she went to get the key to her apartment the next morning, Suzanne was so tired, she collapsed outside the door waiting for the landlord's arrival. She was hardly inside the apartment before she fell asleep.

Brenda moved in immediately, although Suzanne had promised the welfare people nobody would live with her. Ona hit the roof when she found out how her daughter had worked the scam, pulled off another deception. Brenda had forgotten to alert Suzanne to intercept the confirmation letter that would be sent to Ona. The police swooped down on them in the night, only one week later. The welfare people lectured them. Brenda was held in jail. Suzanne went to a home called Maisonneuve in suburban Toronto.

THE FIRST NIGHT in Maisonneuve House, a home for juvenile delinquents, was sheer purgatory. Never had Suzanne felt so alone and ostracized. She was trapped.

Every time she nodded off, the dream overwhelmed her. In the plane, the large, unnatural-looking faces around her grinned and jeered as the speck that was Jamaica receded further into the distance. Three times during the night, Suzanne found herself sitting on the hard cot, bolt upright, with her legs curled under her like a Buddhist statue.

The most vivid image of those dreams was the hands of her mother, hands that flew everywhere, touching and poking. So many hands, so hypnotic, Suzanne couldn't keep up with them. Too many people were pulling at her, all of them hiding behind the evil *voodoun*, wanting to shape her life. Suzanne knew the only reason the dream was so powerful was because they were holding the wrong person. They had let the trickster created to confront her mother, to play along with Joe, fool them and get away.

Throughout the feverish dream was one constant: the drumming. In her mind, in every corner of the room, the drums talked to her, for the most part loudly and sternly. Occasionally, they whispered as quietly as Grandma Nedd praying at an open-air meeting. A Rastafarian lightly tapped the tips of his fingers on the drum's skin in respectful accompaniment, not loud enough to interrupt the prayer, but still a message as potent as the supplication.

Other times, when she least expected it, the rhythm sud-

204

denly pounded in her head, causing her body to rock the bed. All night, the drums kept talking, in a language only she and the drummers understood. She had to get away. She had to be freed. They had to know they were holding the wrong person. Grandma Nedd would tell them, if they only would try to contact her. If they only would let her grandmother rescue her, let her reclaim the child who had received the laying on of the hands by Pastor Grant. The same child of God who didn't even want to come to this country in the first place, who didn't fully understand this foolishness about honoring a mother and a father. Especially a mother and father so hurtful like Ona and Joe. Only the drums understood this. Only the drums tried to tell the truth.

> Boom ka-plak-uh, boom ka-plak-uh,
> Boom ka-plak-uh, ka-plak-uh
> Ka-plak-plak-plak. Boom ka-plak-uh
> Boom ka-plak-plak-plak.

The calypso songs she had heard on her stepfather's stereo refused to leave her alone. Just like the memories of his touches and how they made her cry. The words, the heavy bass beat and the drumming drove her off the bed, to dance, slither, and leap around the room. The same way she used to slide off the bed and try to hide from Joe. As long as she kept moving, she was free. The dance in her feet. The song in her heart. The sway in her hips. The drums; the rhythms in her soul. The animal urgings to grunt and express herself with words that flew out of her mouth, utterings that even she could not decipher. They wanted to set the innocent lamb free. The calypso music, the words, just like on Joe's stereo, set the pace.

> I could feel the Devil in muh head
> Driving muh 'til I want to dead
> In the land of the dread
> Music in muh head.

205

Other times it was the one-drop reggae beat or that funny jazz music her stepfather listened to late at night. While she didn't fully appreciate the strange and sophisticated syncopations of the pianos, saxophones or trumpets of the jazz musicians, there was one redeeming and captivating component of the music: the drumming. It was always the drums that deadened her mind, even in the presence of her stepfather. Everything related to the drum, either as a complement or counterpoint. So was her dancing, either in precise rhythm or counterstep.

On the wall, just like a movie picture, Joe sat and claimed as usual to be appreciating this harmony, all of it, every component so intricate and integral. He nodded his head, either in shame or maybe in acknowledgment of the music. Never once he looked in her direction. But she didn't care. Only the drumming mattered to her.

AFTER JOE HAD his fill of the music, he would come into Suzanne's room. He usually waited until Ona had dropped exhausted in her bed or lapsed into a strong sleep still propped up in that comfortable spot on the sofa. Only once did Ona awake unexpectedly and find Joe in Suzanne's room. Even then Ona didn't enter, but only stared coldly at Joe when he came out. Ona said nothing specifically about Suzanne and Joe, although her eyes and actions betrayed her suspicions. Suzanne didn't care what Ona thought. Or sometimes she wished she didn't have to hurt her mother, didn't have to hurt her own self. Sometimes she was confused about what she thought, about who she was looking at in the mirror, about what she was really trying to explain to Grandma Nedd. The only constant was the music. Especially when the relationship got so cold, nobody bothered talking, and the apartment became a prison.

Suzanne was shut away in Maisonneuve but that didn't

mean she was cut off from this sweet music; the same way that her foreparents, shut away in the craws of slavers and then marooned in the Caribbean, were never so far away they could not fly away home to glory. She only pretended to be dancing; mesmerizing all with her steps. Grandma Nedd said all the Nedd women were born dancers, the curse. When the captors least suspected, she would be long out the door, the same way the other Suzanne used to mesmerize Joe with her dancing. And they wouldn't find her, because she had escaped, following the trail made on the wind by the drums. She would float back home. And when they went searching for her, they would capture the wicked Suzanne, the defiled one, the one that escaped and blamed her, the poor child of the Lamb. They would find the deceiver dancing in one of those taverns downtown, stripping and accepting tips, dancing for the Devil, just as Grandma Nedd always warned. The real Suzanne would never dance for the Devil, would never listen to Joe and his music, would never dance naked for him. Grandma Nedd knew that. And once they captured that other person calling herself Suzanne, she would be free. Free to say to Ona, sorry it didn't work out as we planned and hoped. Free to go back to the arms of Grandma Nedd.

The noise from the attempted flight caught the attention of the matron sitting in the office directly below. This was as Suzanne expected. Her escape had to come with a roaring sound, like the wind, like fire or like the airplane turning around in her dreams and heading back home. Suddenly the reinforced door to the room burst open. The white matron, big and menacing, was standing in the doorway glaring at her. As ugly as Joe when he got angry and frustrated with the dancing.

"What the hell! What's this?" she demanded. "You want to wake up the others? Cut it out right now and get to sleep. Tomorrow morning you have to be up early for another round of tests. I knew from the time you walked in here you were going to be trouble. You *Jamaicans* are always trouble."

No sooner had the door closed and the silence descended than Suzanne heard the drumming again, as distinctly as a long-distance call from the people back home enticing her to flee to safety, to fly away to glory some bright morning. To leave her troubles — Ona, Joe — behind. To clap her hands and sing. To bang out the rhythm of the drums on the walls, and to stomp her feet loudly in time with the sounds on the wind, captured through the transistor in her head.

Suzanne was totally enthralled by the magic of the drums, the African drums. Grandma Nedd and the Rastafarians used to tell her that in the days of slavery drumming was banned. Babylon had feared the beat was enough to inspire even the meekest to rebel and seek freedom. The captors couldn't understand or appreciate the drumming. They couldn't even hear it on the winds. They couldn't know how drumming and dancing could release all the pent-up frustration and liberate the body and mind through sheer exhaustion and delirium. That was why the matron, just like Joe, had come back once, twice, God knows how many times, to do the impossible. To ban her drumming. To stop the wind from blowing. To warn her to be quiet and let others sleep. But a force bigger than Suzanne, bigger even than all the matrons in the world, was driving her on. Like the slaves, Suzanne had no choice but to respond.

I'll fly away to glory (boom ka-plak-uh, boom)
I'll fly away (ka-plak-uh boom boom)
One bright morning when my work is over (ka-plak-uh
*   plak-uh)*
I'll fly away. (plak-uh plak plak plak)

The matron was back in the doorway again. This time two men were with her. "Christ, she's hallucinating," someone said. "Look at her slithering like a snake. That's what those bloody drugs can do to you. She can't handle the withdrawal.

208

I've seen some of them, and it's usually the West Indians, prancing like wild animals, with the strength of animals too."

As if in a dream, Suzanne saw the slave drivers approaching, moving slowly, with ugly smiles on their faces. All she saw were their hands. Hundreds of them. Like in the plane, soon after it took off. Ona was approaching. And she had so many hands, there had to be other people behind her. Maybe the matron and these men were behind her. Joe too. But they couldn't touch the real Suzanne, the child of God. There was a special magic power to protect her, to disrupt the dream just when the nightmare was too awful. It was her dancing. She was dancing at a great speed, twirling, evading.

With the drums setting her pace, Suzanne knew how to dance rings around them. She had the strength. The speed. These slow movers could never catch her. She could out-dance, outrun anybody. Just like how Ona would have out-danced all those pissy boys and girls in the National Dance Troupe and continued on her preferred life course, if the curse hadn't snared her. Grandma Nedd had said so. The music would help Suzanne to remain free, absolutely free and undiverted in her journey.

But too many hands were reaching for her. They were forcing her into a corner. The captors were descending on the little slave girl, the one Grandma Nedd said had brought the curse over from Africa. She couldn't dance away. Louder, the drums were exhorting her to fight back, to dig down deep for that extra strength, to stretch her feet and run. But she couldn't.

"Dance, Suzanne!" the drums demanded furiously. "Dance! Dance, Suzanne!" Only her heart continued to pound as freely as the drums. *Krack-uh boom, boom, boom.*

As the rough hands grabbed her, Suzanne realized she was wide-awake and trapped in the godforsaken home. The people were forcing her into a straitjacket. She was unable to move. If she couldn't dance, she had to do something to get

209

the drumming out of her head. To stop her heart from bursting. She had to shout back and let the drummers know not to send her any more messages. To let them know she was in the hands of the Philistines. They might force the code out of her and decipher the messages moving on the wind, in the sounds of the drums. By taking her away they were ending a long regal tradition in Africa. Replacing it with the curse, just as the ultimate *griot*, Grandma Nedd, recounted. She had to keep shouting to the matron that they were holding the wrong person, to please let her go so that she could dance and be alone by herself and trouble nobody and just be whomever she wanted to be. So that this cup, this curse, should pass from her. If she couldn't dance, she would shout to silence the drums, to summon help before the wicked carried her away and required her to sing a false song. She screamed and screamed and screamed.

The doctor came quickly. She remembered his broad white face near hers, then the prick from the needle on her arm. Then nothing. Just a falling sensation. *My Mother, save me from this cursed hour.* She felt the same way the women did when journeying at Cross Roads, when they swooned and fell to the ground, listless and powerless, unable to hear the drums, lacking the strength to keep wailing. When they realized they could dance and journey until morning light and still not reach the Promised Land. When they understood yet another disappointing night was passing and Elijah's sweet chariot was nowhere in sight, wasn't swinging low, wasn't coming to carry them home.

The next morning, Suzanne found she had lost her voice. The psychologist wrote something on a piece of paper and put it in a brown file folder. She didn't care what he had found out or recommended. This journey back home was much longer than she thought, and now, like the fatigued women back home, she couldn't even talk one language, let alone the inspirational tongues of their worship.

They took her back to the home and the isolation of her

room. Even if she could have, Suzanne was not allowed to talk to her fellow inmates. She refused lunch, supper and the late-night snack. She wished someone would visit her, even her mother, any familiar face. She was denied the use of a phone. All she could do was sit on her cot and listen to the muffled drumming far off in the distance.

The next week the matron of the home, a social worker, and a representative from the Children's Aid Society visited Suzanne in her room. They handed her five pages of the home's rules and regulations and said she would be transferred to a school near the home. They wanted her to get into a routine. It was time to bring her out of the isolation and to start integrating her back into society, but on the home's terms, not hers. This meant getting up by 6:30 every morning and being in bed by 9:30 every night, even on weekends.

They didn't seem to know, much less care, that in Jamaica, even when she was much younger, she had never gone to bed that early, particularly when Pastor Grant held his open-air meetings. She decided not to confront them on the issue. Why not let them think she was cooperating? Let them think they had broken the wild animal in her.

The message was clear, Suzanne thought. Whether she wanted to or not she always had to resort to deception. That was the only way she could survive. It made sense for her not to tell them about the other Suzanne who came to her rescue so often, but who had taken this last trick too far, who had implicated her this time. Obviously, she still needed the other Suzanne. And even if she wanted to break from associating with her, in light of these tough conditions she had no choice but to stick close to her, to let this double stand in for her whenever necessary.

"In this home, you will be expected to earn your own pocket money," the matron said. "This is to teach you what the real world is like. You don't make any money in the real world unless you're willing to work."

While the matron talked, Suzanne looked at the wire mesh

on the window and the bare walls. There was a closet, where her running shoes lay by the door. A laundry basket and a waste-bin sat by a small wooden table, on which were a lamp and a dictionary. If she were free today, she would be in the park in front of the apartment building, hanging out with friends. No. She would be back in Jamaica with Mira Nedd and her best friend Delores.

Instead, she was cooped up in this barren room with strange people lecturing her. She didn't even have her Bible or Grandma Nedd's letters to read. The wings of her thoughts had been clipped. The strong medicine made her so tired when she mused about the outside, particularly about the paradise waiting for her. She was a captive in this home, just like in Grandma Nedd's stories about the slaves of old. Along with her were three other captors with bedrooms on the second floor. Three more were in rooms on the main floor. When she tried to escape it all by dancing, even without music, she felt tired and uncoordinated or someone came immediately and led her listlessly back to the cot.

"To make your money, we will expect you to do chores," the matron droned on. "These include making your bed every morning, assisting with breakfast and helping with the evening meal, which must be attended by all inmates. The evening meal is very important. We expect you to be at the table, even if you're not hungry, to eat what's served and to be courteous to the others, not disruptive."

"When I was with my mother, she never forced me to sit at no table," Suzanne heard a strained voice saying. "If she cooked something I didn't like, I could always make a sandwich and—"

"That will not be allowed at Maisonneuve. You'll be a member of the family here and we expect you to act like one, not to spend all your time sulking in your room. We'll also be emphasizing discipline, making you learn to do things that are necessary, but which you may not like. That's how it's done in the real world. Discipline will be the watchword around here."

"You got to try and cooperate," the CAS worker said. "Don't make things too hard on yourself, Suzanne."

"And another thing," the matron continued, "we expect you to be home from school by 4:15 every evening. That gives you 45 minutes to get home after school ends. You will not be going to church on Sundays. We use Sundays to prepare for the rest of the week."

Suzanne stared at them, feeling dazed from the medication. At one point, the matron had said something about reducing the dosage. The urge to fight back was extinguished, but not the distant, soft drumming emanating from somewhere in the back of her head. The volume seemed to be timed to the dosage. As the medication weakened, the drumming increased.

"If you can't live by these rules, we'll cut your privileges. It's that simple. You would be confined to your room, with no television and no outing privileges with the others on weekends to places like the cinema or the malls. Is that clear?"

Suzanne didn't answer. The matron shrugged her shoulders. The officials exchanged glances. Suzanne tapped her feet.

"And by the way," the Children's Aid Society worker said, "if you have any problems, talk to me. I'm on your side. My job is to look after your interests, to intercede for you. If you need anything—clothes, toiletries—ask me and I'll try to get them for you. We'll work together to get you out of here as soon as possible. Right, Suzanne?"

When there was no answer, the CAS woman continued. "We've also agreed that you can have visitors on weekends. We might even extend that to home visits, if we think things are working out. Is that clear, Suzanne? Do you understand what I've just said?"

Suzanne looked straight ahead. She was familiar with the ruse: one person, the matron, playing the villain; the sweet woman from the society pretending to be her friend. At times, even she and Bobby Ali had tried it, with Suzanne playing the role of the fragile and vulnerable. None of the women was really on her side. Maybe this was where Ona and Mrs. King had picked up their strategy. Suzanne had tuned them out early. Except for the few words about visitors and home visits and the bit about reduced dosages. All she heard was the music in her head.

She remembered how Brenda had warned her to be on the lookout for these government people. The only redeeming thing about this experience, Suzanne thought, was that she had a place to call home, if only for a while. And that for all this she could thank her sweet mother.

THE FIRST PERSON to visit her at Maisonneuve was Joe. He came alone, about a month after she was committed. The visit was unexpected. He turned up about four o'clock on a Saturday afternoon. Looking nervous, he was dressed in his Toronto Transit Commission uniform, so he must have cut work early to see her.

Suzanne wondered if Ona knew he was visiting her. The nervousness was most apparent when the matron talked to him or Suzanne. From the way he kept shifting in his seat, it was obvious Joe couldn't wait to get this formality about rules and conditions of visits out of the way. All the same, Suzanne was overjoyed to see him, even if she had never seen him so compliant.

As soon as they were alone, Joe inquired if she had told the CAS people or the matron anything about them, such as their personal secrets. "You know what we used to do once in a while, not too often, in your bedroom," he said. "You didn't tell them anything?"

He would ask her the same question, sometimes several times, on every visit. But she learned to ignore him. She didn't know why he was so anxious to remind her, when in reality it wasn't even she who had been in the bedroom with him. But obviously he was still confused and she didn't feel like letting him know every little thing about her life.

To escape from the Maisonneuve and the watchful eyes of the matrons, Joe got permission to take Suzanne out driving in his car, just as he used to when she first arrived in Canada.

Suzanne looked forward to the outings across the city as much as she had back then, when she was learning her way around. They stopped at West Indian stores and bought hot peppery beef patties and cinnamon cakes, just like the ones she grew up on at home.

In the stores, she smelled the spices and herbs from the Caribbean, the fragrances that lingered in her memory from visits to her grandfather's store in St. Ann's. Besides the smells, there were pictures, posters and Jamaican flags and all sorts of breads and canned stuff imported from the Caribbean. Around her people talked and joked in their Jamaican and West Indian patois as genuinely as if they were back home. It was like stepping through a door and leaving Toronto behind. A step that took her back to the true Suzanne, the one that even Joe couldn't defile.

Topping it all off was the music blaring from the boom-boxes, the African rhythms, especially the reggae, calypso, soca and drumming. The trips reminded Suzanne of pleasant times, when she was new to the country, trying to feel out her relationship with Joe, her mother and a different society. She was a different person then.

Back then, when she and Joe went shopping, they used to bring home green bananas and plantains, salted meat and fresh goat for currying, all kinds of foods that Grandma Nedd had taught her to cook, but which Ona never bothered with anymore. Foods she wouldn't taste as long as she remained in the delinquent home, forced to eat only tasteless cooking. Several times she asked Joe to bring some of his cooking, but he never did, always claiming he didn't want to travel with stale food prepared the night before. The food might spoil before he delivered it, especially if he had to take a bowl to work and leave the contents unrefrigerated in the hot ticket booth before bringing it to her. The sight of the boxes with the provisions in the West Indian stores only served to remind Suzanne how much she was missing. A Saturday night didn't pass that she didn't cry when Joe delivered her back to the home and signed her in.

Just as she was getting used to Joe's visits, he stopped coming. He gave no explanation. One Saturday she waited for him, but he didn't show up. He never returned. Fortunately, Mrs. King started showing up. She always brought little gifts: fruit, candy and patties. Sometimes Suzanne imagined the presents were from Ona, the same way she used to pretend when she was in Jamaica and Grandma Nedd gave her something special. Mrs. King was friendly, but she wasn't an adequate replacement for Joe. She wasn't as much fun and didn't take her away from the home. And just as quickly, Mrs. King resumed her lecturing, interceding for Ona, trying to make Suzanne feel responsible for all her mother's shortcomings. Still, with Joe no longer coming, Suzanne was glad to have the old woman visit.

"You don't belong in here," Mrs. King said when the matron had left the room to allow their first unsupervised visit.

"I know. I want to get out. I want to go back home."

"That would be good for you and everybody else," Mrs. King said, "but do you know what the real problem is? It's—"

"It's my mother," Suzanne replied softly. "She don't want me around her. She never did. That's why she left me in Jamaica in the first place."

"No, Suzanne. I was hoping the time you done spend in here would help you to realize who—"

"I know who is causing me all this trouble," she insisted. "My own mother. I know that."

"No. You got to take some o' the blame, Suzanne. And the court, the judge, that's another problem," Mrs. King said emphatically. "Believe you me, Ona would take you right back this very minute. It's just that she don't know how she can control you and the judge won't—"

"So how come she never come to see me in here?" Suzanne demanded, interrupting the old woman. "She ain't come to see me, not once."

"You know, your mother can't tolerate a place like this. It reminds she so much of all them bad times in her life, things she still can't forget. I mean, you only have to look at how that matron over there keep looking at the two of we. As if I would take the time to come all the way over here to harm you. As if I'm some pissy little girl she got to approve for a visit like this. Me, a woman old enough to be her mother, but look how she treat me. Think of your mother, a proud woman, going through that kind o' thing time after time."

"That's it, she's always thinking only about she ownself, about what she can get. And when she can't get her own way, she—"

"Then again, maybe she ain't come to see you in here because she didn't agree with sending you here in the first place," Mrs. King said. "Maybe she can't face up to seeing you in here. You ever think for one moment your mother feels the best place for you right now is back at home?"

"In Jamaica?"

"No. No. No," Mrs. King said. "Back with her. But, as I said, the judge is being real tough on she. Can't get him to bend, not even a little bit. And you would have to show that you'll listen to her, that you'll do whatever she tells you, without any back chat, mind you. I know what your mother is thinking and hoping right now. That the longer you stay in here, the more you'll want to listen to her when you get out."

"I don't care what you say, Mrs. King. The problem isn't me. Not at all; it's my mother. She's the one causing me all this trouble. Remember how she used to drive me crazy when all I did want to do was read my Bible? But she always had to have things her way."

"But she was probably only—" Mrs. King began.

"Out of the blue, she tried to stop me from going to church, telling me I should be spending more time on this or that subject from school, telling me nobody in Canada cares a damn about how well anybody can quote the Bible. Now she even has the people in this home believing that I used to spend too much time at the church and not enough time on schoolwork. It isn't true. She just doesn't know the real me. She nagged too much. Even when Grandma Nedd wrote me, she'd find a reason to quarrel. As if it was my fault my granny asked me to read different sections of the Bible and to discuss them with her and my father during Bible study. Lord, you know how she'd hit the roof when I mentioned the letters."

"Listen to me, Suzanne," Mrs. King began again. "Your mother's only asking you to see things different now that you're up here in this country. Remember, you're not in Jamaica anymore. You'll have to make some big changes. After all, Suzanne, don't forget you did a very bad thing back there, I mean getting the money from welfare people under false pretense and letting yourself get mixed up with that so-called rebel daughter. You got to remember them rebels ain't up to no good. You know that so I don't understand what you're doing. What I know is how your mother feel 'bout all this. I talk with her every day and she ain't enjoying all this foolishness. Not one bit."

Suzanne ignored the statement. "Like the time she came across one of the letters, which I was using only as a page mark in my Bible. Lord have mercy, she screamed and shouted so much, I had to hold my head and run to the washroom for a little peace. 'What's this here?' she kept saying, shaking the letter at me. 'What the hell is this?' she continued. 'Didn't I warn you not to listen to what your grandmother tells you? Not to keep writing her? She is accustomed to her ways in Jamaica. She still believes in a lot of foolishness. Old-time foolishness. This nonsense could get you in trouble if you pay any attention to it. It ain't no good for you. Your grandmother don't know any better. You do. You're living in a different country in different times.' Lord, she kept going on and on, so I had to ask her how she could say something like that. She who was raised on the Bible, who was saved by the redeeming power of the Holy Ghost, who was baptized into the Holy Spirit like the original believers and who had received the laying on of hands. How could she say that?"

"What did she say?" Mrs. King asked.

"Some foolishness as usual. Something about how all the Bible teaching didn't get her a big house in Toronto or an important job up here. She forgot that the Bible instructed us not to set thine heart on earthly things, but on those things provided by your Father in Heaven."

"You don't belong in here," Mrs. King said, getting to her feet and checking her watch. "I can't understand how you think at times, how you see nothing wrong, from all the religion in your head, with someone like you joining them rebels to rob a store. Yet you make so much fuss if your mother don't want you to spend all your time reading the Bible. Something just don't add with you. Anyway, I have to go now, but I'll talk to your mother some more. See if we can find a way for she to sign the custody papers. Then we can take them to the judge and see what he says. 'Cause no matter the differences between you and your mother, a little girl like you don't belong in here."

Five months later, one month short of Suzanne's sixteenth birthday, Mrs. King got her way. Suzanne was released into the old woman's custody. Mrs. King was just as strict. Most evenings Suzanne had to be in her bedroom studying with only a little radio keeping her company. It was on this radio that one night Suzanne discovered the Buffalo station with the religious music, with the drumming, testifying and singing like that of Pastor Grant's church meetings. Most nights Suzanne went to sleep with the radio at her bed head, the drum-

219

ming rocking her for the night, with Mrs. King not having a clue what was going on, why Suzanne seemed so willing to live by her strictures.

One day, sitting in the laundry room, she saw a woman pinning a notice on the bulletin board. The notice was for a roommate to take over from a friend who had graduated from university and was going back home. Suzanne struck up a conversation with the woman, Heather, and within a week she had moved up to the penthouse as Heather's partner. Mrs. King didn't object too strongly, although she said she would prefer that Suzanne rejoined her mother.

"You're old enough now," Mrs. King said. "Sixteen years, three months. You can apply for the student welfare you keep talking about without getting into any trouble. So I don't have no problem with you wanting to be on your own. Young people these days are like that. I just hope you put the money to good use, that you remain in school, and that you try to find some way to get on with your mother."

Heather also showed her how to finance the new lifestyle and her newfound independence. She introduced Suzanne to Filmore's, where her previous roommate was a table dancer. Suzanne didn't bother telling Heather, or anyone at the tavern, that it wasn't really she who was the dancer.

CHAPTER 17

TURNING AWAY FROM the wicket, Suzanne stumbled over the stroller with the smiling white baby. Under the Yankees baseball cap, his face looked freshly scrubbed and smooth. It caught Suzanne's attention. As did the smile of the Filipino woman pushing the stroller. With her eyes, the babysitter seemed to be apologizing for creeping up so closely and silently behind Suzanne at the post office window. But it was the baby that interested Suzanne. His clothes were clean, except for the dribble soaking the baseball bib. Only a year or so ago her little brother Telson had been about his size. Suzanne missed taking him walking.

Since her return from the Buffalo prison she had thought almost every day of visiting Telson, and her mother too. But each time she put away the thought, for the same reason she had deferred writing Grandma Nedd. She had nothing to give them, financially or mentally. She needed time to reestablish herself after the Buffalo fiasco. And she had to get over the crushing news about Mrs. King, God bless her soul. Mrs. King was free. She had flown away home one bright morning when her work was almost done. Almost, because she didn't get the victory of convincing Suzanne to make up with her mother, or even to seek the help of the priest Basil Lucas. Every day since her return, Suzanne thought of Mrs. King and how to go about acting on her advice to approach Ona and Reverend Lucas. Telson always seemed the best excuse to get the ball rolling.

Suzanne leaned against the back railing that separated the drugstore from the post office. Once more, she examined the postal order for $25 that she had just purchased. Then she wrote in bold letters in the blank area after the words *Pay To The Order Of*: MIRA NEDD. As she scribbled her grandmother's address on the envelope, she overheard the conversation between the Filipino and the postal workers a short distance away.

"A postal order for five dollars," the woman with the stroller said softly, placing a five-dollar note in front of the wicket.

"That's eight dollars and ten cents," the clerk said. The woman juggled coins in a red purse, fishing out quarters, nickels and dimes. Impatiently, the clerk looked on. "You know, it would save you time and money if you came once a month and bought one big money order."

He was talking slowly, distinctly, as if to someone expected to have difficulty understanding. Suzanne knew he was also speaking to her. He had tried to engage her in the same conversation. That was when she had given him the withering look to which he'd responded by quickly handing over the money order without further comment.

"You'd save money that way, on the handling charges, just as I was trying to tell the person before you." The woman continued slowly counting the coins. "The handling charges are the same if you buy a postal order for five dollars, twenty-five or one thousand."

The woman finally found a dollar coin and pushed all the money toward the teller. Using one hand as a shovel, he pulled the cash over the edge into the cupped free hand. "You can save money. The handling charge is almost as much as the five dollars. So why don't you save up and come once a month?"

"My family waits for the money in Manila," the woman said. "I got to send it back home every week. I got to send it weekly, not by the month. Back home, they can't wait."

The teller sighed in exasperation, shook his head and handed over the money order to the woman. The Filipino woman placed the document in her purse, smiled sheepishly at the clerk and then Suzanne. She pushed the stroller through the door.

Suzanne wondered what her mother was doing with Telson. She must really miss Mrs. King, especially now that Joe was living on his own. Suzanne wondered who was helping Ona with the little boy. When she ran into Joe at the subway station where he worked, he didn't know who was helping out. Said he didn't care really, because that was what Ona wanted. Suzanne wasn't so sure. Too bad, after all these years in Canada, her mother didn't have good baby-sitting for Telson. Didn't even have a proper baby-sitter.

Carefully, she folded the money order in half and then in quarters. She buried it deeply between the two folded hand-written pages. As a final precaution, Suzanne held the letter against the light to make sure nobody doing the same thing discovered it contained the postal order. You could never trust those bastards at the central post office in Kingston, she told herself.

The stories of this kind of tampering were rife throughout the West Indian community, with every nation having its own story. But whether it was Joe having to disguise money he was sending to Barbados or Bobby Ali sending stuff to Guyana, there was always the need for precautions. Everybody knew how the workers at the central stations routinely examined the incoming mail for checks or postal orders. Over the years, she had heard countless stories of how the postal workers de-

223

stroyed the letters. They kept the money orders and checks, cashing them with forged signatures at the same post office, one hand washing the other. If the letter were registered and therefore traceable, they let it through. But a few days later, as sure as there was a God above, some salesman was certain to turn up at the addressee's house with the perfect item to enrich the buyer's life, and with a tongue as sweet to match.

Suzanne was satisfied that short of registering it, and drawing attention to the letter, she had done as much as possible to hide her remittance. She wanted to send Grandma Nedd more money, but she knew her grandmother, in her proud way, was bound to protest. She was even likely to write to scold her that Grandma Nedd wasn't an extravagant woman or a burden on anybody, praise be to God. As an old woman, she wasn't in need of so much money and was getting along quite well, thank you very much, trusting in the saving grace of her savior and in her old-age pension from the Jamaican government. Suzanne, as a young woman alone in this wicked world, treading her way through life with the possibility of not having a man to help her, was to save her few cents and look after herself. Most of all, she was to stop putting so much emphasis on money and the things of Caesar. Rather, she should strive to make her life pleasing to God, the only being she could count on when all else failed.

These admonitions went on forever, just because she sent a few dollars more than what her grandmother felt was reasonable. Twenty-five dollars was adequate, Suzanne told herself. Not enough to throw Grandma Nedd on the defensive; not so little to offend. Anything for a peaceful life this morning, Suzanne told herself.

Sometimes, although Suzanne was reluctant to admit it, it was such a trial dealing with Grandma Nedd. No wonder Ona had given up, especially if she had more immediate things on her mind than wondering what Grandma Nedd, thousands of miles away, was thinking. It had to be so much easier if, in dealing with her grandmother, Suzanne didn't have to go through this deception, the elaborate pretense that was so much a part of Grandma Nedd's life. The old woman would find living in North America unbelievably frustrating; nobody had the time for games, for ferreting out the real person beneath the apparition. Not in a society that moved so fast everyone had to cut directly to the heart and soul on the first try or not at all.

Suzanne would have preferred to send remittances for four or five months together—in one envelope accompanied by a scribbled note of explanation. But this was not the way Grandma Nedd worked. The ritual of appearing to force her grandmother to accept even necessities was part of the old woman's life, an integral part of her proud personal independence. Because she loved her, Suzanne played along with the charade, but she also recognized its costs and frustrations.

She frowned at her thoughts. Somehow, it was only since her return from Buffalo that she found herself thinking of what was so irritating about Grandma Nedd. But what the hell, those things weren't important. So she was just as willing to give her beloved grandmother the benefit of the doubt.

Suzanne licked the stamp and placed it on the envelope. She went through the sturdy, double-layered glass door into the bright sunshine. She opened the red postbox and dropped in the envelope. The red and blue Canada Post van was turning off Wellesley Street into the roundabout in front of the apartment buildings. Suzanne didn't have to check her watch to know it was eleven o'clock on the dot. That was one thing she liked about Toronto; everything was so attuned to the clock. The appearance of the van, even as she heard the muffled sound of the letter dropping inside the box, was reassuring. Her timing was impeccable.

She had planned it that way, sleeping late into the morning and then getting up to shower and grease her skin with baby oil before running down the stairs; no elevator for her in the daily keep-fit regimen, another commitment to herself since Buffalo. Under this plan, she arrived at the post office fifteen minutes before pickup time.

Suzanne adjusted the dark shades on her eyes. Walking with her head high, she headed for the grocery store, contented that the letter was on its way to Grandma Nedd. She had hardly gone ten steps when a male voice called her name from behind. It was a familiar voice but one she didn't place immediately. Timothy, the bouncer at Filmore's? He had a way of hanging around the apartment, looking for her, no matter how much she scolded him. Now that she was back at the tavern, it was only a matter of time before he started tracking her down again. However, Timothy's voice was much deeper. It lumbered like the way he walked. This voice was more pleasant, almost music to her ears.

Suzanne turned in the direction of the voice. Her heart skipped a beat when she saw Henderson, the man whom she had given the slip the night before, for the rest of her life, or so she thought. She was in such an awful mood after the performance, she didn't want to see anybody, didn't want anyone to keep calling her name. She just wanted to get the night over with, the ordeal of having to fall back on returning to Filmore's to make a living, of feeling trapped in somebody else's skin.

The last time she saw Henderson, he had been patiently sitting in the dark of the tavern smoking and pulling at his rolled-up beard, waiting for someone he kept calling Suzanne to pass through on her way home. She had slipped through the back, stumbling over the street people and the drunks sleeping near the vents in the alley. Because he had come to her aid in Buffalo didn't mean he had any claims on her. She wanted to make this point quite clear to him, because she had left the Suzanne Henderson who'd been bailed out of prison behind, at the club. She refused to take that dancer home with her.

At home, she went straight to bed after listening to the Buffalo radio station. The nightmares visited, but by morning

Suzanne felt clean and refreshed. She had reclaimed herself, was mentally strong enough to post the letter to Grandma Nedd.

Henderson must have entered the drugstore through the entrance on the opposite side of the building and seen her walking away from the postbox. It was tempting to turn and walk away, but she changed her mind and allowed him to catch up to her. Henderson looked different. It was as if she were examining him up close for the first time. He was displaying his muscles in a sleeveless T-shirt, and his faded jeans matched the washed-out running shoes. He was carrying a transparent plastic bag containing shampoo, toothpaste and something she was unable to identify. His face looked freshly washed and his hair was well greased, silky and healthy in the warm sun.

In the bright daylight, his beard looked knotted and showed a few bald patches under the chin. Not like the fully groomed beard she thought she had observed in the darkened tavern or on the bus back from Buffalo. The dim lights obviously had hidden some shortcomings, or he had neglected to use a comb this time. He flashed his disarming smile.

"How did you recognize me from behind?" she asked.

"Can't say it," he said, dropping his eyes boyishly to the ground. "You might find it a bit . . . um . . . *offensive?*"

"Go ahead," she said, staring at him through the dark glasses. "Don't be scared. Say it."

"Your ass. It was your ass," he replied, trying to soften the impact by lowering his voice. "I said to myself must be only one woman who lives around here with an ass as tight as that."

He waited nervously for a response, feeling she might be offended by his unintended reference to her trade. "I didn't mean to imply anything," he added quickly. He glanced at her face and quickly looked away.

"I don't mind, you stupid fool," Suzanne said, playfully slapping his bare arm. Once again, she had touched him.

"Boy, I don't think I've ever had to deal with anybody like

227

you," he said. "You can be so moody at times. Just like before you went to Buffalo. You wouldn't talk to me. Then you finally did on the very last day you're in Toronto before crossing the border. Then you shifted again, only to call me from—"

"Don't worry with them stories now," she interjected. "Tell me, though, how you keep finding me? You wait around here looking for me? Or you can smell me out or something?"

"Why you didn't come back out last night as you said you were going to?" he asked. "Why you keep playing me like a yo-yo?"

She was smiling, wondering what kind of a mature man shouted after a twenty-two-year-old whore, a strip dancer, in bright daylight and then apologized for thinking he had offended her. The truth be known, this Suzanne would have been a bit annoyed if, on a day like this, any man hadn't noticed her, the way she was dressed in tight-fitting white shorts, red shoes, blue tank top with no bra and a big red bag over her shoulder.

This was the way her mother encouraged Suzanne to dress and often dressed herself, although her legs were not as firm as they once were. Dressing was probably the only thing, apart from dancing, she had in common with her mother. On the other hand, Grandma Nedd was sure to have frowned at the clothes, even accusing her of courting trouble by tempting the men. That might have been the case once in Jamaica, where women had to worry more about the effects of their clothes on the men, but not here in Toronto.

"You ain't answer me yet. So tell me, what you doing hanging about here?" Suzanne demanded. " 'Cause I'm beginning to think you must be following me or something. Tell me the truth!"

"Why you're giving me so much trouble, woman? Running away from me all the time? When did you leave last night? We live in the same apartment building. I could've given you a ride home."

228

"What number apartment do you live in?" Suzanne asked, ignoring his questions.

"Six-oh-eight. You want to come up and visit me?"

"Never. Nothing so fresh." She was laughing now, like a little girl, as free and uninhibited as if she had been friendly with him for a long time. All along Suzanne had known this was the way Henderson was capable of making her feel, and she was enjoying herself. She also recognized the effect she was having on this man so many years older. Her happiness, especially her laughter and the flailing of her hands, was making him uneasy.

"I thought you told me last night you're leaving Toronto today, or was that another big-foot move to get rid of me?" He was being persistent as usual.

"No, man. We're leaving this evening. For Buffalo." She hoped he didn't notice the cringe on her face for being so foolish to say Buffalo. Why, of all places, *Buffalo*.

"Again?" he said, the tone of his voice leaving her unsure whether he believed her. "After what happened the last time. Buffalo?"

"Uh huh," Suzanne said. "No problem, this time."

Henderson didn't respond. An uneasy silence descended on them. Suzanne continued to smile. Then she turned to walk away toward the grocery store, expecting him to follow her.

"Where you going now, if I can ask you that, Miss Buffalo?" he asked.

"The store," she replied.

"Would it be too forward of me if I ask you to have lunch with me again? At our old spot?"

Finally, his tone suggested he was fighting back rather than begging. She knew it was best to turn him down and be done with this relationship. It was safest to stop fooling around. Looking him straight in the face, she ought to say: *Thanks, Henderson, for coming to help me out in Buffalo and all of that. Not that I'm ungrateful or anything, but we can't see each other no more. And please don't come visiting me at Filmore's no more. It ain't that I don't like you. Or that I don't appreciate you visiting or the fact that you always want to talk with me. It's just the best thing for the two o' we.* That was sure to be the final rejection he would take from her. After all, how long could one of these macho West Indians continue to beat his head against a wall?

But she had no spirit for another battle. She wasn't in a disagreeable mood. Neither did she feel like shopping and returning home to a hot apartment to cook and then eat alone. Moreover, she was hungry and her stomach was making funny noises.

"So what do yuh say, woman?" he pressed. "You coming or not? I don't see why it taking you so long to make a flipping decision."

"Okay, but only a quick bite," she said slowly, surprising herself. He returned the smile.

"Fine with me, Miss Buffalo," he said.

As they walked away, Henderson reached for her hand. She quickly pulled it away. "Now, none of that foolishness before I change my mind," she snapped. "Why you men always got to be touching, touching so much? None o' this touching up business, you hear me."

"Okay. If you say so, but don't blame me for trying. The old people back home got this saying which you probably know that nothing ventured, nothing gained. Besides, everybody done know that if you're a man, you got to make a play if you see something you want real bad."

Grandma Nedd had spoken the very same words to her countless times. It was refreshing and reassuring to hear someone who appreciated the wisdom of the older generation back home. Perhaps Henderson wasn't that bad after all. At the same time, to mention the old people back home reminded Suzanne of Grandma Nedd's warning about married men and their curse. No problem here, Suzanne thought, she knew how to deal with this one. Nothing much could come out of having lunch together.

They cut across the car park to Wellesley Street. Deliberately she let her hand brush against his. It was somehow different from the touches of other men she knew.

CHAPTER 18

"I STILL DON'T understand why your mother didn't bail you out," Henderson said, as he stopped the pickup truck in front of a row of town houses. Parked cars lined both sides of the street, a clear sign they were arriving late at the party.

"Nothing don't surprise me no more," Suzanne said nonchalantly. "In fact, you should hear what she keep telling people 'bout me. If you want to know anything about me, at least from my mother's point of view, all you have to do is ask any of them women she always hanging out with. You know, them West Indian women that always getting together and whining about what's happening to the next generation. Instead of examining themselves and seeing why the same people they like to call the next generation having things so tough. But not them. All they want to do is form these useless support groups, as they like to call them. Lots o' these groups popping up all over the place. You know, where these women spend all this time talking about this, that and the other and doing nothing. Talking 'bout getting involved in things like politics. In showing that we ain't just immigrants no more. No more planning to pull up stake and go back home someday, but that all we

232

here in this country to stay. You should go and check them out for yourself, if you doubt me. See who like to turn up at these meetings. That's how you can find answers to any question you got 'bout me. And about other young people too."

Henderson finally squeezed the front of the truck between two cars, leaving most of it parked illegally in the street.

"What they'd say if I asked?"

"Ask them yourself. Don't take my word for it. As I just tell yuh, them women like to talk a lot. And besides, some of them are the same age as you. Right now, Ona got all of them turned against me. As if I care."

Most of the day, Suzanne had been in a touchy mood. He had taken care not to say anything to spark an argument. But as the time got closer for them to dress and leave for the party, her spirits had lightened. She seemed determined to shed the self-doubt and brooding from being unemployed and short of money, or anything that might just upset her when she was in such moods. Obviously he had misread her again, Henderson thought. He had chosen the wrong time to settle a matter that had bothered him for the four months since he'd received that unexpected call from Buffalo. Somehow the time was never right for such a discussion. He decided to let the issue drop and concentrate on their plans for this summer night.

"I still think we should go to a nightclub," Henderson said. "I think I'd feel a lot safer at a nightclub. 'Cause I'm tired of reading every damn week about some shooting at one of these parties. Some kid or the other shot dead or in the hospital. Look what happened this morning. And in bright daylight too, in front of a million people."

"Nothing will happen, man," Suzanne reassured him. "You're with me, so no problem. People here know me."

As they walked across the street, they heard the reggae music playing so heavily it seemed to shake the earth. The music reminded him of an incident earlier in the day, one that had brought out a weird side of Suzanne, as if she relished the danger of the moment.

233

About ten o'clock, he and Suzanne had driven up to an intersection on the way to the community center to pick up his son from morning basketball practice. Suddenly, loud music and the sound of blaring car horns shattered the pleasant quiet of the tree-lined neighborhood. The green streetlight was flashing, giving him the go-ahead to turn onto the side street.

Without warning, a black car appeared out of nowhere to block the intersection. A man in the back was holding a camera, filming the stream of cars with funeral signs on their hoods. It wasn't the usual funeral procession; no police escort was in sight. The occupants of the cars were black youths, dressed casually, in dark shades, baseball caps and sleeveless T-shirts that displayed their muscular arms. The lights changed to red but that didn't stop the unescorted procession.

"What the hell is this?" Henderson had asked.

"Must be the funeral for Lenny," Suzanne said. "He got shot up at a party somewhere around here. Them youths are serious people, man. They don't allow no police near these funerals. No grown-ups either. Maybe one or two o' the relatives can come. But that's all."

"What happened to this guy?"

"Lenny took three slugs, one in the head," Suzanne said.

"Anybody arrested yet?"

"Nah, man. Nobody ain't that crazy to go cooperating with no police," Suzanne replied. "Not if they don't want to end up like Lenny. 'Cause nobody 'round here don't like informers, especially if they dealing with white police. And the drug people even worse when they got to deal with people ratting on them. In any case, I think the hit men that got Lenny were back across the border in Buffalo, Detroit or wherever they did come from long before anybody could tell what happened. Maybe they're even from New York or Miami. Who knows?"

"I see," Henderson said. "Some kind of weird people you hang out with, eh?"

"I guess so. At least, that's what my mother thinks."

234

"Like that Bobby Ali fellow," Henderson said. "Always walking around with his beeper and talking nonsense about controlling the illegal business in the community. He's heading for really big trouble, if you ask me. I don't understand why you still like to hang out with him. Since he beat that drug rap, all the young people around here treating him like a real hero. I think he's real trouble, man."

"Not Bobby. He's O.K. He got a nice cellular phone now and another BMW after the Buffalo police confiscated the last one. Business must be good for him. He's even getting a cut from the illegal business in Buffalo, even though he's a marked man at the border. They still can't keep him out when he's ready to cross the border. Too many back roads."

When the funeral procession was almost through the red lights, someone in one of the blocked cars started to shout at the occupants in the car blocking the road. This was followed by a cacophony of blaring horns. The head of the driver blocking the intersection disappeared momentarily. When he reappeared, he was pointing a large sawed-off shotgun in the air. Shots rang out. People screamed. Suzanne dropped to the floor of the truck. Henderson remained transfixed at the wheel. The horns went silent instantly.

Just as quickly, the shooting ended. The black car with its two laughing occupants sped off up the main street after the procession. The traffic rushed out of the intersection. Back in her seat, Suzanne clapped her hands and laughed. In the distance they heard the screeching tires of the car and the popping sounds of what must have been more shots.

"Did you see the look on the people's faces?" she asked. "I tell yuh, Lenny's getting a real good send-off. A real salute. And them youths really showing who controls the streets." She was laughing but to Henderson it sounded respectful, as if she had thoroughly enjoyed the occurrence. This frightened him. By the time the police showed up, the streets were deceptively quiet and uneventful, just as they always appeared in Toronto.

For the rest of the day, Henderson couldn't recover his nerve. Not even when he and Suzanne took the subway to and from the waterfront for a picnic.

SUZANNE PLACED THE tape in the Walkman strapped to her hips and handed Henderson one of the two sets of earphones. They had just turned into the subway station. "Here, take these," she ordered. Compliantly, he received them. He wasn't in a mood for another fight with her. Henderson just wanted to get home after the afternoon at the lakeshore park, where he had taken Suzanne to cheer her up. Everything appeared to be returning to normal. Prospects for the rest of the evening looked good.

"All that dumb music you like so much only sounds like gibberish to me," Henderson said, still hoping to sway her that they should attend a different fete instead of the house party later that night.

Henderson pushed the two penny-sized speakers into his ears. The volume almost lifted him off his feet.

They came off the escalator onto the subway platform just in time to catch a train. As they were settling into their seats, a woman squeezed through the closing doors, her hands loaded with two plastic bags bulging with what looked like knick-knacks. Despite the blackness of her face, the grime was clearly visible; the clothes were dirty and her shoes were bursting at the sides.

Henderson saw the flash of anger on Suzanne's face, the coldness in her eyes. The stranger stopped in front of them, reacting as if she recognized friends. She put the bags in the aisle and, after rummaging in one of them, pulled out a figurine of Jesus Christ adorned with a crown of thorns. The middle-aged woman waved it in the air, staring at the two of them. In the corners of her mouth was what looked like a mixture of spittle and bread.

"The only true friend we got is Jesus," she started. "We black people, a prodigal people journeying back home, we must come back to our true faith. The way of life we accustomed to."

She waved the figurine, but it slipped from her fingers and crashed to the floor. The head broke off and rolled between Suzanne's feet. The woman appeared momentarily paralyzed. Her mask had slipped, perhaps the result of the cold stare on Suzanne's face. She dropped to her hands and knees, frantically gathering up the pieces. Angrily, Suzanne kicked away the head and its crown of thorns and sprang to her feet. The sudden jerk pulled the earphones from Henderson's ears.

"Come, we getting off here," Suzanne ordered. "Let we get out here. Right now."

The train was slowing to enter the King Street station, four stops short of their Wellesley station. Henderson followed Suzanne out of the train. The door closed and the woman resumed her search on all fours.

"Did you smell her breath?" Suzanne asked. "And that stale sweat. As if she didn't bathe for weeks."

"Obviously, the woman ain't right in she head," Henderson said. He didn't like how Suzanne was switching moods again.

"Then she shouldn't be getting on the train harassing people," Suzanne snapped. "She's not back in the West Indies, where you can do these things. It's not the same thing like if somebody is preaching back home, where you expect certain things. This is Canada. Not back in the West Indies. And you know better than to say you defending that woman."

"But she was only—"

"Who give she the right to embarrass other black people with all that shouting and screaming on the train?" Suzanne interjected. "I always learned that there's a time and place for everything. And she was certainly out of place, behaving as if she ain't know no better."

Henderson stopped arguing. Fortunately, Suzanne's sour mood didn't last long.

SUZANNE AND HENDERSON joined a trickle of young black adults, several with distinctive haircuts, with the marks and signs shaved into their scalps daily. They were walking toward the source of the music, a brightly lit door in the middle of the row of town houses. Outside, several young men and women were standing around, talking loudly, and defiantly breaking the law by drinking beer in the open and smoking ganja. The group was exclusively black.

Although she was out with him, something at the back of her mind told Suzanne she was seeing too much of this married man. But with so much free time on her hands, at least Henderson was helping her to while away the empty hours. Apart from the odd night at Filmore's, her manager was unable to find continuous work for her in Toronto, so she had lots of time to herself. Most of it she spent with Henderson.

Most mornings they met in front of the drugstore in the apartment building. As the early workers hurried to the bus stops nearby, Suzanne and Hendy would chat for about forty minutes. Then he would get into his truck and go off to a factory somewhere in the suburbs, where he made high-priced furniture for a big department store.

In the evenings, Henderson usually dropped by her apartment for a drink. Sometimes he stayed for supper. Often they went to a movie or took long walks along Yonge Street, or across the viaduct and ravine to the Danforth, into the Greek area of the city. She liked Greek food, particularly the salads.

"I still don't think I'll be comfortable at a party like this," he said.

Suzanne knew why a man of Henderson's age was afraid of the parties. Few parents allowed children still under their control to attend such gatherings. Too many of them were getting criminal records because of the shootings and the drug and weapons charges brought by the police against those arrested at these illegal basement parties. But Suzanne was an adult, no longer needing parental approval for anything. And because she was old enough, Suzanne could buy as much beer and booze as she liked without fearing an undercover cop might claim the owner of the house was selling alcohol to minors.

Suzanne and Henderson pushed through the crowd into the house, then down the stairs to the basement. With every step, the air became more acrid from the ganja and the music even louder. At the bottom, three beefy men stood in front of a table with a lamp and a cash box on it.

Henderson fished out the thirty-dollar admission for the two of them. They slipped past the table into the darkened room but two men stopped them. One, with a menacing-looking ring in his nose, told Henderson to spread his legs and arms for a body search. The men moved quickly and professionally. Finding nothing, they motioned Henderson inside. Nobody challenged Suzanne, but the women behind her had to empty their handbags. One of the men searched the hair of the women, running his fingers through the bleached blond hair. Several of these women had the characteristic multicolored hair, with fiery red, green and yellow highlights. All were daringly dressed in the skimpiest of shorts exposing the cheeks of their arses or in flimsy see-through dresses that clearly revealed nothing was underneath. The rebel daughters talked loudly and boastfully, the jewelry hanging from their wrists, necks, ears and noses. So many people were coming through the door. Henderson wondered how the bouncers kept up with the security checks.

"Shaba Ranks," one of the rebels shouted as soon as she was through the door. Immediately she broke into a dance, raising one foot and winding her waist like a propeller. "Play Shaba, man. Me want to hear Shaba and dance-hall music all night. Throw in a little calypso, too, and a bit o' rap music. But give me Shaba all night." She pushed past Henderson and headed for the darkened part of the room. A line of her associates followed her.

"Mr. DJ, you hear me? Just pump up the volume, man," she shouted. "Pump it up loud, loud. 'Cause tonight, me come here for a good time, not a long time."

"Hey, yo-yo," the DJ called over the sound system.

"Yo-yo-yo," the rebels called back. The music blared. The rebel daughters kept moving, dancing.

"All you party animals out there, let me hear you say ah-yo-yo," the DJ intoned.

"*Yo-yo.*"

"Yo-yo-yo," he shouted.

"*Yo-yo-yo.*"

"Music!" the DJ shouted. The drumming through the speakers announced another calypso. The crowd started rocking. And shouting. And jamming one another. And sweating. The smell of the burning ganja was overpowering. It staggered Henderson, who was still feeling queasy from the body search, something that he had never experienced before and didn't want to endure again. He stumbled over the upturned edge of a carpet and brushed hard against a man standing in the shadows.

"Hey, what the fuck there, man?" the young man shouted over the music. Henderson was just as surprised to find someone standing in the darkness. No wonder he had thought the room was empty. The sides of the room were crowded with the men and women dancing against the wall and in the shadows. Several of them were dressed in dark colors, so that they blended easily into the background. "You blind or something, old man? What the fuck you doing here, anyway? This is a party for young people, man. You spying for the police?"

"No problem, man," Suzanne interrupted. "He's with me. He ain't no problem, man."

"Oh, it's you, Suzanne," the man in the shadows said, suddenly no longer angry. "I think Bobby was looking for you a few minutes ago. Like he left already, though."

Henderson's eyes were adjusting to the darkness. The young

man's head looked square, because the hair was cut low around the ears and back and rose to a flat muff at the top. This was the trademark cut of the young people, unlike Henderson's universally low cut, not so much for style, but to hide the emerging gray.

The music stopped, but the young man continued to shout. "We haven't seen you around recently, sister. And what you up to these days, I mean, hanging out with an old fogey like this guy here? He ain't a cop, is he?"

The last question brought loud laughter from those around him. Henderson looked around the basement, but could make out nothing but the glowing tips of cigarettes.

"I tell you to leave him 'lone, man," Suzanne said, protectively taking Henderson's arm.

"I'm not so sure we should trust some of these old-time West Indians, you know," the man said. "They're just plain useless, man. The same people that like to stand by and let the white people in this country do all this foolishness for so long. You know, so that this certain people in this country still expect other people like me and you to be just like the old-timers. You know, the ones still cleaning toilet bowls in hotels and restaurants. Man, I know some people don't like me to say them things, but we got to put the blame where it belongs."

"Henderson is okay," Suzanne reassured him. "Anyway, let me go and buy a drink. Give respect my brother."

"Respect due," he called back.

"Christ, he's a rough guy," Henderson said when they were out of his earshot. "Angry as hell too. I mean, I just brushed against the guy, and he was ready to eat my arse off. You know, we can still get out o' here and go to a club before it's too late."

"Chill out, nuh man!" Suzanne rebuked him. "I like these people. They're like me. Tell me, why would I want to go to a club with all old people? The next thing, you'd be wanting me to spend the night in the damn Hole among all those people from my mother's time."

241

She guided Henderson to a corner with the largest knot of people. They had to pick their way between groups of young men and women forming a chain and grinding their pelvic areas together in a sensuous dance. Some people were dancing in twos and threes and even individually, with all of them concentrating on winding their waists to the music, some with one foot in the air, others simulating sex by dancing against poles and against the walls. The music was jumping and so was everybody in the basement. The strong smell of curry and the spices of the specially prepared jerked chicken and pork wafted through the air. Most of the smell came from steaming cardboard plates in the hands of the revelers coming down the stairs from the kitchen.

Suzanne seemed totally at home in the setting. She put her leather bag over her shoulder and placed her hand in the crook of Henderson's arm. Around them, several young men and women were dancing; others were leaning against the wall, smoking.

"Good shit and cheap," said a man standing beside Suzanne, offering her a package. Until he spoke, it seemed he was just waiting in the darkness.

"Nah," Suzanne said. "Don't want."

"Good shit, woman. The best you can buy."

"No, man."

"Ah, come on. Don't give me no hassle, sistren," he persisted. "I got the best stuff in this fuck-hole place, eh girl. A rock for *vous*, madam? And what about the gentleman?"

"Look, I said I don't want nothing," Suzanne shot back. "You understand. Nothing. So stop pressing, man!"

"What about you, brother?" the man said, turning to Henderson. "Good stuff. Blow your arse-mind, bro. A rock?"

"Look, guy, beat it," Suzanne said angrily. "Carry your arse and leave the two o' we 'lone, nuh man. Do we look like rasscloth crackheads like you?"

"Who the hell you talking so to, you little cunt?" the man

said, raising his voice. "You don't know, I now feel to bash yuh face, one time?" As he spoke, he turned over the back of a raised hand as if to smack Suzanne.

Henderson felt his heart pounding harder. Suzanne was his date. He had to defend her. He had to act like a man and protect her if there was violence. The mere thought of confrontation caused his legs to weaken. The blood throbbed loudly behind his ears. His guts growled as he recalled what Suzanne had told him about Lenny. Nobody in the crowded room would dare to identify a murderer, his killer.

"Who the hell you think you chatting to, girl? Is me the bossman 'round this place long time now. It's me that control everything 'round here. Straight from New York. Must come through me. Everything, is me controlling it. A-1 stuff and you—"

"Ah, shut the fuck up, you idiot," Suzanne shouted. "Stuff the shit up your arse." Henderson had never seen Suzanne in such a defiant mood. Anything could happen. So often, something happened in their relationship to deepen his suspicion that he was dealing with more than one personality.

The tottering dealer swung at her. Suzanne ducked and adeptly sent him flying into the crowd with one push. He knocked over a bar stool, then sprawled on his face onto a seated couple, as though he wanted to hug both people at the same time. Plates of rice and chicken went flying in every direction. Young men and women began to shout. A fight broke out as curry and gravy splattered on the expensive shirts and dresses of those standing nearby.

"Let we get out o' here real quick," Henderson whispered. He grabbed her elbow. Suzanne angrily shook him off and made as if she was going after the sprawled man.

"Him got a gun," someone shouted. "Run!"

Several people were already heading for the narrow stairway, but only a few could make it up. Henderson heard the first loud bang, then another and another. Somehow he was on the floor, spread-eagled among many who had also dived for cover. The shooting went on for what seemed like minutes. When it stopped, someone turned on the basement light. Several men were roughly bundling the gunman up the stairs.

"Kick in his ass," a woman shouted over the hubbub. "The crackhead idiot could have killed somebody."

"Yes, man, make him get some sense in his head," another voice suggested. "Teach him to leave his piece at home. Teach the mother him some respect."

People were standing around, talking loudly. The music had ended abruptly during the melee. Henderson brushed off his clothes. His heart was pounding loudly. He tried to look calm. Suzanne was in heated conversation with two men.

"Let's party, man," the DJ announced over the sound system. "Let's have a good time now that little shithole is out of here with his toy. Now he's out on the street popping off shots. If he ever try to come back in here, we'd kick his arse real good. Tell him that, if he's listening. If he thinks that toy he has is something, wait until he sees the pieces the brothers at the door have."

The music resumed. The lights went out. Some young men lit cigarettes.

"Yo-yo," the DJ called again. But the refrain was half-hearted. Couples moved to the center of the floor to dance. There was a stiffness, a stiltedness, in the room.

"Come, let we get out of here before the police come," Suzanne said.

"Yeah," Henderson agreed.

Several couples were racing for their cars as Suzanne and Henderson scampered across the road to the pickup truck. In the distance, they heard the approaching police sirens.

"You asked me earlier why my mother won't bail me out, now you know why," Suzanne said as the truck backed into the middle of the street. "She claims it's because I like to hang out with people like these damn assholes at this party when I should know better. Sometimes I think she's bloody right. I mean if I say I don't want drugs, I don't want any." She was still livid. "He should understand that, man. No is no. Let's go to this nightclub you've been bugging me 'bout all night. Come, man."

"First I got to go home and change my clothes," Henderson said. "I smell stink o' ganja."

"Me too. God. Can you imagine what my mother would say if the police had busted me again?" Suzanne asked. "And for what? Because o' that stupid idiot. This time I wouldn't even have you to turn to. Your ass would be right there in jail beside me."

Henderson pressed harder on the accelerator, as if he were fleeing the very thought. The flashing lights and blaring sirens were approaching quickly. The music was still as loud. However, nobody was standing around outside anymore.

AS SOON AS Henderson pushed open the door to Suzanne's apartment, loud drumming and chants hit them with a staggering force. With the volume cranked up so loudly, the music filled the air, echoing off the walls. It came from the small radio in Suzanne's bedroom.

"The clock radio came on," Suzanne said apologetically, turning on the lights and mashing off her shoes. "Christ, it's that late, eh?"

"What's that playing on the radio?"

"My Buffalo station. I try to listen to the religious music every Saturday night. I have the radio set to come on at eleven every night. I don't like to miss the program."

Her voice was lower and flatter, as though she had suddenly deflated. The spirited woman who had spent the day and most of the night with him was transformed by merely stepping over the apartment's threshold.

"Anyway, I think I changed my mind. I don't think I want to

go out any more tonight," Suzanne said, holding the door open. "I think you should go home now."

"What's happened?" Henderson asked. The frustrations of the day and the night were bubbling over. "Christ, sometimes I just can't keep up with you. You're always having these mood swings. One minute, you're going out with me. Then we just stop by here for you to get some flat shoes, and you change your damn mind. I mean, it's like being on a roller-coaster dealing with you."

"I'm sorry," Suzanne said softly. "I'm tired and want to sleep. I'll listen to the spirituals on the radio and fall off to sleep that way."

"You getting too caught up with them Shouters over there, if you ask me," Henderson said. "You got to be careful. Real careful. Why do you want to mix with these kinds o' people, anyway? I mean they're people that used to hide out in swamps across the U.S., worshiping their African idols while pretending to be Christians. You're always saying you want to be a Christian. That you can't wait for the day when you can return to the church. So you shouldn't be listening to them people so much. You don't have to hide and pretend like them. They're funny people."

"They're the same people as in the Pocomania at home, or the Shakers and the Tie Heads as you like to call them," Suzanne said softly. "You don't have to tell me about them. I'm a Pocomania, remember."

"Let me say right now, Suzanne. If we're going to have a re-lationship, I can't keep having these changes," Henderson said angrily. "What am I supposed to do for the rest of the night?"

"I don't know," Suzanne said, swinging the door back and forth, causing the hinges to creak, the swaying a clear indica-tion she was impatient for him to leave. "Go to Filmore's. See if you can find someone like me there. Better yet, go home to your wife. What God has joined together let no man put asunder."

246

"Damn," he swore. "Sometimes I just don't know who I'm dealing with. You don't have to lecture me about my wife. You know it was only a marriage of convenience. I'll get out of it as soon as possible, you know that. Maybe, when me and you can—"

"Not me," she said sharply. "Don't bother with that. Not me and you in anything."

She pushed the door wide open. He stepped through. Outside he turned to face her and puckered his lips. She swung her head at the last moment, offering her cheek for a peck.

"Good night," she said.

Behind her, the drums were talking and snarling, loud, proud and victorious. As the music grew more aggressive, she tapped her feet more vigorously, leaving Henderson unsure whether it was a sign of impatience or a desire to dance. The drums had taken hold of the room and apparently of Suzanne in a way he never imagined.

"What you're going to do now?" he asked, still hopeful.

"Sleep."

> Crack, back-uh lack lack lack,
> Crack, back, back back crack
> Crack back-uh lack lack lack
> Back lack, back lack, back lack, lack lack.

Suzanne glanced over her shoulder as if to chide the drums for contradicting her.

" 'Bye," Henderson said finally.

She closed the door behind him and walked into the bedroom. Taking off her clothes, she held the ends of her skirt open wide, danced in a whirl, smiling at the approving picture of Grandma Nedd in the corner of the bureau.

Henderson must have been still in the elevator when Pastor Grant phoned collect. He said he had been trying to get Suzanne all evening. Grandma Nedd had suffered a stroke and was in the hospital. The situation was looking bad, he said, and could Suzanne pass on word to Ona as he had been unable to get through to her? When Suzanne put down the phone, the urge to dance was gone.

CHAPTER 19

THE FIRST SURPRISE for Suzanne stepping off the aircraft was the immediate blast of natural heat on her skin. Somehow she didn't recall Jamaica being that hot. Nothing like North America, where she had grown accustomed to the weather alternating between hot and cold, but cold more often than hot.

Four hours away, it was summer in Toronto, but the weather was already turning cool. Mentally, she had started to prepare for the cold. She should not have forgotten that no matter how the seasons changed in Canada, Jamaica was consistently hot. The direct heat actually stung the skin, as if the rays were trying to revitalize her entire body by boring through the pores. Suzanne was surprised at how much she had forgotten in what she considered a relatively short time away from the island.

But the surprises didn't end there. The waiting at the carousel for the luggage also shocked her, as did having to endure the long line to get through immigration and customs. In an age of computerization, why did these government officials still have to process things by hand? she wondered. Obviously, Suzanne wasn't alone in thinking this. As she waited impatiently for the first chance to see her grandmother, she heard the mumbling in the snaking queue. Many returning Jamaicans were as impatient, perhaps even more so, as the tourists. Suzanne had grown used to the speed up north. Her expectations were that the entire world moved at the same faster pace to which she had, evidently, now become accustomed.

Suzanne had rushed home on the first flight after getting the news about Grandma Nedd two nights earlier. She had told the travel agent she didn't know how long she was going for. All that mattered was that she planned to stay as long as needed to help Grandma Nedd get back on her feet. That was the least she could do for this woman who had been so kind to her, who in many ways was the only real mother she'd ever had.

But Suzanne also knew that this trip home had more meaning. It was to be a test of herself. In the back of her mind was the nagging wish that maybe this was the opportunity to return to her natural home for good. The chance to start life all over. The opportunity she had been searching for so desperately since the incident in Buffalo earlier in the year. Not one day had passed since her Buffalo experience that she didn't think of changing her life. But it was so hard to switch courses in Toronto. Once you started on one lifestyle, you were virtually locked in it. At least, everybody treated you as if first impressions were all that mattered. If she were lucky, she wouldn't even use the return portion of the ticket.

The travel agent, in her wisdom, had recommended Suzanne buy a fourteen-day ticket. For one thing, she could get one of those cheap last-minute tickets with fixed dates for travel. Once she was on the island, it was easier to decide whether to extend the stay. Suzanne wasn't prepared for what she encountered on the island, starting with the airport.

Pastor Grant had agreed to meet her there. But she walked right past before he called out to her. It was strange how he'd recognized her instantly. It was no wonder she'd almost missed him. She was expecting a tall, slim man. In her mind was the image of this man immaculately dressed in his white and black robes with the bows around his waist. The man who sweated under the street lamp when they went journeying.

Instead, standing in front of her was an old man with sunken cheeks. Bones underneath his eyes jutted out, stretching the skin on a face showing all the scars of time and a tough life. Pastor Grant needed a shave. The stubby white beard was something Suzanne didn't remember.

It must have been the long trip, Suzanne thought. Or maybe the extended wait in the heat affected her. Perhaps it was all these things, plus the anxiety of seeing Grandma Nedd that was confusing her. Pastor Grant didn't look anything like the figure of authority he had been in her youth.

GRANDMA NEDD WAS stretched out on the cot when Suzanne arrived at the hospital. She had insisted Pastor Grant take her there right from the airport, not bothering to stop off at home. Several times during the trip, Pastor Grant said he had to talk to Suzanne privately. Every time she put him off, telling herself the chat could wait. What Pastor Grant wanted to discuss, she assumed, was how she was doing in Canada. Maybe he wanted to know whether she had spoken to Ona and if she and her mother were still living the faith he had taught them. These questions were best left for a later time. She had to see Grandma Nedd right away. And in any case, try as she did for a day and a half, she had been unable to get through to Ona. The woman was perhaps the only person in all of North America who did not have a telephone answering machine.

The hospital wasn't like any Suzanne had visited in North America. Not that she really expected the same type of institution. It was just that she didn't like the way it looked. Neither did she fancy the strange smell of disinfectant that reminded her of sickness.

In her mind was the picture of Ona in the hospital. She and

Joe had gone to visit Ona and to see the little baby for the first time. Joe had turned up at her apartment earlier in the day and told her that she had a brother. "A lovely little boy," he had said. In the afternoon, they went to the hospital. Ona was sharing a room with another woman. It looked like a hotel room. The baby was in the nursery and had to be rolled in.

In the presence of the other woman, she and Ona made small talk and pretended to get along. Suzanne couldn't help feeling that her mother looked embarrassed, a bit distraught. At first she thought this was the lingering emotion from childbirth after a twenty-year break. Only later did she discover that the look on Ona's face was the apprehension from pondering what she was doing having a child in such a hostile country. And when she was almost forty years old and already so tired.

When Suzanne saw the baby, she fell in love with him: with his tiny hands and feet, the smoothness of his face, his pink little mouth. Suzanne recalled touching him and feeling how hot he was. And then he smiled. The first smile for her, perhaps for anyone. The ward smelled sweet, scented with all the flowers people had sent to the room, primarily for Ona's roommate. Somehow she had imagined Grandma Nedd in a similar semiprivate room where her pride would be protected from prying eyes.

The nurse was pulling back the curtains around Grandma Nedd's cot when Suzanne arrived. Suzanne waited until she had finished adjusting the cot and the night table before introducing herself.

"You say this is your granny?" the nurse said. "I didn't know she had any family here."

"I'm from Toronto," Suzanne whispered.

"From overseas, eh," the nurse said. Instantly, Suzanne felt her stature increase tenfold in the woman's eyes. "Well, it's good to see that you've come back down to see your granny. She wasn't doing too good when we first brought her in, but she's a fighter. A real strong spirit."

Suzanne stepped closer to the cot. The woman on the bed

252

did not look like Grandma Nedd. Her hair was almost white and badly needed combing. Nothing like the well-groomed locks Suzanne remembered twisting between her fingers as a child when they preened each other. She twitched a lot, kicking one foot, while the other remained paralyzed.

"Grandma," Suzanne whispered. There was no answer. The old woman was in a light sleep. She was breathing loudly and laboriously through her mouth.

"Grandma," Suzanne said again. "It's me. Suzanne. Me. Suzie."

The eyes fluttered open, stared unfocused at the ceiling, as if Grandma Nedd was responding to a distant call in her head, a plaintive cry from somewhere in her youth, which she quickly dismissed as a trick of the mind.

"It's me, Suzanne," she said again. This time she reached for the old woman's hand.

"Suzanne? Suzanne, you say," the old woman struggled. "Suzanne in Canada."

"No, Granny. I here, now. I've come back to see you. To be with you. How you feeling?"

"You want Suzanne? I see. Canada."

But Grandma Nedd didn't see much. She abruptly fell into a deep snoring with Suzanne still holding her hand. Suzanne sat by the cot watching her. All the time, she remembered the grandmother who used to dance so well, who was so full of energy. But who from the looks of this drawn person on the cot was now almost spent.

She sat and watched as people came and visited other patients; and she was still at the side of the bed when visiting hours ended. She helped the nurse clean her grandmother and feed her the spoonfuls of mush she accepted so unwillingly. Occasionally, Grandma Nedd mentioned Suzanne's name in her incoherent rambles, as if still wrestling with the earlier conversation. When Suzanne finally left the hospital, she felt thoroughly drained.

Exhausted, Suzanne went home, intending to stretch out

and relax, maybe watch the television while she adjusted. But when she got home, she realized Grandma Nedd didn't have a television, or a phone. Anyway, who would she call even if there was a phone? She wouldn't know how to get hold of her friends of ten years ago. And, if she did, what was she to tell them? The last she had heard, her childhood friend Delores was living somewhere in the United States, in either New York or Boston.

Suzanne sat in the darkened room feeling like a prisoner. If there were a phone around, she would call Toronto. Maybe Bobby Ali, inviting him to come down for a vacation. Or Henderson.

"I DON'T THINK there's much more you can do for your granny by hanging around here," Pastor Grant was saying as they sat in the old house. Finally they were having the conversation requested by Pastor Grant and it wasn't what she had anticipated. It was about what kind of recuperation, if any, to reasonably expect for Grandma Nedd.

Suzanne had thought the same thing several times since she had returned to Jamaica. She had gone to the hospital every day and had grown used to talking to Grandma Nedd even when she did not respond. Some days were better than others. It was at the end of the first week, just when Suzanne had to start thinking seriously whether to extend the stay, that Grandma Nedd showed some improvement. By then she seemed to know to whom she was talking. Yet there wasn't the enthusiasm Suzanne had expected, thereby robbing them of moments of any real intimacy.

"You helping your mother?" Grandma Nedd asked. "She got the little boy. . . . "

"Telson," Suzanne said, sensing that the old woman was struggling over the name. "He name Telson."

"You . . . you . . . help . . . yuh . . . mother, yes?"

Suzanne's first thought was to tell Grandma Nedd the truth. Now was the chance to unload. The opportunity to disclose all that had happened from the day she left Jamaica for Toronto. To relate how she did not get along with her mother, how Ona was a fraud and had misrepresented what life was like in Toronto. How she had always planned to post a letter containing these confessions to her. She thought of telling her that life wasn't as good in Toronto as in Jamaica and that she was even thinking of returning home to live.

There were so many things she wanted to tell Grandma Nedd just to set the record straight, just to let her know what kind of daughter she had in Toronto and how she, Suzanne, had struggled to keep the faith she had learned in Pastor Grant's church. How Ona and others had forced her to fail once or maybe twice. How she knew her grandmother was always willing to forgive her any transgression, no matter how big or small.

But she didn't. What's the use? Suzanne thought. What difference would it make? Grandma Nedd had never lived in Toronto, never lived outside the Caribbean for that matter. She would never understand some things in Suzanne's life. In any case, all Suzanne was capable of telling her was old stuff, things that probably didn't matter anymore, if they ever had.

Suzanne looked at the old woman stretched out on the cot. She knew she still loved this woman; she was her mother in the truest sense. But she felt the distance between them. Grandma Nedd knew of only one kind of life. She never had to pull up stake and start all over in a strange new country, with the only guiding light blind ambition and a belief that life simply had to get better.

Grandma Nedd knew how to draw up the plan. She never had to live it. While Mira Nedd had instilled ambition in both she and Ona, fortunately for the old woman, she never felt trapped by such teachings. She was never imprisoned by strong pride and loving loyalties, never had to see dreams aborted and then hang around putrefying.

255

Grandma Nedd had taught them how to nurture the dream. But she never told them how to bury it once it was smothered. She never told them dreams and ambitions had a life of their own. Once they died, they had to be mourned like a living thing and then thrown out. Otherwise, they just hung around and rotted, affecting every conversation, every relationship. Grandma Nedd hadn't seen the immigrant dream die.

And Suzanne felt glad that she had never sent those letters she had written. How childish they probably sounded. Ona was right not to let her post the letters, even if she got carried away with the constant quarreling.

"Yes, Grandma. I help her," she lied without any pangs of conscience.

"Help her. The only family you got. The little boy. First boy we ever had. Help with him. The little boy."

"Yes, Grandma. I'll help her with Telson."

"I don't know. A boy," she mumbled, " . . . the curse only women."

"Don't worry your head," Suzanne said. "I'll help with him and I'll help you too. I'll stay here and help you get better. So that you can go out and journey some more. Remember how we used to go journeying at Cross Roads?"

"No. Not me. Don't do that no more. The legs, you see." Pastor Grant had told Suzanne the same story earlier. He and Mira Nedd seldom journeyed at night, he said. He had corrected her in a tone that suggested she should have expected certain changes that came naturally with age and maturity. He and her grandmother were a bit too old for those things now, Pastor Grant explained slowly. As to be expected, a younger generation had taken over at the church. This was only natural, he continued. People like himself and Grandma Nedd were the elders, the spiritual advisers. They didn't have to do all that preaching and praying late into the night. For them, nights were for sleeping.

So much had changed and all this was news to Suzanne. Still, she had raised the idea of Grandma Nedd journeying because she felt the need to humor her grandmother. Or maybe because her senses had not yet fully come to terms with what she had observed since returning.

"I on a different journey," Grandma Nedd said. "It soon done."

"What you saying, Grandma?" Suzanne said. "I'll stay down here and go journeying with you."

"No. You have to journey alone. You still young. Mine soon done."

Suzanne felt the warm tears in her eyes. She knew Grandma Nedd was right. Yet she felt she had to steer the conversation away from this finality.

"But the curse," Grandma Nedd said. "It soon done, too. Your mother now have to deal with it. I've done my bit carrying it until now. So help her. And the little boy. He's different."

"Yes, Grandma," she said. "Yes, Grandma."

Suzanne sat in silence as the nurse bathed her grandmother and prepared her for the night. She was glad Mira Nedd was in no mood to talk or to remember. Suzanne didn't have anything to say on the night she had always longed for so badly, the first opportunity for her and her grandmother to just talk.

PASTOR GRANT CAME to see Suzanne early the next morning. They sat in the little room once again looking uncomfortably at each other. "I know you want the best for your granny. But we all done know how Sister Nedd was blessed with a full and long life. She's at peace with her God. She wouldn't want to be a burden to anyone, especially you. The Sister Nedd I know won't want a bright young woman like you sticking around this place, wasting precious time. She would want you to live your life. And what can you do to help? The only way you could help her is to take her back up with you to Canada where she could possibly get better medical help. But that ain't possible."

"I know," she said.

"Then you should go back up."

"I know," she whispered.

"And don't worry. We down here will continue to take care of your grandmother for the rest of her stay with us. I'm sure your mother will feel the same way. I plan to have a good chat with her too," he said. "As you know, in our customs there are certain duties expected of Ona. I guess I'll have to spend some time reminding her of a thing or two about our rituals and celebrations."

Then there was nothing left to say. She and Pastor Grant were strangers. Once Grandma Nedd was removed from the conversation they didn't have anything to really talk about. Soon after, he left. Suzanne sat in the house for most of the day, in the chair with the broken leg which was propped on a brick. She didn't feel hungry or thirsty, just numb and hot from the heat of the tropical sun.

On her way to the hospital, Suzanne stopped at the airline's office to confirm her return flight in two days. The weight of the world fell from her shoulders when she came out into the hot sun. She felt at ease too. For the rest of her stay, she visited with Grandma Nedd and helped to bathe and feed her, but she also spent time buying gifts to take back home.

The evening before she was to return to Toronto, she visited Mr. Heron the shopkeeper and asked him to help with Grandma Nedd if anything happened. He nodded his head in agreement and accepted the long white cotton dress, one of the type Grandma Nedd kept for journeying and that Suzanne wanted to remember her wearing. Mr. Heron took the neatly folded dress and put it in a plastic bag. He also arranged for the taxi to pick up Suzanne for the airport.

Then Suzanne went to the hospital. The final thing Suzanne did for Grandma Nedd was to grease and comb her hair, and after the bath dressed her in the cotton nightgown she had brought from Toronto. She tied her head with a white scarf and snapped a picture of her. A new, more realistic picture for her wall. Then she sat and watched her. Fully dressed, Grandma Nedd looked as though she were on a journey, just as Suzanne remembered her. At 10 o'clock the matron politely told her it was time to leave and suggested she should come back the next day. When Suzanne was leaving, Grandma Nedd stirred, as if sensing her departure.

"Good night, Grandma," she whispered, bending low to kiss her cheeks. "Good-bye."

Grandma Nedd twitched but didn't appear to wake. Suzanne patted her head and walked away. She carried the strong smell of Grandma Nedd's favorite bay rum with her. She smelled it all night.

THE SUITCASE IN the middle of the room looked almost as big as the house itself. This had to be the only explanation for why Suzanne was constantly tripping over the valise and the handbags stuffed with bottles of rum for Henderson and Bobby Ali. Suzanne didn't remember the house ever being so small, so cramped and so cluttered as if Grandma Nedd never threw away a piece of cloth, a biscuit tin or even broken furniture. The three pieces of luggage in the middle of the room appeared to have sucked up all the space in the house, leaving no leeway for walking or even for Suzanne to stretch out her feet. The last place she saw so cluttered had been Mrs. King's apartment, and perhaps Ona's room only once or twice.

This was not what she remembered about this house. The same way nothing on the island had been as she expected. This was not the Jamaica she carried around in her head and kept calling her home. Canada was so much bigger in every respect. She had grown used to the bigness and surprisingly, after only two weeks, she missed it. Jamaica was too confining. Suzanne was glad she'd taken the agent's advice.

Sitting in the little house in which she had grown up, she had time to think about what she would do when she returned home. Even the thought of calling Toronto home surprised her. After all, Jamaica had always been her home. She had come back to help nurse her Grandma Nedd back to health, the most important person in the world. So why was she so anxious to get away?

As she waited for the taxi, Suzanne wondered what had changed so much in the past ten years. So that she hardly recognized the things around her, or felt close to the people she'd always loved and respected. Why was the sound of the rain falling on the roof not as soothing and calming as she had remembered? The pitter-patter of the raindrops sounded too close to her head. The rhythm wasn't the same lullaby that had soothed her to sleep as a child. Why was it that the strange silence of the night made her crave the nonstop sounds of cities that never slept? Why did she feel so trapped in the middle of the night, when sleep deserted her, and there was nothing to do in this village but stay in bed and think? She always remembered how every night the drums played in the distant hills, their rhythms carried on the wind. Yet they were noticeably silent on her return.

THE TAXI TURNED into the hospital driveway. Suzanne got out and walked slowly through the casualty ward and up the stairs to the public ward. In another three hours, her plane was leaving. She stopped by the bed where her grandmother was sleeping, the one good foot moving as if in irresistible dance. She had to hurry so as not to miss the flight.

"I thought you're going back up today," the nurse said.

"I come to see her for the last time. But she's sleeping."

"Should I wake her?" the nurse asked and moved to shake her.

"No. No," Suzanne said. "Don't wake her. Just tell her I stopped by. Just tell her that her grandchild stopped in on the way to airport. Just tell her I love her."

"Why don't you tell her yourself," the nurse said. "She'd love to hear it from you herself."

"I can't. . . . Tell her I said good-bye."

"All right," the nurse said, relenting. "Have a safe trip." Suzanne gave the nurse a big tip to ensure continued good treatment. This was the least she could do for her grandmother.

INSTEAD OF TRYING to change back the last of her Jamaican money into Canadian currency, Suzanne went to the duty-free store at the airport to look for a special gift. She had to get something extraordinary for Telson, even if she didn't know how she'd get it to him.

With nothing else to do in Jamaica, she could not wait for the plane to take off. At the Toronto airport, she quickly cleared immigration and customs. The flight arrived an hour late and Bobby Ali still wasn't at the airport as promised.

"Probably in jail," she snorted. Suzanne thought of calling Henderson to ask him to come and get her.

"What the hell," she said. "I can't keep waiting for people."

Pulling her luggage behind her, she walked over to the stand for the downtown bus. That night, after she got home, the drums went crazy.

CHAPTER 20

THE SECOND SUNDAY back from Jamaica, Suzanne went to see Reverend Lucas, arriving midafternoon when she thought he would have time to talk with her. This was the only way she knew to confront her fears and apprehensions. The only way to stop herself from being pulled in two directions by some unknown force.

Suzanne knew it was time she came to terms with this internal struggle. It was not possible for her to continue living a life of deception, doing one thing at night and then disowning it by day. There had to be a consistent way of doing things. She had to remove the sense that she had to be someone different from the usual Suzanne to get ahead in Canada.

"Is it really true?" she asked haltingly as soon as she and Lucas had dispensed with the briefest of greetings. She was so anxious just to talk to someone capable of explaining everything. "I mean what the Bible says, that the sins of the fathers, and the mothers for that matter, descend on the children unto the third and fourth generation? I have a grandmother who used to tell me all these things were true."

"Ah, you're the young woman Mrs. King was so fond of,

aren't you?" he asked. "Mrs. King lived a full life. One of the few West Indians I've known who at the end of her days was able to say that her life was made so much better by coming to this country. Such contentment. Certainly there's a lesson in that."

The look on his face further confirmed in Suzanne's mind what Reverend Lucas meant with his seemingly innocuous statement. For a moment, she felt like turning around and walking away. This was definitely a futile quest. This man, although he was black and respected by Mrs. King, would never understand her. How was she to expect him to give her meaningful advice, to help her think through the things bothering her so much?

Suzanne looked around the empty and dark church, with the beam of light struggling through the stained glass. Why had she even given a second thought to Mrs. King's suggestion to make this visit? This place felt so bleak and alien, so sterile and foreign. Even the light from outside was struggling to pierce the darkness.

Since her arrival in Canada over a decade ago, this was the first time she had willingly turned to an establishment for advice. And it had taken a lot to arrive at this point. She knew she needed help. Help to reassess everything in her life; to re-examine many things she once took absolutely on faith. And by standing before this priest, she had turned to a church that had no real appreciation for the rituals and beliefs of her true religion, the Pocomania. How far did she have to go to get another opinion? At least she was willing to try to help herself, to explore beyond her limited circle and to follow the advice of Mrs. King.

But now, from Lucas's tone and the look on the face of this priest, Suzanne felt it might all be for naught. Obviously he didn't understand how much it was taking out of her just to make the visit. From the impatient way he was looking at the door, it was plain Reverend Lucas didn't realize how difficult a step this was for her, how she needed time to get it all off her chest. Not to be rushed by his glances at the door. She must have been crazy to expect anything different. Life was so confusing now. Nowhere to turn for advice. Nothing to help her think through all those strange ideas she had brought back from Jamaica, notions she had spent the two weeks in solitude wrestling with, but getting no further ahead on her own. It was so frustrating, she thought. It was impossible to get a clear grip on anything, on even her true feelings.

"I am not joking, Father Lucas," she said. As she talked, she wrapped the long floral dress from Jamaica around her. The dress fell loosely around her shoulders and hips, as if it were too big by two full sizes, as if she had lost too much weight since buying it.

Then she told him about Grandma Nedd. She confided in him, reaching out for a hand across the gulf. She asked him if she was bad or even evil for wanting Grandma Nedd to die quickly, in the care of the trained staff of a hospital, instead of having to return home and live in a small ill-equipped house. She would rather Grandma Nedd were to die right away, to simply walk up the stairway to the King's highway and glory, instead of hanging on and suffering only to die alone in the little cramped house. "That would be the ultimate curse, if you ask me," she said.

"Well, what do you really mean when you talk about a curse?" he asked. "Can you be more specific? I thought we were talking about something else. If your grandmother told you something specific and it is bothering you, why not let it out?"

Suzanne told him about Henderson and of her ambivalent feelings for this married man. She confided how much she feared she was headed uncontrollably for a relationship with Henderson, the ultimate fulfillment of Grandma Nedd's prophecy about the curse of the Nedd women. She didn't have the strength to break off the relationship, she confessed. "So I'm asking you if it's true that certain things in this life are set from

264

birth? Things that can't be changed no matter how much you try. Some people back home say that it can happen."

"Everyone is responsible for his or her own soul," he said, rather flippantly. "Remember the old Baptist spiritual:

> It's me, it's me, O Lord.
> Standing in the need of prayer.
> Not my brother; not my sister, Lord.
> It's me standing in the need of prayer."

"But what if there's a curse on you?" she had asked. "What if you feel you got jinxed? What if you feel your mother and your mother's mother carried the same curse, and you can't escape it?"

"How old are you, Suzanne?" he asked.

"Twenty-three next April. Why?"

"I'm just wondering why anyone as young as you should be having such terrible thoughts. You don't really believe in this idea of a curse, do you? Let's be realistic. I hope you are not using this talk about a curse to hide any shortcomings you might have. We might want to examine this avenue in our discussion. What do *you* say to that?" His voice was harsh and cold, so unexpectedly distant.

Slowly she rose from the pew and got ready to leave. Lucas knew he had hit a nerve, but showed no regret. How could she even try telling him about Joe and how what they did had always affected her? How could she broach the subject when this priest wouldn't even ease up, wouldn't give her a safe opening to raise the matter?

"I don't think you understand what I'm trying to do," Suzanne said, dropping her voice. "You just don't understand West Indians. We are not like you, black but Canadian born. You don't understand how we have to put up with changes. How we have to square the things they taught us back home with what we know we have to do to get ahead here. How we

265

have to learn things all over again, with nobody to show us anything."

"What is there to understand?" he shot back.

Suzanne couldn't continue. She was sure he wouldn't understand. How could he? He didn't know about journeying at Cross Roads well into the early hours of the morning, about singing and dancing under the single streetlight, about having the dreams of the runaway slaves and the Maroons conferred on you whether you wanted to accept them or not, about being sent out to realize those dreams without anyone to guide you beyond merely pointing you in what was assumed to be the right direction, about being left at the foot of the stairs of the plane. No, he wouldn't understand the heavy burden of the dream.

Suzanne walked out into the late summer sunshine no clearer in her mind than when she entered the church. But at least she knew she had tried to come to terms with her problem. Doing something, anything, was important. Perhaps it was the first tentative step to her finding a solution. She planned to return home and reinstate her self-imposed solitary confinement. Like in the dream where she was in the mourning room before setting off on the most important journey of her life. Except, unlike the dream, there was no pointer to assist her.

Without Mrs. King, she had hoped Reverend Lucas would play that role, become her Canadian pointer, but he couldn't understand her journey. She must return to her place of mourning, pull the curtains across, pray, meditate and examine herself, just as Daniel had done. No pleasant bread or wine would pass her lips. Until she received some definite sign of how to regain control, she must remain sequestered within the walls of her apartment.

CHAPTER 21

SUZANNE HELD HER head in her hand. She pulled some of the rolled braids, tugging the limp plaits at the roots, scratching her skull where it itched. After all this time, the voices were still flailing angrily, the same way the drums tended to take control by drowning out everything else.

Through squinted eyes, she saw the blur of the men standing in front of her. One was Bobby Ali; the other was Henderson. She adjusted her eyes. They were sensitive in the bright light. They had grown accustomed to all those days and nights in absolute darkness. Bobby had switched on the lights as soon as he came through the door. The sudden jolt gave her no time to prepare for the sharp bright flashes surging through her head. Now her head was spinning, as if everything that was settling down in her brain was again rising in upheaval. Why did she answer the intercom? She should have ignored it, the same way that until this morning she had deliberately refused to answer the telephone or apartment door buzzer. If anybody wanted her, they had to get past her answering machine first.

Unexpectedly, Bobby had shown up at her apartment that Friday night, five weeks after her return from Jamaica. His timing was impeccable. She was beginning to feel the need to get away from the drums and voices in her head. They had beaten her head hollow. She felt soft and tired. And she was beginning to weary of the journeying. Bobby Ali must have sensed something was wrong, that she was brooding. Or maybe after all these weeks he had suddenly remembered not showing up at the airport and wanted to make amends.

When he arrived, Henderson was there, having no success in trying to coax her out of the apartment. They had spent more than an hour sitting in the darkness. Letting Henderson into the apartment was the first sign she must have been weakening, Suzanne thought, as she watched Bobby going through the apartment flipping on lights. Bobby Ali was taking control. Not once did he stop upbraiding her for hiding out.

"A weekend like this, and you say you're staying home," he said. "With all this sweet music all 'round town. Millions of people from all over the world dancing on the streets, mashing down Toronto. And you say you're staying at home. Look, don't make me laugh. Get up off your arse and enjoy life. You coming with me. I ain't leaving you alone in this place. I know a Caribana fete that is just the thing for you. The medicine the doctor ordered."

"He's right, Suzanne," said Henderson, "you need to get out of this place."

Suzanne felt like telling them the only thing she needed was a tonic to help her completely reconcile her feelings about Grandma Nedd. But she was too washed up and weak to argue. She looked at Henderson and shrugged her shoulders, as if to signal that she no longer had the will to fight someone as persistent as Bobby Ali.

Up to then it had been a deliberately boring, but thoughtful withdrawal. Returning from the meeting with Basil Lucas, Suzanne felt her depression was heavier than usual. It was certainly more ponderous than before she had spoken with the priest. No matter how she tried to rationalize it, she still felt bad for having to leave Grandma Nedd. Yet she knew there was nothing more for her to do. At least physically; nothing beyond journeying with Grandma Nedd in the spirit, and waiting for the inevitable bad news. Every day she listened for the phone call from Jamaica, for Pastor Grant to leave a message on the answering machine because she knew she couldn't speak to him when he called.

It also bothered her that she had not talked to Ona. Somehow she was unable to bring herself to speak to Ona about her surprised discovery of the real grandmother, a woman so fragile and spent. To tell this to Ona was almost like revealing not only a part of Grandma Nedd but something personal about herself as well. Something still best kept hidden, at least for the moment.

And how much could she tell Ona without challenging even the images her mother had? The very recollections that kept Ona going in the face of her daily struggles. What right did she have to paint different pictures, even if they were drawn with words and images of an adult, about this woman who had such impact on both her and Ona? A woman who, after all, had to be different from them because of her times, experiences and accident of geography.

Suzanne didn't know how much to tell Ona, if anything at all. For these reasons, she felt guilty for not telling her mother the real story, the truth that was capable of shaping the memories of Grandma Nedd long after she was gone. For in the end, those precious thoughts would be the only agents keeping Mira Nedd alive and strong in their minds, their connection to the past and what gave them strength for the future. The memories and her teachings. Suzanne felt she had no right to tamper with this legacy. She had no right to help Ona select what parts of her mother she was going to keep with her, perhaps even to the very end of Ona's own journey.

Several times, Suzanne found herself thinking of how she would react to the unexpected news that Ona had died. What would she remember of her mother? And what could anyone say Ona taught her? The thought of Ona dying always startled

Suzanne. It was so different now from when she was a youth, when she barricaded herself in the bedroom and prayed to the true and living God to smite her mother.

Ona was her mother. Something physical and biological. These facts alone must count for something. There was an important blood bond, even if the channels of love had atrophied too early for them to be repaired. Still, a bond was a bond. The same had to be true for Ona and Mira Nedd. For in the achievements and deaths of a mother were the clearest reminders of an offspring's own limits and mortality. A clear indication of how far up the stairs the succeeding generation begins the next leg of the journey to the ultimate dream.

But beyond telling Ona the obvious news about her mother's ailment and of the poor long-term prospects, Suzanne didn't know what else to share with her about the woman she had rediscovered. She decided to leave the chore of explaining anything to Pastor Grant whenever he linked up with Ona.

With the decision made not to bother Ona with meaningless details, Suzanne began to feel her resolve to continue journeying waver. Suzanne felt the need to celebrate her grandmother's completion of a long and eventful voyage and of her own desire to let the outside world back in again.

"I've been looking all over for you. Everybody I talk to keep saying they didn't see you around. You ain't hanging out no more," Bobby was saying. "It's like Henderson here's been hiding you for everybody. I even checked at Filmore's and somebody say you ain't work there for a whole month now. And then when I call, you playing you ain't answering the damn phone. Where you've been all this time?"

"Nowhere," she answered softly. "And don't bother asking me no more questions. And if you want me to go with you to this Caribana fete, let me go and put on some clothes."

Getting dressed for the celebration allowed her to escape, if only temporarily, while she showered and prepared for her coming out. She didn't feel up to answering any questions, or to talking about Jamaica and her mixed feelings about everything. Spending three weeks, like Daniel, in solemn thought was enough for her. That stage of her journey had ended. A different Suzanne had to emerge. The real one. Or so she hoped.

"Wow, look at that rebel," Bobby said when she reappeared, dressed extremely provocatively, in the ways of the rebel women around Toronto. Henderson whistled appreciatively. The compliments lifted her spirits, making her feel alive again. As if her personality had snapped back, or another more fun-loving side had taken over. This was the way she felt after a really vigorous dance on the stage. When she heard the customers screaming and shouting for her to continue. When she felt the warm perspiration running down her body and her heart pounding in celebration. She pushed a black cap on her head and turned the peak backward. The sleeveless T-shirt was cut and frayed at the waist. The already short jeans were further rolled almost to her hips. A pair of running shoes and a small leather bag completed her attire. Henderson stepped aside to let her walk by in front of him.

"Now you look like the real Suzanne I know," Bobby Ali said. "None of this hiding-and-sulking business that you've been getting on with. No more o' that, you hear me? So, come let we party."

The house in the suburbs was already crowded when the three of them arrived. The music from mammoth speakers made the windows rattle and the cups and glasses clatter. It vibrated under her feet and reverberated through her body, like the numb tingling of electricity. Suzanne felt sorry for Henderson. He looked terribly out of place and self-conscious. By far, he was the oldest in the house and obviously the most awkward.

Maybe he did like her after all, she mused. Even to the point of exposing himself to possible ridicule from people half his age. All of this just to keep her spirits high. When she needed him, Henderson was always there for her, even to the exclusion of his family. Maybe she should stop giving him

271

such a hard time, even if he was still married. She must stop
thinking of how much he reminded her of Joe. Of how in
those really trying years with Ona, Joe, like Henderson now,
was the only person she could rely on. Even if she knew what
she was doing to get his affection and attention had been
wrong and sinful.

"Come and dance, man," Suzanne said, grabbing Henderson's elbow. Around them, the men and women were gyrating, bouncing and heaving gracefully to the music. The
rhythm seemed to do something to Suzanne, to transform her
again, making her lighter on her feet. With the long thin
straps of her clutch bag over her shoulder, she instinctively
found herself bending at the hips, dipping and grinding her
pelvic area against him. Next to her, a fat woman was bent
from the waist, touching her toes, while pushing her arse into
the groin of a skinny man, rubbing vigorously against him
with the most sexually explicit moves.

All around her people were having fun. They were shouting
and whooping, encouraging one another to be even more daring, egged on by the racing tempo of the music. Enthralled by
the intoxicating beat, the women in their extremely short
pants and skimpy tops were even less inhibited than the men.
Henderson was simply captivated by the movements. A broad
smile spread across his face and Suzanne felt good for him.
And for herself too. The dances he was watching reminded
him of growing up in the Caribbean, he told Suzanne. Reminded him of a time when he used to peer through the bars
of the windows of the dance halls to see the men and women
doing-bad on the inside. Back then, he recalled seeing men
and women tying the ends of their shirts and blouses together.
They would wind and grind their waists in unison, in a com-
petitive showdown, until they were on the floor. Until their
bottoms, and then their backs, swept the floor.

In those days, the older folks had told him these *worthless-
nasty* dances were brought over from Africa to Barbados. And
they moralized that self-respecting Christians would never be

caught dead conducting themselves so disgracefully in public. The saving grace of the Lamb had rescued them from this life and lowness. For, after all, this was the dance of slavery and backwardness, of the uncouth and uninitiated. But somehow this dancing had been preserved on every island in the Caribbean. And here in North America, so many years later, the young exports from these islands were carrying on in the same manner, and quite publicly, behaving no differently than the original slaves.

"I can't remember when last I see something like that," Henderson shouted to Suzanne. His eyes were drawn to one couple in particular. They looked to be hardly in their teens and were dancing at the edge of the crowd. Even when fully prostrate on the floor, the man still wriggled on his back and the woman squatted and jammed between his legs, like two snakes in mortal combat. Suzanne and Henderson stopped dancing just to admire the couple. Others must have been watching too. When the music, and the ritual dance, finished, everyone near the couple applauded loudly.

Another calypso started and the couple on the floor was instantly forgotten. "Get something and wave," the DJ exhorted. The horn music blared, the drums pounded, everybody screamed. A sea of hands swayed in the air and to the music. Looking around her, all Suzanne saw were hands. *Hands, hands everywhere.* Like those hands on the plane in the dream. And as in the dream, the hands were approaching her. Except that their reach seemed beyond her, reaching for some invisible flag that everyone wanted to touch and wave. And then she saw it. A flag just like the one hoisted by Pastor Grant at Cross Roads in St. Ann's. The same kind of flag with its colors of red, gold and green. All the hands were reaching for it, or saluting it from a distance or mimicking the actions of the flag as it drifted on the wind.

At the urging of the music and the DJ, the revelers were jumping, waving hands in the air, pumping and swinging or pointing their fingers toward the sky, all in symmetry. A frenzy took hold of the crowd with every drum solo. Every man, woman and child hopped up and down to the cascading rhythms, to the sweet nostalgic beat. Even as they swayed and hopped and jumped, they mimicked the movements of animals: the beasts of the wild, the panthers, the donkey and even the snaking conga line. *The prancing panthers*, Suzanne remembered. Pastor Grant had called them the blackest and proudest of the African animals. All around her people were acting like animals, no different from those under the light at Cross Roads in St. Ann's.

She heard the people grunting and saw them prancing. She found her own self also on the floor, some stranger locked between her legs, just dancing, with Henderson and Bobby Ali cheering her on. Around her the bass drums were pounding. *Boom, kcrack-uh boom. Boom, kcrack-uh boom. Boom boom.*

They were driving her on, daring her to dance and to be free. Back on her feet, she heard men humming from their chests the strains of the calypso and reggae. *A humba-humba humba. A humba-humba humba.* The women singing sweetly. And it was great. It felt so good, this mixture of her dream and reality all coming together on this one day. All serving to liberate her. Everything proving that she didn't have to hide or suppress one personality so that another might live. Grandma Nedd danced only for her God. But she also danced for liberation. On this day, Suzanne knew it was possible to do both.

Suzanne looked at the sweat on Henderson's face. He appeared fatigued. There was no way he could keep up with her. She just wanted to cut loose. Nobody was going to hold her back. Nobody was going to get in the way of her celebration of Mira Nedd. Dancing was the only way for her to pay homage to this dear old woman. Dancing was her only means of expression. Dancing was the only message Mira Nedd understood. She abandoned Henderson, leaving him dancing with a strange young woman who kept looking up into his face and smiling. With everybody jammed together so tightly, she thought, he was unlikely to notice she had disappeared. In the two hours since they'd arrived, another one hundred or more people had shown up, all of them marching straightaway onto the dance floor. The bodies created a rhythm that swept them along.

"Music sweet for so," a young woman said to Suzanne. She threw a handful of plaits off her face, momentarily revealing thin mixed Asian features and a long chin before the hair fell back in place. "This is Caribana, man. This is we culture. Too bad it's only once a year. This is when we can really be West Indian right here in this cold-arse Canada."

She pressed a container into Suzanne's hand. She took a sip and felt the sting of alcohol.

"Just wait 'til tomorrow morning when the parade begins downtown," the woman continued. "Real fun begins tomorrow, we'll start mashing down Toronto with we dance. From morning 'til night. We ain't sleeping. It's nice, nice, nice."

As far as Suzanne knew, this party never ended. About nine o'clock the next morning, the young woman and a group of friends took her back downtown for the annual Caribana parade. But even then, people were still arriving at the party. Along the lakeshore of the city, they joined hundreds of thousands of revelers dancing along the streets or behind the elaborate costume floats which depicted virtually every aspect of life. Even more people were lining the sides of the streets, standing on top of buildings, watching the parade and rocking on the spot. Around Suzanne was every color of the rainbow and much more. The colors created a vibrancy that was life itself. As if all these people had heard the command *Come Out* and had been resurrected.

Somehow Henderson found her. Even among the hundreds of thousands of people on the streets of Toronto she was unable to avoid him. And he was in a mood for dancing, a spirit that she had never seen in him. On his breath she sniffed the white rum he must have been drinking straight.

"Let's join in a band," he said. "No use standing here, just watching." Suddenly the doubts were returning. Suzanne felt tired and hungry. She had not slept during the night, she said. The all-night feting had left her hips and calves sore. Her lower back ached. And she wondered if Pastor Grant had finally called and left the message on the machine.

"I think I'll rest a while. So I can think what to do next," she said. "I'm still not too sure—"

"What you're talking about," he interrupted. He grabbed her hand and the swift current of bodies dragged them along. Henderson put his palms on Suzanne's shoulders, stepped into the arc created by his arms and legs and began jumping to the music. Every time he moved forward, she felt her bottom bang against his legs and waist. They must have danced for miles and hours. Under the broiling sun. Suzanne's toes were trampled at least a million times. But she felt exhilarated, tired, but yet renewed. She felt the demons of doubt vanish.

Several hours later, they collapsed in a park on the grass under a tree. Suzanne dropped her head on his chest and promptly fell asleep. One more section of the journey had ended for her.

CHAPTER 22

ONA ROLLED OUT of the bed and in frustration tossed the light blanket and sheet aside. One of her pillows was on the floor, and she flung it back onto the bed. Through the bedroom window, she saw the darkness outside and wondered why, on the only day she could really sleep in late, she had to wake up so early. There was just no explaining some things. But she just couldn't sleep any longer.

Ona stretched and yawned loudly. She felt rested but also agitated. Like those times, and it was happening with increasing frequency of late, when her body just crashed from exhaustion. When she fell into such a good, deep sleep, she did not remember dreaming and lost all sense of time and place.

When that happened, she usually awoke feeling refreshed. As if she had really slept. As if her body had decided it had stored up too much weariness. And it had to throw off some of this tiredness, because she had reached a threshold represented by a physical barrier that she could no longer press against. A specific point when everything just had to collapse physically and mentally. When her body took over its own administration and tried to unburden itself. After crashing, she was usually good for several months.

This morning was different. Yes, she felt rested. But today she felt as if something had awakened her. As if things had not run their natural course to the desired end. Something had purposely intruded to rob her of that which was so special. Again, she felt without control over her own life. The same way that at times she had no real say over when her body collapsed into a deep sleep. It was almost as if someone, something really, had awakened her abruptly, had decided without consultation that it was time to disrupt and to rouse her.

As soon as Ona became aware of the room and of being awake, she felt the numbness and cold chills from the dread and disappointment. It was a deep hollowness of expectations, the somber sensation that something untoward was about to happen, and that she had no say in the matter. She could only be on guard, to reduce the element of surprise when whatever it was happened.

For a while, she told herself that her body was probably fighting off a cold. The shivering and feeling of foreboding were just symptoms of a weakened body, tired and run-down; of her immune system calling on all its resources to beat back the invading viruses. That was why she felt a bit weak, a little down, the kind of feeling that always left her feeling deflated and hopelessly depressed. No, her body was only adjusting to some virus, she told herself without conviction. It couldn't be anything more. She must remember to wrap herself more warmly now that the seasons were changing and colds were in the air.

Going into the kitchen, she put on the kettle and watched the electric grill glow as it heated. Without bothering to turn on the lights in the kitchen, she rummaged through the cupboard. Her fingers searched among the half-empty packages of curry power, black pepper and baking soda, among other things, until they found a dried, hard piece of ginger. Ona cracked the ginger and smelled it to see if it still carried an aroma, if it had some potency. Satisfied that it could still offer flavor and healing, she dropped it into the cup and poured the boiling water onto it.

While the ginger tea steeped, she decided she might as well start preparing the day's lunch. A good Sunday lunch, something nice for Telson. Maybe a baked chicken. A small one, just enough to last the two of them no more than a couple of days. The little boy still wasn't eating any more than a wing or a drumstick and she would end up eating most of the chicken. Maybe she should cook some red beans and rice. Just like her mother used to cook on a day like this, on Sundays after church and the mingling with the brothers and sisters in Christ.

For some unknown reason, at that moment Ona found herself missing her mother most acutely. Maybe this was just another sign that she wasn't feeling too well. For it had been years since she actually *missed* Mira Nedd. A long time since she really felt like talking to her, wanted to discuss what they should cook for lunch, or just longed to talk about the ways of the world. She had received the information several weeks ago that her mother was sick in the hospital and every day the news stayed on her mind. Mira Nedd flashed into her mind so often. Of late, Mira even turned up in her dreams. Maybe that was why she couldn't sleep in this morning. Her mother had toyed with her all night. The only escape was to be awake, except that it left her feeling hollow, expectant and defeated.

Ona poured the beans from the package into a cup and then added the last of the hot water from the kettle. She also dumped in two heaping teaspoons of baking power to help soften the beans before cooking. God, she thought, how I wish I could afford a half-decent pressure cooker. Here I am in this country all these years, supposedly living in the lap of luxury, and I'm still cooking red beans the same way Mama would back home. Boiling them for hours and hours to make them soft, just like Mama taught me, when a pressure cooker would do the job so much better.

The smell of the ginger releasing into the water wafted through the kitchen. Ona put a spoonful of sugar in the tea and stirred it. She still had those chills, that feeling of dread. She knew the hot ginger tea would break the air in her stomach and make her belch. But that was all she could expect. It would not settle her nerves. It wasn't going to help her feel better, even if the heat from the cup and tea warmed her hands and chest.

Ona took the frozen chicken from the fridge, put it in a wooden bowl and placed it beside the beans soaking. For some reason, just looking at the beans and the chicken gave her a great urge for some good West Indian food. Maybe a piece of peppery jerked chicken with the rice and beans cooked in coconut milk and mixed with all those scallions, peppers, onions, pimento—all those extra ingredients Mira Nedd always added to a pot to make it smell and taste so good—would satisfy her urge. She had not tasted that type of food since Joe had disappeared to God knows where. It was food that Ona just didn't have the knack to master even though she knew all the ingredients.

From underneath the kitchen counter, Ona took out the plastic bottle of vinegar. She poured a generous portion of it on the chicken. She would let it thaw, with the vinegar, salt and the fresh juice from a green lime seeping into its bones. Then she would baste it with some jerk seasoning Joe had left in one of the jars in the cupboard.

Ona was covering the container and the chicken with a soup bowl when she heard the first knock on the door. Soft and intrusive it came, causing her heart to jump. She glanced at the clock on the stove and noticed it was 4:27 and wondered if Fanny had gone to a dance in the Hole and, on the spur of the moment, had decided to drop by on her way home. If it were Fanny, she must remember to tell her that the two of them weren't young yams anymore. They were responsible women. Instead of spending all night feting and dancing up, they should be at home resting their bones and sleeping.

280

The knock came again, louder. This time she thought she heard keys rattling, as if someone was trying the lock. Her heart leapt to her mouth in fear. Suppose this was the dread happening. At this very minute. The curse of the Nedd women's ability to predict things. That's why she had awakened feeling so frail and shuddering. The chills of expectation ran through her body. The same way she used to feel back home. The same kinds of feelings her mother described as a sign someone had just disturbed the eternal resting place and spoiled the sleep of the grave. Ona knew something was wrong, or that something wrong was going to happen, and now she was confronted by a possible burglar. Maybe some vile person had been watching her. And had noticed that she lived with only a little boy, no man to protect them, and was now coming to violate her, at the hour of the morning when she would be sleeping and most vulnerable. The muses were right to warn her, to awaken her, so she'd be ready.

The knocking came again, more urgently. The rattling of the keys was louder. Ona took up the cup of tea, just in case she had to defend herself by scalding the intruder. She advanced quietly to the door, walking on the balls of her feet. Holding her breath, she peeked through the spy hole in the door and almost dropped the cup when she realized who it was.

"What you doing out there at this hour?" she asked, opening the door and stepping aside to allow free entry into the apartment.

"Like you changed the locks on me, eh." Joe walked in, smelling smoky, looking tired, with a sheepish grin on his face. "Guess you never expected me back. So my old keys ain't no more use."

"You'd be the last person I'd expect to see at this hour."

"I was hoping you'd be up," he said, mashing off his shoes at the door. "I gotta talk to you."

"What 'bout?" Ona walked away, sipping the ginger tea. She curled up in her favorite position on the love seat and put

281

the cup on the floor. The tea tasted as if it needed more sugar, but Ona knew that would stifle the crisp taste of the ginger. Or maybe the ginger was too old, so that the tea was too weak. Her mouth still felt tasteless after a few good sips.

"I got lots to talk to you 'bout. But tell me, how come you never come looking for me? Not even once since . . . since you know . . . since . . . "

"What for? If you'd want to see me and your child, you'd come and check we out long time now."

"I was talking about, you know, it just ain't like you. At first after I left here, I thought: ah she's soon going to come after me. I don't mind telling yuh. But I was thinking all this time that you'd come along and talk about how the two o' we should get back together for Telson's sake. So that he won't grow up without a father to look after him. You know, all them things you always used to talk about. And I had all these answers ready for you, just waiting for yuh. But you never turned up. You really surprised me, I don't mind telling yuh that and—"

"People change, I guess," Ona interjected, sounding as if she were a little bored with the conversation. Yet she didn't have the urge to fight back and to order Joe out of the room. Another time she would have flown off the handle at him. How dare he just walk back into her life when it suited him, when he'd never sent one cent to support Telson, or helped her with the bills he left behind? But she felt too drained to argue with him. And anyway, it was her fault for opening the door. It was she who was breaking her solemn promise not to let this brute back in her yard.

But she couldn't just throw him out without hearing why he had turned up in the first place, what was on his mind that couldn't wait. There had to be a reason for Joe turning up at this hour. He said he wanted to talk to her. Maybe she should just surprise him and keep her mouth shut, not interject or tell him what was bothering her. Then he couldn't fling the accusation at her that she never listened to him, never gave him a chance to talk.

Ona picked up the cup again and took another sip. This time she did belch. Loudly. The sound seemed to surprise Joe, still standing as if he expected Ona to order him out of the apartment. Ona noticed a few other things that were strange about Joe. He was nervous and jumpy. His voice sounded husky, the way it always did when he was out with his friends smoking, drinking and probably gambling.

"I just ran into your daughter," he said. Ona could tell that Joe was still beating around the bush, that he still couldn't bring up what he really wanted to talk about.

"Where you see she now?" Ona asked, playing along with him, but also welcoming the news about Suzanne.

As he closed the door behind him, Ona noticed how small Joe looked, as if he had lost weight. His eyes moved around the apartment trying to come to terms with the changes since he'd been banished from the apartment. For a moment his eyes rested on the old family photographs of Ona, Suzanne, Telson and himself that were still on the walls. He seemed almost relieved that the pictures were still there, in the same spot right above the television.

"I saw she in St. James Town."

"I guess she's back in town, then," Ona replied. "When did you see she?"

"About a hour ago."

"Bitch. She was probably out working the night," Ona said. "I don't know what's going to come o' that girl. A young woman like that got no right coming home at this hour of the morning."

Purposely, Ona continued to talk calmly, hardly raising her voice or showing any traces of annoyance at this intrusion. She noticed how Joe tried to hide the puzzled look on his face when he had to prick his ears to hear her, and even had to ask her to repeat some statements.

283

"Boy, you sure are different tonight," Joe said. "On my way over here, I keep thinking you was going to give my arse one good cussing and I probably deserve it. To tell the truth, I was hoping to ease in here and stretch out on the floor over there without you even knowing I was in the apartment until the morning. Except that when I turned up, I found out you changed the damn lock on the door. My keys ain't no more use, just like how I don't have the key to your heart no more, eh."

"Was that supposed to be funny?"

"See what I mean," Joe said. "You really changed, girl. I mean, I don't even know if I can tell you what I got to tell you. I don't know if you'd even care, or even try to help me."

"What's wrong?" she said, again speaking slowly and measuring her words.

Although he had tried to joke about it, his hesitancy showed that Joe still couldn't put his finger on what was so different about Ona. Something kept telling him that a piece of the puzzle was missing. No longer did he hear in her voice the tone or edge of the impatient woman who was always egging him on, taunting him to reach higher and further and to be a real man. Now, maybe because of the hour of the morning and the lingering drowsiness from sleep, there was abandonment in her voice, a cry of resignation almost as loud as his.

"I don't know why I didn't do like all them other mothers with own-wayish children. I should've send she right back home when it looked like things weren't working out," Ona added. "But I keep trying and trying, always hoping things would turn around."

Joe said nothing, letting her talk, allowing her to take the pressure off him by indicating when she wanted him to add to the conversation. Obviously she was more concerned about Suzanne than about any of his problems. So maybe he should not keep pressing and trying to interest her with his problems. Later in the day, after he had some sleep and a chance to think and plan, he would try again. By then, he hoped, the old

284

Ona would have returned. The Ona that was forever cussing his arse, the one he now missed so much.

"Out on the streets at this hour. The police don't even care who they shoot," Ona said. "Look at how they shot that young black woman right in her car, and now she's crippled. The same kind o' thing is happening all over the place. Like in Montreal, with the police handcuffing that young man and then taking target practice at his head, only to get off later before some tribunal."

To Joe, the words and the voice were the same. But the fighting spirit was missing. It was like a part of Ona had died and she was merely mouthing stock speeches.

"I can't keep worrying my head. I just hope it's better when Telson gets bigger, 'cause I can't afford to lose him too."

"How's it without Mrs. King to help out with Telson?" Joe asked, again searching for a way to her.

"Tough."

Ona spread a blanket over her feet and sipped from the cup.

"Real tough. By the way, Mama back home sick bad."

"Yeah?" he asked, sounding not too interested.

"Real sick."

"You know, I want to have a good talk with you. Maybe we can still make a go at it if we get back together. I was thinking that the three o' we can go out to eat a little bit later today. And that afterwards me and you and Telson could go walking in the park. So we can talk and discuss things. You know, try doing some things together that we never had the time to do."

"The last time I talked to Pastor Grant from back home, he said Mama ain't looking too good, so you know what that means," she continued. "And the thing about it is that I'm too shame to even let Pastor Grant know that I haven't been able to tell that daughter of mine what is happening to her grandmother. How can I let Pastor Grant know that me and that girl don't even talk, that I don't even know where to find her? So that whenever he calls and I think he's going to say something

285

about Suzanne, I have to change the topic real quick and try to get him off the phone. Well, I'm glad to hear you say you see she a short while ago. Maybe she'll get some o' them messages I, like a damn fool, keep leaving on the answering machine. And maybe she'll call me back."

"As I was saying, maybe we can start doing a few things together. Things that you never had time for because you and me was always too busy."

"You mean things that you never wanted to do," she shot back. "At least not with me."

"Maybe it was me. But you know I was thinking that you're the only person I can turn to in this whole world when things get down. As I was trying to tell yuh, I might be in a spot o' trouble. I might need some help from you again, 'cause you're the only person that could help me. I might have to ask yuh to lend me a bit o' money, you know to pay some debts, but I'll pay you back."

"Well, now she's back in Toronto, I hope she'd pick up the phone and call me before she talks to Pastor Grant and he finds out the truth, that me and she don't even talk so I couldn't tell her the news earlier. Maybe I'm getting lucky tonight. First you show up out of the blue. So maybe Suzanne will surprise me and call."

"Boy, you can cut that sarcasm with a knife," Joe said. "Anyway, as I was saying, I got to find a bit o' money to pay back some money I borrowed. Otherwise I'm in trouble."

"What trouble you talking 'bout?"

"I'll tell you. But not now."

"Tell me now."

"I'm too sleepy and tired from hanging out with the boys." Joe dropped his voice, as if failing to accept a challenge. "In any case you sound like you got other things on your mind."

"You and them boys." Ona sucked loudly on her teeth. "None o' them ain't no good. But suit yourself."

"We'll talk later."

Testing his limits, Joe avoided having to explain his situation by retreating into the bedroom. When unchallenged, he stripped and dropped into the unmade bed. Joe noticed Ona had repositioned the bed, perhaps her way of expunging the memories of him and that woman on the bed. He also noticed that the picture of the two of them was missing from the wall. Joe wrapped his hands around Ona's pillows and crushed them against his face. Ona's unique smell was all over the sheets and pillow. He buried his nose in the smells and got comfortable. And he closed his tired eyes in a desperate bid to suffocate the night's bad memories. It had been a long, tough night. Yet he knew the worst was still ahead. He had to tell Ona about the gambling and the TTC money. But first he had to wait until both he and Ona were in the mood for such a discussion.

ONA WAS DOZING when she heard the firm, authoritative knocking. She fumbled in the closet for a housecoat and wrapped it around her. Peeking through the peephole in the door, she was startled to see two burly policemen, their caps and faces distorted by the lens. Her first thought was that Suzanne was in trouble. Otherwise why would they be knocking on her door so early in the morning?

"Mrs. Morgan," one of the policemen said. "We're looking for your husband, Joe Morgan. We thought we saw him come into this building a short while ago. Is he here?"

"What'd he do?" Ona asked, admitting the men.

"Theft from his work," the policeman answered. "When you gamble big and lose, you better be using your own money."

"Shit," Ona said. One of the policemen walked past her and headed for the bedroom.

"His pants are on the floor by the door," the policeman said.

"Please," Ona said. "Look, he's sleeping. There ain't no

way out of the bedroom but through this door. Let me go in and wake him. Let him put on some clothes before you arrest him."

"Why?"

"You know. He does sleep . . ." She lowered her eyes.

"Naked?"

She dropped her voice. "Yes."

Ona walked into the bedroom. Probably sensing her presence, Joe turned on his side and mumbled something, saliva running out of the corner of his mouth. Bending over, Ona touched him, for the first time since they'd parted. Gently she shook his shoulder and whispered his name.

"Joe, Joe, get up," she said. "Some people here to see you."

He sprang from the bed with such force he almost knocked Ona to the floor. Seconds later the policemen were on the bed, restraining him.

Telson came into the room to see the policemen dragging away his father, naked and handcuffed, with Ona trying to put a pair of pants on him.

"Where they taking you, Daddy?" the boy asked.

"Daddy will be back soon," Ona said.

When they were gone, Ona held the child and cried. And she hugged him for a long time. When he eventually ran away to play, she remained seated on the edge of the bed, her mind whirling. Apart from Telson's voice, no sounds intruded into her apartment, not that of the radio or the television. The only noise she wished to hear was the ringing of the telephone.

She knew what she had to do, the only thing she could do, when the phone rang. She planned to tell whoever it was that she had decided. On principle, she was going to tell them, she could not bail Joe out nor even provide money for a lawyer. Not after what she had told her own daughter. She had the arguments and answers all sorted in her head. She had no choice. The same way she had to harden her heart against Suzanne, had ruined their relationship by sticking to her word. Principles were principles, even for Joe.

She was taking the chicken out of the oven when the phone finally rang. Ona took a deep breath, preparing herself for the voice asking her to help Joe. Instead, she heard the static and the unmistakable echo of a long-distance call. The feeling of dread was almost overpowering. She could feel something moving in the pit of her stomach, her legs trembling, the breath gushing through her mouth and nostrils. The operator was asking if she was Ona Morgan. A Pastor Nathan Grant was calling collect from Jamaica.

"Mama," she whispered at the first sound of the pain in Pastor Grant's voice. And thoroughly deflated, she started crying all over again.

CHAPTER 23

PASTOR GRANT WAS pleasant but firm in summoning Ona home. Mira Nedd's mantle awaited her, he said.

"As soon as I'm finished talking with you, I will take up the old bell I got sitting on that table over there and I'll give it one good ringing," he said. His sorrowful voice was just loud enough for Ona to hear it over the static from the distance.

Ona listened in respectful silence. She heard and felt every painful word as if Pastor Grant were standing in front of her bouncing words carefully aimed at her, like a ball off the wall. Words that hit sore and bloodied spots, striking so many strategic sites on her body she didn't have enough hands to protect and cover them.

"As is our custom," he said slowly, measuring every word, stretching out every syllable, "I shall turn to the four corners of the earth. And I shall ring my bell to my heart's out to summon home our dearly departed sister. Such is my duty to an elder, as an anointed leader. With my bell, as old, tired and worn as me itself, I shall call the flock from all over the world to come home. Everybody must come to celebrate a great and wonderful life. And with my bell, I shall remind those that have reached the end of the journey ahead of us to reach across the River. To welcome your dear mother with open arms. To hide her in the bosom of Abraham until she has rested from this crossing."

"My poor mother," Ona heard herself whispering.

"Yes," he continued. "I shall ring my bell as a message to those in the land of the living too. To start the dancing and to prepare for the feast, the sustenance to keep them going until we have completed the journey of our forefathers and mothers. My bell and the flag I shall raise, the flag of the undisputable conqueror, will fly over the church and over your mother's home. That's my duty as a man of God and a true friend of the family."

"I understand," Ona said.

"But there's only so much I can do, Ona. Your mother was special, very special to all of us. Many things she did will not die with her. They must be carried on. And as a man of God I must tell you, Ona, even in this hour of personal sadness and physical loss, that it is incumbent upon you to come back home and see that your mother receives the sleep of the saints, the peaceful rest of those who know their work is ended and who can say my Lord, my God, my soul is ready, for I have made the crooked road straight. I've helped the blind to see, I've washed the feet of travelers and I've passed the torch into hands that are perhaps better than mine."

Ona answered the call. She had no choice but to return home to perform the age-old final rites and duties to her mother. Only she could oversee the special Pocomania wakes, the fasting and then the celebrations of dancing, the drinking of overproof rum and feasting that had been handed down over the centuries from her African forebears.

So it was Ona who, at the appointed hour, reached for one of the bottles on the table and unscrewed the cap to officially start the mourning and rejoicing. It was she who let the rum fall to mix with the dust, all the while thinking: dust we were even before the beginning and to dust must we return. It was she who respectfully offered the first drinks from the first bottle to the unseen guests and visitors that answered the summons of the bell; she who gave generous first sips to the four corners of the room, while everyone watched as the stains from the rum spread across the floor in various shapes, all forms of animals recognizable and unknown, creatures of this world and the one into which Mira Nedd was newly born, the final mixing of past, present and future.

And in the middle of the night, she was the one to carry out the crucial ninth-night ritual. She tossed her mother's old coconut-fiber mattress out of the house in final liberation. With this act, she told her mother's spirit that it was no longer to remain in the abode of the familiar. It had to set off fearlessly on its final journey into the spirit world with the full assurance that all was well with those left behind, that the mantle had been passed on and accepted, that the diadem had found a new head to adorn.

Heaving the cumbersome bed through the window, Ona told her mother that she had become the new mother, the font of wisdom and caring, and that Mira Nedd was now somebody else's child. The cycle was complete yet again. The curse and the blessing were ready to be repeated, or to be lifted in reprieve of the next generation. Ona had completed the transformation. She had done a daughter's job.

Ona's last act before returning north was just as significant. She could not leave without one last visit to her mother's final resting place. At the grave site, four days after tossing out the mattress, with Telson running among the plots reserved by the government for the poorest, Ona received the message that her mother would be unable to rest peacefully until the two of them were reconciled, until Ona was ready to complete the journey her mother and her ancestors had started. Until she too had prepared herself as the next in line to accept and embrace the bitter gall. Even from the grave, Mira Nedd seemed to be telling Ona that she did not want this to be the end, that

292

she wanted the cycle to continue, that she wanted Ona to be happy in accepting her wishes.

Ona stood silently at the grave, admiring the flowers still fresh because of the rain, looking at the mound that gave off a fresh, earthy odor. She listened to her mother and to herself too. Occasionally she heard a happy squeal from Telson as he tripped over clumps of dirt or ran after a butterfly. Every time she heard her son's laughter mixing with the effusive chirping and singing of the birds, mingling with the wind in the trees around the graveyard, she said to Mira Nedd: "Mother, you pinching or you tickling the poor child?" And every time she asked, she heard Mira Nedd, and possibly the wind, chuckle.

Later that night, alone in her mother's house, Ona felt herself being absorbed into the room. She liked the smell of things around her: the flowers, the books, the old musty papers and the rotting wood flooring. She liked the quietness broken only by the chirping of the crickets and whistling frogs. And she liked the feel that things were small and controllable, that she was the center of everything. The next day, she and Telson were leaving for Toronto and its problems. Toronto with Joe possibly still in prison, with Suzanne too busy working the streets to take time off for her grandmother's funeral.

Toronto was always out of control. Here, this little porous shack with every downpour rotting the wood, was home. And yet it wasn't. She had been away too long. Were she to die on this island, she could not possibly expect the same number of people at her funeral or for them to venerate her as they had her mother. Not in the way they had come from far and wide to crowd the church and to wave Mira Nedd on to another world. In this manner, Ona could not compare herself to her mother, no matter how much she accepted the mantle entrusted to her.

These people knew her mother intimately, in a way they would never know Ona. They unquestioningly accepted Mira Nedd as part of their community, these people from whom her mother drew strength; friends and acquaintances who, with a smile in the morning or a nod in the evening, indicated that, like all of them, she was just as important as one of the rocks Pastor Grant put on the white cloth in the center of the circle. When they sang at her funeral, danced every night of the wake, they celebrated a life they knew and shared. A life that for Mira Nedd's only daughter, was filled with too many blank spots.

Ona acknowledged that she would never be accepted back fully. So why had the leadership role been passed on to her? She had been tainted by life abroad and she had not put in the consistent years of being part of this community. The Ona that was being groomed for this very day had stopped receiving the training, stopped melding with the society, when she went overseas. She was out of synchronization. Even if Ona were to pull up stakes and return to Jamaica for good, she could not really come back and step, as if from a dream, into this community and start functioning as an important member, much less a leader. She would have to adjust again, or readjust. Re-accept the cultural heritage she had thrown off. It would be so difficult, because her personal reacceptance was not guaranteed, because she would always see things through different eyes, would always be skeptical and unbelieving of some things the community would require her to accept by faith alone. She could come back to live in this village; but she must be willing to accept that she would be subjecting herself to a life of isolation, constantly having to pass one test after another to prove she had successfully renounced her foreign ways, that she had reclaimed the Ona of her childhood. She was like one of the Old Testament prophets called to be a leader, knowing that the leadership was despised, that the leader was condemned to walk in the wilderness with a rebellious and unsympathetic crowd a mere arm's length behind. She would be like Mrs. Small, the teacher the children called Miss English Woman, never fully trusted, a foreigner in her own land.

Mentally, Ona knew she was not ready for this challenge. To attempt another change. Ona had seen the effects of such makeovers on the faces of the few friends she knew from Toronto, people who had returned home for whatever reason. There was something, some small way in which they approached her, or hugged her, that signaled that this was really their community—the outsiders trying to make it back in. They didn't have to tell her how difficult it was for them to readjust, to compensate for the blanks in their personal development while overseas. Of course, they joked, the readjustment could be eased if they all had money and were able to sedate themselves with wealth and travel.

It was the members of this outside community who unintentionally broke Ona's heart by telling her that Suzanne had been back to look after her grandmother. They talked about what a good job Suzanne had done, how Ona had to be pleased that when she couldn't get away Suzanne had leapt in and done such a commendable job. All the time Ona had to act as if she weren't hearing the news for the first time. She had to swallow the disappointment that Suzanne never bothered telling her anything, not even that she knew Mira Nedd was sick.

"Suzanne really did a great job," Mrs. Small had said, not realizing how every word was piercing Ona's heart. "You should be proud of her, you know. Looks like she's turning out to be a real responsible young woman. She did represent you well and she did love her grandmother."

"Umm," Ona said. "I know. I know." What she really wanted to say was that she finally knew that Suzanne would never be her daughter. Ona had no choice in the matter. She had to admit it: Mira Nedd was really Suzanne's mother. That was how Suzanne saw it. With that admission, Ona felt the coldness of failure overtaking her body, the chills from the final realization that she and Suzanne could never ever be close, would never bridge the gap. Otherwise, how could Suzanne have done this to her? How could she return to the island without telling her? How could could Suzanne then re-turn home to Toronto without telling Ona what had hap-pened? Strangers had to tell her. How could she? Ona asked herself. How could Suzanne reject her so?

Ona had no illusions as to what she was going back to in Toronto: a life on the periphery, stuck in a no-man's land of never being fully West Indian and yet not Canadian. Toronto would never be home. No place in North America could be home because it was not bred in her bones. Once you arrived as an adult, nobody was willing to extend the hand of friend-ship to draw you into their inner circles and clasp you to their bosoms. Ona missed out on the excitement of feeling like a vi-tal part of that community, from feeling that Toronto needed her, like the people of St. Ann's needed Mira Nedd. Her mother had lived, not merely resided, in St. Ann's. This would always be her predicament; once she left home she cut those umbilical ties forever; but she could not find a replacement in her adopted land because she would always be the outsider.

This wasn't a problem for her alone, Ona thought; it was for every immigrant she knew. Every one of those imports arriving with a suitcase full of clothes and a head full of dreams paid this price; must have found themselves, even decades later, stretched out in bed in the dead of the night, asking Why am I here? All the time knowing that each passing minute made a return to the old country even more difficult.

Were it not for Telson, she would not even entertain the thought of going back to Toronto. Her home, spiritually and otherwise, was in this little wooden shack. But the future had to be with her financial home in Toronto—not *her* future be-cause it had all been spent—but the hopes and aspirations for Telson, the one person she could not afford to lose.

In the distance, Ona heard the drums beating softly. The Rastafarians were up to something. The violence of the rhythm was gone, but the melody floated on the air. In a few hours, she would be returning to Babylon. Ona's feet instinc-tively began to respond; she felt what must have been a firm hand on her waist. It gently pushed her out of the chair and into the center of the room with the boxes, broken chairs and musty-smelling books and magazines. Ona danced. Not once did she feel she was dancing alone. She held out her hand as if holding a partner and she moved effortlessly as the partner glided on air, guiding her, dipping her, just leading her. She danced and abandoned herself to her own music, to the voices and memories in her head and in her heart, to the harmony of the Rastas floating on the wind. Holding Mira Nedd close, she tried to merge with the apparition, to become one with it.

On the plane back, Ona cried. She was tired and spent. And she wished to God that she would not have to wait until it was too late, until death itself, for her own chance to be at one with Suzanne. For she knew she was bound to regret always that she had stayed away from Mira Nedd so long. Too long before she celebrated the dance of peace with her mother. She did not want this for her daughter. And it was somewhere over the Atlantic Ocean, that vast body of water that over the years had separated and drowned so many millions of her people and their dreams, when it was as dark down below as in the hold of the first slaver, that the thought first occurred to her: maybe there was a reason for passing the leadership to her. Maybe it wasn't intended for her to journey among the people of St. Ann's, but perhaps among the lost souls in the new Ninevah, that great city Toronto.

ONA LEFT HOME early, not knowing whether she was going to work or to court. Common sense told her to go to work and secure the only thing she still had. If she jeopardized her job, what would happen to Telson? Would the little boy turn out like his sister, another delinquent, or like his father, simply lost? She ought to be putting what strength she had into saving the little boy. Realistically, she knew she should simply abandon everything so that Telson, despite his sex and color, would

297

not be part of that group heading for extinction through an early grave or prison.

"I can't let Telson turn out like Joe," she murmured to herself. "I can't let him grow up like all them worthless men, those damn lowlifes who simply gave up on the struggle. No, I can't let that poor child become like all those people so willing to accept their place as the misfits in this society. That's not for my Telson. I want him to grow up and learn. Telson has to learn the tricks of surviving in this country."

But she also had a duty to Joe Morgan. When he knew the noose was tightening, he had returned to her. Ona had refused to put up Joe's bail because she just couldn't. She hoped that someday he understood that principles were principles. Fortunately, Joe had gotten hold of Suzanne. She had managed to scrape together the four thousand dollars from God only knew where. In any case, the money Ona would have tied up with the bail had been needed for the funeral.

On this morning back in Canada, it wasn't easy to make any decison, let alone the right one. In the six weeks since she'd returned, the peace of mind and confidence Jamaica and the funeral had brought her had long evaporated. So had the clarity with which she saw some things. Ona wanted to help Joe, but she lacked the will and confidence to make a decision. The self-doubt was deeply embedded in her. Everything she had touched over the years had gone sour, as when unwashed hands touched pure milk.

Ona felt jinxed. Everything in her life proved it. Both in Jamaica and in Canada. Her daughter didn't even contact her anymore, not even after she had swallowed her pride and left a message about Mira Nedd's death and funeral on her answering machine; her husband was before the courts, angry with her and living where she didn't know; her son was facing a life in a strange country without family.

Ona walked the streets with her head in a fog. Her eyes settled on a sign atop a little house. The flashing lights beckoned her. A woman was standing in the doorway, smiling, as though she had been waiting for Ona.

"Here, take this," the woman said, handing Ona a yellow piece of paper. "Read it. Come and see me. I can help you. You are not alone with your troubles, my sister."

Ona took the paper and stuffed it in her coat pocket. Her legs felt tired from the long walk. Her face stung from the winter cold. Her heart felt as if it would burst. When she went into a doughnut shop for a coffee and was searching for change, she pulled out the leaflet. She read about the amazing works of Mrs. Jumpter, *"gifted card & palm reader & adviser on all problems of life."* The telephone number, address and hours of business, 9 A.M. to 10 P.M., were displayed in a poorly designed circle, representing the signs of the zodiac, the same ones she had seen on tracts by her mother and Pastor Grant.

"Lucky days & lucky numbers," she read. *"Mrs. Jumpter tells all. Readings confidential. Guaranteed help within days."*

Ona immediately thought of her mother and of all those people who had come to her with troubled dreams. She couldn't resist the urge to go back to Mrs. Jumpter, if only to get some idea of what kind of life was awaiting Telson. At that point, she cared absolutely nothing about herself.

"There's no problem so great she can't solve. Tells you how to hold your job when you've failed, & how to succeed," Ona read.

Back home in Jamaica, some people had claimed to have the power to predict the future. The obeah men claimed the power, as did Pastor Grant, who always relied on a mystical revelation to help solve problems. Her mother had sworn such things were possible and that this all-knowing gift, as part of the family curse, was handed down from mother to daughter in the Nedd family, the same way a queen passed down her treasures in African matriarchal societies. Maybe Ona had fooled herself all these years by pretending she didn't believe that her mother and Pastor Grant knew what they were talking about. For even in Canada, wasn't she always the head of her family, seemingly awaiting her mother's mantle even in this strange land? Wasn't it preordained then that men would never stick around them because the Nedd women always had to be the head of their homes, because the men always felt overpowered? Her mother had said so.

Ona looked at the paper in her hand. Now, here she was living in a supposedly more sophisticated society and someone was claiming to have the same powers as Pastor Grant, her mother and the obeah men. Someone to show her the way, a kind of John the Baptist, perhaps preparing her, this reluctant messenger, for her rightful calling.

"Calls your friends & enemies by name without asking you a single question. Tells you your troubles & what to do about them. Reunites the separated. Upon reaching womanhood & realizing she had God-given powers to heal, Mrs. Jumpter devoted a lifetime to this work. Removes evil influence."

Ona's mother, God bless her soul, and Pastor Grant had used the very same language. When Ona closed her eyes, she could hear them echoing these words on the tract.

Mrs. Jumpter was sitting at a table, eating a sandwich and drinking coffee, when Ona showed up. A bell tinkled softly as she pushed open the door. The woman stood up to greet her. A large colorful flag, which Ona didn't recognize, was spread and pinned on the wall behind her. When Mrs. Jumpter sat, it looked like the end of the flag was brushing the crown of her head. No sooner did Ona sit down at the table than Mrs. Jumpter reached out to pat her hand and told her not to despair about her little boy.

"How do you know I got a little boy?" Ona asked. She was baffled that this stranger could zero in on her most troubling concern.

"I know many things," Mrs. Jumpter said confidently, her voice soothingly soft. "But that's not important. What's important is that times are tough right now. They'll get better. You have to make some decisons and pretty soon." She patted Ona's hand reassuringly, like an older sister knowingly coaching another through the most painful point of childbirth. "Listen to your heart. You've been running away from something all your life, but you can't run forever. You shouldn't pretend to be different."

"I know," Ona whispered, accepting her sentence the same way Joe Morgan was submitting to the court miles away.

"Every one of us has been placed on this earth for a purpose," Mrs. Jumpter said, looking Ona straight in the eyes, staring into her soul, stripping away the guilt, fear and indecision. "You have a purpose on this earth. You will never be happy until you stop running, until you stop denying."

"How will I know what that purpose is?"

"In your heart, you already know," Mrs. Jumpter said. "But God will send you another signal, a reminder. It will happen very soon. Don't ignore it. Come and see me again. I will help you to cross that river."

Ona paid the suggested fee for five visits, taking advantage of the twenty-percent discount, and walked back out into the cold morning. Only on the outside did she pause to reflect that the woman had actually given her a receipt for professional services. This was so unlike Mira Nedd, who never accepted money for her readings, for it was a gift from God to be shared freely, although occasionally she would accept a cock or a dozen eggs or a few yams and potatoes merely as a token of appreciation, but definitely not as payment. "What the hell," Ona mumbled dismissively. "This is Canada, North America." Now she knew that everything, including even the gifts of God, had a cost.

On the street, a man approached her and pushed a religious tract into her hand. "Take this," he said in a tone so similar to Pastor Grant's last summons. "This is my last one. You must read it and open your heart. The Lord God will show you the way." Just as quickly he disappeared. If it hadn't been for the pamphlet in her hand, Ona might have thought him a figment of her imagination.

She stared at the brochure. "*A prodigal son returns*," it said.

"There comes a time when we must stop running from the true God. We must stop and listen." Ona read the entire pamphlet on the spot. This was a genuine signal, another one. The signal she had been waiting for. The big sign Pastor Grant and Mrs. Jumpter had told her about. She knew it. This had to be it. Otherwise, why had this man been waiting for her, keeping the very last flyer just for her?

Ona didn't go to the courthouse. Nor did she return to work. She went home, took out her Bible and spent three weeks steadfastly reading the scriptures, waiting for God to send her another signal. Even visits by the Children's Aid Society investigators, checking on what they said were complaints of a naked, dirty and hungry child running through the apartment building didn't faze her. She was through dealing with these representatives of Caesar and told them so. She had no choice but to return to the things she had rejected in the hope of making it in Canada. She had no choice but to strip away all the masks she had packed on top of her real self, on the Ona that in Jamaica had been baptized and chosen. The real Ona that never died despite attempts to smother her, to lock her away, to pretend she no longer existed.

Her life had been a failure, particularly her time in Canada. And there was a reason for this failure: she had strayed too far from her teachings, tried to become the person that in her soul she wasn't. The only thing salvageable was her faith, what she had known all along, from those days when dancing in the House of the Lord and at the old school had brought her so much pleasure.

Without a job, Ona committed her life and well-being fully into the hands of her God and the city's welfare department.

CHAPTER 24

SUZANNE AND HENDERSON joined the crush of people at the entrance to the Eaton Centre where they had gone to buy a few gifts, primarily to pick up something for her little brother, Telson. She also intended to use the Christmas present as an excuse to visit her mother. Ona had at least made the effort to leave Suzanne a message about Grandma Nedd's death. Maybe she could try seeing Ona again.

In the south mall they ran into Bobby Ali and a group of youths. She gave him the usual high-five hand slap and he didn't leave her hanging. It was some weeks since they had seen each other. "We're casing a few places for a smash-and-grab tomorrow," Bobby had whispered to Suzanne. "If you want to join us, you know for some quick money to pay for all them Christmas gifts you buying, meet we here at three o'clock. On the dot. You know, in the Christmas Eve rush, anything we do has to be a breeze."

Before she responded, a familiar voice and the ritualistic ringing of the bell caught her ear. The shrill shouting bounced around the cavernous building, seemingly out of harmony with the clamor and rhythm of the place. Suzanne also noticed people hurrying away from its source, unwilling to take the harangue.

"Good Lord," Bobby Ali said. "Look, it's your mother. What the hell she's doing now?"

"Preaching," Suzanne replied. She was totally amazed by the sight of her mother.

Wearing a shabby white dress, so unlike the pristine clothes of the Spiritual Baptists or the Pocomania back home, Ona was prancing up and down the mall, waving a Bible above her head, a bell in the other hand, shouting at anyone willing to tolerate her presence. Around her head was a scarf in the familiar colors of red, yellow and green. All that was missing was the drumming.

"These are the last days," Ona cried out. She looked utterly weary, as though she were running on some inner strength, maybe on a power she didn't even know she had. From her looks, undoubtedly Ona's body wanted to go home and to go to sleep. But Suzanne could tell that something was driving her on, the same source from which the gibberish was spewing forth.

"Put your faith in the Lamb of God that taketh away the sins of the world," she shouted. "Don't put stock in material things, searching for this thing we like to call the better life, believing it will satisfy your heart. Listen to me: Silver and gold hath I none. Like the three wise men, I'm on a long journey to save souls. And I can't turn back. Not until I'm at the very end."

Three security guards, dressed in brown jackets and blue trousers, closed in on Ona. Gently but firmly, they escorted her through the mall's doors designated for staff only. The crowd returned to its shopping as though nothing had happened, but obviously relieved to be free of this intrusion. Suzanne could not recover from the shock. She rested on a bench to recompose herself.

Soon the astonishment gave way to a great sense of sympathy for her mother. For the first time in so many months,

Suzanne felt pity for her, for her mother in such condition mentally and physically. The image of Ona, filthy, with long dirty fingernails, was indelibly marked on her mind. This was definitely not the Pocomania Grandma Nedd had taught them. This image, although somewhat familiar, wasn't right, as if Suzanne had found herself in the wrong dream. She was unable to put her finger on what was so wrong with the Ona she had just seen.

"Preaching!" Suzanne said. "My mother journeying, here at the Eaton Centre. My mother, ringing bell and all! Makes me wonder where little Telson is all this time."

THE DRUMS WERE violent all night. They barked, growled, hissed and boomed like thunder. As soon as Suzanne's head hit the pillow, the big bass drums pounced, like animals impatiently waiting for night. The soprano ones came later, then the steel pans, all creating an unspeakable dissonance. The bells also rang out, long and sharp screams. *Bang! Clang! Balang! Calang!* The same way Pastor Grant had rung them for benedictions.

So vicious was the drumming that Suzanne grunted and whined in her sleep. *Krack, back-uh crack, uh kcrack, uh kcrack.* Harsh and brutal, painful and mourning. The pain was in the bass drum, but the bells were so soothing. It reminded Suzanne of sitting in the shade of a tree, but leaving her feet in the scorching Jamaican sun.

In this dream, the flight attendant made an announcement in preparation for the landing in Kingston, Jamaica. But when Suzanne looked out the window, what she saw below was the sprawling monotony of Toronto. Nowhere was the ocean bathing the serene shores of a paradise island. Instead she saw the bilge-water Lake Ontario, the needlelike CN Tower and thousands of tiny cars zipping along the maze of highways covering the land.

The drumming became ferocious as Ona reached out to touch her with those menacing fingernails, all the while cackling like a deranged bird. Never in previous dreams had Ona gotten this close to Suzanne, never was she able to look into her mother's eyes, into the empty cavern of her mother's soul.

As usual, Ona led the dancing in the aisle of the plane. It was a dance of sacrifice, a corruption of the Pocomania thanksgiving celebration around the altar laden with fruits of the harvest. Suzanne was pinned against the side of the aircraft, where she could either look out at the sterile city or stare directly into her mother's face and submit.

Everyone on the plane was celebrating, laughing and winking behind Ona's back. They had tricked her into thinking Toronto was as personal as Kingston, as pretty, as fulfilling and rewarding. They had fooled her. More than that, they were scorning her. Ona had been conned by these people, who wanted only to use her. It was so plain. Even when they were duping Ona by cheering her on against her own daughter, these hypocrites despised Ona, couldn't accept her. She would never become one of them no matter how much she sacrificed her daughter, the way the original Israelite had offered his firstborn in the bush.

Ona was a pawn, a monkey dancing to a grinder's organ, to the powerful demands and taunts of "Dance! Dance! Dance!" They had bewitched her into making her daughter just like her, like the monkey teaching its young to dance, and to collect pennies and peanuts, condemning her offspring to a life no better than her own. These deceitful people had betrayed Ona into selling out her daughter, and finally herself. Once they were finished with her, Ona had no choice but to return adulterated to what she had repudiated: her customs, culture and religion.

These people were now asking the same price of Ona's daughter. *"Dance, Suzanne, Dance!"* they demanded over the drums, tossing money at her feet, the same kind of money and treasures so many children had dreamed about in the Caribbean. *"Dance, Suzanne, Dance!"* The same coins and bills they tossed at her feet while she was onstage and on those little boxes.

The voices were rising, drowning out even her mother's cackling. The drums were trying valiantly to suffocate the laughter and the demands. But for the first time, the drums seemed to be losing their potency. They were less able to protect, to call up the powers of the ancestors. Ona and the defilers, the true sources of all those manipulating hands, continued to advance on the shrieking Suzanne.

"No, no!" Suzanne screamed.

Suddenly she bolted upright on the bed in the darkened room, hugging her knees to her chin. The pillows were on the floor. The twisted sheets told of violent struggles. Cold sweat covered her face, back and breasts. The radio announcer was giving the weather report in calm measured tones that belied the concerns over yet another ferocious snowstorm, and just in time for Christmas, he was saying.

She reached for the telephone on the side table, but stopped abruptly. Who to call? Henderson? Bobby? She didn't really want to talk to them. But who else was there to call? Grandma Nedd and Mrs. King, the two women she always relied on, were dead, gone from this world, perhaps into the land from which the drumming came. She scrambled off the bed and paced the floor. The nightmare had been too real, too frightening.

SUZANNE SHOULD HAVE been in a better mood. With Christmas two days away, she should have been happy, free of the stress that brought on such dreams. But that wasn't the case. So many things had gone wrong.

In the evening, she had attended Filmore's annual Christmas party for the staff and the dancers, hoping the festivities

307

would distract her and get her in the mood for work later in the night. It should have been a happy occasion. Her manager had announced he had signed a four-month contract for her with Filmore's, the longest in the tavern's history.

"You girls don't have to worry about Buffalo anymore," he had said, laughing.

Margaret, Suzanne's dancing rival, with a young child at home, had announced she was packing in the club scene to go on welfare, creating a vacancy in the troupe. She wanted to spend more time, particularly the evenings, with her son.

"The government will provide the day care and they're paying me to go back to school for a computer programming course," she explained. "It starts in the new year."

"Good for you," Suzanne had said, trying to hide her glee to be rid of her. "I'm glad you're getting out of this rat race."

"Careful with your language," Philmore Leach had warned. "We don't want to scare off our most recent recruit. Come here, Debra."

The young shy girl of about sixteen years came to the center of the room. Suzanne's jaw dropped. She instantly recognized the girl as the daughter of Anita Watkins, the West Indian woman who lived in Mrs. King's old apartment building. Suzanne knew how much hope the mother had had for this girl. She remembered the times they talked and she knew how Mrs. Watkins had struggled to get her daughter from the Caribbean before she was too old. Knowing Mrs. Watkins, Suzanne realized there was no possible way Anita would stand by idly and allow her daughter to be a table dancer. "I'll kill her first," Anita had sworn over a lesser transgression.

Debra's eyes fixed on Suzanne's, in the way black people signaled one another in a crowd, but also with pride, as though she were now on the same level as a mentor.

My God, Suzanne thought, what is she doing? She should still be in school. Her mother, like so many West Indian parents, wanted her to be a doctor, even if it meant the old woman had to spend the rest of her life scrubbing floors to see the girl through university.

Suzanne couldn't bring herself to welcome Debra into the group, to even talk to her. If she did, the only advice she had to offer was for the girl to run home as quickly as her legs could take her. Suzanne wasn't looking forward to meeting Anita Watkins again.

Later, Suzanne realized why the management was so anxious to sign up the young woman and to retire Margaret. When she danced, Debra absolutely brought the house down. Nobody who saw her onstage was likely to believe she was the shy little girl Suzanne had passed so often outside the apartment building. Debra was expressive, totally uninhibited, showing no first-night jitters.

Maybe it was because of Debra's performance, or because Suzanne was listless onstage, but for the first time in her career Suzanne found little demand for her services. Everybody wanted Debra. As the night grew older, the new recruit became even bolder.

SUZANNE STOPPED PACING the room. The clock radio showed 5:02 A.M. Christmas Eve. She went to the window. Nothing was moving on the street. The snow was falling quietly on the sleeping city where, so deceptively, everything seemed to be at peace. Through the window, Toronto looked so quiet and pure, so innocent. Any rage in the city had to be inside her.

Suzanne decided to take a chance. She picked up the phone and dialed. She knew how much Ona detested getting calls at such hours, but maybe Ona had changed in that respect too.

"Hi, Mom," Suzanne whispered into the phone, "just thought I'd call and find out how you're doing?"

"I'm fine," the sleepy voice said. Suzanne was amazed at how much it sounded like her grandmother's. And then, intuitively, Suzanne realized what had bothered her since seeing Ona preaching. In the Eaton Centre, she had encountered the Ona she had expected to find when she first came to Canada. The one she had always hoped to see, the God-fearing woman that Grandma Nedd talked about, the child of Christ so steadfastly committed to the ways of the Lamb. This was the Ona that had remained hidden from her. But now that she had seen it, Suzanne didn't like that side of Ona. It looked too bush-league, as if Ona wasn't ready for the big city. As if she were incapable of making the mental adjustment, of appreciating that living in Canada was different from in the Caribbean. As if she were no better than those dirty and miscast preachers on the buses and subway with too many rough edges that should have been smoothed by now. She had felt embarrassed seeing her mother looking like such a cultural misfit.

"How's Telson?" Suzanne held her breath. She was hoping for an opening to tell Ona that she had seen her in the mall. And to ask how the guards treated her. Maybe they gave her a fifty-two-dollar ticket for trespassing. Maybe they forced her to sign a statement saying that, on pain of being arrested the next time, she was never to return to the mall. The same kind of bond security guards all over Toronto were forcing youths that were black, Filipino and Chinese to sign to keep them out of the malls.

"He's okay, sleeping. Why?" Ona sounded calm and composed, nothing remotely approaching the woman Suzanne had seen journeying in the mall.

"Oh, nothing. Just that I miss him. Tell him I'll come and see him for Christmas. Maybe he can spend a few days with me. I'll call you before I come over."

"Okay with me," Ona said. "I've got to go, though. I've a hard day ahead of me. This is the last day before the big day: before the coming of our sweet savior into this world. I got so much to do to prepare for that day, to help other people get ready. I can't even think of going back to sleep now you wake me. I got so many things to do."

"I know," Suzanne said. " 'Bye. Tell Telson I love him, and I'll come and get him if anything—" The disconnection happened before she had finished. She didn't get the chance to raise the matter of preaching in the mall. But her mother sounded fine, at least physically.

Suzanne slept soundly well into the morning. The nightmare didn't come back. The drums were silent; the bells didn't ring. When she awoke it was to the telephone's ring.

"Bad news, girl," Fanny said. "Sorry to be the one to break it to you, but they come this morning and take your mother to the madhouse, to the Clarke Institute."

"What?" Suzanne gasped.

"Bright and early this morning, she's up and down the streets, preaching like the ministers back home, dressed only in a flimsy nightgown on a cold morning like this. Saying God will protect her from the cold, that her mother was watching over her. That Christ was coming back. What a scene! The neighbors were out there. It breaks my heart to have to be the one to tell you this. Me and some of the girls are talking about what we can do to help."

"What about Telson?"

"I tried to get him, but the Children's Aid people took him away," Fanny replied. "I ain't family, although the boy does call me Auntie, so they won't give him to me. I was the only person that could come close to getting him. A little boy like him doesn't deserve to be in a home, to be on this slippery slope so early in life."

Suzanne switched on the television to catch the morning news. From the way she had talked, it obviously didn't even occur to Fanny that there was another family member to take care of Telson; not once did Fanny even consider Suzanne might want to help Telson.

As she flipped to another channel, Suzanne came across an

advertisement from one of the malls telling shoppers about the post-Christmas bargains that were already available in time for the big day. It was then that she remembered Bobby Ali's invitation to join the band of thieves later that very day.

CHAPTER 25

THEY WERE ALL waiting patiently when Suzanne, Telson and Henderson arrived. Telson had been the last stop for her, up in the suburbs where the authorities had placed him pending a permanent decision by the courts. The immigrant women, most of them Ona's age, with the same brutal wear and tear showing on their faces and hands, were standing in the hallway of the apartment building—just waiting. Many of them Suzanne didn't know. Others she had seen in passing, kindred spirits her mother had stopped momentarily to talk to while pushing a shopping cart down the aisle. Yet she instantly understood why they had come, and had waited for so long. Why they refused to go home, to show any sign of defeat, although never knowing exactly when Suzanne would turn up.

Every one of them was part of a community. They had hurried over to offer their support at the first news of Ona's tragedy. Nothing—not time, not last-minute Christmas shopping, not falling snow—was going to prevent them from paying their respects to the family, or from doing so in person.

The women made a path for Suzanne as she approached the apartment door. Many of them mumbled words of comfort, mere utterances that Suzanne did not really hear, her mind refusing to focus long enough for her to decipher them. But instinctively Suzanne knew what the women were saying, even though she saw only the movements of their lips and the pained looks in their eyes. She nodded in acknowledgment as she passed by them.

Stopping in front of the door, she searched her bag for the key that she had not used for so many years, but which she had always kept as some unexplained reminder. She fumbled with the lock, unaware that Ona had changed it when she'd thrown Joe out. Finally she located Ona's set of keys in the bag of her mother's belongings. The thought of her mother, of how she'd left her at the institute, cut her heart. Ona probably didn't even know that Suzanne had collected her clothes and few possessions.

The door unlocked, she stepped in with the women following, some of them immediately taking charge of the food, drink and music. Telson ran to switch on the television. Fanny turned it off and lifted him onto her knees. Telson didn't rebel. Something must have told him that this was, indeed, not a moment for outside intrusions but for all the people gathered in this apartment to look inwardly and to draw strength from one another. Certainly that was the way Suzanne saw it.

She had spent the morning doing all the necessary chores to achieve her goal and to keep her last promise to Grandma Nedd. Henderson had come early to drive her around the city. The visit to the psychiatric institute had left Suzanne devastated and numbed, drained of all emotions and expectations. She was glad she had not taken Telson to see their mother. Ona was heavily sedated, her eyes glazed over, and she did not recognize Suzanne or Henderson, who quickly left the room.

Occasionally Ona got off the bed and walked around the room, unable to stop herself from journeying and dancing. Every time she did, Suzanne wrapped her hands around her mother's shoulders and led her back to the cot, the same way she had seen the men back home lead the spent women to the area of resuscitation at the all-night journeying sessions at Cross Roads. Ona acted just like those women, except that she had not fainted under the spells of the spirits of the departed elders or the animals taking possession of her body and soul. And she didn't grunt, groan or snarl. She just danced, sometimes causing Suzanne to jig along with her just to keep up. And she said absolutely nothing.

Suzanne stayed with Ona in the eerie silence until it was time for her mother to be fed. She took the meal from the tray, and with the plastic spoon lifted small morsels into Ona's mouth. When this proved too laborious, Suzanne asked for a real spoon, only to be told that she must take great care to hand back the utensil when she was finished and not to leave behind any implements that could hurt her mother. Whether she knew it or not, Suzanne thought, Ona was in a prison.

Henderson returned for Suzanne just after the medication had put Ona to sleep. She was curled on the cot in a fetal position, not even stretched out in the proud, queenly, majestic way Suzanne had left Grandma Nedd on her hospital bed.

The lawyer said he was sympathetic but felt Suzanne had no chance of getting Telson. "Quite frankly," Anthony Rice, the black family law specialist, said, "you don't have a very good case. You know how demanding the Children's Aid Society people can be. You've been in their care. After all, you make your living . . . *table dancing*. What will you answer to their charge of moral defilement?"

"I'll say he's my brother," Suzanne said calmly. "Simple as that: he's my brother. We're the only family we got."

Joe Morgan had promised to sign any papers needed for Suzanne to get custody. He seemed beaten down and complained about the treatment he was getting in prison and about the bad-tasting food. More than anything, he missed his own cooking. When Suzanne told him about Ona, he looked straight at the wall, mechanically brushing back his short-cropped hair, smacking the top of his head with his palm every time he brushed.

"I ain't no use to anybody, not in here," he said softly, as if whispering to himself. Joe looked at Henderson and then at Suzanne. "No use whatsoever. This is what my life has been reduced to. No use."

He began pacing the room. To Suzanne, Joe looked older and thinner. His hair was much grayer than she remembered, even though it was shorter than he normally wore it. But it was the eyes that told the story. The fire in them had been dimmed by resignation; the ambition that used to propel him so viciously had gradually slipped away, leaving him hollow, confused and helpless. A cold numbness came over Suzanne. She didn't know what feelings she had for Joe, if anything more than pity. And shame that this man had once had such power over her. Had used her to hurt her own mother. But his help-lessness was her liberation. She could put the demons to sleep, or at least quiet them for a while. "I ain't no goddamned use to anybody," he said again, "not even to my goddamned self. So yes, I'll sign the bloody papers, anytime."

Telson was already dressed and waiting when Suzanne arrived at the posh suburban home where the foster family lived. He appeared well scrubbed and his hair was greased and combed. The shirt looked new, as did the winter coat and boots. Resting on the chair beside him was the stuffed toy Suzanne had bought for him in Jamaica. On their way over to the apartment, Telson said he was hungry. They stopped at a fast-food restaurant to give him a treat and to let Suzanne pause long enough to gather her strength for the rest of the day. Her last promise to Grandma Nedd had been to help Ona with Telson. She intended to do whatever it took to keep her word.

"Just look at them pictures up there," Fanny was saying. "Such a nice-looking family, I tell yuh." The people around her gazed at the wall and at the family portraits hanging above the television. Although Joe and Ona were absent physically, their spirits were just as strong in the apartment. Who could forget them when shoes, plates, glasses, clothes, pictures—and memories—were present? "Such a nice-looking family. I remember when I did meet Ona for the first time. Me and she hit if off good, good, just like that. A real nice woman. And the only thing she ever used to talk about was getting you back."

Fanny was not talking directly to Suzanne. As if she were paying homage to a dearly departed and had now to shore up the spirits of those left behind. "Getting you up here to join her, so she could make something of her life. Now, I can't begin to tell you how good my heart feels to know that you went over to visit your mother this morning." Suzanne closed her eyes momentarily. It was uncanny. Fanny sounded so much like Mrs. King. And it wasn't her Barbadian accent alone, but the timbre of her voice. The way she emphasized things. The way she was sounding like a woman no longer young, talking the language and imagery of the old. "I feel real good about that, like the God above answered my prayers, in truth. And I plan to do anything I can to help Ona get back on she two feet and to see that she is she old self again. I know she'd do the same for me if the tables did turned. And who can tell in this country? Who can tell? It could be any one of we in here, instead of Ona, resting we troubled souls in that damn place right now."

The door opened and Anita Watkins came in, not bothering to knock. She brought a slab of dark fruitcake in a pan covered with foil. It looked as if it had come straight from the oven. Anita placed the pan on the table beside the sandwiches, cakes, coconut breads and bun-bun that the women had brought, every one of them contributing in an uncoordinated way to the celebratory feast.

"My Debra told me she's run into you," Anita Watkins said to Suzanne. "I guess she tell you she's working. Good for my little Debbs, eh." She was talking to everyone in the room, spreading the news of how her daughter was making her proud. "Making real good money, she tell me. Promised me a

317

real good Christmas gift and she gave me one or two dollars to help with the shopping. All I can tell her is to praise the Lord and to make sure that she saves a few dollars for university. I tell her that now she has this job paying so much money, she don't have to go running out and renting no apartment, not yet. She can stay with me a bit longer. Taking yuh time ain't laziness, I tell she."

"I'm too glad to hear the good news," said a woman standing by the table. "Things 'round here so tough for some people. My Jocylin can't find anything worthwhile to do. And don't talk about my biggest boy, Trevor, it's like he'd never find no work, if you ask me. If I didn't have this job as a nursing assistant in the hospital, I wouldn't know what we'd do as a family."

Suzanne's eyes popped open. She recognized what was happening and what was the only possible outcome. Someday, perhaps very soon, Anita Watkins would find out the truth about Debra. Then the mother and daughter would begin journeying on the same path as Ona and Suzanne. Maybe she should prepare Anita Watkins by telling her the truth. Maybe even drop a hint, so that when she did find out, the truth wouldn't hit her so hard. For in her boasting statement was already planted the virus of destruction. But even then Suzanne knew she couldn't approach Anita Watkins with such news.

But she also felt she had to do something. Maybe she should try talking to Debra, try reasoning with her. Perhaps, as someone closer to her age, someone who had gone through the wringer, she could help turn Debra back and save Debra and Mrs. Watkins from an afternoon like this. She was sure Anita Watkins would sooner accept some cock-and-bull story about Debra being unlucky enough to lose her first job after only a few days than live with the knowledge that her daughter danced naked on tables for expensive tips.

"So you're going to try and keep the little boy until your mother's back on her feet again, eh?" Anita Watkins asked. "I mean, if I had my way I would take the boy my own self. But you know how things are up here in this country. Ain't like back home, where everybody is family. All the same, I agree with you taking him. I don't like the idea of that little boy growing up in no white people's home, no matter how much they can provide for him. Apart from filling his belly and putting a shirt on his back, what can they teach him about himself and about his people and culture? It just don't sound too right to me. But the courts in this country don't understand certain things."

The women nodded in agreement. There was absolutely no doubt or disagreement that Suzanne, by rights, should have Telson. The only doubts were in Suzanne's mind as she continued to search for a more potent and less emotional answer to her lawyer's question. *"What will you answer to their charge of moral defilement?"*

Before she responded Henderson came through the door with bottles of pop and booze from the store. Indeed, how could she answer that question with someone else's husband always hanging around her? Suzanne thought. And suppose the Children's Aid Society people came early and found him in the apartment and questioned what kind of example she was setting? He was a perfect example of this moral defilement, of the curse that followed the Nedd women.

Henderson did not hang around for much longer. Suzanne took him into one of the bedrooms and spoke with him. Then she kissed him and walked him out. Suzanne was certain that he fully understood why they were never to be that close again, why there was no future in their relationship. Telson was simply too important. But obviously he hadn't appreciated what she was doing, because he stormed out of the bedroom. He knew that this time her decision was final. There was to be no more waiting around until she snapped her fingers.

Suzanne rejoined the group to find that the early tension in the apartment was abating as the port wine and rum loosened the women's tongues. The voices were rising as they talked

about plans for Christmas dinners and of the last-minute shipping and packing that still awaited them. Obviously life had to
move on. They had to attend to other business and to renew
the hopes and dreams. Some of them were talking about
Christmases in Ghana, London, Birmingham, Jamaica, Trinidad, Barbados, New York, Halifax and elsewhere. Joe's radio
was playing loudly. The West Indian Christmas songs that
were never heard on regular radio serenaded them from one
of the pirate black stations cropping up all over the city. But
the sudden jolt coming out of the speaker was enough to capture everybody's attention. It was almost as if someone at the
station had accidentally turned a knob, inadvertently increasing the power, running the risk of blowing the speakers.

"Brothers and sisters, we interrupt this music for some important news," the announcer said. "There's a hostage-taking
at the Eaton Centre. The police have the place surrounded.
They asking people not to go to the mall. I have with me a sister who was at the mall. What happened, sister?"

"It like these youths, you know, they like they went to rob
this store," the woman began. She sounded out of breath. "But
like something went wrong, like somebody knocked over
something or the other. And the security moved in. Then the
youths had to run, but the security was blocking the door
through which the youths was trying to get out. So them
youths decided to hold some of the shoppers until they can get
out. I think one or two people got killed in the shooting."

"So what happened next?"

"Well, in no time the place was crawling with police. Both
the regular ones and the ones from the Emergency Task
Force. Them all over the place. The police closed down the
mall and a whole lot of people just get mad, 'cause they still
got lots o' last-minute shopping to do. And everybody cussing
and setting up their face, asking why anybody had to go and
rob people on Christmas Eve when everybody's out shopping
and looking to have a merry time tomorrow. I mean, it just
ain't right."

"You going back over there?"

"Not me. Not me," the woman answered. "I going home to where I damn well live. I got my family waiting for me home and I making sure nobody ain't shooting me before Christmas. What presents I ain't buy yet, we'll have to do without."

The women exchanged anxious glances. Instantly there was a rush for the phone. Suzanne heard one mother after another inquiring if this or that son was home of if anyone knew where was such and such a person. The panic remained in their voices until the assurance came that their son was accounted for. Then the phone was passed to another anxious mother. Those too apprehensive to wait their turn had rushed downstairs to the public pay phones in the lobby or at the corner of the streets, or had gone to friends' apartments on other floors. The outside reality they had resisted letting into the room had intruded with great force, shattering the communal spirit and reducing them to a collection of individuals concerned only with self-preservation.

By the time the radio reported an update of the grim news, only a few people were around to hear it, only those who had spoken directly to their children. Yet they all bowed their heads and reached for the bottle of rum as the announcer raised the death toll and they realized that Christmas was now spoiled for all of them. They would have to make their way over to the homes of the dead and console the families. The final Christmas cooking, baking and present wrapping would have to wait.

As the last woman left, Suzanne closed the door and dropped into the love seat, Ona's favorite place to sit. If circumstances had been different, there was a great possibility that Suzanne might have joined Bobby Ali in the robbery. And in all likelihood, like any member of Bobby Ali's gang, she might now be dead or badly wounded. Suzanne couldn't help thinking that maybe, just maybe, Ona had saved her. But then, Suzanne thought, even without her mother's sickness to distract her, she might have been busy on a day like this. She might not have even remembered Bobby Ali and his childish foolishness of robbing stores.

THE TIME WAS approaching for the Children's Aid Society people to pick up Telson. Suzanne kept looking through the window onto the circle below where the cars entered off the main road and parked. Every time she saw lights turning, her heart leapt and she got even more nervous.

Suzanne remembered her first morning in this apartment so many years ago. How she had looked down on the same streets below and saw them so dark and dull. Now it was even quieter. No movement. As if the city had imploded and everyone had rushed home, as if there were no externality to the city. Below her on the street were only the quiet and the slush of the black snowbanks.

"Do you think you would like to live with me?" she asked Telson.

"Yes, Suzie."

She did not continue the conversation. What more could she say? That she hoped he could. That she planned to work her ass off to get him. That she had to get him, no matter what it took. Back home in the Caribbean, it would have been so natural for her to take Telson in. But up here everything took time. Lots of time. But why, then, should she waste precious time comparing what happened in the Caribbean? She had no choice but to approach this problem with the acknowledgment that she was living in Canada, so there was no use trying to impose some solution no matter how well it worked in some mother country. She must find a way to reduce the time these things took.

The knock on the door intruded on her thoughts. The official came in and stood awkwardly just inside the door, jingling the keys in her hand, in much the same way Suzanne had seen her clients jingling coins and wads of paper when they

322

wanted to encourage her to dance and to go beyond. "Are we ready, Telson?" she asked.

For his response, Telson jumped off the seat and clung desperately to Suzanne's leg. Reaching for his coat and boots, Suzanne coaxed him into a sitting position. She knew she had to be tender with him. She didn't want to further frighten or alarm him.

"You have to go now, Telson," she whispered. "Remember. Tomorrow. Christmas. Santa Claus is coming tonight and you've been a very good boy. I'll come and see you. Go along, Telson."

He clutched his stuffed toy and walked away with the woman, looking back and stumbling until he was through the door. Suzanne followed them to the elevator.

" 'Bye, Telson," she said. "I'll come and see you. Tomorrow."

" 'Bye, Suzie."

The elevator made a thumping sound and the door slid open noisily. Then it closed.

Suzanne slammed the apartment door on the world outside. She knew what had to be done; what had to be her main purpose until her mother recovered, if ever. She had to do whatever was necessary to get Telson. The very next day, she would start preparing a plan and executing it. And it wouldn't take her as long as it had taken her mother to get her back. With the new year would come renewed hopes, the knowledge that even the longest and darkest night, as Grandma Nedd used to tell her, could only run until morning caught up. Then there would be a chance to resume fighting and for the reborn hope of winning.

But for this night, almost the longest of the winter, she wanted to be alone with herself and with Ona and Grandma Nedd. She planned to have three strong shots of the overproof rum. One each for her grandmother and mother because she had not celebrated them, not in the same way others had, and one for herself. She would willingly accept the diadem until Ona was well again. And by doing her best to mother Telson,

323

Suzanne hoped her grandmother would rest more securely in the knowledge that the curse that so blighted the Nedd women had finally ended. No future generations would be sacrificed on this altar of making amends.

She would teach Telson that all is forgiven, that the punishment handed down unto the third and fourth generations had been finally and permanently abandoned. For if there had ever been a curse, there was never any provision in it for a male member of the Nedd family. Even on her deathbed, Grandma Nedd had had to wrestle with this unexpected development. Telson, as a black male in North America, might be marked for extinction. But at least in his short two years he had already achieved one very important thing. Or had it been Ona who had ended the curse by conceiving Telson, a son?

She lingered over the third shot, sipping the rum straight so she could feel the sting in her mouth and the burn in her chest, bringing water to her eyes. The sting reminded her of the tough times still ahead. She planned to spend the rest of the wake sitting in Ona's love seat and just thinking: of Mira Nedd and Ona Morgan; of Bobby Ali and of Telson; of all those West Indian kids living and dying in this country, in all of North America.

There was no time for brooding over herself, no more confusion from trying to decide who she really was. Those personal decisions of what constituted her character had been made, were now confirmed in her mind as unchangeable. She realized that every immigrant must assume a different personality to survive. Everyone must set aside the old self he or she had been for so long, the being that even while suppressed was always an integral part of the entire person. Only in the dark, or among immigrants like themselves, did they dare show the personalities they were supposed to have left behind. Only then the stifled voice was released, gushing forth like a bird set free on a stream of the most brazen and titillating vernacular, the very spirit and essence of the islands. This was wrong. Nobody should have to hide a part of themselves as if it were

324

some illegitimate or deformed child, something to be ashamed of. Instead they should be encouraged in this new land to nurture such indispensable and unique possessions.

Now she understood not only the need to take on a new voice in the hope of integrating, but also the importance of not silencing the old and faithful voice. Of learning to waltz like Canadians but still being able to wind the waist in pleasant outlandishness like West Indians, like Africans. To hear the drums and to dance freely and openly.

She appreciated the wrenching struggle in her own body. She had learned to arbitrate and temper the fight when one personality felt it was about to be rubbed out, made extinct. How in a bid to survive on the same footing as the new character, the old self, like a sibling feeling threatened by the newborn, believed it had no choice but to fight back and to scream and shout. Had no choice but to keep reminding of the dreams and aspirations, of all the unfulfilled promises made to it as a child, but which were now overlooked in preference to this newcomer.

She had finally grasped what her mother had tried to teach her, the strategies Ona had adopted as her own survival techniques. And, in the new year, she planned to be strong, to be whole again, to clear the air of the putrid stench.

"Sleep on, beloved," Suzanne whispered into the glass. "Sleep and take thy rest."

ABOUT THE AUTHOR

CECIL FOSTER was born in Barbados and moved to Canada in 1978. His first novel, *No Man in the House*, was published to critical acclaim in the United States and Canada. Since leaving his position of senior editor at the *Financial Post*, Foster has worked for CBC radio and television and written for several leading magazines.